1222

ANNE HOLT

Translated by Marlaine Delargy

LARGE PRINT

Oxford

First published in Great Britain 2010
by
Corvus
an imprint of Grove Atlantic Ltd.

Published in Large Print 2011 by ISIS Publishing Ltd.,
7 Centremead, Osney Mead, Oxford OX2 0ES
by arrangement with
Grove Atlantic Ltd.

LP

British Library Cataloguing in Publication Data
Holt, Anne, 1958–
    1222.
    1. Storms - - Norway - - Fiction.
    2. Travelers - - Crimes against - - Fiction.
    3. Murder - - Investigation - - Norway - - Fiction.
    4. Detective and mystery stories.
    5. Large type books.
    I. Title II. One thousand two hundred and twenty-
    two III. Twelve twenty-two
    839.8'2374–dc22

        ISBN 978–0–7531–8806–4 (hb)
        ISBN 978–0–7531–8807–1 (pb)

    Printed and bound in Great Britain by
    T. J. International Ltd., Padstow, Cornwall

*This book is a little bit serious
and a lot of fun, Iohanne.
That's why it's my first little book for you.*

BEAUFORT SCALE 0

CALM

Wind speed: 0–1mph

Snowflakes fall vertically, often with a side-to-side motion.

CHAPTER
ONE

As it was only the train driver who died, you couldn't call it a disaster. There were 269 people on board when the train, due to a meteorological phenomenon that I have not yet understood completely, came off the rails and missed the tunnel through Finsenut. A dead train driver comprises only 0.37 per cent of this number of people. Given the circumstances, in other words, we were incredibly lucky. Although many individuals were injured in the collision, these injuries were mostly minor in nature. Broken arms and legs. Concussion. Superficial cuts and grazes, of course; there was hardly one person on board who wasn't physically marked in some way after the crash. But only one fatality. Judging by the screams that ripped through the train minutes after the accident, one could have gained the impression that a total disaster had taken place.

I didn't say anything for quite some time. I was convinced that I was one of only a few survivors, and besides I had a tiny baby I had never seen before in my arms. It came flying from behind when the impact occurred, brushed against my shoulder and hit the wall right in front of my wheelchair before landing on my lap with a soft thud. In a pure reflex action I put my arms around the bundle, which was yelling. I started to get my breath back, and became aware of the dry smell of snow.

The temperature dropped from unpleasant static heat to the level of cold that threatens frostbite within a remarkably short time. The train listed to one side. Not very much, but enough to cause pain in one of my shoulders. I was sitting on the left in the carriage, and was the only person in a wheelchair on the entire train. A wall of dirty white was pressing against the window on my side. It struck me that the enormous quantities of snow had saved us; without them the train would have jack-knifed.

The cold was debilitating. I had taken off my sweater back in Hønefoss. Now I was sitting here in a thin T-shirt, clutching a baby to my chest as I realized it was snowing into the carriage. The bare skin on my arms was already so cold that the whirling, blue-white flakes lay there for a chilly second before melting. The windows had caved in all along the right-hand side of the carriage.

The wind must have increased in strength during the few minutes that had passed since we stopped to allow people to get on and off the train at Finse station. Only two passengers had disembarked. I had noticed how they leaned forward against the wind as they struggled across the platform towards the entrance to the hotel, but it didn't seem any worse than normal bad weather up in the high mountains. Sitting here now, with my sweater tightly wrapped around the baby and with no chance of being able to reach for my jacket, I was afraid

4

that the wind was so strong and the snow so cold that we would freeze to death within a very short time. I curled my body over the tiny baby as best I could. With hindsight I can't actually say how long I sat like that, without any contact with anyone, without saying anything, with the shouts of the other passengers like disconnected fragments in the dense howling of the storm. Perhaps it was ten minutes. It might have been only a few seconds.

"Sara!"

A woman was glaring furiously at me and the child, which was entirely pink, from its cardigan to its tiny little socks. The small, clenched fists that I was trying to cover with my own hands, along with the furious, yelling face, had a pale pink tinge.

The mother's face, on the other hand, was blood-red. A deep cut in her forehead was bleeding freely. That didn't stop her from grabbing the baby. My sweater fell to the floor. The woman wound a blanket around her daughter with such speed and skill that this couldn't possibly be her first-born child. She tucked the little head inside the folds, pressed the bundle to her breast and yelled accusingly at me:

"I fell! I was moving along the carriage and I fell!"

"It's OK," I said slowly; my lips were so stiff that I had difficulty speaking. "Your daughter isn't hurt, as far as I can tell."

"I fell," sobbed the mother, kicking out at me without making contact. "I dropped Sara. I dropped her!"

Freed from the troublesome child, I picked up my sweater and put it on. Despite the fact that I was on the way to Bergen, where I was expecting pouring rain and a temperature of plus two, I had brought my padded jacket. Eventually I managed to get it down off the hook on which it was still hanging, miraculously. In the absence of a hat, I knotted my scarf around my head. I didn't have any gloves.

"Calm down," I said, tucking my hands into the sleeves of my jacket. "Sara's crying. That's a good sign, I think. But I'm more concerned about . . ."

I nodded in the direction of her forehead. She paid no attention. The child was still crying and was determined not to be consoled by her mother, who was trying to tuck her inside her own fur coat, which was far too tight. Blood was pouring from her forehead, and I could swear it was freezing before it reached the sloping floor, which was now covered in snow and blood and ice. Somebody had trodden on a carton of orange juice. The yellow lump of ice lay in the middle of all the whiteness like a great big egg yolk.

The warmth refused to come back into my body. On the contrary, it was as if my thicker clothing was making the situation worse. True, the numbness was slowly receding, but it was being replaced by piercing, stabbing pains in my skin. I was shaking so hard I had to clench my teeth to avoid biting my tongue. Most of all I wanted to try to turn my wheelchair around so that I was facing all the cries, facing the weeping of a woman who must be right behind me, and the torrent of swear words and curses coming from someone who sounded like a teenage boy whose voice was just breaking. I wanted to find out how many people were dead, how badly injured the survivors were, and if there was any way of securing the windows against which the wind was pressing as it increased in strength with every passing second.

I wanted to turn around, but I couldn't bring myself to take my hands out of the sleeves of my jacket.

I wanted to look at my watch, but couldn't bear the thought of the cold against my skin. Time was as blurred to me as the whirling snow outside the carriage, a chaos in grey with strips of blue-lilac glimmers from the lights that had started to flicker. I couldn't grasp the idea that it was possible to be so cold. More time must have passed since the crash than I thought. It must be colder than the train driver had said over the loudspeaker on our way into Finse. He had warned the smokers: it was minus twenty, and not a particularly clever idea to try to grab a couple of minutes' pleasure. He must have been wrong. I have experienced temperatures of minus twenty many times. It has never felt like this. This was a deadly cold, and my arms refused to obey me when I decided to check the time in spite of everything.

"Hello there!"

A man had forced open the automatic glass doors leading to the luggage racks. He stood on the sloping floor with his legs wide apart, wearing a snowmobile suit, a thick leather hat with earflaps and a pair of bright yellow ski goggles.

"I've come to rescue you!" he bellowed, pulling his goggles down around his neck. "Just take it easy. It's not far to the hotel."

His accent indicated that he was local.

I couldn't quite work out what one man was going to be able to do in this carriage full of wailing people. And yet it was as if his very presence had a calming effect on us all. Even the pink baby stopped crying. The boy who had been swearing non-stop since the crash yelled out one last salvo:

"It's about fucking time somebody turned up! Fucking hell!"

Then he shut up.

I might have fallen asleep. Perhaps I *was* in fact on the point of freezing to death. At any rate, the cold was no longer so troublesome. I've read about that sort of thing. Even if I can't claim that I felt the pleasant drowsiness that is said to precede death from the cold, my teeth had at least stopped chattering. It was as if my body had decided on a change of strategy. It no longer wanted to fight and shake. Instead I could feel muscle after muscle giving in and relaxing. At least in that part of my body where I still have feeling.

I'm not sure if I fell asleep.

But something has disappeared from my memory. The rescuer must have helped quite a lot of people before I gave a sudden start.

"What the hell . . ."

He was bending over me. His breath was burning against my cheek, and I think I smiled. Immediately after that he squatted down and examined my knees. Or rather my thigh, as I would soon learn.

"Are you disabled? Are your legs crippled? From before, I mean?"

I didn't have the strength to answer.

"Johan," he shouted suddenly, without getting up. "Johan, over here!"

He was no longer alone, then. I could hear the sound of an engine through the storm, and the gusts of wind from outside carried with them the faint smell of exhaust fumes. The roaring noise came and went, grew louder and then faded away, and I came to the conclusion that there must be several snowmobiles at work. The man called Johan knelt down and scratched his beard when he saw what his friend was pointing at.

"You've got a ski pole through your thigh," he said eventually.

"What?"

"You've got a ski pole right through your thigh."

He shook his head in fascination.

"The loop snapped off when it hit you and caught on your trousers, but the pole itself . . ."

His head vanished from my field of vision.

"It's sticking out about twenty centimetres on the other side," he called out. "You've bled a bit. Well, quite a lot, actually. Are you cold? I mean, are you colder than . . . It looks as if the pole is slightly bent, so . . ."

"We can't pull it out," said the man with the yellow goggles around his neck, so quietly that I only just heard him. "She'd bleed to death. Who's been stupid enough to put a pair of poles in here?"

He looked around accusingly.

"We need to get her out of here right now, Johan. But what the hell are we going to do with the pole?"

I don't really remember anything else.

And so of the 269 people on board train number 601 from Oslo to Bergen on Wednesday 14 February 2007, only one person lost his life in the crash. He was driving the train, and can hardly have grasped what was happening before he died. Incidentally, we didn't crash into the mountain itself. At the foot of Finsenut, a concrete pipe has been sunk into the rock, as if someone thought that the ten-kilometre tunnel wasn't long enough as it was, and therefore needed to be supplemented with several metres of ugly concrete in the otherwise beautiful landscape around the lake known as Finsevann. Subsequent investigations would show that the actual derailment occurred exactly ten metres from the opening. The cause was the fact that the rails had acquired a comprehensive covering of ice. Many people have tried to explain to me how such a thing could happen. Two goods trains had passed in the opposite direction during the course of an hour before the accident happened. As I understand it, they had pushed the warmer air in the tunnel out into the increasingly colder air outside. Just like in a bicycle pump, somebody told me. Since it is more difficult for cold air to retain moisture than it is for warm air, the condensation from inside turns to droplets, which fall to the ground and turn into ice. And more ice. So much ice that not even the weight of a train can crush it in time. Since then I have thought that although I couldn't see the point of the concrete pipe at the time, it was probably put there to create a gradual cooling of the air inside the tunnel. So far, nobody has been able to tell me if I am right.

It lies far beyond my comprehension that a weather phenomenon that must have been known since time immemorial can derail a train on a railway that has been in use since 1909. I live in a country with countless tunnels. We Norwegians should have a good knowledge of snow and ice and storms in the mountains. But in this hi-tech century with planes and nuclear submarines and the ability to place a vehicle on Mars, with the ability to clone animals and to carry out laser surgery that is accurate to the nearest nanometre, something as simple and natural as the air from a tunnel coming into contact with a snowstorm can derail a train and smash it against a huge concrete pipe.

I don't understand it.

Afterwards, the accident was referred to as the Finse disaster. Since it wasn't in fact a disaster but rather a major accident, I have come to the conclusion that the designation has been coloured by everything else that happened in and around the railway station 1222 metres above sea level in the hours and days following the collision, as the storm increased to the worst in over one hundred years.

CHAPTER
TWO

I was lying on the floor in a shabby hotel reception area when I came round. An all-pervasive smell of wet wool and stew assailed my nostrils. Just above my head a stuffed reindeer was staring glassily into the distance. Without looking I was aware that the room was full of people, weeping, sitting in silence or babbling agitatedly.

Slowly I tried to sit up.

"Don't do that," said a voice I recognized from the train.

"I have to get going," I said blearily to the reindeer.

The man in the blue snowmobile suit suddenly appeared in my field of vision. Bending down with his head between the animal and me, he looked as if he had antlers.

"You're going to have to stay here for a while," he said with a grin. "Like the rest of us. My name is Geir Rugholmen, by the way. What's yours?"

I didn't reply.

I wasn't planning on making acquaintances during this trip. True, Finse has no road links with the outside world. Even during the summer the historic Rallarvegen is closed to general traffic. In the winter it is, at best, a snowmobile track. With a wrecked train across the railway track on the Bergen line and a snowstorm that to all intents and purposes appeared to be gaining in strength, I still thought it was only a question of time before Norwegian State Railways' enormous snow ploughs would be able to battle their way up from Haugastøl or Ustaoset in the east, and would move us all safely. I wasn't going to get to Bergen this time, but none of us would be staying in Finse for very long.

CHAPTER
THREE

It turned out there were eight doctors among the passengers from the train that had crashed. A fortunate over-representation that could be explained by the fact that seven of them were due to take part in a conference at Haukeland University Hospital on the treatment of burns. I was also on my way there when the train was derailed. Not to the conference on burns, of course, but to see an American specialist on the complications following a broken spine. Since I was shot in the back and paralysed from the waist down one night between Christmas and New Year in 2002, the rest of my body has begun to suffer. It was a while before I discovered that I couldn't hear as well as I used to. I banged my head on the floor when the shot hit me, and the doctors had concluded that the aural nerves had been damaged in the fall. It doesn't matter. I don't have to use a hearing aid, not at all, and I get by perfectly well. Particularly in view of the fact that I rarely talk to other people, and that television sets are equipped with a volume control button.

But I do have breathing difficulties from time to time. And sometimes a pain like a kind of cramp stabs through the small of my back. That kind of thing. No more than bagatelles, really, but I had allowed myself to be persuaded. This American was supposed to be brilliant, after all.

So seven of the eight doctors from the train were specialists in a type of injury from which none of us was suffering. The eighth, a woman in her sixties, was a gynaecologist. Like an unexpected gift from the gods, all the doctors had got off very lightly in the accident. And even if they were in fact experts in skin and women's reproductive organs, they were still working their way blithely through cuts and broken bones.

I myself was taken care of by the dwarf.

He couldn't have been more than 140 centimetres tall. As if to compensate for this, he was exactly the same width. His head was far too big for his body, and his arms were even shorter, comparatively speaking, than those I had seen in persons of restricted growth before. I tried not to stare.

I stay at home most of the time. There are several reasons for this, including the fact that I can't cope with people staring at me. Bearing in mind that I am a middle-aged woman of normal appearance in a wheelchair, and therefore should not really be of particular interest to anyone, I could only imagine what it was like for this man. I saw it immediately, as he walked towards me. Someone had placed a cushion beneath my head. I was no longer compelled to gaze up at the reindeer's muzzle, where the fur had worn away and rough seams revealed the taxidermist's appalling work. As the little doctor moved through the room with an odd, rolling gait, the crowd parted before him like

Moses parting the Red Sea. Every conversation died away; even the complaints and cries of pain stopped as he passed by.

They just stared. I closed my eyes.

"Mmm," he said, kneeling down beside me. "And what have we here?"

His voice was surprisingly deep. I had expected some kind of helium voice, as if he were an entertainer at a children's party. As it would be extremely impolite not to look at the doctor when he was speaking to me, and my closed eyes might suggest that I felt worse than I actually did, I opened them.

"Magnus Streng," he said, taking my reluctant right hand in a thick, stubby paw.

I mumbled my name and couldn't help thinking that the doctor's parents must have had a very particular sense of humour. Magnus. The Great One.

He peered at me for a moment, and raised his index finger. Then his face broke into a huge smile. "The policewoman," he said enthusiastically. "You were the one who got shot in Nordmarka a few years ago, weren't you?" Once again his face acquired an expression of exaggerated thoughtfulness. This time he placed his finger against his temple before smiling even more broadly. "By that corrupt chief of police, isn't that right? It was —"

"It was a long time ago," I interrupted him. "You have a good memory."

He toned down the smile and concentrated on my leg. Only now did I notice that the omnipresent Geir Rugholmen had sat down next to the doctor. The snowmobile suit was gone. His woolly jumper must have dated back to the war. His bare elbows protruded through holes in both sleeves. His knee breeches had presumably been blue once upon a time, but had faded to an indefinable dark-greyish shade. The man smelled of wood smoke.

"Where's my chair?" I asked.

"The pole just slipped out," Geir Rugholmen said to the doctor, adjusting his plug of snuff with his tongue. "We weren't going to pull it out, but we had to break it off outside the wound before we brought her here. And it . . . it just slipped out. But she's not bleeding so much any more."

"Where's my chair?"

"I know we should have left the pole in," said Rugholmen.

"Where's her chair?" asked Dr Streng, without taking his eyes off the wound; he had ripped open my trouser leg, and I had the feeling that his hands were quick and precise in spite of their size and shape.

"Her chair? Her wheelchair? It's on the train."

"I want my chair," I said.

"Bloody hell, we can't go back and . . ."

The doctor looked up. He fished a pair of enormous horn-rimmed spectacles out of his breast pocket, put them on, and said quietly: "I would very much appreciate it if someone could fetch this lady's wheelchair. As soon as humanly possible."

"Have you any idea what the weather's like out there? Are you aware —"

The index finger, no longer quite so comical, pushed the spectacles up the doctor's nose before he fixed his gaze on Rugholmen.

"Fetch the chair. Now. I imagine you would find it quite unpleasant if your legs were left behind on a train while you yourself were helplessly carted off. Having seen you and your excellent colleagues working out in the storm, I presume it's a relatively simple matter to go and fetch something that is so important to our friend here."

Once again, that big smile. I got the feeling that the man consciously made use of his handicap. As soon as you began to overlook the circus-like appearance, he made sure he resembled a clown once again. His mouth didn't even need the traditional red paint, his lips were thick enough as they were. The whole thing was very confusing. Which must have been the intention. At any rate, Geir Rugholmen got reluctantly to his feet, mumbled something and headed for the porch, where he had left his outdoor clothes.

"A man of the mountains," said Dr Streng contentedly before taking his eyes off him. "And this wound looks fantastic. You've been lucky. A good dose of antibiotics just to be on the safe side, and you'll be fine."

I sat up. It took him only a few seconds to bandage my thigh.

"We really have been lucky," he said, tucking his spectacles back in his pocket. "This could have gone very badly indeed."

18

I wasn't sure whether he meant my injury, or the accident itself. He brushed the palms of his hands against each other as if I had been covered in dust. Then he waddled off to the next patient, a terrified eight-year-old boy with his arm in a temporary sling. As I tried to haul myself over to the reception desk in order to find some support for my back, a man positioned himself in the middle of the floor in the big room, his legs spread wide apart. He hesitated for a moment, then used a chair to help him jump up on top of the five- or six-metre-long rough table that was standing by the windows facing south-west. Since he was several kilos overweight, he almost fell off. When he had regained his balance, I realized who he was. Around his neck he was wearing a red and white Brann football club scarf.

"My dear friends," he said in a voice that suggested he was used to speaking to large groups of people, "we have all suffered an extremely traumatic experience!"

He sounded absolutely delighted.

"Needless to say, our thoughts go out to Einar Holter's family, first and foremost. Einar was driving our train today. I didn't know him, but I have already been told that he was a family man, a much loved —"

"His family hasn't yet been informed about the accident," a woman's voice interrupted loudly from the other side of the room.

I couldn't see her from where I was sitting, but I liked her immediately.

"It's not exactly appropriate to hold a eulogy under the circumstances," she went on. "Besides which, I think —"

"Of course," said the man on the table, holding the palms of his hands up to the congregation in a gesture of resignation, "I merely thought it was the right moment, now that we know we are all safe and no one has been seriously injured, to remind ourselves that in our mutual rejoicing at —"

"Brann are a crap team," someone yelled, and I immediately recognized the tough kid from my carriage.

The man on the table smiled and opened his mouth to say something.

"*Brann are crap*," the boy repeated, and burst into song. "Vålerengaaa, you are my religion, you're one in a million, a proud old tradition!"

"Great," said the man with the Brann scarf, smiling contentedly. "It's good to see that young people today are committed to something. And it really does seem as if things are beginning to sort themselves out, both in here and out there as well."

He pointed vaguely towards the entrance. I had no idea what was going on over there.

"I merely wanted to point out . . ."

I almost felt sorry for the bloke. People were sniggering. A few were booing quietly as if they didn't want to give themselves away, but did want to vent their contempt. This might have had some effect on the man. At any rate he had abandoned the joyous hallelujah tone when he tried to complete the sentence.

". . . that for anyone who is interested, I will be holding a prayer meeting in the hobby room in quarter of an hour. If anyone needs help with the stairs, please let me know. I am surely not alone in —"

"Shut your gob!"

The boy wasn't giving up. He was on his feet now. He was standing only a couple of metres from where I was sitting, and had formed a megaphone with his hands.

"You!" I said sharply. "Yes, you!"

The boy turned to face me. He couldn't have been more than fourteen.

His gaze was searingly familiar.

Perhaps they know it. Perhaps that's why they always try to hide their eyes, darting to and fro, behind their hair or beneath half-closed eyelids. This boy had pulled his cap down way too low over his forehead.

"Yes, you," I said, waving him over. "Come here. Shut up and come over here."

He didn't move.

"Do you want me to tell everybody why you're here, or would you like to come a little bit closer? So that we can maintain a certain level of . . . discretion?"

Hesitantly he took a step towards me. Stopped.

"Come here," I said, in a slightly more friendly tone of voice.

Another step. And another.

"Sit down."

The boy leaned back against the reception desk and slid slowly down onto his bottom. He wrapped his arms around his knees, not looking at me.

"You're on the run," I stated quietly, not bothering to ask. "You live in a care home for young people. You've had several foster homes, but it all goes pear-shaped every single time."

"Bullshit," he mumbled.

"I'm not really interested in having a discussion about it. A fourteen-year-old like you, travelling alone . . . Or perhaps you're part of a fairytale family who just decided to take a trip, as the weather was so nice? Can you show me who you're travelling with?"

"I'm not fourteen."

"Thirteen, then."

"I'm fifteen, for fuck's sake."

"In a year or two, maybe."

"In January! A month ago! Do you want proof, or something?"

Furiously he pulled his wallet out of a pair of jeans that were way too big for him. It was made of nylon in a camouflage pattern, and was fastened to his belt by a chain. As he pulled out a credit card I noticed that his cuticles were so badly bitten they were bloody.

"Wow," I said, without looking at him. "Credit cards, no less. All grown up. We'll say fifteen, then. And now you're going to listen to me. What's your name?"

He was just as interested in making winter friends as I was.

"What's your name?" I repeated sharply, catching a glimpse of the name on the card before he pushed it back in his wallet.

He glared silently and absently from beneath the peak of his cap. There was a stale smell all around the boy, as if someone had washed his clothes and not bothered to air them properly before putting them away.

"Adrian," I said wearily. "Right, now I'm going to tell you something."

The boy gave a start, ran his hand over his cap and stared at me for three long seconds.

Adrian was fifteen years old, I knew nothing about him, and yet I knew everything. He was hardly in any condition to fight, he probably didn't weigh any more than fifty kilos under those oversized clothes. He was foul-mouthed. A thief, without a shadow of doubt, and I was convinced that he was already well on the way into a destructive cycle of substance abuse. A petty criminal, a little shit who hadn't yet learned to hide his expression.

"Are you psychic, or something? How do you know —"

"Yes, I am psychic. Now just shut up. Are you hurt?"

He moved his head a fraction. I interpreted this as a no.

"Your chair!"

Geir Rugholmen brought with him a cold draught from outside. Only now did I realize that the large lobby was gradually emptying.

"We need to find a room for you as well," he said, putting together my wheelchair with surprising expertise. "Most people have already got a bed here at the hotel. We've used the private apartments as well."

He waved vaguely in the direction of the stairs before attaching the last wheel.

"Fortunately the hotel was more or less empty. It's not exactly high season. It will soon be the winter break; things would have been much more difficult then. We've moved most of the youngest and fittest adults over to the buildings around the station. So now we need to find a room for . . ."

He broke off and squinted at Adrian.

"Are you two together?" he asked sceptically.

"In a way," I said. "For the time being."

"I think we've got space for you in one of the closest rooms. There are already two people in there, but with a mattress on the floor your pal here will also be able to —"

"Let's make a start then," shouted the man wearing the Brann scarf, beckoning to a group of youngsters who were sitting at the table eating what I thought was stew, but which I later found out was hot soup. "We're gathering down here, everybody! We've organized coffee and biscuits too!"

The response obviously hadn't matched up to his expectations. The priest eagerly grabbed the arm of a woman passing by, but let go immediately when what he presumably thought was a proper mountain ski hood turned out to be a hijab.

The teenagers continued eating in silence. They were in no hurry. Quite the reverse, in fact; without even looking at the man, they casually helped themselves to more soup. Somebody started humming an incredibly irritating nursery rhyme. One of the girls giggled and blushed.

24

"Can't somebody put a bullet in that fucking priest's head," mumbled Adrian, before raising his voice: "And I'm not fucking sleeping in the same room as other people. I'm just not."

He ambled over to the table and threw himself down on a chair as far from the others as possible.

Geir Rugholmen scratched the dense, blue-black stubble on his chin. "Quite the little hard man, your pal."

He moved to help me up.

"No," I said. "I can manage. He's not my pal."

"Good job."

"Don't worry about him."

"I'll do my best. Wouldn't you like me to —"

"No!"

My tone was sharper than necessary. As it often is. As it almost always is, if I'm perfectly honest.

"OK, OK! Take it easy! God. I only wanted to —"

"And I don't need a bed either," I said, adjusting my position. "I'd rather just stay here."

"Tonight? You're going to sit in that chair all night? Here?"

"When are you expecting help to arrive?"

Geir Rugholmen straightened up. He placed his hands on his hips and looked down his nose at me. That look from those who are standing up, the tall ones, the ones whose bodies work perfectly.

Strictly speaking, I think it's perfectly OK to have mobility problems. I want to be immobile, that's the way I've chosen to live. The chair doesn't really hamper me significantly in my everyday life. It can be weeks between the occasions on which I leave my apartment. The problems arise when I am forced to go out. People are just desperate to help me all the time. Lifting, pushing, carrying.

That's why I chose the train. Flying is a complete nightmare, I have to say. The train is simpler. Less touching. Fewer strange hands. The train offers at least some degree of independence.

Except when it's derailed and crashes.

And I really don't like those looks, up and down, from those who are healthy and mobile. That's why I didn't meet his gaze. Instead I closed my eyes and pretended I was settling down for a sleep.

"I don't think you've really grasped the situation," said Geir Rugholmen.

"We're snowed in on the mountain."

"You could put it that way. We certainly are snowed in. At the moment a full storm is raging out there, with gusts of hurricane force. A hurricane on Finse! It's not exactly an everyday occurrence. We're in the lee of —"

"I'm really only interested in one thing: when can we expect someone to come and get us?"

There was complete silence. But I knew he was still there. The smell of wood smoke and old wool was equally strong.

"I asked you a question," I said quietly, keeping my eyes closed. "If you can't answer, that's fine, of course. Personally I was thinking of having a little nap."

"You're like an ostrich."

"What?"

"You think nobody can see you if you shut your eyes."

"The ostrich buries its head in the sand, as far as I know. And in any case, that's supposed to be a myth."

I gave an enormous yawn, still with my eyes closed.

"Nobody can say I haven't tried," said Geir Rugholmen sourly. "If you're just going to sit here being awkward, well . . . Sod you."

His ski boots clumped across the floor and disappeared.

I'm good at that sort of thing.

I might even have dozed off for a little while.

BEAUFORT SCALE 1

LIGHT AIR

Wind speed: 1–3mph

Barely noticeable. Snowflakes drift
visibly on the wind.

CHAPTER
ONE

The Crown Princess had been on the train, according to what people were saying.

Nobody knew where she had gone.

When I insisted on having my wheelchair fetched from the train, it wasn't only because I felt helpless without it. As far as my mobility went, it didn't really make that much difference. I had to stay in the lobby anyway. The toilets were on the same floor right next to the main staircase, which made it possible for me to empty my bags with comparatively little embarrassment, thank God, but apart from that there was nowhere I could get to without help.

The most important thing about the wheelchair is that it creates distance.

Not physically, of course; as I said I am constantly stared at and bombarded with offers of help. I strive more for a kind of mental distance. The chair makes me different. It defines me as something completely different from all the rest, and it is not uncommon for people to assume that I am stupid. Or deaf. People talk over my head, quite literally, and if I simply lean back and close my eyes, it's as if I don't exist.

You learn a great deal in this way. My relationship to other people is — how shall I put it — more academic in its nature. I would prefer not to have anything to do with them at all, something that can easily be interpreted as a lack of interest. This is incorrect. People do interest me. That's why I watch a great deal of television. I read books. I have a DVD collection that would be the envy of many. In my day I was a good investigator. One of the best, I would like to think. That would be impossible without a certain curiosity when it comes to other people's stones, other people's lives.

It's having people close to me that I find difficult.

I am interested in people, but I don't want people to be interested in me. A very taxing situation. At least it is if you surround yourself with friends and colleagues, and if you have to work in a team — as you do in the police. When I got shot and almost died, I ran out of strength.

I was perfectly happy sitting there, all by myself.

People were staring, I could feel it, but it was still as if I didn't exist. They were talking openly about everything. Despite the fact that many had disappeared for a while when the rooms were allocated, it was still too early to wind down for the night. Most of them came back before long. A few were standing chatting in the reception area. The shock of the accident had begun to subside, edging towards laughter. The situation was no longer threatening, in spite of the fact that the storm outside the old hotel was more violent than anything any of us had experienced before. It was more the fact that the shabby, melancholy air of the hotel was having a calming effect on us. Its crooked brown architectural patchwork had withstood both wind and storms for almost a hundred years, and it was not going to let anybody down tonight either. The doctors had worked their way through the queue of those needing help. A few of the teenagers were playing poker. I had positioned my chair at just the right distance from the long wooden table, and I could hear both the youngsters and the stream of people coming back from their rooms to find out the latest news, to compare their injuries and to stare at the huge windows as the storm tried in vain to batter its way through to us at Finse 1222.

I was listening to what people were saying. They thought I was asleep.

And now that everyone had been taken care of and fed, when there wasn't much more to say about where exactly they had been on the train when the crash happened, and glasses of red wine and beer had started to appear, most people were more interested in where on earth Mette-Marit had got to.

The rumour had already been circulating on the train. Two middle-aged women just behind me had talked about virtually nothing else. There was an extra carriage, they whispered. The last carriage looked different from the rest of the train, and this wasn't the way the normal morning train to Bergen looked at all. What's more, the far end of the platform had been cordoned off. It had to be the Royal Carriage. True, it didn't look particularly royal, but there was no way of knowing how it was equipped inside, and besides it was widely known that Mette-Marit was scared of flying. It could be Sonja, of course, she adores the mountains, I mean everybody knows that, but on the other hand she wouldn't be leaving home right now, just before the King's seventieth birthday.

I breathed a huge sigh of relief when the two ladies got off at Hønefoss.

I rejoiced too soon.

The gossip had caught on, and was well on the way to becoming the truth. Strangers were chatting to each other. The train became less and less Norwegian as it climbed towards the high mountains. People were sharing their sandwiches and fetching coffee for each other. One person thought they knew something they had heard from someone they knew, and a girl of about twenty-five had definitely heard that somebody she went to school with who now worked in the royal protection team was actually going to Bergen this week.

When we left Oslo, there was quite simply an extra carriage on the train.

By the time we were approaching Finse, the carriage had turned into the Royal Carriage and everybody knew that Mette-Marit and her bodyguards were on board, along with little Prince Sverre, no doubt. He was still so small, after all. He needed his mummy, the little darling. An eager, elderly man thought he had seen a little girl through a window before he was brusquely turned away by the police, so Ingrid Alexandra was there too.

But where had they gone, all these members of the royal family?

Sometimes I realize a little more clearly than usual why I would prefer not to have anything to do with other people.

CHAPTER
TWO

Her voice was characteristic, bordering on parody.

It is said that opinions in themselves are never dangerous. I'm not so sure.

Whether it is Kari Thue's views or her missionary zeal that frighten me most it's difficult to say. At any rate, she is still very adept. She could play the main character in a play by Holberg, with her absurd logic, her way of distorting the facts, and her impressive belief in her own message. Besides which, she has such a bloody high profile. She's everywhere: on the television, on the radio, in the papers. Kari Thue frightens nervous people into becoming aggressive, and seduces otherwise sensible men into insanity. The woman with a voice as sharp as the parting in her thin hair had already started a quarrel. There were two Muslims at Finse this afternoon; a man and a woman. Kari Thue is a bloodhound of note, and she had scented the problem long ago.

"I'm not talking to you," she almost screamed, and I just had to open my eyes a fraction. "I'm talking to her!"

A short man with an enormous beard was trying to position himself between Kari Thue and a woman to whom he was married, judging by appearances. She was wearing dark, full-length clothes and a headscarf; she was the person the priest had tried to drag along to his prayer meeting in the hobby room, in his confusion. I presumed they were Kurds. They could of course just as easily have been Iranians, Iraqis, or even Italian Muslims, when it came down to it, but I still settled on Kurds. Ever since I got to know Nefis, who is a Turk, I have become pretty good at noticing details that I can't define, strictly speaking, but which mean I rarely get it wrong. The woman was weeping, hiding her face in her hands.

"There, you see!" shouted Kari Thue. "You've —"

The priest wearing the Brann scarf, who was at least as well known from television as Thue herself, moved towards them.

"Let's all just calm down, shall we," he intoned, placing a calming hand on the shoulder of the agitated Kurdish man. "My name is Cato Hammer. We should all be friends and have some consideration for each other in a situation like —"

He ran his other hand down Kari Thue's back. She reacted as if he had been anointing her with sulphuric acid, and turned around so fast that she almost dropped the little rucksack she carried over one shoulder.

"Get off!" she hissed. "Don't touch me!"

He removed his hand at once.

"I really do think you need to calm down a little," he said in a fatherly tone.

"This has nothing to do with you," she said. "I'm trying to conduct a conversation with this woman!"

She was so preoccupied with the genial priest that the Kurd seized his chance. With a firm grip on his wife's arm he hurried away from the reception desk and disappeared in the direction of the stairs, where a sign carved in wood announced that you were now entering St Paal's Bar.

I don't like priests. I dislike them and imams in equal measure, although I haven't actually come across many of the latter. I did once meet a rabbi who was quite decent, but that was in New York. On the whole I have little time for religion, and particularly for those who act as stewards for various religious beliefs. I find priests the most difficult of all to tolerate. Naturally, they are also the ones I am most accustomed to. And I react against priests like Cato Hammer most strongly of all. They preach a theology of tolerance where the boundaries between right and wrong are so vague that I cannot see the point of having a religion at all. They smile piously and open their arms wide. They love everyone. Sometimes I suspect that priests like Cato Hammer don't believe in God at all. Instead they are in love with a Jesus cliché, the good man in sandals with the velvety gaze and welcoming hands. Suffer little children to come unto me. I just can't cope with it at all. I don't want to be embraced. I want sulphurous sermons and threats of eternal flames. Give me priests and bishops with straight backs and burning eyes, give me implacability and condemnation and promises of punishment on the other side. I want a church that whips its congregation onward along the straight and narrow, and makes it crystal clear to the rest of the world that we are heading for eternal damnation. At least that would make it easy to see the difference between us. And I won't have to feel involved, something I have never asked to be.

So I didn't like the man.

Without pre-empting events, I would still like to say at this point that the first thing I thought when I heard that Cato Hammer was dead a few hours later was that he hadn't been such a terrible person after all, in spite of everything.

"Don't get so agitated," he said to the raging fury. "You create distance between people, Kari Thue. Muslims are not the same as Islamists. The world is not like that. You divide us up into —"

"Idiot," she snapped. "I've never said or implied anything of the kind. You've fallen for the naive Norwegian political correctness that is allowing this country to be invaded by . . ."

I closed my ears.

If religion is, as I believe, basically a scourge for mankind, then I still see no logic, not to mention decency, in arranging believers in some kind of rank order. Religion comprises tyranny and civilization, rejection and conformity, love and oppression. And why Islam in particular should be regarded as worse than other faiths is beyond my comprehension. But it is not beyond Kari Thue's comprehension. She is the leader of a movement that reserves the right to stand up for all women, children, foetuses and everything else that forms part of "Norwegian values".

I am allergic to the word "values".

Combined with the concept "Norwegian", it becomes utterly loathsome. In her fanatical desire to strike back at the "Islamic world threat", Kari Thue and her increasingly numerous and terrifyingly influential campaigns are making life very difficult for hard-working, well-integrated Norwegian Muslims.

The other feeling that struck me several hours later when I heard about the death was therefore a sense of annoyance that it wasn't Kari Thue who was lying there frozen stiff in a snowdrift instead of Cato Hammer.

But you can't really say that sort of thing.

CHAPTER
THREE

"Are you asleep?"

"No," I said, trying to sit up straight in my chair. "Well, not any more."

I was starting to feel stiff. Despite the fact that I couldn't feel the wound in my thigh, it had become clear that the rest of my body had also taken a considerable beating. My back was aching, one shoulder was sore and my mouth was dry. Dr Streng had pulled up a chair beside me. He offered me a glass of red wine.

"No thanks. But a glass of water would be great."

He disappeared for a couple of minutes.

"Thanks," I said, emptying the glass in one draught.

"Good," said Dr Streng. "It's important to take in fluids."

"Definitely," I said, smiling stiffly.

"Terrible weather," he said cheerfully.

I don't respond to remarks like that.

"I tried to go out for a while," he went on, unabashed. "Just to feel the cold, that's all. It's impossible! It's not just that there's a hurricane blowing, they say the snow is worse than anyone up here has seen before. It's piled high against the wails and windows, and the temperature is down to minus twenty-six, and with the wind-chill factor it's going to feel . . ."

He thought for a moment.

"Freezing cold," I suggested.

I put the glass down on the floor. Released the brake on my chair and nodded briefly to the doctor before setting off slowly. He didn't take the hint.

"We can go and sit over here," he suggested, trotting after me with two glasses of red wine in his hands in the hope that I might change my mind. "Then we can look at the weather!"

I gave up and parked by the window as he suggested.

"Not much to look at," I said. "Whiteness. Ice. Snow."

"And wind," said Dr Magnus Streng. "Just listen to that wind!"

He was right there. For one thing, the roaring from outside was so loud that everyone had to raise their voice in order to be heard. What was more remarkable was that the wind was making the window panes vibrate, as if the storm were a living thing with a loudly pounding heart. The view was completely devoid of reference points. No trees, no objects, even the walls of the rooms at right angles to reception had disappeared in a whirling chaos of snow, without anything to focus on.

"Nothing to worry about," said a voice behind me. "Those windows will hold. They're triple-glazed. If one goes, there are still two left."

Geir Rugholmen was clearly not a person to hold grudges. He sat down on the edge of the table and raised his glass in a toast. It looked like Coca-Cola.

"Absolutely," I said.

"Fascinating," said the doctor happily. "These windows aren't quite as big, but in Blåstuen" — he was referring to the hotel's common room on the lower floor — "you really do see the proof that glass is an elastic material. Now, Rugholmen, what can you tell us about these rumours that there's royalty among us?"

I actually thought I saw a slight shift in the expression on the face of the mountain man. Something watchful, a flicker in his eyes before he sought refuge behind the glass he was holding.

"Nothing but talk," he said. "You shouldn't believe everything you hear."

"But that carriage," Magnus Streng protested. "There was definitely an extra —"

"Is everything OK with you?" asked Rugholmen, looking at me with a little smile, as if he wanted to draw a line under our earlier discussion.

I nodded, then shook my head as Magnus Streng once again offered me the glass of red wine.

"Everybody should be sorted for tonight by now," said Rugholmen. "And we must be grateful that people were moved across to the other buildings in time. Right now it's absolutely impossible to be outside. The wind would just blow you off your feet, and the snow is something else."

"When is somebody going to come for us?" I asked.

Geir Rugholmen burst out laughing. His laughter was happy and melodious, like that of a young girl. He took out a tin of snuff.

"You don't give up, do you?" he said.

"How long is the weather going to be like this?" I wondered.

"For a long time."

"What does that mean?"

"Hard to say."

"But surely you must be in contact with the Met Office," I said, not even trying to conceal my irritation.

He tucked a fresh plug under his lip and slipped the tin into his pocket.

"It doesn't look good. But you should just take it easy. There's enough food here, and warmth, and plenty to drink. Make yourself at home."

"If it had to happen," said Magnus Streng, "it's fantastic that we were only a few hundred metres from the station. As far as I understand it, that's why we weren't travelling too fast. Less than seventy kilometres an hour, they said. We really can talk about a blessing in disguise. And then there's this hotel! What a place! What service! Nothing but smiles and kindness. You'd think they took in accident victims every single —"

"Who's actually responsible?" I interrupted, looking at Geir Rugholmen.

"Responsible? For the hotel?"

I sighed.

"For the accident?" he asked sarcastically, throwing his arms open wide. "For the weather?"

"For us," I said. "Who's responsible for the rescue operation? For getting us down from here? As far as I know, it's the local police who carry the operational responsibility. What does that involve? Is it Ulvik police district? Is there a local representative? Is the Mountain Rescue Service in Sola —"

"That's a hell of a lot of questions you've got there," Geir Rugholmen interrupted me, speaking so loudly that those sitting nearby stopped talking and looked over in our direction. "It's hardly my job to answer questions like that!"

"I thought you were part of a rescue team. The Red Cross?"

"You're wrong there."

He slammed his glass down on the table.

"I'm a solicitor," he said irritably. "And I live in Bergen. I've got an apartment here and I've taken a week off work to sort out the kitchen before the winter skiing break. When I heard the bang it didn't take much imagination to work out what had happened. I've got a snowmobile. I helped you and plenty of other people, and I'm not asking for any thanks for that. But you could at least try to be a little bit more pleasant, don't you think?"

His face was so close to mine that I felt a fine shower of saliva as he hissed: "If you can't be grateful, you could at least be a little bit more polite towards a bloke who instead of painting his kitchen has been shuttling back and forth in this fucking awful weather to bring both you and your bloody chair to safety!"

45

I'm used to people going off and leaving me alone. That's what I want. It's a question of finding the balance between being rude and reserved. Too much of the latter simply makes people curious and more intrusive, just like Magnus Streng, who had clearly decided to get to know me better. But I had obviously gone too far when it came to the former.

"I do apologize," I said, trying to sound as if I meant it. "I am of course grateful for your help. Particularly for the fact that you went to get my chair when the weather had worsened. Thank you. Thank you very much indeed."

I was lying. Geir Rugholmen looked at me expressionlessly for a few seconds, then shrugged his shoulders and gave a wry smile.

"Good," he said. "And I can tell you that we're holding an information meeting in . . ." he glanced at his diver's watch made of black plastic, "half an hour. It's going to be held here. Because of you, in fact. It was my idea. And just so we're clear: it's going to take a while before anybody comes to fetch us. It's impossible to say how long. The power lines are down to the west of Haugastøl. The snowstorm is so severe that not even diesel snow ploughs can get through. There's no chance of a helicopter in weather like this. We're simply cut off. So you might as well try and relax for the time being. OK?"

Without waiting for an answer he finished off his drink and walked away.

Adrian had found someone.

This surprised me. I had noticed it a little earlier; he sauntered across the rough, worn wooden floor with an older girl trailing behind him. She might have been around eighteen. It was hard to say, actually. She reminded me of a less attractive clone of Nemi, the cartoon character. Thin as a rake, and dressed all in black with coal-black hair. Only the mouse-coloured roots showing along her parting, a silver-coloured piercing in her lower lip, and her pale skin diverged from the monotonous black. Her make-up was so thick she could have been fifteen or twenty-five. The two of them sat down on the floor with their backs to the wall and their arms around their knees right next to the kitchen door. They didn't appear to be talking to one another. They just sat there like two mute, antisocial individuals in a group of people who had become positively relaxed during the course of the evening.

"Are you sure you wouldn't like a little drop?"

Magnus Streng was offering me the glass of red wine again.

What I really wanted to do was to remind him that he was a doctor. That I had just been involved in a major accident, and had suffered loss of blood due to a ski pole penetrating my thigh. I really wanted to ask him if alcohol was appropriate medication for a middle-aged disabled woman with an indubitably lowered general state of health.

There are limits, even for me.

"No thank you."

But I didn't smile. Which was equally effective, in fact.

"No, right," he said, getting to his feet. "Enjoy the rest of your evening, then, I'm going to try and sort out this royal mystery."

My mobile rang.

Well, it glowed silently. I always have the sound switched off. Up to now it had been in the pocket of my padded jacket. It had fallen out onto the floor when I was looking for a piece of chocolate. It showed fifteen missed calls.

Presumably the accident had been reported across the media. Since the satellite dish in Finse had either been blown down or buried in snow, there were no working televisions in the hotel or the private apartments. A few people had been listening to the radio during the afternoon and evening. None of them had anything new to report on a rescue operation. It seemed as if the matter was not being pursued at present; it could hardly be said that we were in great danger. I have to admit that it seemed pointless to risk life and limb in order to rescue survivors who were safe and warm, cosily installed in a charming hotel. And I don't suppose the dead train driver was in any hurry to get down from the mountain. As far as the mysterious extra carriage was concerned, it seemed as if those passengers were also safely settled in the top, and doubtless most luxurious, apartment in the wing.

Basically, everything was more or less OK.

Apart from the fact that I had forgotten something.

I too have people who are close to me: a woman and a child.

I'd forgotten to call home.

Despite the fact that I was dreading speaking to Nefis, and was busy trying to come up with a strategy before I gathered the courage to call, I couldn't quite forget Geir Rugholmen's reaction to the question about the mysterious carriage. It was highly unlikely that Mette-Marit would be on the train. But there *was* an extra carriage. There *had* been security guards on the sealed-off area of the platform at Oslo's central station.

"I'm alive," I said before Nefis had time to say anything at all. "I'm perfectly OK and things aren't too bad at all."

The telling-off lasted so long that I stopped listening.

If the people in the last carriage weren't members of the royal family, then who were they?

"Sorry," I said quietly when the tirade on the other end of the line finally petered out. "I really am sorry. I should have called straight away."

Whoever had been travelling in that last, completely different carriage between Oslo and Bergen, it was incomprehensible that nobody had seen them after the accident. That couldn't possibly be true. Somebody must have helped them. Somebody from the rescue team must have helped them along the route from the tunnel opening to the hotel. As the rumours about the royal party grew, the only explanation I could come up with was that the people in the last carriage must have been taken out first, and were therefore already indoors and settled in the top apartment before the rest of us started arriving at Finse 1222.

"I'm sorry," I said. "Really I am."

Nefis was crying at the other end.

BEAUFORT SCALE 2

LIGHT BREEZE

Wind speed: 4–7mph

Clearly perceptible in extreme cold. Snowflakes moving horizontally rather than vertically.

CHAPTER
ONE

I was alone in the reception area. The large room was actually just as much a social area for guests, with the table along the windows facing south-west, a couple of capacious wicker chairs next to the staircase, and shabby sofas and chairs in what could, with a little bit of goodwill, be described as the bar at the other end. Someone had switched off most of the lights. In the semi-darkness I rolled my chair over to the corner behind a robust pedestal table where flasks of coffee had been laid out, along with a little machine that evidently provided hot chocolate. Above the bar hung another of the roughly carved signs: *Millibar*. I almost smiled. For a moment I thought about settling down on one of the two small sofas for the night. It would definitely be more comfortable. I decided against it.

It was quarter past one, and I was completely alone.

The information meeting had been less than informative. We had been told that it was snowing more than anyone could ever remember. That it was windy and extremely cold. That the derailed train was blocking the track to the west, and that there was no hope of getting any help from the east for some considerable time. Help from the air was obviously out of the question. We were assured that there was sufficient food and drink for everyone for several days, and that the electricity supply was not a problem either. There was a generator if the situation became critical.

The last point was the only thing I didn't know to start with.

A very boring meeting.

But afterwards I was still glad I'd been there.

CHAPTER
TWO

The total number of people residing in the hotel and wing was now 196, not counting the passengers in the mystery carriage. This included the hotel's seven employees, plus four men and one woman from the Red Cross rescue corps who had fortunately been in Finse getting everything ready before the start of the winter season. Three German tourists were the only ordinary guests. Two of them had arrived on the same train as the rest of us; they were the ones I had seen battling their way across the platform just before the train left Finse. They seemed pleased about the storm, and drank vast quantities of beer before being the very last to go to bed. The rest of the passengers from the train had been installed in the nearby buildings, which had names that fitted well with both the railway and the mountains: Finsenut, Elektroboligen and Tusenheimen. The distance between the main hotel and these buildings was no more than one hundred to three hundred metres, we were told. However, given the prevailing weather conditions, there was no possibility that they could come back for the meeting.

Of course, 196 people is not a valid number from which to draw statistical conclusions. There were, for example, too many men to allow a comparison with the normal population. And far too few people over sixty, as far as I could see. In addition, I had only managed to count four children under ten, plus the pink baby from the train, which I hadn't actually seen since the accident. Nor did I know much about the professional background of the passengers, even if it subsequently emerged that the number of priests and church employees was alarmingly high. A whole swarm of them were on their way to a conference on church matters in Bergen. Among them was the not universally popular football priest. Although after the confrontation with Kari Thue, I at least had begun to look at the man through new eyes. During the information meeting he sat alone behind one of the pillars by the bar, making it impossible for him to see the woman in knee breeches who calmly and slightly too quietly asked us to be patient, this will take some time. Before I lost sight of him I noticed that he looked unusually serious. Kari Thue really could frighten people out of their wits.

Despite the limited number of people, and given the excessive proportion of both the servants of God and the medical profession, I still had the impression that I was observing a representative group of Norwegians. Sitting there up against the wall by the stairs leading down to the hobby room and up to the old railway carriage that was suspended in mid-air, forming a bridge between the hotel and the private apartments, I was looking at an almost entirely white collection of individuals. Apart from the two Kurds and the three Germans, there was just one person of non-Norwegian origin: a dark-skinned man in his fifties, who judging by his accent came from South Africa.

And of course there might be the odd Swede or Dane hiding amongst us.

Since the number of foreigners resident in Norway comprises barely 9 per cent of the population, we were a little way off reality. But otherwise we had most elements. Self-confident young people in horrendously expensive clothes who didn't exchange a single word with dross like Adrian and his miserable girlfriend. Stressed businessmen with top-of-the-range laptops, desperately trying to get an internet connection. Screaming kids and middle-aged women. A handball team of fourteen-year-old girls were completely incapable of grasping the point of showing some consideration for others. They made a racket all over the hotel, arguing loudly over who was going to share a room with whom. Some adults were demonstratively uninterested in what was going on, while others chatted animatedly about everything from the allocation of beds and the unexpectedly delicious food to the bridge tournament that was under way down in the hobby room. What we had in common, and what distinguished us from the Kurds, the Germans and the South African, was that nobody was really all that worried. While the two Muslims constantly cast terrified glances at the windows and shrank before both Kari Thue and the roar of the storm, the rest of us were more or less having a nice day out. The Germans did seem excessively delighted at being able to add a hurricane to their list of experiences, but even after six large strong beers none of them was able to hide their respect for the storm and their fear of its consequences. The South African seemed to have a more scientific fascination with the whole thing. He often went over to the window where he would shake his head, place one hand against the glass and peer myopically out into the whirling snow as if he were searching for something. A couple of times he clambered up onto the windowsill and rested his forehead against the cold glass, seemingly lost in dreams.

The rest of us just sat down in our Norwegian way, and turned into a little piece of Norway.

Which, when I thought about it, was bound to lead to a crime sooner or later. A quick calculation told me that it would happen within five days, from a purely statistical point of view, taking the average and making no adjustments whatsoever to allow for current circumstances.

But in five days I would be far, far away from Finse.

We all would.

I'd better mention the dogs as well. There were four of them on the Bergen train when it came off the rails, and they were all rescued. A poodle, a Gordon setter, and something that I later discovered was a Portuguese water dog.

The fourth and final dog frightened the life out of everybody around it, and the owner had to lock it up, keeping it away from children and other sensitive souls.

CHAPTER
THREE

I had fallen asleep.

Fortunately I realized this straight away when Geir Rugholmen shook me by the shoulder. I quickly turned my head away and wiped my mouth with my sleeve. I dribble terribly in my sleep.

"Is it true what the doctor said?"

He was speaking quietly in a strained whisper.

"What?"

I straightened up in my chair and raised my arms. He was too close.

"Are you with the police?"

"I was. It was a long time ago. Can you move a bit further away, please?"

I drew my head back irritably to show how I was feeling. I glanced at the clock, which was showing five thirty. In the morning.

"What sort of police?" he persisted, without moving.

"Norwegian. I was a perfectly ordinary Norwegian police officer."

"Don't be difficult. What did you work on?"

"I was with the Oslo police for twenty years. I worked on all kinds of stuff."

"What rank were you?"

"Why are you asking me all this?"

Geir Rugholmen flopped down heavily on one of the chairs.

"Enough," he said drily, "I don't understand why you have to be so unpleasant. There's a body out there on the porch. Frozen stiff."

He covered his face with his hands, resting his elbows on his knees.

It struck me that I liked his smell. He smelled of mountain and man and fresh air. I'm not all that keen on mountains or men or being outside. Not that I actively dislike any of those things, but they have no importance in my life. And yet the smell of his clothes reminded me of something I couldn't quite get hold of, something warm and safe that I had presumably tried to forget.

"It was pretty stupid to go out there," I said. "Talk about asking for it. Freezing to death, I mean."

"He didn't freeze to death."

I tried to look uninterested, Geir Rugholmen got stiffly to his feet. Shook his head, smiled wryly and pointed over at the windows, which on sunny days presumably provided a fine view of Finsevann and the mighty Hardangerjøkulen glacier on the far side of the lake. The windows were deep and the ledges served as seats.

"Your pal doesn't seem to need much in the way of comfort," he said.

I hadn't been alone after all. Adrian was asleep on the window ledge in an icy draught, with a jacket under his head and a blanket over him. His feet were sticking out in their worn-down trainers, and the cap was still pulled well down over his eyebrows. His breathing was regular.

"What happened?" I said as Geir Rugholmen turned to leave.

"I've had enough."

"You said the body was frozen stiff. But he didn't freeze to death. So what happened?"

He stopped without turning around.

"Are you finally giving in? Do you really want to help?"

I didn't want to help at all. The only thing I wanted was to be brought down from the mountain, away from all these people and the storm and the bloody snow, which as time went by had made it difficult to see out. Trying to focus on something in all that chaos where there was nothing on which to focus made me feel sick and dizzy.

I didn't reply, but he stayed where he was.

"He was shot," he said. "At close quarters, as far as I can tell."

"Shot."

He slowly turned around. Took a couple of steps towards me before stopping, wiping the snuff from the corners of his mouth with his thumb and index finger, and taking a breath before saying something.

"My name is Hanne Wilhelmsen," I said, pre-empting him. "And many people would probably say that I can be a little difficult."

Geir Rugholmen took my outstretched hand without smiling.

"They'd be right. Geir, as you have no doubt forgotten."

"No. So who's out there?"

He didn't let go of my hand.

"Cato," he said after a brief hesitation. "The football priest. Cato Hammer."

For some reason I was not surprised.

That surprised me.

In order to avoid giving away what I was thinking, I looked over at Adrian. I was trying to come up with a reason why I had thought of Cato Hammer even before Geir Rugholmen answered my question. My own antipathy towards the man could of course be the reason, but then it struck me that I would have much preferred to see Kari Thue dead. Leaving aside the fact that I didn't really want to see anyone dead. Let alone murdered.

I just wanted to go home.

Adrian snored a little, and turned over in his sleep. Then he curled up into a ball and his breathing became calm and even once again.

He reminded me of a stray dog that has been badly treated.

CHAPTER
FOUR

"We've taken pictures from every angle and every side as best we could in the storm," said Geir Rugholmen, groaning beneath the weight of what until recently had been Cato Hammer, a priest at Ris church in Oslo, born in Trondheim, raised in Kristiansand, and with an inexplicable connection to the Brann sports club.

The woman with the quiet voice who had spoken at the information meeting was looking around as if she didn't know what to do. I remembered that somebody had introduced her as the director. She herself preferred a less pretentious title.

"Berit Tverre," she said seriously. "I'm the manager of Finse 1222."

Her hand was ice-cold, her skin chapped and rough. She was wearing blue knee breeches, khaki socks with a woven pattern, and a thick, beige woollen jumper. Her hair was blonde and caught up in a ponytail, and her eyes were as blue as those on a poster girl for Nazi Germany. A healthy, beautiful hotel manager aged about thirty-five.

"I was the one who found him," she said, clasping her hands in front of her mouth and blowing on them.

"Bloody hell, it was cold holding that camera. I hope the pictures turn out OK."

She held out a digital camera to me as if I had suddenly been elected to lead the investigation, without any indication of agreement on my part. I didn't take it. Berit Tverre hesitated, then put the camera down on a large industrial oven. I hoped it was a while since it had been switched on.

"I don't really know if the kitchen is the most suitable place to keep a corpse," I said. "But I don't suppose environmental health will be paying us a visit in this weather."

Geir tipped the body onto an island in the middle of the room. The island was made up of a gas hob, a large sink and an old-fashioned oven with an iron grate. Each part was a different height from the rest. Berit had placed a lid over the sink. Above the whole thing hung a fan, a rectangle several metres long made of frosted glass with aluminium fittings. For a moment it made me think of a coffin, which might descend on the corpse at any moment.

Cato Hammer definitely looked uncomfortable lying there. His eyes were wide open. His mouth was gaping, his tongue pressed against his palate. The entry wound went through the left cheek immediately below the eye, and you didn't need years of experience as a police officer to see that the shot must have been fired at close quarters. I would even hazard a guess that the barrel of the gun had touched the skin. A bluish circle was visible around the hole. As soon as Geir hauled the corpse inside, I had noticed that the exit wound was large. I felt no compulsion to look at it more closely.

"Shouldn't we," Geir began breathlessly, "shouldn't we take his temperature? To find out how long he's been dead?"

"If you feel like sticking a meat thermometer in his liver, carry on." I brushed the dead man's face gently with my hand and went on: "You could try with the brain. Or some internal organ. Personally, I wouldn't bother. We won't learn much from a measurement without precise instruments."

"But what about you? I mean, you said . . ."

"Once upon a time I was a tactical investigator," I said. "As a lawyer you ought to know that's something completely different from what the crime scene technicians do on *CSI*."

"I work in property development," said Geir. "As a police officer you ought to know that's something completely different from criminal law. And I don't waste time watching television programmes. What do we do now?"

I slowly wheeled my chair around the corpse. There wasn't much room, and I got stuck for a while by the windows. It looked as if Cato Hammer might have broken his arm. Without touching it, I leaned forward. There was something about the angle of the lower arm. The palm of the hand looked unnatural, lying there with the thumb in the wrong place.

"I'm afraid that's my fault," said Geir. "As far as I know, nothing was broken when I picked him up. I — I dropped him on the floor out there. I'm sorry. As I said, we have got photos of him as he really looked. What do we do now?"

Both the entry and exit wounds showed that Cato Hammer had been shot with a heavy-calibre weapon. A revolver, in my estimation.

"They make a loud noise," I said.

"What?"

"Where did you actually find him?"

"Two or three metres from the door," said Berit Tverre. "And it was a close thing."

"What was?"

"Well, he was practically buried in the snow. I could see his hands and a bit of his left leg. I only went out to put up a new thermometer."

"Remember that."

"What?"

"Remember how much of the body was visible," I said, without taking my eyes off the dead man.

In spite of the fact that the corpse looked terrified, on closer inspection there was something trusting about his expression. It looked as if he had been enormously surprised at first, and had then happily decided that the surprise was a positive one. Perhaps he had caught sight of his God in time, and realized that things weren't so bad after all.

"What in the world could he have been doing out there?" asked Geir. "Outside? In this weather? Or do you think he was shot first and then dragged outside afterwards by —"

"That," I broke in, "is probably a key question. If we find out what Cato Hammer was doing outside in a snowstorm in the middle of the night, we've got the murderer on a plate. Unfortunately, it's not that easy to get any answers out of poor Cato here."

"I mean, he is pretty well used to the mountains," said Berit, looking at the corpse with an expression that suggested melancholy rather than grief. "He ought to know better than to go outside now. In this weather. I don't understand it. He knows . . . he knew the mountains."

"How do you know that?" I asked.

"He's been here before. To the hotel, I mean. Several times. Most of those who say they know the mountains are lying. But he . . ."

I thought I could see the hint of a blush on her face. On the other hand, she did have rosy cheeks anyway.

"He was also pretty cautious by nature," said Geir, looking sceptically at the dead man.

"Did you know him as well?"

"Well, I don't know if I'd go that far. I'm on the board at Brann. Which means it's more or less impossible to avoid bumping into this idiot."

"But . . . cautious? What do you mean by that?"

Geir shrugged his shoulders.

"He kept his guard up. Tried to be nice to everybody, kind of. A bit . . . polished around the edges. Wanted to please everybody. That sort of thing."

He wrinkled his nose and adjusted the snuff.

"I had the opposite impression," I said. "I mean, he must be regarded as controversial, surely?"

Geir didn't reply.

"Have you got one of those dolls they use to teach CPR?" I asked.

"A what?"

"One of those . . . It's called Resusci Annie, or something like that, isn't it? The doll you use to learn mouth-to-mouth resuscitation?"

"No," said Berit Tverre sceptically.

"It's a bit too late to try mouth-to-mouth on Hammer."

Geir laughed. Under the circumstances, the shrill, girlish laughter made him seem even more unsure of himself.

"Some other kind of doll, then," I said. "Life-sized. Have you got anything like that? If not, maybe you could make one. Out of blankets and a cabbage, for example."

"And why would we want to do that?"

It really is amazing how slow people can be. Even educated people who are familiar with the mountains. I looked at Berit Tverre, waiting for the penny to drop.

"Oh," she said eventually. "We put the doll in the snow in the same spot, and see how long it takes for it to get covered in snow to the same extent."

"That would at least give us some kind of indication of the time of the murder," I said, nodding. "If the weather remains as bad, more or less. And it would be a useful thing to do. For those who will end up investigating this eventually. Which will be incredibly straightforward, of course."

I had seen more than enough. So had Cato Hammer, I expect. I ran my hand over the staring, dead eyes. The body had already begun to thaw, and it was easy to close his eyelids.

My chair was halfway across the floor before Geir pulled himself together.

"What shall we do with the body?"

"Put him in the freezer," I suggested. "Or put him outside again. Find a sheltered spot and cover him up with a tarpaulin or something along those lines. Use your imagination. There ought to be enough cold places up here. Where's the train driver?"

Without waiting for an answer I moved off and added:

"Let the dead take care of the dead."

"Hang on a minute!"

I stopped, and even managed not to sigh.

"What are we going to do?" Geir persisted. "There's a murderer out there, and as far as I know you're the only one with any kind of police experience, and —"

"Listen to me," I said, turning my chair around. It isn't completely impossible for me to be nice if I want to be. "This so-called Royal Carriage," I said, drawing quotation marks in the air. "As far as I understand it, the passengers from that carriage have been installed in the top apartment in the wing. I have no idea who was on board. But at any rate, I certainly don't believe they were royals. Our royal family simply doesn't behave that way. But as the platform *was* actually cordoned off in Oslo, and as the whole thing is surrounded by such enormous secrecy, then I have to conclude that there must be police officers among them. Security guards, perhaps, if not from the palace. And since this is

69

definitely a case for the police, it would be an excellent idea to seek them out and explain the situation."

There was of course an ulterior motive to my sudden attack of volubility. I was looking directly into Geir's eyes as I was talking. Once again I saw that faint flicker I couldn't quite interpret. He licked the corner of his mouth as if he wanted to divert attention from the fact that he was blinking too often.

"I think you both know who's up there," I said with a smile.

Neither of them said anything, but nor did they exchange glances. Berit Tverre was looking downwards at an angle, and I was unable to see what she was studying so carefully. In the silence between us I realized I was afraid of the hurricane for the first time since I woke up on the floor in the reception area after having been rescued from the train. The gusts of wind were so strong that we could hear the clink of glass and the rattle of tins. At brief, irregular intervals we heard loud thuds and bangs against the outside walls, as if the weather gods were beginning to believe that it might at last be possible to tear down this building, after all those stormy mountain winters.

"I think you know," I repeated, moving towards the door leading into the lobby. "But that's none of my business, of course. None of this is, fortunately. But I'm still —"

A violent gust of wind against the wall brought me to an abrupt halt.

"I'm still going to give you a piece of advice," I went on when the unexpected surge of fear had abated.

70

"Fetch one of the doctors. There are plenty of them around. Not because they can be of any help to Cato Hammer, but because it would be a good idea to conduct a preliminary examination. When it comes to the actual murder, that can wait. There's no point in starting an investigation here and now. Wait for better weather. Wait for the police. Let them do what they can, and this will all be cleared up in no time."

I had reached the door; I pushed it open and rolled out of the room.

Nobody made any attempt to call me back.

CHAPTER
FIVE

I couldn't sleep, of course.

I had moved over to the long table, and I didn't really know if it was because I wanted to get closer to Adrian, or further away from the kitchen. Geir and Berit had emerged and walked past me without a word. I had no idea what they had done with the corpse out in the kitchen. With the roar of the storm it was impossible to say whether they had bundled Cato Hammer into the walk-in freezer or whether he was still lying on the metal worktop; the thought reminded me that I was hungry.

Adrian was still curled up on the window ledge with his back to the storm. The blanket had partly slipped off. I was close enough to pick up the smell of badly dried clothes and sweaty feet, but far enough away for him not to notice when I turned my chair to look at him more closely. He was completely motionless.

Once upon a time I had been able to sleep like that too.

The boy looked good. As he lay there now, not screwing his mouth up in that practised, dismissive expression, I could see that his lips were full. Even though they were dry with flakes of loose skin and a sore right across the centre of his lower lip, the half-open mouth gave away how young he was. His teeth were white and even, his tongue pink and happy, like a puppy's tongue. A little spot by the side of his nose was the only defect on his beardless face: you could call it a beauty spot. I was tempted into pushing the cap up from his eyebrows. I didn't complete the movement. He sat up with a jolt, a protective hand held in front of his face.

"It's only me," I said quietly. "Wouldn't you rather lie down on the sofa over there?"

"Shit," he mumbled. "I was dreaming."

I hadn't seen the sweater he was wearing before. It was a bit too small, even for a skinny boy like him. He was still wearing his own thick hoodie underneath the sweater; it was sticking out at the neck and wrists, as if he were caught in a cocoon and were trying to escape.

"You shouldn't go to sleep in clothes that are too tight."

"I'm cold," he said, yawning.

"Try it the other way round. Put the sweater inside with the hoodie on top."

"It's too bloody scratchy."

"Would you rather be itchy or cold?"

He didn't reply, and pulled a face as he turned his head.

"You can borrow my padded jacket to put over you," I said, pointing over towards the sofa by the bar.

I wouldn't get any more sleep tonight.

"Veronica lent me this," he said, looking down at his chest. "She knitted it herself."

"So her name's Veronica, then."

He grinned and looked up.

"Look at this . . ."

He lifted the sweater slightly. Just above the lower part at the front, Vålerenga's logo had been knitted into the pattern, roughly and with letters that could be made out only with difficulty. Adrian laughed, a dry, unfamiliar laugh,

"It's a bit stupid having the logo so low down, really."

"Not very Nemi, being interested in football," I said. "Shouldn't you try to get a bit more sleep?"

Instead of replying he stretched and put his feet on the floor. He gave an enormous yawn. His breath was musty and smelled of stale alcohol.

"Who's been giving you drink?"

"Somebody."

"The somebody who gave you the sweater?"

"Mind your own fucking business."

I moved away.

"Anyway, it's not fair," I heard Adrian mumbling. "Some people were allowed to bring their luggage from the train. I wasn't. Were you?"

"I was unconscious," I said, struggling to get a drink of hot chocolate out of the machine in the bar. "So the answer is no."

"My iPod's still there. And my clothes. I haven't even got a toothbrush."

"You can buy one down in the kiosk."

The machine must be switched off. There were no lights showing. I was manoeuvring my chair behind the counter to look for the plug when a thought struck me.

74

"You were awake during the rescue operation," I stated casually. "Did you notice whether most people managed to bring their stuff with them?"

"Noooo . . ."

Adrian considered the question.

"That woman with the pink kid was yelling because she got it into her head they weren't going to take the buggy. And then there was some idiot who wanted to take a massive great trunk with him. They wouldn't let him. I didn't really think about my own bag. At the time. I just wanted to get away from . . ."

"Were you brought out early?"

"Early?"

"Yes, were you among the first to arrive at the hotel?"

I'd given up on the chocolate machine, and was looking at Adrian. He flushed red.

"I'm fifteen years old, for fuck's sake. I keep on hearing that I'm just a kid, only a kid." He put on a voice that was presumably meant to represent a middle-aged, female childcare expert. "In which case it's only right that I was among the first to be rescued!"

"That's absolutely true. But that means you were here when people started to arrive. Do you remember anything else about that business with the luggage?"

Adrian stood up and came over to me. With quick, sure movements he examined the front and back of the machine before getting down on all fours, fishing out a plug and inserting it in a socket that I couldn't see.

"It ought to work now," he said. "Can you reach?"

"Yes. Thank you."

"There wasn't actually all that much luggage," he said thoughtfully. "Now you come to ask. People just came pouring in, all cold and bad-tempered. But there were a few of those arseholes, those business types in suits and so on who had their laptops with them. They clung to their computers like that woman from our carriage clung to her kid. And then there was an old woman with a knitting bag. At least, that's what she said it was. And then there were loads of girls with ordinary handbags. And then of course Veronica had her black bag. And then —"

"Can you write this down for me, Adrian?"

"You what?"

"Could you possibly be very kind and write down everything you can remember about the luggage? Who had what?"

"Write it down! I can't see a computer around here. Can you?"

"By hand, Adrian. You can write things down by hand, can't you?"

He was suddenly preoccupied with getting a cup of hot chocolate from the machine.

"I don't care how bad your handwriting is," I said.

"I can't," he said. "Anyway, why should I?"

"Because I'm asking you nicely. And because it's actually important to me. And because I think you're a really sweet, lovely boy, deep down."

At least he was old enough to appreciate irony. He could smile. Chocolate came frothing out of the dispenser.

"Sweet and lovely," he repeated. "Absolutely."

He burnt his mouth on the hot drink.

"Paper," he said, sucking cool air onto his tongue.

"There's bound to be some over there," I said, pointing towards the reception desk. "And a pen."

He shrugged his shoulders and ambled across the floor with the cup in his hand. He was still wearing the tight woollen sweater that made his upper body look small and misplaced on top of the wide jeans that were far too long.

I heard footsteps on the stairs. At first I thought the noise was coming from outside.

"What are you doing here?" said Adrian in a churlish tone of voice. "Can't you tell the time, or something?"

In spite of this, Magnus Streng nodded pleasantly at the boy as he walked across the room, followed by Geir Rugholmen, and stopped in front of me.

"I hear you've been informed," he whispered. "It would be a great help if you could come with me to the kitchen to take . . . a closer look at the whole thing."

"I've already seen everything worth seeing," I said quietly, keeping an eye on Adrian who was searching rather too intrusively behind the reception desk.

"Adrian! You're supposed to be finding some paper, not poking around in other people's belongings!"

"Please? I'd really appreciate it."

Dr Streng was persistent. I hesitated for a moment, turned my chair around and gestured towards the kitchen door, where a large metal sign informed us:

It is dangerous to go near the electrical wiring with a fishing rod or line.

Adrian was left alone once again.

When I got back it turned out that he had made a remarkable list. First of all, it was packed with detail. He hadn't observed every single passenger as they arrived at the hotel, but he had written a precise description of some fifty passengers and what they had brought with them from the train. Adrian had only named six of them, which was perfectly reasonable; he hadn't known anyone before the train crashed. The rest were so accurately described that I immediately knew to whom he was referring. The boy was unusually observant, particularly in view of the fact that he walked around with his cap pulled down over his eyes the whole time. It was also clear that he had the ability to work quickly; I could hardly have been away for more than forty minutes.

However, the most remarkable thing of all was the appearance of the list. His handwriting was as elegant and even as if it had been print, with a style that has not been taught in Norwegian schools since before the war. Although the paper was blank and unlined, it looked as if Adrian had used a ruler. There were full stops and straight margins, graceful loops and beautiful capitals, like something from a textbook on calligraphy. Nor could I find one single spelling mistake in the six-page document.

But I knew nothing of this as I followed Dr Streng and Geir Rugholmen into the kitchen. The only thought that struck me as I glanced at the boy for the last time before the door closed behind me was that I would really like to know what time he had settled down to sleep on the window seat.

I was hardly the only one who had heard what he said when Cato Hammer was standing on the table holding what was to be his last address to a large congregation.

I could only hope that no one had taken much notice of Adrian's outburst.

No one apart from me, I mean.

CHAPTER
SIX

"Actually, I think he was a good man," said Dr Streng as he slowly moved around Cato Hammer's corpse with his rolling gait. "Even though he did a lot of stupid things. He had his demons, that's for sure. From time to time he struggled terribly. Both with his God and the one downstairs."

"It sounds as if you knew him," I said.

The doctor didn't reply. He merely nodded slowly and meaningfully as he examined details on the dead body. The nose, with its strange, bluish-yellow colour. The eyes, which were open, frighteningly. I knew I had closed them earlier. He stopped by the damaged arm and leaned forward, looking at it closely. Geir Rugholmen hastened to explain his little accident while moving the body. Dr Streng waved his right hand airily and moved on.

"I am bound by my vow of patient confidentiality," he said eventually, without taking his eyes off the corpse. "But given the circumstances, I can tell you that Cato Hammer was once my patient. Just a few years ago, in fact. I had quite a small private practice alongside my post at the university. Since I can safely say that Cato Hammer's needs when it came to medical treatment lay outside my field of competence, I referred him on after two or three consultations."

He stopped, placed his hands on his back and rocked back and forth on the balls of his feet. He reminded me of a penguin on patrol.

"Mmm," he said several times; I hadn't a clue what he was confirming to himself.

"What was it?" I asked.

"Sorry?"

Streng sounded surprised.

"What was he suffering from?"

"The incurable loneliness of the soul. Yes indeed."

"He didn't exactly seem to be lonely," mumbled Geir.

"I am talking about the spirit, my good man. About cracks in the soul. About the eternal inner struggle between good and evil. Or in Cato Hammer's case, between God and Satan. It's not easy, that kind of thing. Not easy at all."

Well I never, I thought, but managed to hold my tongue.

"I referred him to a psychiatrist," said Streng after taking a deep breath. "Even though I was of the definite opinion that the best thing for him would be to talk to an educated and experienced theologian. Which I told him, in fact. But it didn't help. I think he simply didn't dare to go down that road."

Silence descended over the kitchen, as if we were all rather embarrassed to have learned that the boastful TV celebrity Cato Hammer had been in need of psychiatric help.

"It would have been helpful . . ." said Dr Streng so suddenly that I jumped. Then he stopped. Peered at the bullet hole. His head was just on a level with the corpse, but he didn't look for anything to stand on. "It would have been helpful," he repeated, "if someone had taken the trouble to check the temperature of the body when he was found."

Geir caught my eye. A little twitch at the corner of his mouth was all he allowed himself. And he didn't give me away. Instead he shrugged his shoulders apologetically and said: "There are only electronic thermometers here in the hotel. For medical use, I mean. And we didn't think it was a good idea to take the temperature inside the ear of a corpse."

"Hmm," said Streng. "But the best thing would have been the liver. A meat thermometer would have done the job perfectly. There must be one of those around, surely? I mean, the brain is a bit of a mess," carefully he lifted Hammer's head and examined the brutal exit wound, "so the simplest method, which is to shove the thermometer up here . . ." he pointed at the priest's nostril, "and into the brain would presumably have told us very little. When was he brought inside?"

Geir looked at his watch. "Just over an hour ago."

"It's quite simple to work out, actually," said Magnus Streng. "In principle it takes twenty-four hours to halve the difference in temperature between the body and its surroundings. In other words, if it's minus twenty-five outside and we start with the premise that Hammer was an active, healthy man with a body temperature of thirty-seven degrees, then the difference will be . . ."

82

"Sixty-two degrees," I said.

The doctor smiled and nodded.

"In other words, twenty-four hours in the snow would give our man here a core temperature of six degrees," I added. "Thirty-seven minus half of sixty-two, which is thirty-one. Six degrees. I'd call that dead. But he wasn't lying out there for that long. And he's been lying in here for a while. And he was partly covered by snow, which protected him. Plus the strong wind out there is an uncertain factor when it comes to the actual temperature. Plus . . ."

Streng smiled again and held up his chubby hands.

"I got your point quite some time ago."

Berit Tverre came into the kitchen. She was out of breath, and hadn't got round to removing all her outdoor clothes. Her voice almost disappeared as she made her way around the partition screening off the washing-up area, struggling to take off her capacious anorak.

"It's pointless. I've tried three times. The first time, Mr Cabbage Head was completely covered in snow in four and a half minutes. The second time it took almost quarter of an hour. The last time it happened so fast I didn't even have a chance to check how long it took."

"Ergo," I said, "in this case we will just have to rely on good old tactical work."

"Which should be easy, according to you."

I looked enquiringly at Geir.

"That's what you said when you were in here earlier," he insisted. "You said this investigation would be incredibly simple. Or something along those lines. Is that what you think?"

I nodded.

"We have a very limited number of suspects, all of whom are trapped up here. A limited geographical area to examine, to put it mildly. I think the murder will be cleared up in a day or two. Once the police have taken over, of course. I mean, they have to make a start first."

"But in the meantime . . ." Berit Tverre said hesitantly.

"In the meantime you can do as I said, and fetch one of the police officers I assume are in the top apartment. Or you can do what you've told everybody else to do, just chill out and relax. This storm has to die out at some point."

In the meantime, I thought, there's a murderer with a heavy-calibre weapon wandering around amongst us. In the meantime we can only hope that the intention of the person in question was to kill Cato Hammer, and that he or she would not dream of harming anyone else. While we are waiting for the police, I thought without saying anything, we could pray to the gods every one of us must believe in that the perpetrator was rational, focused, and did not suspect any of us of knowing who he or she was. And that he or she would have no reason to suspect that anyone might be starting to investigate the case here and now.

"Take it easy," I said. "Everything will be fine."

BEAUFORT SCALE 3

GENTLE BREEZE

Wind speed: 8–12mph

Wind clearly perceptible, can be troublesome.
Falling snow appears to move more rapidly
horizontally than vertically.

CHAPTER
ONE

I was definitely getting rusty.

When Adrian gave me the list he had made, I was impressed. The only problem was that I couldn't work out what I wanted it for. Perhaps I had hoped it would be complete when I asked him to do it. I took the fact that I could even think such a thing as an indication that I was further away from the Oslo police district than I had felt in many years. And not just literally.

The document would have been useful if it had contained a complete overview of all the passengers and what they had brought with them from the train. The compilation of such a list presupposed that someone had been given the task before people started arriving at the hotel. A thorough registration process, like in a prison. The papers the boy handed me with an embarrassed gesture barely supplied more than the obvious. Their artistic appearance was impressive, and they told me something new about Adrian.

"Thank you," I said, and meant it.

"OK."

I looked up at him when I had finished going through the list, folded the sheets and tucked them in a pocket on the wheelchair. He just stood there looking awkward with his hands dangling by his sides, his eyes downcast.

"You did have someone," I said. "In spite of everything. So did I. For me it was wooden houses."

"What?"

"For me it was cottages built of wood. I had a neighbour when I was a child. He was a carpenter. A caretaker. To be honest, he was the only person who was really there for me. The other adults around me didn't waste much energy on my existence. But I'm bloody good at building wooden houses."

Adrian looked sceptically at my chair.

"Was." I corrected myself with a nod. "I was good at building wooden cottages. Bloody good."

"What's the list for?"

"It could be useful. Who did you have? Who taught you this? This fantastic, elegant handwriting?"

"Has something happened?"

He was scraping at the worn, uneven floorboards with his shoe.

"Yes."

"What?"

I was saved from coming up with an answer. Geir Rugholmen rushed in, grabbed hold of my chair without a word and pushed me towards the kitchen. Adrian followed a few steps behind, but stopped dead when Geir snapped at him,

"I don't like being pushed," I said as the door closed behind us.

I could see that the corpse had disappeared. Since they couldn't have taken it through reception without my seeing them, I assumed they had used the walk-in freezer. On the other hand, I wasn't really sure whether there might be another way out of the kitchen.

The thought of the freezer reminded me how hungry I was, and I placed a hand on my stomach.

"Now listen," said Geir, placing himself directly in front of me. "Listen to me." His voice was higher than usual. "I did what you said."

He coughed and crouched down so that his head was lower than mine, but I didn't really know if it was a great deal better than looking up at him.

"I went up to the top floor. There are actually three apartments, numbers seventeen, eighteen and nineteen. They're all on the same corridor. And there's a guard up there."

As if he wasn't sure whether I was listening properly, he waited for a reaction before he was prepared to carry on.

"I see," I said, shrugging my shoulders. "A guard. With all this secrecy, that shouldn't really surprise you. Of course there's a guard."

"An armed guard."

There are a few individuals who have really known me. Not many, of course, and until I was twenty it was only the carpenter who lived next door who sometimes made an honest attempt to see who I was. Since then, many have tried. Far too many, an exhausting number in fact, but I have been strong enough to prevent most of them from succeeding. When I started to run out of strength, I stopped letting anyone try.

But there are a few. They've all said the same thing, complaining and accusing me. Hanne shuts down. In any discussion, from a noisy quarrel to the simplest conversation, sooner or later I reach a point where I no longer have anything to contribute. Usually sooner, so they say. Always too soon, they've all said.

But I always think best alone.

"Hello!"

Geir placed a hand on my arm and shook me.

"Did you hear what I said? There's an armed guard in the corridor outside the three apartments on the top floor!"

"What sort of weapon is he carrying?" I said into thin air, mostly in order to have something to say.

"How the hell should I know! A rifle. Or an automatic rifle. Or an automatic pistol maybe; it looked like something in between."

"Haven't you done military service?"

"Community service. I pushed old people around in their wheelchairs in a care home."

"Don't you hunt?"

"No I bloody don't! I know nothing about guns, but even my five-year-old son would have realized he was carrying a gun."

"Was he a Norwegian?"

"What?"

90

"Was this armed man a Norwegian?"

"Of course he was a Norwegian! It's hardly likely that some foreign squadron has been scrambled out here at Finse, is it!"

"They have squadrons in the air force and the navy," I said. "Not in the army. And anyway, we're not really talking about the military here, are we. How do you know he was a Norwegian?"

Geir stood up and sighed demonstratively.

"He spoke Norwegian. He looked really Norwegian. In other words, he was totally Norwegian."

"What did you talk about?"

This was actually beginning to resemble a conversation, and Geir calmed down slightly. He looked around for somewhere to sit.

"I said hello," he said, and hitched himself up on the work surface that until quite recently had been the resting place for the remains of Cato Hammer. "And then I introduced myself. I didn't get any further."

He waited in vain for my response.

"He just told me to go away," he continued impatiently.

"Did he aim the gun at you?"

"Did he . . . No. He told me very firmly to go away. I had only just got through the door, and I half-closed it before I tried to say anything else. He interrupted me and repeated the order. Go away. That's what he said. Several times."

This was the final, irrevocable proof that the royal family were not in Finse on this stormy February night.

They would neither need nor demand such protection. The question now was who did.

The answer that immediately struck me was terrifying.

An enormous crash made me jerk back in the chair so suddenly that I almost tipped it over.

The cold rushed in through the broken window, and it took only a few seconds before the floor was covered with snow several metres inside the room. The air turned dirty white with whirling snow and howling wind, and I found it difficult to breathe. Berit Tverre came racing in. Glass and paper swirled around the room, and I bent forward in my chair with my hands linked behind my head, as if I were in a plane that was about to crash and could do nothing more than hope for the best. I had noticed that there were a dozen or so scoops and ladles hanging from a pole beneath the fan. Now they were flying around the room, and one of them almost hit me on the head.

In the old days I had a good sense of time.

I could pinpoint a given period of time with great precision, without using my watch. It was useful. That ability, or perhaps it was more a question of intuition, has disappeared. I get mixed up. I fumble and I have no idea how long it was before silence fell once more. The storm was still roaring, of course, but at least it was on the right side of the wall. Compared with the raging bedlam when the window caved in, this was total silence.

I unlocked my hands from the back of my neck and slowly raised my head.

Berit and Geir were sitting under the smallest window in the food preparation area, completely out of breath. They had secured the window with a solid wooden panel. It was still freezing cold in the room, but the snow on the floor was already melting.

"Thank you," I managed.

They both started to laugh. They gasped for breath and laughed. They each waved a hammer in the air as if they had just won a life and death struggle. Which they had, in a way.

"Wow," came a voice. "Bloody hell. Could that happen to these windows in here?"

Adrian had come into the kitchen without our hearing him. He took a few steps from the washing-up area, screened off by a partition, and came into the main kitchen.

"Is there anybody else out there?" I asked.

"No. They're all asleep. Could the big windows go as well?"

Berit stood up and held out her hand to Geir to help him up.

"No," she said firmly. "This window has needed fixing for a long time. I should have secured it when the storm started."

Adrian grinned as if he were choosing how much of Berit's assurances to believe, and was looking forward to the chaos to come.

I brushed the snow off my sweater and my chair. If nothing else, the storm's sudden attack on the hotel had put a stop to a conversation I wanted to avoid.

"Come on," I said to Adrian, heading for reception. "Let's leave these people to clear up."

The metal on my wheels was so cold that it made my palms smart as the door closed behind me. I was seriously concerned, but unfortunately my anxiety had nothing to do with the weather.

CHAPTER
TWO

"What's actually going on?"

Adrian had sat down on the window ledge with his back to the glass and his feet on the table. His arms were folded demonstratively across his chest. I chose to ignore him. He sat up straight.

There was no chance of keeping the murder of Cato Hammer a secret. I had realized that as soon as I saw the body. The priest had been one of the most conspicuous people on the train, and he hadn't exactly made himself invisible the previous evening. Even if many of the passengers had expressed their scepticism and displeasure, there were clearly a number who liked the man. As far as I understood it, there had actually been some kind of service down in the hobby room. Quite successful, I had heard from an elderly married couple who thought I was asleep, and quite well attended. Hammer might well have had plans for the morning too. Besides which, he was a member of a larger party.

Sooner or later somebody would start asking questions about the football priest's disappearance. The question was whether I should lie to Adrian in the meantime.

"Are you deaf, or something? What's going on? What do you all keep doing in the kitchen?"

I looked at the boy.

Strictly speaking, there were 193 suspects in the case, since I could only say with absolute certainty that the pink baby and I were innocent. Bearing in mind the force of the raging storm, if it was at all physically possible to move from place to place in the village of Finse, then the circle of potential perpetrators would have to be extended. Apart from the passengers who had been provided with accommodation outside the hotel complex, I had heard that there were others out there too — the odd cottage owner and four Polish joiners who were busy restoring one of the apartments in Elektroboligen.

An uncertain but limited number of possible murderers.

Adrian was one of them.

"What the fuck's the matter with you? Hanne! Hello!"

It was the first time he had used my name. I don't know how he knew it. He must have eavesdropped on the conversation between Dr Streng and me when he was dressing my wound.

Adrian had been pretty aggressive the previous day. But I was convinced that his outburst against the priest had been an expression of general contempt for adults. And for authority. And in particular for any football team other than Vålerenga.

"Look at me," I said eventually.

"What?"

He pulled his cap further down.

I leaned forward and pushed it back.

"Look at me," I said again. "What have you got against Cato Hammer?"

"Cato Hammer? That idiot who supports Brann?"

I couldn't see the slightest hint of shame or fear. On the contrary, his eyes narrowed in contempt and when he looked away and glanced around the room, it was as if he were hoping the priest might pop up again for a fresh mauling.

"You don't make jokes about football," he snapped. "Brann suck. And that wanker doesn't even speak with a Bergen accent! He's never even lived there! He isn't —"

"Not many Vålerenga fans were born and brought up in eastern Oslo," I broke in. "Were you?"

Stupid question. No doubt Adrian had grown up all over the place. And nowhere. He didn't bother to reply.

"Cato Hammer is dead."

He looked completely floored for a few seconds before screwing his eyes up again, this time in disbelief. When he eventually opened his mouth to say something, I thought I could see a hint of fear in his eyes. At the same moment we heard a racket on the stairs. I turned around in a reflex action. A family of four were making their way noisily down with the Portuguese water dog pulling on the lead. It barked when it spotted me.

"It's seven o'clock," the father trilled enthusiastically. "A new day, new opportunities!"

"What were you going to say?" I asked Adrian quietly, trying to catch his eye again. "You looked as if you were going to say something?"

It was too late. He shrugged his shoulders and tugged at that bloody cap.

"Nothing."

"Nothing?"

"Sorry to hear that, maybe. Or oh, how dreadful. Is that what you mean? Whatever."

"I find it odd that you haven't asked how he died."

Adrian sighed.

"How did he die?" he asked.

"He was murdered."

"What?"

"He was shot."

"When?"

The question surprised me. I concentrated more on trying to interpret his facial expressions than really listening to what he was saying.

"Last night," I said briefly.

"Where is he now?"

"You're asking some very odd questions."

"Just like you," he said, nodding in the direction of the coffee machine. "Do you want a drink?"

Adrian was a child in many ways, and even if I have allowed myself to be fooled by adults for some reason, I have yet to meet a young person who can carry off that particular role.

"Don't say anything to anybody else," I said. "For the time being."

He stared at me for a second before shaking his head. "Keeping something like that a secret," he muttered. "That's bound to go well. Do you want a drink or not?"

Adrian was himself again. The annoying thing was that I couldn't be completely certain what I had seen in his face when the noisy family with the dog disturbed me.

But it could certainly be compared to fear, and I couldn't work out why this made me so uneasy.

CHAPTER
THREE

I had no way of knowing if it was Adrian who had given the game away. Probably not, given that when the boy did communicate with anyone other than me, it was through sullen words of one syllable. Apart from with Veronica, I assumed, although I had only seen them together in mutual silence. In any case, the girl hadn't come down to breakfast yet. On the other hand, everybody else had. Kari Thue was complaining loudly about how well she had slept.

"It's a disgrace," her thin voice sliced right across the room to me. "It's absolutely indefensible, allowing people to sleep so heavily and so late under these circumstances. Many of us could have suffered concussion in the accident without realizing it. And if that happens, the person is supposed to be woken up at regular intervals!"

The lobby had been transformed into a transit hall, and rumours were buzzing as people came and went. Everyone seemed to be en route to somewhere. They stayed just long enough for the gossip to start up again, exactly as it had on the train before the accident. I sat there utterly fascinated, listening to one improbable tale after another. The rich flow of stories had only one truth in common: Cato Hammer had disappeared.

The dining room was in the wing that stuck out towards Finsevann, with an entrance leading from St Paal's Bar. As far as I knew, the staff also used a conference room further in, on the other side of the wall from Blåstuen. My food had been served on a tray by a woman who for some reason was smiling the whole time. I had noticed her the previous evening. She was obviously employed at the hotel, and treated me with a friendly air of collusion that I was unable to understand. Even if I had taken part in the unpleasant events of last night, and was also in a unique position because of my inability to leave the reception area, there was no reason to treat me like a member of some kind of Finse club. I immediately assumed that she knew what had happened to Cato Hammer. It would be difficult to deal with both the corpse and the practical problems linked to the murder without informing the staff. At the moment she was wandering around like some kind of mountain Pollyanna, dispensing smiles and laughter in all directions. Which was remarkable in itself, really. The atmosphere among all those coming and going from the dining room, some carrying plates and coffee cups, was becoming more and more intractable as the questions came thick and fast and nobody seemed capable of providing any answers.

"Everybody will be told what's happened." She smiled in a doomed attempt to calm the masses.

"There will be an information meeting in here at nine thirty! Everybody will be told then."

I didn't like her, but the food was good.

"Is it true?"

One of the girls from the handball team was staring at me. She was slender, flat-chested and lanky. Her tracksuit was red, and she was wearing new trainers from which the laces had been removed, for some reason. I frowned.

"Is it true?" she repeated with a smile.

Her teeth were enclosed in a sturdy metal framework. I smiled back.

"Is what true?"

"That he's dead, that bloke. That priest."

"Why are you asking me?"

"Well, at least you're sitting still," she said, looking around before perching on the table and swinging her legs. "All the other adults are just wandering about all over the place."

The teenagers, who had been playing poker all evening and had shamelessly sneered at the dead priest, were determined to believe that Cato Hammer had tried to get to Haugastøl on a stolen snowmobile. Since several people thought they had heard the sound of an engine during the night, and Kari Thue was pretty sure the weather had improved slightly at about three o'clock, the story of Cato Hammer's wild mountain adventure took off. Somebody insisted they had heard shouting and screaming at about that time, and by the way, where were the Red Cross people? Had there been a fight? A very shaken woman, who later turned out to

102

be the cause of all the fuss, maintained over and over again that she was supposed to have had a meeting with Hammer at eight o'clock, which was now over an hour ago, and that he was not the kind of person to miss a meeting. She knew him very well, she explained, fighting back the tears. It was out of the question that Cato Hammer would leave them all in the lurch in this godforsaken place. As he wasn't in his room, and nobody, absolutely nobody, had seen him since eleven thirty the previous evening, he was definitely dead or seriously injured. Perhaps he was lying helpless in the snow, and couldn't somebody go out and look for him, for God's sake?

"I don't think it is exactly godforsaken here," said the girl with a grin, her brace glinting in the light. "It's quite a nice hotel, actually. Don't you think so?"

A man in jeans and a blue blazer was standing motionless in the middle of the room just a few metres away from me. He looked bewildered, a marker post for all those rushing to and fro. I had noticed him the previous day. He was part of the large church delegation. When Cato Hammer was trying to gather people together for a service, the man in the blazer had seemed troubled, almost embarrassingly agitated. A couple of times he had tried to tug at Hammer's sleeve, as if to calm the over-energetic priest. Now he was just standing there looking lost, running a hand nervously over his thin hair.

"Is it true?" the girl from the handball team persisted. "Is he dead, or has he done a runner? But then why would he do that? Is it possible to run away in this weather? Do you know what's happened?"

"Hi," I said, nodding to the man who had taken a couple of steps towards me and the girl in her red outfit. "Is there something I can help you with?"

He gave a thin smile, took the last few steps and held out his hand. "Roar Hanson," he said, not quite sure whether to acknowledge the girl as well.

"Hanne Wilhelmsen," I nodded. "You looked as if you were wondering about something?"

"We all are, aren't we?" said the man, pulling up a chair. "I must say I am a little anxious."

"Do you know Cato Hammer?" I asked. "Or . . ." I gave a little laugh. "How well do you know him? I saw you talking to each other several times yesterday, and —"

"We're friends," said Roar Hanson seriously, then hesitated. "Yes. We are friends. Not very close friends, it's fair to say, but we were at college together and . . . I don't understand . . ."

He stopped.

I tried to follow his gaze. The noisy family with the water dog were trying to find somewhere to sit. Adrian wasn't all that keen on moving for their sake. Instead he made room for Veronica, who was wearing just as much make-up as the previous day. On her feet she was wearing a pair of red woollen socks that I had seen Adrian wearing with his trainers only last night. I thought this business of swapping clothes was more common among kids younger than these two. Perhaps it was romantic. What do I know about that kind of thing.

The dog was barking and his good-natured master threw some scrambled egg on the floor before holding a strip of bacon up in the air and making the dog jump. The children clapped. Roar Hanson wrinkled his nose.

"They're pretty liberal when it comes to dogs in this hotel," he said, seeming more depressed than annoyed.

"So you're a priest as well," I said.

"Yes. Well, I'm an ordained priest, but at the moment I don't have a parish, I'm working as a secretary within the national church commission. We're on our way to . . . We were supposed to . . ."

For some reason he was unable to tear his gaze away from the family with the dog. The animal was now working its way through a large helping of cornflakes with jam. It was splashing milk everywhere. Adrian was amusing himself by tossing bits of salami into the sweet mixture. Veronica remained expressionless, as ever.

"You were going to Bergen," I said. "We all were. How did you . . ."

"Is he dead?" Roar Hanson whispered. His mouth was trembling.

I was beginning to wonder if I had police officer stamped all over me. The only thing that distinguishes me from everybody else is the fact that I'm in a wheelchair. And that I might be slightly more dismissive than most people. Both these elements tend to lead to the same result: people keep away from me. Right now, you would think I was suffused with some kind of empathetic magnetism. People kept coming up

105

to me, asking questions, poking about. It was as if my stationary sojourn in a room where everyone else was simply coming and going made me so different that I had been accorded the status of oracle; an omniscient authority, a position to which I had never asked to be elevated.

"Why are you asking *me* that question?" I wondered as he kept his eyes fixed on mine.

"Is Cato dead?" he repeated. "Is he . . . Has someone killed Cato?"

We had both forgotten the girl from the handball team. She leaned towards us, her mouth half-open. She smelled of peppermint, and carried on chewing loudly without bothering to hide her excited smile.

"Is it true?" she whispered, "A real murder?"

"Yes," said Roar, rubbing his eyes. "I think it is true. But I can't believe it."

I didn't know what to say. There was quarter of an hour left before the information meeting. I still had no idea what was going to be said. As a general principle I tend towards the view that honesty is always worthwhile. As I let my gaze wander from the girl's expectant expression to the priest's anxious, tear-filled eyes, I was no longer so sure.

The best thing would probably be to come up with a first-class lie.

CHAPTER
FOUR

I escaped.

I was saved by a terrible noise that at first made me think another window had succumbed to the storm. Fortunately, I was wrong. The racket was coming from the stairs, where two lads came rampaging through with ski boots on their feet. They were yelling and screaming, and at first it was impossible to make out what they were saying.

The atmosphere at Finse 1222 had not survived the night.

After the traumatic experience on the train, the feeling of security offered by coming indoors and being supplied with hot food and plenty to drink, by the sense of community, a bed to sleep in and a few games of cards had bound us together. Since none of the passengers knew the train driver, his dramatic death had not put a damper on the air of joyful gratitude. On the contrary. Poor Einar Holter's tragic demise gave an extra pinch of spice to the experience, a reminder of how lucky the rest of us had been.

The morning had brought with it a growing, sour impatience. True, the family with the black dog was still relentlessly bloody cheerful, but as the hotel's communal lounge began to fill up at around eight thirty, I soon noticed the change in atmosphere.

For one thing, the storm was beginning to get on our nerves. It was getting worse and worse, and none of us could understand how this was possible. The storm had been raging earlier, with constant hurricane-force gusts, and the wind gauge on the pillar dividing the reception desk in two was indicating that it could hardly go any higher. Berit Tverre kept going over to check. From time to time she glanced briefly at the large windows, and a furrow I had not noticed earlier had appeared at the top of her nose.

Cato Hammer's disappearance made things even worse. At first I didn't think people would be particularly concerned. I mean, obviously they would react if they got to know the brutal truth about how he died. But so far no one knew, apart from the staff, Dr Streng, Geir Rugholmen, Adrian and me. The general unease over the fact that one person hadn't turned up for breakfast was therefore striking. After all, Finse 1222 is a real old haunted house of a building, with lots of hidden nooks and crannies and narrow, forgotten corridors. Bearing in mind Cato Hammer's theological flexibility, something he had constantly stressed in public, he could just as well still be lying in a warm, comfortable bed, which according to the Bible he shouldn't be doing.

But then there was this woman. She was hysterical, to put it mildly. It was driving us all mad. Most people were already in a somewhat unstable frame of mind by the time the two lads hurtled down the stairs and into the lobby, both bawling at the same time.

"He's shooting! They're shooting up there! On the top floor! They've got guns!"

Six or seven people were standing at the foot of the stairs; two of them were girls from the handball team. They started shrieking as if a boy had surprised them in the shower. From my position diagonally across the room with the long table between me and the stairs, I saw an elderly man give such a violent start that he threw a full cup of coffee up in the air. It rotated slowly on its way down to the floor. In his confusion the old man lost his balance. The bouncy dog got red hot coffee on its nose, and barked, howled and whimpered in turn as it zigzagged among all the people, searching for its owner. When the old man fell to the floor, the girls put their hands to their faces and took a deep breath before letting out an ear-splitting, atonal scream. Someone shouted for a doctor. The dog owner yelled imaginative curses at the lot of us before he finally managed to grab the dog; he clutched it to his chest and rushed into the men's toilets. Roar Hanson, who for some reason was standing right in the corner behind the counter in the Millibar, where strictly speaking nobody was allowed except the staff, threw himself on the floor and disappeared from my view. I noticed that Veronica, Adrian's black-clad friend, was standing on the same side of the bar. She started to laugh, a surprisingly hoarse, deep laugh that in no way matched the rest of her spindly figure. The Kurd also hurled himself down, but unlike the priest he was thinking of others, not himself. He lay down on top of his wife, covering her with his body. The movement was so quick that it must have been something he had been trained to do. A woman who had been sitting on her own knitting throughout the previous evening started sobbing loudly. The pink baby, whom I hadn't seen since the accident, woke up and started yelling in her mother's arms. The noise level in reception threatened to drown out the storm. Shouts about guns and shooting were still coming from the stairs. One of the businessmen — I thought I might have seen his photo in *Dagens Næringlsiv* but I couldn't think of his name — quickly closed his laptop, wriggled out of the window seat and started to run towards St Paal's Bar with the computer under his arm.

"They're going to shoot us!" somebody bawled. "They're on their way!"

The man increased his speed. Several people followed him. A four- or five-year-old boy with his mouth full of food and a roll in each hand was knocked over by a tall woman as she ran. I tried to move so that I could help the child, but I barely had time to release the brakes before Geir Rugholmen came racing out of the kitchen. He picked up the child and placed him on my knee in one smooth movement before climbing up onto the table, raising his arms in the air and bellowing:

"Stop! Stop! *Shut up, the lot of you!*"

It was like flicking the switch on a circuit breaker.

Not only did everyone stop talking, but all the people who were running, pushing and waving their arms around froze like the players in a game of statues when the music stops.

Afterwards, I thought of that moment as a turning point. The atmosphere had shifted long ago. And yet it was only now that I really began to feel afraid. Not of the storm. Not of the murderer at liberty in our midst.

"Right, listen to me!"

Geir was no longer bellowing. There was no need.

"He's dying!" a feeble voice shouted from the stairs, at the far side of the lobby. "Elias is dying! Somebody help me!"

Geir gazed out across the room, at all the faces turned towards him. Before he found what he was looking for, Dr Streng and the female gynaecologist were hurrying across the floor in a slalom race between the motionless figures. The female doctor was the first to reach the man on the floor. She bent down, and I could no longer see her or her vertically challenged colleague.

The boy on my knee was weeping quietly.

"Stay exactly where you are," hissed Geir Rugholmen. "Nobody is shooting. Do you hear me? *Not one single shot has been fired, and not one single shot is going to be fired.* Is everything OK over there?"

Nobody answered him. I could hear rhythmic counting from the other end of the reception area, and assumed that Elias's tired heart had been unable to cope with so many exhausting experiences in less than twenty-four hours.

I heard cautious steps behind me, and half-turned around. It was the woman who had knocked over the little boy without stopping. She stood on the short staircase between St Paal's Bar and reception, next to the businessman who had also come back, crestfallen and red-cheeked. Some of the others who had tried to flee from the imagined shooting drama were slowly moving closer. The woman was staring at me with eyes that reminded me of why I had begun to feel so afraid.

A sense of unease was spreading through the room. The counting stopped. I looked up at Geir, who could presumably see what was going on from his elevated position. He rubbed a hand over his eyes.

"I'm very sorry," said the female doctor, far away.

The only sounds that could now be heard above the storm were the sobs of the little boy I was holding, and the weeping of the woman who had just become a widow.

The Finse disaster had just claimed its third victim.

The woman behind me came up to my chair, held out a thin, uncertain hand and said, "I'm sorry. You must forgive me!"

I didn't look at her. Instead I met Geir Rugholmen's gaze. He was still standing on the table, his legs wide apart; he was strong, but there was an air of resignation about him. We were both thinking the same thing.

The people who were snowed in at Finse 1222 had begun to let go of their dignity. And only eighteen hours had passed since the accident.

CHAPTER
FIVE

After Elias Grav's ill-timed heart attack, people did at least seem to be trying to pull themselves together. The two young men who had started the whole thing by yelling about guns being fired seemed quite upset. Geir had not given up until they had loudly and clearly admitted that maybe there hadn't been any shooting. But they had definitely seen guns! There was a man, or maybe even two, standing in the corridor outside the top floor apartments with an automatic weapon in his hands. They stuck to that, the boys, even if that business about the shooting might possibly have been cracking and banging caused by the storm. They might have misheard. They really didn't mean to scare anyone, they said in their defence, but when the rumours started about the guards on the top floor, they felt they had the right to investigate the matter. Geir repeated his clear instruction: everyone was to respect the cordon he had set up in front of the door leading to the narrow corridor; Berit Tverre then took over and informed the assembled company that unfortunately Cato Hammer had passed away during the night. He had been carrying out a small errand down in the lobby at about three o'clock, and had fallen over. The cause of

113

death was presumed to be a massive brain haemorrhage. Magnus Streng confirmed this, weighed down with seriousness, his hands joined together as if to show respect for the dead man's profession.

"And it's almost true, after all," I said. "It certainly was a real bleed in the brain."

Nobody cracked a smile.

We were in the kitchen: Berit Tverre, Geir, Dr Streng and I. We couldn't hear a sound from the lobby, and not only because of the noise from outside. The old man's heart attack had been a shocking thing to witness. The widow's lack of self-control hadn't exactly improved the situation. People moved away in silent embarrassment, and when the sad explanation for Cato Hammer's disappearance was delivered, most of those present had had more than enough. Some went back to their rooms. Others chose to stay in the communal areas without really knowing what to do. The continuation of the previous day's bridge tournament had been postponed for the time being. Evidently playing cards was regarded as inappropriate under the present circumstances. It didn't stop the gang of poker-playing teenagers, but at least they'd had the decency to withdraw down to Blåstuen. On the whole, people seemed to have swallowed Berit's lie hook, line and sinker. However, I was still somewhat concerned about how the murderer might have reacted to the story. I had tried to look for any changes in facial expression as Berit was giving her little speech, but it was pointless to try to read anything from the small number of people I could see from the position I was in. If the perpetrator had actually been in the lobby when Cato Hammer's death was announced, we could only hope that he or she accepted the incorrect cause of death as a temporary declaration of peace from the hotel management.

People must be kept calm at all costs.

Including the perpetrator.

"Who's actually up there on the top floor?" I asked, looking from Geir Rugholmen to Berit Tverre. "I really do think I ought to be told at this point."

They were spared the need to answer the question.

"It's rather difficult to prepare food for almost two hundred people when my kitchen has been converted into some kind of conference room," the chef interrupted us crossly.

He was surprisingly young, with a thin beard and short, spiky hair. Despite the cold draught coming from the broken window, he was wearing only a vest over his full-length apron. Both items of clothing were dazzling white and freshly ironed. He was chewing on a toothpick. Behind him stood two assistants, a woman and a man.

"Could you at least move a bit further in? Over there?"

"It'll be a bit cramped," said Berit, shrugging her shoulders apologetically. "But I suppose we can . . ."

She pulled two bar stools that had turned up during the morning towards a door I had never opened. I followed slowly, with Geir and Magnus Streng right behind me.

We were standing in a storeroom with three substantial doors on the right-hand side. Freezer, fridge, and another cool room.

"This is where we have our deliveries," said Berit, banging a metal door with her hand. "As you can tell, the insulation in here isn't much good. But we'll just have to put up with it. We do have an office behind reception, with no steps," she nodded in my direction, "but I've got three men in there trying to keep in touch with the outside world. This is the only place on this floor where we can be left in peace, to a certain extent. Don't worry about the kitchen staff. They're concentrating on what they're meant to be doing."

"I'm perfectly comfortable sitting here," I said.

Nobody thought that was funny either. Magnus Streng hopped up onto the high bar stool with surprising agility. Berit took the other. Geir Rugholmen leaned against the wall and folded his arms.

"So," I said.

"We don't really know much," said Geir, scratching at his beard.

I waited in vain for him to continue. Berit and Geir looked enquiringly at each other, as if they hadn't really decided who was going to speak.

"When the train crashed," Berit began hesitantly, stopping to take a deep breath before going on. "When the train came off the rails and crashed, we heard it. In spite of the fact that by that stage the weather was already unpleasant, to say the least. The Red Cross people rushed over."

116

I remembered somebody mentioned the Red Cross depot, a building attached to the wing of the hotel on the opposite side.

"But the strange thing is," Berit said, taking her time. "The strange thing is that there was a phone call. It can't have been more than two or three minutes after we heard the crash, and the telephone rang. At first I was intending to ignore it, I was convinced something serious had happened to the train and I really wanted to get the rescue operation under way. But somebody . . ."

She shook her head, as if she were trying to come up with an explanation for her own behaviour.

"I answered the phone."

From the kitchen I could hear the clatter of pans and a whining noise that I took to be an electric meat saw. By now the draught from the door leading to the delivery area was so strong it felt like a breeze. I shivered.

"Who was it?" I asked, when nobody seemed keen to continue.

"I don't really know."

"Right. What did this person want?"

"He . . . It was a man. He mentioned a name, but I didn't hear it properly. What I did grasp, however, was that he was from the police security service, PST. His voice was . . . insistent, I'd say. Authoritative. As if he was totally used to giving orders. And everything happened really quickly."

"But what did he say?" Magnus Streng asked impatiently. "What did the man whose name you can't remember want, and what did you do?"

"He said the last carriage had to be emptied first. They had their own snowmobile with them, he said, but they would need more than that. One more."

"Their own snowmobile? A snowmobile? On the train?"

Magnus Streng reminded me of a clown again, just when I had forgotten how funny he was.

"Yes. It turned out to be true. Not one of the biggest, but big enough for a driver and one passenger to get here long before the others. Perhaps twenty minutes or so. But the strangest thing of all was that he knew where they were to go."

"Who?" I said. "The man on the phone, or the one on the snowmobile?"

"Both, actually. But I meant the man on the phone. 'Put them in Trygve Norman's apartment,' he said."

Streng's mouth fell open. I don't suppose I looked all that much more composed. We looked at each other and closed our mouths simultaneously.

"Yes."

Berit raised her hands in a gesture that was half resigned, half eager.

"That's what he said! That's exactly what he said. And Trygve's apartment is indeed the one right at the top, furthest to the west. It's the best apartment here at 1222, if we ignore the director's residential quarters which are of course . . ."

She shook her head and broke off.

"It's no secret that Trygve owns that apartment, on the contrary, he's one of the driving forces when it comes to keeping this place going and . . ."

Once again she stopped. Cleared her throat and went on:

"But the whole situation left me so confused that I didn't say a thing. And then . . . then he gave me a mobile number. But that was only after he . . ."

Her eyes suddenly filled with tears. I could see the muscles in her cheeks twitching as she gritted her teeth. She was breathing deeply through her nose.

"Everything's fine," said Dr Streng, placing his chubby hand over hers.

She merely nodded. Then she swallowed once more.

"We are *not* in a dangerous situation."

"The man on the phone," I reminded her. "First of all he did or said something. Then he gave you a telephone number."

"Yes. First of all he said it was extremely important that I did what he said. That the people in the last carriage must get here before everybody else. He did actually use the word 'extremely'. Then he added that it was" — she searched for the right words — " 'a matter of national security'. Isn't that what they say?"

"Yes," I said. "That's what they say. If that was what he meant. And the number?"

"I just had time to scribble it down. He said I could call that number if I didn't believe him. But that I would have to hurry, if that were the case."

Suddenly she started rummaging in her trouser pockets. She couldn't find what she was looking for on the right-hand side, but she pulled a folded scrap of paper out of the left-hand pocket.

"I chose to believe him. I didn't think I had any choice. So I never called the number. Instead I made sure they went straight up to the apartment as soon as they arrived. The first two, I mean. One of them spoke Norwegian. He was polite, but stressed. Or . . . very snappy, somehow. The other one didn't say anything. He was wearing so many clothes that I'm not even sure about the sex. But I think it was a man. He was . . . big. Powerful, I think. But of course that could just be the clothes. Hat, hood, anorak, ski goggles . . ."

I held my hand out for the piece of paper. She passed it over.

"Did the number of the man who rang come up on the display?" I asked her, looking at the eight numbers on the paper.

There was no area code.

"No. It said *number withheld*. But he did give me that number."

"Do any of you have a phone like that?" I asked without looking up from the piece of paper. "With a hidden number, I mean, so that you can't see who's calling?"

"Here," said Magnus Streng, passing me his. "I've got two mobiles — one for work, and this one for family and other important people. It has a hidden number. Sometimes it's nice not to be at everybody's beck and call."

He grinned broadly and said:

"I expect it's the same for all of us."

Without replying I keyed in the number. It rang twice before someone answered. A man gave his name.

I was no longer aware of the storm or the penetrating racket from the three chefs in the kitchen. I could no longer feel the troublesome draught. On the contrary, a wave of warmth flooded through my body, I felt light-headed.

Empty of thoughts.

Afterwards I would regret hanging up. I didn't say a word, I simply broke the connection when the man had twice asked who was calling, without getting an answer. When I tried to call again later in the day, I was informed by a mechanical voice that the subscriber has changed to a new number. *This subscription has been terminated at the subscriber's request. No redirection details available.*

I should have said something when I had the chance. Because it was not difficult to recognize the man on the other end of the phone. He had answered, introduced himself with his full name, without any intermediary, without some secretary or adviser or *please wait while we try to put you through to the Foreign Secretary.*

The number Berit Tverre had been given by a stranger just a few minutes after the train crash went straight through to the private telephone of the Norwegian Foreign Secretary.

Or one hell of an impressionist.

Whichever it might be, I didn't understand a thing.

CHAPTER
SIX

"Who was it?"

"Nobody."

"Nobody? But I heard somebody answer!"

"It was nobody," I repeated, clicking my way through to Magnus Streng's *numbers called*.

With a couple of clicks the number I had just called was deleted from the phone's memory, I passed the elegant, steel-grey phone back to Dr Streng. He took it and looked at it enquiringly, as if he expected it to start chatting away by itself.

I pushed the piece of paper into my trouser pocket.

"That was of no relevance to our situation," I said. "Let's move on."

"Move on?"

"Geir," I said, taking a deep breath. "You have an irritating tendency to repeat what I say."

"And you have an irritating tendency to avoid answering my questions."

"Think," I said. "Think."

Geir opened his mouth and I could see from his face that he was about to repeat what I had said yet again, with a big question mark after "think". He managed to stop himself.

"I think we ought to let the mad woman in the attic run her own race," I said with a smile. "Or the man, for that matter. Given the current situation we ought to concentrate on our own problems. Let's leave the people upstairs in peace. They have nothing to do with the murder of Cato Hammer. And even less to do with the storm. Besides . . ."

It was obvious that Geir had to exercise considerable self-control to stop himself coming out with a fresh torrent of questions. I smiled at Berit and nodded towards reception.

"I was impressed with that lie you came up with out there. Very wise. It actually looked as if people believed you. Perhaps it was the old man's heart attack that did it. Reminded us all of our vulnerability, I mean. How quickly something can happen. How fragile life is. Under normal circumstances I'm not really in favour of lying, but in this case . . ."

"You're in favour of keeping quiet," said Geir.

"Well, yes," I said, shrugging my shoulders. "In this case it was at least sensible to come up with a story. Probably. Given the hysteria that broke out when those boys came rushing in, who knows what would have happened if people had found out about a veritable execution. By the way, how could you be so sure they hadn't actually heard a shot? As far as I could see, you came out of the kitchen, not down the stairs."

"Pure guesswork," said Geir. "I just assumed they were wrong. It's very clear that we're dealing with professionals up there. It's not particularly professional to fire at civilians when you could probably frighten them off by shouting boo. Nor is it particularly professional to shoot at unarmed lads. Besides which . . ."

He scratched the back of his neck and pulled a face I couldn't quite interpret.

"If they *had* heard shots, I had to try to get them to believe they were mistaken. As it is people are already feeling sufficiently . . ."

We knew exactly what he meant.

"I'd better get back in there," said Magnus Streng after a pause that left us all feeling somewhat troubled. "To my patients. There are dressings to be changed. Broken bones to be attended to. I'll be much more useful in there than in here. If I may be so presumptuous, Adieu, ladies and gentlemen!"

I laughed and waved a hand in his direction. He was a man at whom you waved. By and large, Magnus was a person it was impossible to dislike, in spite of my efforts to do so. I decided to give up as I watched the small figure walking towards the kitchen door. Time had long since moved on from Dr Streng's kindness and archaic language. At the same time he had the aura of an old-fashioned gentleman, a little bit too pushy and sometimes slightly ridiculous, but even so. Magnus was a nice man. I seldom meet men like that. I seldom allow myself to meet men like that. I don't want to.

"Hello!"

I gave a start as Geir waved a hand in front of my eyes.

"Where's Berit?" I mumbled.

"Sometimes you look as if you're in a trance," said Geir; it was difficult to tell if he was irritated or worried. "She left. Didn't you see her go?"

I didn't reply. Instead I stared at him as if I had never seen him before. His eyes were an indeterminate grey-brown colour. His face was dark for the time of year. Beneath the black stubble I could see a pale grey area of dry skin. He must be younger than me, the deep lines around his eyes and on his forehead had been caused by sun, wind and cold. Not age. I guessed that he was around forty. I had noticed that he took snuff all the time, but now he suddenly got out a packet of cigarettes and offered one to me. I surprised both of us by accepting, placing the cigarette in my mouth and leaning forward for a light. We both turned our backs on the clattering coming from the kitchen.

That first drag.

You never forget how good it is.

All cigarettes should be put out after the very first drag.

"Has it been a long time?"

Geir smiled and lit one for himself.

"Many years. I've got a kid."

"Me too. Three of them, I still smoke. In secret, mostly."

He laughed out loud, that delighted, girlish laugh.

He still smelled good. A scent of something I didn't want to think about, but it was so strong right here and right now that I couldn't help it.

Once upon a time I had someone called Billy T. He was my best friend, and that was why he had to go. I barely have room for Nefis in my life. The fact that it is possible for us to share a life that is sometimes both good and secure is down to the fact that she's the only person in the world who has mastered the art of being close and completely absent at the same time.

And then I have Ida. She has ice-blue eyes that look at me with a love I didn't believe existed. Ida still thinks I am a good person. But she's still only three years old.

We also have a kind of housekeeper, our little family, an old sparrow with a broken wing who sort of moved in without anyone actually asking her. But I'm not fond of Mary. She is simply there, like a human piece of furniture, and I have learned to live under the same roof as her.

That's enough for me: Nefis, Ida, and a tired, dried-up whore who cooks our meals.

I never think about Billy T any more.

Perhaps it was because of the smell of Geir Rugholmen. Perhaps it was because of the endless noise of the storm and the wind raging around Finse 1222, lumping us together into more than just 196 separate individuals, or rather 194: Hammer and Elias Grav had already been removed from the register. And perhaps that was what it was. Two dramatic deaths in less than twenty-four hours had proved too much even for me.

Once upon a time I was knee-deep in corpses. Literally, on a couple of occasions.

I really was out of practice. In police work as well as everything else.

It had cost me too much, letting people into my life. So I stopped trying. Only now, after many years of self-imposed isolation, was I beginning to see what hard work it was, keeping people at a distance. And I thought about Billy T for the first time since I don't know when.

"You're doing it again," said Geir, stubbing out his cigarette on the floor with his heel.

"Doing what?"

"Disappearing."

"I don't think you should leave the butt there," I said. "We are in a kitchen, after all."

He held out his hand for my cigarette, dropped it on the floor and stood on it before picking up both butts.

"What do you think about the people upstairs?" I asked slowly.

He frowned.

"A little while ago you said we ought to forget about them!"

"Yes. But now it's just the two of us. What do you think?"

"Everything and nothing. I really have no idea who they might be."

"In that case, you haven't looked closely at the facts we already know."

"Which are?"

The chef suddenly appeared in the wide opening leading into the kitchen. His hands were on his hips, and he looked furious.

"Is someone *smoking* in here? Well?"

"No," said Geir and I in unison.

Geir slipped the butts unobtrusively into his pocket. I caught myself hoping they were still burning slightly.

127

"It stinks in here," said the chef, wrinkling his nose. "One more time, and that's it — no more using this for your meetings. Got it?"

We both mumbled heartfelt assurances of cooperation.

He went back to the food. I could have released the brakes on my wheelchair and said thank you for the cigarette. I could have gone back to reception and started to look forward to lunch. I had so many opportunities to upset Geir all over again.

"They're Norwegians," I stated instead. "They have something that requires a particularly high level of protection. An object or a person."

"A person," said Geir firmly. He was perched on the bar stool Berit had left. "They didn't bring any luggage from the train. It would be somewhat over-dramatic to have all those guards up there if they're supposed to be guarding something that's been left behind in an empty train wreck."

"The object could be small. They could have had it on them."

"They could have looked after a small object down here. There's no need to barricade yourself in an apartment because of a small object."

"Exactly."

"But you said . . . I thought . . ."

"I'm only going through the possibilities. I totally agree with you. There's a person up there who requires protection. Who requires that?"

"What?"

"Who requires high-level protection?"

128

"Politicians, the royal family, superstars . . ."

"We're in Norway," I interrupted him. "None of our politicians or royals need that kind of protection. And we're not exactly falling over superstars. In any case, even Madonna or Robbie Williams wouldn't want this kind of fuss. They'd rather have —"

"A prisoner," he suddenly broke in.

"Exactly. A prisoner. Since the Norwegian National Railways would hardly have cooperated with anyone other than the national authorities when it came to something as irregular as adding an extra carriage to the train, we must assume that this is about transporting a prisoner."

The draught from the door to the delivery area was starting to get me down. My muscles were aching, and I regretted leaving my padded jacket in the lobby.

"A prisoner who needs to be moved," I summarized. "How are prisoners moved?"

"How are prisoners moved?"

I smiled. Before I had time to point out that he had already fallen back into his old, sinful ways, he went on:

"By plane. By car. But by . . . train?"

"Completely impractical," I nodded. "In fact, I've never heard of such a thing. The train is bound by the track. It is driven by others. It starts and stops according to a timetable. Horror of horrors. Of course the same thing is more or less true of a plane, but at least it's fast."

"Perhaps the prisoner is afraid of flying?"

"In that case they could use a car, easy as pie. Even if the journey across the mountains in winter isn't exactly a pleasure, travelling by car would be considerably easier than attaching an extra carriage to a train full of civilian passengers. To be perfectly honest . . ."

I was looking, presumably longingly, at the cigarette packet in his breast pocket. He took it out and offered it to me.

"No. I don't want the chef after me."

"You said you were going to be honest."

"Yes. We've already established that it must be a prisoner. With all the fuss we can safely assume that it's a high-risk prisoner." The cold really was painful. I clasped my hands together and held them up to my mouth. Blew. The warm air made me shudder. "And in that case, nobody," I said emphatically, "not one single guardian of the law on this earth would voluntarily transport a high-risk prisoner on a passenger train. Least of all on the Bergen line in the middle of winter. They were obviously aware of the risks imposed by storms and snow, since they brought their own snowmobile with them. Impressive. And that one detail tells us more than a lot of other things. This is a journey they have dreaded. A journey they have been planning for a long time. A journey that has scared the shit out of them."

"So why did they do it, then? And who are *they*, anyway? Police? The military? The prison service? Why couldn't they just . . ."

He stopped dead as he saw me smiling broadly for the first time. Perhaps the sight frightened him.

"They had no choice," I said, wheeling my chair towards the door.

"They always have a choice, surely . . ."

"Not in this case."

I made a quarter turn.

"We're not just talking about a dangerous prisoner here. We're talking about a dangerous prisoner whose position is such that he can make demands. There is no other explanation for choosing to take the train; the prisoner himself must have insisted on it. For whatever reason."

The last comment was a straight lie. The reason why a prisoner would prefer to take the passenger train to Bergen rather than travel by plane or car was terrifyingly obvious. But there were limits to how much I was prepared to share with Geir Rugholmen. For the time being, at least.

"And there aren't many things more dangerous than a prisoner who can get the police to do something as idiotic as this," I went on. "So I'm sticking to my recommendation: leave the people on the top floor alone. I'm absolutely certain they have nothing to do with the murder of Cato Hammer. The problem of having a murderer in our midst is, to put it mildly, considerably greater than having a gang of nervous guards upstairs."

I moved away from him and out through the door. The beginnings of a headache reminded me how tired I was. In spite of the fact that the conversation with Geir Rugholmen had been interesting, at least for him, I had not stopped brooding for one minute about the telephone number Berit Tverre had been given by someone working within the police security service minutes after the accident.

The kitchen was filled with the aroma of chicken soup, and the chef was no longer in a bad mood. On the contrary, he gave me a small portion to taste in a coffee cup.

"An hors d'oeuvre," he said. "To stimulate the appetite."

He called it mulligatawny. I didn't correct him, even though there were neither pieces of apple nor rice in the greasy, rich soup, with the oil forming little beads on top of golden brown deliciousness.

It was the best thing I'd ever tasted.

Soup for the soul, that's what the Americans call that kind of thing.

And we certainly needed it.

BEAUFORT SCALE 4

MODERATE BREEZE

Wind speed: 13–18mph

Unpleasant out in the cold, with noticeable resistance. Falling whirls away in the wind. Snow lashing the face is very unpleasant.

CHAPTER
ONE

Time was passing noticeably slowly. Perhaps it was because I felt hungry all the time. We had barely finished a huge lunch before I felt the pull in my midriff that had me looking around for something to put in my mouth. When I didn't find anything I leaned over to Adrian and tucked a hundred kroner note into his hand.

"Will you go to the kiosk for me, please? Get some snacks. Crisps or peanuts. And half a litre of cola."

"I'm not your fucking errand boy. And you eat a hell of a lot, I have to say. That can't be good. You'll end up looking like a . . ."

He wasn't sure what I'd end up looking like. I can understand that. I have a certain amount of self-awareness. I look younger than I am, and I weigh sixty-four kilos. Slightly less than I should, since my height is 172 centimetres. If I'm measured while I'm lying flat out on the floor, that is. Which I never do, but my height was written down in my passport at the time when I was able to stand. Getting fat isn't a problem, but I often feel hungry. Almost all the time. A psychologist who was once forced on me ages ago got a little bit too hung up on that particular point.

"Are you a good boy or are you not a good boy?"

Adrian was actually good-looking when he smiled.

"I'm a very good boy," he laughed.

He was a mystery in many ways, was Adrian Droopyjeans. When he tucked the note in his pocket and set off, Veronica stood up and followed him. I still hadn't heard her say a word. She moved surprisingly silently. Since there was no longer any trace of snow or dampness on the floor, most people had started going around in their stockinged feet. The woolly socks she had borrowed from Adrian looked very strange with the Nemi-inspired clothes. She reminded me of a slinking black cat with bright red paws. And she had a magnetic attraction when it came to dogs — they always came up to her wagging their tails, no matter how deeply asleep they appeared to be when she walked by.

Cracks had appeared in the windows facing out towards Finsevann during the course of the morning. Only in the outer panes, to be fair, and Berit Tverre had dismissed the whole thing as a normal sign of wear and tear when one cracked; a silent flash of shattered glass. When the rest of the pane followed, she shrugged her shoulders and reminded us that there were two layers left. Nothing to worry about. Absolutely nothing.

The strange thing was that people believed her.

The dramatic events of the morning had once again altered the atmosphere. While the previous evening had been relaxed and the new day had begun with a sullen nervousness, it now seemed as if most people had succumbed to silent resignation.

We were simply waiting.

136

We were waiting as best we could, for the storm to abate, for help to come. We were waiting to go home. In the meantime, there wasn't much we could do. Since we were all travellers, there was plenty of reading material to swap with each other. There was a pile of well-read paperbacks on the long table. And there was a relatively well-stocked bookshelf down in the hobby room. Several people had taken the opportunity to buy books from the hotel, despite the fact that the selection was severely limited. One was about Roald Amundsen and one was about the history of Finse. Also on offer was a not particularly tempting coffee table book about the Bergen railway.

That was it.

The gang of poker players had put away their cards, but not in order to read. They were sitting at the longest table in St Paal's Bar. All wearing earpieces, with their mp3 players on cords around their necks. Some were humming quietly and morosely along. I felt a rising antipathy towards the leader of the gang, a broad-shouldered lad in his twenties with a pink handkerchief tied around his head. The others called him Mikkel. His hair was presumably blond, but was dark with grease and hair gel. His eyes were blue, almost powerful. His face would have been attractive but for the mouth, which was set in an expression of spoilt discontent. The rest of the group behaved like puppies around him. So far I hadn't seen Mikkel fetch his own beer once. He had also won a fortune off the others at poker. I would bet that same fortune on the fact that he was cheating, and the others knew it.

Without doing a single bloody thing to put him in his place.

I looked away from him.

Beyond the cracked glass in the window, the air had taken on a strange colour.

It was too light, somehow.

Up to now the whiteness had actually been grey. The daylight was filtered through heavy clouds and vast amounts of falling snow. Finse 1222 had been surrounded by a muted light that was almost semi-darkness. Something was different now. Above the lashing wind and the violently swirling snow, the cloud cover must have broken. At least, I couldn't come up with any other explanation for the dazzling whiteness that made it even more difficult to see out. Perhaps it was a good sign. Perhaps the weather was beginning to change. I pushed that optimistic idea aside as a series of thuds, bangs and thumps from the eastern wall made people look up anxiously from their books and old newspapers.

Roar Hanson came padding towards me. He hesitated and was about to turn away when I gave him an encouraging smile.

"Am I disturbing you?" he asked softly.

"Not at all," I said, nodding towards an empty chair. "You might even be able to help me with something I've been wondering about."

"What's that?" he asked, without returning my smile.

He seemed just as despairing as he had been earlier. He kept on rubbing his shoulder. It had been dislocated in the accident, and it seemed as if it were still causing him considerable pain. His eyes were damp, but without tears. There was something white at the corners of his mouth, and I wished he would lick it off. His hair, thin with the hint of a comb-over, looked unwashed, and when he sat down I caught an acrid smell of sweat that had nothing to do with physical activity.

"Are you feeling stressed?" I asked, regretting the question immediately.

"What was it you were wondering about?" he mumbled.

"Well. These dogs . . ."

I pointed at the setter, sleeping peacefully on the floor next to its owner, who was sitting in the Millibar with a cup of hot chocolate. Nobody had seen any sign of the Portuguese water dog since it got red hot coffee on its nose.

"Where do they go to the toilet? They can't get outside, and I assume they have to pee from time to time?"

"I've made them a toilet in the cellar."

Berit Tverre placed a hand on my shoulder. I hadn't heard her coming. She smiled and went on: "We've got lots of strange rooms in this hotel, and I've covered the floor in one of them with old newspapers. One of the staff rooms, actually. We empty it and wash the floor four times a day."

"Wow," I said. "There's nothing wrong with the service here!"

Roar Hanson made a move to get up. I gave Berit Tverre a look, hoping she knew me well enough to interpret it correctly.

"See you later," she said, hurrying away.

"Sit for a while," I said pleasantly to Roar Hanson.

He adjusted his position slightly on the chair. I wheeled my chair a little closer and leaned forward.

"This business with Cato Hammer," I said quietly. "I can understand that you're upset. He was your friend, or so I've heard. And —"

"I don't believe what they said about the brain haemorrhage," he whispered.

I tried to catch his eye, but he refused to meet my gaze. Instead he kept looking back over his bad shoulder, as if he were afraid somebody might touch it.

"Why not?"

"I think he was murdered."

"What makes you think that?"

"Was he murdered?"

"What makes you think Cato Hammer was murdered?"

"Because no one can run away from his sins. Not for all eternity."

Oh God. I swallowed and tried to sound neutral.

"But we're all sinners, aren't we?" I ventured.

"In God's eyes, yes."

"And now God has taken Cato home."

I really am terrible at this kind of thing. I might have blushed. I haven't set foot in a church since I was forced to go to a christening almost ten years ago. But I had to make an attempt to get the man to talk, and to prevent myself from laughing at all costs. Roar Hanson was showing all the signs of an imminent breakdown.

"Nonsense," he said, looking me in the eye for the first time. "A ridiculous thing to say. God doesn't take anyone."

I know I blushed this time. I had to try and get onto safer ground, talking about something I was more comfortable with than this.

"So what kind of sins was Cato guilty of? A crime of some kind?"

"Greed and betrayal."

Like most of us, I thought. But this time I kept quiet.

"And the betrayal was worst of all," said Roar Hanson. "You can make amends for greed. There can be no forgiveness for betrayal."

I thought everything could be forgiven. Just shows how wrong you can be.

"Crisps," said Adrian, dropping the bag on my lap. "And Coke. There you go. Veronica and I are going to see if the table tennis table is any good."

The young woman was waiting for him a few metres away.

I took the bottle of cola.

Later I would try to recreate the moment that followed. I was so busy making sure I didn't drop the packet of crisps on the floor, and so annoyed that the boy had chosen paprika flavour that I was a bit late in looking up, and didn't entirely grasp what was happening.

"Wash your hands daily," said Roar Hanson.

He was always so quiet that I had to look at him in order to pick up everything he said. However, when Adrian yelled back, it was impossible not to hear:

"Fuck you!"

The boy turned on his heel and disappeared.

"What was that all about?" I asked.

"No idea," said Roar Hanson, getting to his feet. "I have to go."

"Where are you off to?" I asked in an attempt to prolong the conversation.

He didn't turn around. His back looked somehow narrower than it had done earlier as he walked towards the stairs and I lost sight of him.

I didn't understand him at all. On the one hand he sought contact. On the other, he communicated in cryptic sentences and left me as soon as he had come out with a couple of them. Why he should be reminding Adrian about hand hygiene was completely beyond me. What I really wanted was to say sod the bloody priest; I found his appearance repellent, and he was obviously mentally unstable.

Which was a serious problem.

I didn't think this group of people would be able to cope if one of us broke down. After the episode when most had been overcome by panic and far too many had proved they were not exactly reliable in a crisis, Geir, Berit and I had realized that the most important thing over the next few hours was to keep the atmosphere as low-key as possible. God knows what would happen if Roar Hanson really lost it and started hurling accusations of murder around.

"Adrian," I said sharply, trying to beckon him over.

He was sitting on the stairs leading down to the side wing with his right trouser leg rolled up. The bandage around his knee was soaked in blood. I had no idea he had been injured in the crash. His trousers were so scruffy I thought the tear across the knee had been done on purpose.

"I think it needs changing," he said gloomily, pulling a face. "It's worse now than it was yesterday. Am I going to get gangrene or something?"

"No," I said. "Come over here for a minute."

He got up reluctantly, limping demonstratively as he took the three or four steps towards me.

"Ouch. Fuck."

"It's not *too* bad," I said. "Why didn't you say anything yesterday when I asked you if you were hurt? Here. Take these."

I popped two painkillers out of the pack I had in a side pocket of my wheelchair.

"What's going on with you and Roar Hanson?"

"That pig? With all that white gunk around his gob?"

Adrian pushed the tablets into his mouth and washed them down with cola.

"Roar Hanson," I said again.

"He's a bastard. He was after Veronica last night. Twice."

"Says who?" I asked.

"Veronica, of course! I saw him too. He was all over her. Creepy!"

"Perhaps he just wanted to talk. Be nice. He is a priest, after all, and Veronica doesn't exactly seem like the most popular —"

"Oh, don't start! Veronica knows loads of people! Celebs, I mean. She hangs out with the kind of people you can only imagine — in your wildest dreams! And she's a black belt, second grade Tae Kwondo, and she teaches people you just wouldn't believe."

"Right. Absolutely. But what made you so angry just now?"

"That's got fuck all to do with you."

"Adrian . . ."

"Shit. I thought you were different."

"Thank you," I said.

He pulled his cap down even lower over his face.

"For what?"

"For not saying anything. About what we discussed this morning. About . . . you know. I decided to trust you, and I'm glad I wasn't wrong."

The boy hesitated. I had gone for a cheap trick, but Adrian wasn't exactly surrounded by people who trusted him, and I had to use what I could. He opened and closed his mouth a few times before he finally began:

"He said . . . That dickhead said . . ."

Something was going on over by the reception desk.

"He's been shot!" shouted a girl's voice. "That priest, he can't have had a brain haemorrhage. He's been shot in the head!"

Adrian swung around in the direction of the noise. I tried to raise my upper body from the chair by supporting myself on the armrests, but I still couldn't see who was shouting. The first thing that struck me was that I was witnessing a diametrically opposed reaction to the explosion of panic this morning. This was more like an implosion. People were heading into the reception area. Nobody said anything. I tried to move forward.

"It's true," sobbed the voice. "I was just having a look around, that's all. I was just . . . There's a big hole in his face and he . . ."

It was the handball girl in the red tracksuit.

"There, there. It's all right."

A male voice was attempting to console her.

"Is this true? Have you been lying to us?"

There was no mistaking Kari Thue's voice. I changed my mind and rolled back. The people who had been in the side wing up to now were on their way up to us. They were moving slowly and hesitantly, as if they didn't really want to believe the story that was travelling from mouth to mouth, and which eventually made everyone hurry along. Mikkel, wearing his pink handkerchief, was pushing his way through to the reception desk. I could see Adrian out of the corner of my eye. He had climbed up onto the table where the flasks of coffee had just been refilled for the fourth time since lunch. For some reason he had taken off his cap, but he quickly put it back on again.

"Liars!" yelled Kari Thue. I couldn't see who she was talking to, but assumed Berit Tverre was her target. "Isn't it obvious that we all have the right to know that we're trapped here with a . . . *murderer!*"

It was as if someone had turned a gigantic volume control up to the highest level. People were pouring endlessly from the stairs and from the wing where the staff had started to lay the tables for lunch. They crowded into the reception area, talking over one another. Everybody was moving in towards the same spot: a terrified fourteen-year-old girl dressed in red, whose youthful curiosity had led her to trip over Cato Hammer's earthly remains.

Geir Rugholmen shot out of the kitchen. He stopped, took a deep breath, and was obviously searching for someone with his gaze. It turned out to be me. He stared at me for several seconds before silently forming these words with his lips:

"What do we do now?"

You could have made a better job of hiding the corpse, I thought. Then it occurred to me that I didn't actually know where it was. Later I would learn that they had put the dead priest in the delivery area outside the kitchen, just inside the uninsulated door keeping the storm at bay. It was minus ten in there, I was told, so from a preservation point of view it was absolutely fine. However, if the intention had been to keep the murder a secret, they could have come up with something better. Nor was I completely sure what the chef thought about having a corpse lying in the area where he received fresh produce and equipment on a daily basis. Presumably he had no idea it was there.

"What do we do now?" Geir mimed again.

I was unable to come up with an answer.

CHAPTER
TWO

"The only sensible course of action is to split up," shouted Kari Thue. "I have the right to decide for myself who I can trust. Who I choose to be snowed in with. At any rate, we ought to form two separate groups."

I couldn't believe my ears. Or eyes. I must have looked like an idiot sitting there, right in the corner by the kitchen with a coffee cup on a rustic cupboard beside me, open-mouthed with astonishment as more and more people gathered around Kari Thue at the other end of the room. The girl in red had already been forgotten. She had done her bit, and I couldn't see her anywhere. I hoped one of the adults had gone with her to her room. Thank goodness nobody even glanced in my direction. For the first time since the accident I considered asking Geir to help me get away. To a room where I could be by myself. With a key in the lock enabling me to keep everyone else at a distance until the storm was over and I could make my way home to Krusesgate without needing to exchange a single word with anyone. That might well be worth the humiliation of being carried.

But Geir was busy with an entirely different matter.

The long table had been elevated to a kind of speaker's platform following the train crash. Kari Thue was standing on its broad surface talking loudly and quickly, with much gesticulation, while Berit Tverre tried in vain to get her to come down. Geir was pushing his way through the crowd to help out.

"Since we have access to two buildings," yelled Kari Thue, "I would suggest that one group takes whatever food and drink they need over to the apartment wing, while the other group remains here. The train carriage linking the two buildings can easily be blocked off at each end. And guarded, of course. I would like to volunteer to serve on a committee responsible for dividing everyone into two groups. This committee should consist of . . . three members. You . . ."

She pointed at the knitting woman, who clutched her work tightly and looked as if it was all she could do not to break down completely.

"And you . . ."

The finger curled over and beckoned the business-man I thought I recognized, but whose name I couldn't recall.

"I suggest that the three of us spend the next hour coming up with a split that most people will be happy with. As far as I understand it . . ."

At this point her voice shot up to a falsetto. Berit had grabbed hold of Kari Thue's forearm and was determinedly trying to pull her off the table. Kari Thue jerked her arm violently upwards. Berit let go and would have fallen, but for the press of people behind her.

148

"Get down from there!" shouted Berit. "At once! I'm the one who . . ."

The rest of the sentence was lost in the racket, and I could no longer see her. So far about fifty people had gathered in the lobby. There were still approximately three times as many scattered around the two buildings, and more and more were steadily arriving. Mikkel, the lout from St Paal's Bar, had brought his gang along and stationed them behind the crowd, where they were amusing themselves by shoving everybody forwards. They seemed totally uninterested in what was going on, except as an opportunity for some entertainment. A few started shouting out that they agreed with Kari Thue. Others tried to help Berit. The man from South Africa had climbed up on the window ledge and was standing with one foot on the table, earnestly pleading with Kari Thue to calm down. I was picking up only odd words in broken Norwegian, but it was enough for me to understand that the man was seriously concerned. Moreover, he was the only one of us who was still as neatly and correctly dressed as when the accident happened; he was wearing a grey suit with a narrow stripe, a shirt that was still clean, and a deep red silk tie, perfectly knotted. It didn't help much. Kari Thue flung her arm out at him, but missed. She was still talking non-stop.

"We're dealing with a brutal murder here! We're much safer if we split up! I have the *right* to choose who I —"

Geir had climbed up onto the opposite end of the table. He ran towards her, bent his head just a hair's breadth from the lamps suspended from the ceiling, and without a second's hesitation he flung his arms around the skinny woman and locked her down. Her little rucksack was crushed between his stomach and her back, but Geir didn't even seem to notice.

"Calm down. *And shut your mouth!*"

In order to stress the seriousness of his words, he gave her an extra squeeze and lifted her bodily off the table.

"Do you understand?" he yelled, before whispering something in her ear. I have no idea what he said, but it worked.

Kari Thue collapsed like a rag doll in his arms. Carefully he made sure her feet were touching the surface of the table before he slowly let go. She didn't lash out. She didn't scream. And neither did anyone else. Even Mikkel's gang moved back imperceptibly, as if they had realized with sudden embarrassment that they could have hurt someone.

"Get down," I said loudly. "Get down from the table and we will decide what we are going to do."

Suddenly I was looking into fifty faces, all of whom seemed more surprised that I had said something than if I had got to my feet and walked. To tell the truth, I was equally surprised myself.

"First of all, Berit Tverre is the person in charge here," I said. "And secondly, there is no reason whatsoever to split into two groups."

Since I had actually opened my mouth, I should have said something less obvious. My voice sounded strange. It was a long time since I had had any reason to speak loudly. On the other hand, what was actually being said didn't seem to be the most important thing; it was the way it was said that mattered. Kari Thue allowed herself to be helped down from the table. Geir was already down. People slowly started moving closer to me. I held up my hands and they stopped like obedient dogs. Only Kari Thue, Geir and Berit pushed through the wall of people who were now standing four metres away from me. The South African was the only one who no longer wanted to be involved. He marched angrily towards the stairs and disappeared. I also noticed the Kurd on the fringe of the group, a little distance away from the rest. He was the only one who had already stopped looking at me. Instead he was examining a stuffed raven in a glass case on the reception desk. He was staring into the shiny eyes, apparently uninterested in anything apart from the black bird. The woman in the headscarf, whom I had assumed to be his wife, was standing next to him. Until now she had seemed unusually reserved, a shy creature who shunned any attempt at contact from other people. Now she was looking straight at me. Her eyes were large and green with brown flecks. It struck me that I hadn't really looked at her before. The headscarf drew attention away from everything else. Which was no doubt the intention. Her face was broad without appearing masculine, extremely and surprisingly open, with symmetrical features and an expression around her mouth that I could not interpret.

"Carry on," whispered Geir; I hadn't even noticed that he had come right up to me.

151

"Who the hell gave you the right to decide?"

Mikkel got there before me. Even when he smiled he looked discontented. He was standing next to Kari Thue with his arms folded. His head was tipped back in order to underline my status as a cripple.

"I'm not making any decisions," I said. "Berit Tverre is the person who will make decisions."

"And who decided that?"

I have to admit that I do have a number of prejudices.

In the past I thought it was worth trying to do something about them. In recent years I've stopped bothering. I've given in, so to speak. Since I spend most of my time at home, I don't really see the point in wasting my energy on trying to be a better person. It's probably too late, anyway. I'm rapidly approaching fifty. In three years I will pass the meridian, and I prefer to expend my energy on other things, rather than dealing with rich daddy's boys from Bærum who suffer from an excess of self-confidence. He must have been fifteen years younger than Kari Thue, yet he was allowing himself to be devoured by her eyes, while she was clearly having to restrain herself from touching him.

"*I* have decided," I said. "And so has everybody else whose intelligence is more or less intact. We are Berit Tverre's guests. Start acting that way."

"We live in a democracy," Kari Thue said in her loud, grating voice. "A democracy that does not cease to exist simply because we are cut off. If the majority of people here agree with me that it would be safer to —"

"You're never going to find that out," said Berit, walking into the middle of the floor. "Because there isn't going to be a vote. Hanne Wilhelmsen is absolutely right. You are my guests. I make the decisions. And right now my decision is —"

The crash that interrupted her came from a different world.

As time went by we had all more or less grown accustomed to the roar of the storm outside, the thuds and blows against the walls and the intense whining of the wind as it swept around the hotel and its outbuildings. It was as if the howl of the storm had become a carpet of sound that we recognized, just like the lapping of waves on the coast or the constant rush of the waterfall at some old mill.

This was something completely different.

At first I thought it was a massive explosion. My ears were singing and the walls shook. Powerful vibrations in the floor made my wheelchair move. The sound of clinking glass came from the Millibar. The setter, which was the only dog I could see at the time, leapt up with a high-pitched howl before flattening itself against the rough floorboards. It was as if it thought the ceiling was about to come down. It wasn't the only one. People sought shelter underneath the table. A few ran towards the side wing, which might have been a wise move; the deafening crash came from the opposite side of the lobby. Geir and Berit were running against the tide of people, and had already reached the stairs. I lost sight of them as Mikkel and his gang rushed past me and down to St Paal's Bar. Only Kari Thue remained completely motionless. She was sobbing, with her face in her hands. Her shoulders were narrow and so bony that they almost sliced through the thin fabric of her blouse. She was expecting to die, and in a different situation I might have felt sorry for her.

Right now I had neither the time nor the opportunity to do so.

The terrible noise was still going on. The first crash was followed by a piercing, high-pitched noise interspersed with a series of short bangs and thuds that were much worse than anything the storm had come up with in almost twenty-four hours. Even the sound of screaming people searching for refuge wherever they could find it was drowned out by the noise that couldn't possibly be an explosion.

Explosions are brief. They pass.

This went on and on.

And the temperature was dropping.

I didn't notice it at first. Only when I had gained some kind of overview and noticed who was running where, and where people were trying to hide, did I realize how cold it had become.

It was getting even colder, and it was happening fast.

The sound of whatever it was that couldn't be an explosion was dying away. Instead it was as if the howling of the storm had moved indoors. A biting wind swept across the floor, picked up a chocolate bar wrapper and carried it off towards the kitchen in a wild dance.

Suddenly Adrian was standing in front of me. He was holding Veronica by the hand. They looked like a big sister dragging her little brother along. Her face was pale and expressionless, but she slowly let go of his hand and put her arm around the weeping boy's shoulders. He sobbed:

"Are we going to die, Hanne?"

I wished I could give him an answer. I had no idea what had happened, or what lay before us. Despite the noise I could hear my own heart pounding beneath my breastbone. I felt sick with fear. But something was happening. I no longer felt incapable of doing anything. The adrenalin, which continued to course through my body with every bang and gust of wind, had sharpened my senses instead of leaving them dulled. I was noticing everything. I had noticed everything. Now, several months later, when I close my eyes to recapture the events of those seconds and minutes at Finse 1222, it's like watching a film in slow motion. I can recall every detail. But at that precise moment, there and then, as my teeth began to chatter with shock and cold, there was actually only one detail that was worth noting.

When the racket started and total chaos ensued, the Kurd opened his grey-brown jacket and reached for a gun he was carrying in a shoulder holster. With lightning speed he dropped down behind the pillar by the reception desk in the firing position — one knee on the floor, the other foot in front. Shocking in itself. However, the biggest surprise, and something that I couldn't understand at all, possibly as a result of my own prejudices, was that the Kurdish woman did the same thing. In contrast to the man she took her gun out of its holster and aimed it at an imaginary foe by the stairs. Her loose, shapeless dress was obviously specially made, and did not hinder her from drawing her gun or moving at lightning speed. Only when the cold from the stairs reached her and it was clear that nothing else appeared to be threatening us did she slip the revolver back in its holster.

During the minutes that followed I was able to establish that no one apart from me had noticed this peculiar behaviour. At first this struck me as rather strange. However, on closer consideration it seemed logical; everybody had either been on the move, or had sought protection in a reflex action with their faces covered. The two Kurds hadn't seen me, and quickly reverted to their roles as the over-protective immigrant and his terrified, weeping wife.

I decided to leave it at that for the time being.

Perhaps they weren't Kurds at all.

Perhaps they weren't even married.

BEAUFORT SCALE 5

FRESH BREEZE

Wind speed: 19–24mph

It becomes difficult to ski against the wind. Drifting snow along the ground whirls up so high that visibility is restricted. Driving snow lashes the face.

CHAPTER
ONE

For some reason I was thinking of Cato Hammer.

The murder of the controversial priest was actually the least of our problems. I was sitting in my chair by the kitchen door, where I had more or less helplessly witnessed rather too much in the course of just about half an hour. Kari Thue's attempt at mutiny had been quite threatening. Nor was it easy to digest the idea that two apparently typical representatives of our new underclass had behaved like highly trained agents. However, the violent event that had taken place somewhere near the western wall was the worst thing. As I tried to suppress my fear by sorting out all the thoughts I had had about the murder of Cato Hammer during the past few hours, I had serious doubts that the western wall was still standing. The temperature in the hotel was dropping at an alarming rate. During the past twenty-four hours we had lived in an atmosphere of coffee, food, sweat, and dog. Now all the smells were gone. Only a dry, menacing cold seared my nostrils. Outside it was still almost minus thirty, a fact I couldn't quite manage to assimilate. I had put on my padded jacket and wrapped a blanket around my crippled legs. That was when I discovered that the wound in my thigh

159

had opened up. A red flower was growing on the chalk-white bandage, and had already spread to the ragged edges where my trouser leg had been cut open. I looked around for another blanket.

And I was still thinking about Cato Hammer.

The remarkable thing was that so many people had known him. I don't mean they'd *heard* of him, most of us had. As I struggled with my anxiety over what could have caused the temperature to drop so sharply, it struck me that almost everyone I had encountered after the accident had willingly admitted to some kind of link to Hammer. He had been Magnus's patient. Geir knew him from the board at Brann football club. I'm absolutely certain Berit Tverre blushed when she mentioned the priest's earlier visits to the mountains. There was nothing odd about the fact that Roar Hanson knew Hammer, of course; they had known each other at college, and worked together.

Adrian had just been furious.

Furious and foul-mouthed. He had behaved quite differently towards Cato Hammer than to anyone else from the train.

"The carriage!"

Geir was standing in front of me. I recognized him only when I saw the yellow ski goggles. They covered virtually his entire face before he pulled them off and leaned on my chair, panting.

"The carriage has fallen down!"

The carriage.

I had of course noticed it when we were in the station, unaware that just a few minutes later we would be sitting in a derailed wreck. The hotel and the wing containing the apartments, both of which were so close to the railway that they looked like part of the station complex, were joined together by an old railway carriage. It was suspended some three or four metres above the ground, and made it possible to move between the buildings without going outside. It looked like a big toy train, a rusty red reminder that Finse was the country's only genuine station community; you could get here only by train. The carriage didn't even fight with the architecture. The whole complex was just one big piece of patchwork in any case, and the suspended carriage was an amusing salute from the residents of Finse to Norwegian State Railways. From all the conversations I had listened to over the past twenty-four hours, I had gathered that the carriage was filling up with snow. The fixings were old, and gaps had appeared by the wall of the wing. Not large gaps, but more than enough to make some people anxious early this morning. Quite rightly, as it turned out.

"There are huge amounts of snow packed tight between the buildings," said Geir, gasping for breath. "So the carriage didn't fall all that far. It's lying at an angle on the snow. The other end is still attached to the wall, and it looks as if the only damage is that the door leading into the carriage is still on the wall. On our side a whole chunk of the wall has been torn away, taking the door with it. Thank goodness nobody was inside the carriage when it fell."

"Yes," I said. "We certainly have been incredibly lucky on this trip."

He looked at me.

"Everything all right with you?"

I nodded and said: "I just need Dr Streng to have a look at my leg. It's started bleeding again. I'm sure it's nothing serious. How are you?"

He was a little surprised; he frowned and straightened his back. He took his time inserting a sizeable plug of snuff, and smiled.

"This stuff is good for you!"

"What are you going to do about the hole?" I asked.

"Johan's fetching the Poles. We've got enough material in the cellar. I should think we'll get —"

"Fetching the Poles? The joiners? In this weather? From up in . . ."

Geir started tucking the blanket more tightly around me. His breath turned into a light mist, hitting my face in warm puffs and making me feel even colder. As far as I knew, the four joiners were in one of the buildings several hundred metres away.

"Johan can drive a snowmobile at the South Pole in June," said Geir with a smile. "It's winter down there when it's —"

"I know," I interrupted him. "When it's summer here. But I had the distinct impression that nobody could get away from here. That nobody could be outside at all."

"Well, Johan can. He wouldn't have done it if it hadn't been essential. But he *can*. When he has to."

I pushed him away when he started lifting my feet so that he could tuck the blanket around them.

"Tell me about this Johan."

162

"He was born up here. One of the few. According to the local mythology he was born outdoors in a winter storm and grew up in a snow cave at Klemsbu, but of course that's just nonsense. His father was the stationmaster, and they lived very well. But it's true that he could ride before he was five years old. His older brother fixed up a snowmobile for him so that it was physically possible for such a little scrap to reach the accelerator and the brakes on the handlebars. Nowadays Johan lives at Ustaoset and owns a wilderness centre. He attracts filthy rich Americans and scares them to death out in the wilds. There's money in that kind of thing. But he's often here. Fortunately he was here when the crash happened. There are some fairly rigid restrictions when it comes to driving snowmobiles, so he's a member of the Red Cross, which allows him to drive often enough. Anyway, you've met him. Don't you remember? He was the one who brought you here."

"But . . . in this weather!"

"As I said: Johan is probably the only person in Norway, in the whole world for all I know, who can cope with any kind of weather. If the snowmobile can do it, then Johan can do it. He's as bowlegged as a cowboy. It's just that his horse is called Yamaha."

There was snow in the air.

The door with slender panels of glass that had separated the stairs from the grotesque hole in the wall had been torn open and smashed by the wind.

Although I was still sitting over by the kitchen door, separated from the hole in the wall by the entire lobby,

163

a flight of stairs and half a floor, I could clearly feel and see the snowflakes dancing in the moving air. So far they were melting as soon as they hit the floor.

"Perhaps he ought to get a move on," I said, thinking about Cato Hammer once again. "I have a feeling time is short."

Geir clapped his gloved hands together. Then he leaned towards me once again with one hand on each wheel. Fortunately, the brakes were on.

"It might not look like it, but we have actually got this under control. I can promise you one thing: as long as people stay indoors" — the feeling of being indoors wasn't actually all that palpable at the moment — "then nobody will freeze to death at Finse 1222. You have my word on that."

I almost dared to believe the man.

CHAPTER
TWO

And I had good reason to do so, as it turned out.

It was four thirty. It was still unpleasantly cold, but at least it had stopped snowing in the lobby. As I quickly calculated that we would soon be on our second day at Finse, I almost couldn't believe it. For many years I have lived according to a slow routine that suits me. Nothing happens and nothing is going to happen. Everything is predictable and can take its own time. I have more than enough time, and I am happy to fritter it away. However, the past twenty-five hours had been so eventful that for long periods of time I had forgotten how tired I was.

"Are you asleep?" asked Geir in surprise.

He had undone the top part of his snowmobile suit. It was dangling down and flapping around his hips. He reminded me of Ida when she comes rushing in after she's been picked up from nursery, and hasn't time to take her outdoor things off before she climbs up on my knee for a hug and a ride around the apartment.

I must remember to call home.

"No, of course not," I said in confusion, blinking furiously.

I really must remember to call.

165

"We've secured the hole," he said, raising his fist in a victory gesture. "With planks and sheets of metal and whatever else we could find. Then we packed the whole thing with blankets and nailed them to whatever we could. It's as cold as hell up there, and the draught made it almost impossible to get close to the damaged part of the wall. Plus the entire corridor is full of snow. But . . ." He knotted his sleeves around his waist. "We're still here. It's starting to warm up again. In an hour or two it will at least be habitable in here."

It was about time. My lips had gone numb, and my jaws were aching from pressing my teeth together to avoid biting my tongue.

"What about the other side?" I asked. "Have they managed to seal up that opening too?"

"Yes. Two of the lads from the Red Cross and one of the joiners got a couple of men from the train to help them. It was easier from that side. They were finished before us."

He patted his breast pocket.

"Good old Telenor. The mobile coverage has been brilliant. We were in touch all the time."

I took a deep breath and tried to lower my shoulders. But the cold sank its claws into me once again, and every muscle in my body tensed. I looked around for Magnus Streng. The wound at the top of my thigh was still bleeding. I hadn't dared to look at the other side.

The doctor was nowhere to be seen.

"Come with me," said Geir, beckoning me after him as he set off.

"What do you want?"

"Come with me."

It was obvious that I was more troubled by the cold than others were. I was bleeding, and had been sitting still for a long time. I had probably fallen asleep as well. Following Geir might not be such a bad idea. He headed for the main entrance and opened the door to a narrow passageway before helping me into the outside porch. The kiosk, which was on the left at the bottom of a small flight of stairs, and which couldn't be more than twenty-five square metres in area, was packed with people who didn't really know what they wanted. The scenario struck me as a confused symbol of western culture: we had all looked death in the eye, and immediately sought consolation in the quest for something to buy. Pollyanna was sitting at the till, smiling broadly. She was, as far as I could see, the only person who had a reason to be in a good mood. In general the atmosphere was subdued, anxious and oppressive, just as it was among those who had settled down in the lobby when it became clear that the damage to the wall could be repaired.

Adrian and Veronica were looking at sunglasses on a stand. It was obvious the boy had been crying, and when he raised his head and caught sight of me, he instantly grabbed a pair of dark glasses and put them on. Roar Hanson was standing right next to him. He was feeling at a pair of orange Ulvang socks, and didn't even look up when I tried to say hello.

"Beyond here," said Geir, banging the outside door with his fist, "we're just going to let the snow block the door. Even Johan says it's not worth wasting energy trying to keep it clear. It would just be too much. Since strictly speaking he's the only one who can stay outside for any length of time, we're not going to bother."

"Fire," I said.

"Fire?"

"What do we do if there's a fire?"

"Jump out of one of the upstairs windows. Tear down the insulation we've put up where the carriage was. Something like that. But there isn't going to be a fire. There has to be a limit to what we're expected to suffer . . ."

He smiled faintly.

"Have you worked out," I said when he had helped me get my chair over the threshold into the lobby without being asked, "how many of us there are in here now?"

"Fewer and fewer all the time," said Geir with forced cheerfulness as he pushed me further into the room. "When the carriage fell there were seventy-nine people in the wing. We were 196 in total in the entire complex . . ."

"194," I corrected him. "You have to take out Elias Grav and Cato Hammer."

"Exactly. And you have to add four joiners. One of them is over in the wing. The other three are here. So that makes . . ."

"118," I said. "There are 118 people left in the hotel."

Kari Thue had gathered a little court around her at one end of the table. The conversation stopped abruptly as Geir and I got closer. At that precise moment I

168

wished she had got her way. I wished she had taken her subjects to the wing and stayed there.

Twenty-four hours ago, there were 269 people on board a train. Then we became 196. When two men died, we were 194. Now there were only 118 of us left.

I thought about Agatha Christie's *And Then There Were None*.

I immediately tried to dismiss the thought.

And Then There Were None is a story that doesn't exactly have a happy ending.

CHAPTER
THREE

"I expect it's the shock," said Magnus contentedly, shovelling down a large piece of salmon, "that's made you start bleeding again. Perhaps you've bumped into something. At any rate . . ." he raised his knife like an exclamation mark above his plate, "there's nothing to worry about! You'll be absolutely fine!"

It was eight thirty in the evening and I felt anything but fine. I was so tired I was finding it difficult to concentrate on anything other than the food. My own body odour had begun to bother me. The only consolation was that everybody else smelled just as bad. Which was more reprehensible on their part; they had access to showers and hot water. On the other hand, we had all had other things on our minds apart from personal hygiene.

"I must say," said Magnus Streng, mopping up sauce with a piece of coarse bread, "that the kitchen here really does maintain an excellent standard. I mean, this fish must have been frozen, but even so. Delicious! Do you realize that while all these terrible things were going on, all this business with the carriage and so on, our friend the chef and his faithful companions were in the kitchen baking bread. Baking bread! That's what I call a dedicated professional!"

He laughed delightedly and popped the last piece of bread in his mouth before emptying his glass of red wine in one draught.

The temperature had returned to a reasonable level. It was probably no more than fifteen degrees, but compared with the level during the hours after the carriage fell, this felt positively tropical. For the first time I had capitulated when it came to the stairs leading down to the dining room. Geir had insisted. Johan had helped him to negotiate my chair down the three steps before I managed to gather my strength for a real protest. Perhaps I was too tired. Perhaps I really wanted to do it. To sit at a table. To eat in a normal way, along with other people. To eat good food in the company of other people.

And I had actually called home.

I didn't say much, but I did call.

Nefis was pleased.

Her friends can't understand how she puts up with me.

I meet them from time to time, of course. Nefis gives parties. She invites people to dinner. She goes so far over the top when it comes to celebrating Christmas that you can easily forget she's a Muslim. Last Christmas Eve there were so many of us around the extravagantly laid table that it looked like a scene from *Fanny and Alexander*. And I can live with that, I hardly ever say anything, and Nefis's friends stopped talking to me long ago, apart from a few absolutely necessary and as a rule completely meaningless phrases. But I am there. I sit there at the far end of the table, eating and listening and looking at Nefis, at how happy she is. I always go to bed early. As I fall asleep to the murmur of voices from the dining room, I know they can't understand what she sees in me.

I think I know; I never have any doubts.

From the moment I met her at a pavement café in Verona, when I was trying to escape from a sorrow that I thought would cost me my life, I have been sure about Nefis and me. When I was shot in the back a few years later and lost my mobility, and no longer had the strength to do anything other than to push away those friends I still had, I held on to Nefis. She was the one I wanted there, by my sick bed. She was the only one who was allowed to come when I tried in vain to regain some movement in Sunnaas Rehabilitation Hospital, and she was the one I wanted to come home to.

In late winter four years ago she woke me in the middle of the night. I had been allowed home from hospital for the first time, two months after the accident. We had had such a lovely evening. Now she was weeping quietly, overcome with guilt. She was pregnant. I had said no to children, over and over again, ever since the question had come up on the very first night we were together, and I explained that I didn't want to burden any child with a mother like me. Nobody should have a mother like me, and since then there had never been an ounce of doubt: we were not going to have children.

But now we were.

172

I smiled in the darkness that night. I think I said thank you. It was impossible to sleep. I have never been so happy.

I never have any doubts about Nefis and Ida and me. In times like these, perhaps that's enough.

I was missing them both.

This feeling of longing is something I have never known. Except when I was a child, and I yearned for so much that I never really knew what it was. This longing was something quite different, a warm, lovely pull in my stomach that almost made me smile.

"You look as if you're about to fall asleep with food in your mouth," said Berit.

"That's all right," I said.

"Coffee," said Geir, placing a cup in front of me. I hadn't even noticed that he'd left the table. "Drink. It's red hot."

I curled my hands around the cup. The heat alone made me feel good. I blew gently and drank.

Roar Hanson had been glancing surreptitiously in my direction all through the meal. He was sitting with his colleagues from the church commission a couple of tables away from us, in the main dining room. Every time I looked over, he glanced down. In my mind I cursed Magnus Streng who had been so determined to bring up my police background when he treated me that first time. If he hadn't done that I would have been spared it all. The intrusiveness. The worry. And the annoying curiosity about what it was that Roar Hanson actually wanted to tell me. I had no doubt that he was pondering whether to confide in me about something.

Veronica and Adrian had become inseparable. They had tried in vain to get a table to themselves, but every chair was needed, which meant they had to share with others, so they had taken their food up to reception and disappeared. I hadn't exchanged two words with the boy since the carriage fell. He was obviously embarrassed, and I had been too tired to try to distract him.

Many people had tried to get a seat at Kari Thue's table. Despite the fact that it had filled up as soon as she sat down, several others had pulled their chairs over and were sitting with their plates on their knees. I could only guess what they were talking about. They were speaking quietly, consciously avoiding looking in our direction. Berit shrugged her shoulders and put down her knife and fork.

"She's hardly likely to try again."

"Don't count on it," I said. "Even if it's no longer possible for her to seek refuge in one of the apartments, she could still demand that some of us are locked in."

"An intelligent person, that Kari Thue. Very intelligent." Magnus Streng refilled his glass, almost to the brim. "But not very sensible," he added, raising his glass in a toast. "A very dangerous combination, in my considered opinion. I've seen her film, *Deliver Us From Evil*. Fascinating. What about you, Hanne? Have you seen it?"

"No."

"It's good, unfortunately. Extremely politically correct, apparently. Not exactly Michael Moore, if I can put it that way." He beamed as dessert was placed in

174

front of him. "The problem is that the film is basically unethical, in terms of both methodology and content."

I wasn't up to this.

"Of course you're not up to this," said Magnus Streng, waving over one of the waitresses. "I don't suppose it would be possible to have a little more of this fantastic strawberry sauce?"

He patted his stomach and picked up his spoon again.

"You know . . . People like me don't frighten other people. Not really. As long as I can remember I have been met with . . . mainly curiosity. Silence also, of course; as a child I sometimes found it quite difficult to deal with the silence that always came down over me like a cheese-dish cover whenever I moved outside my own little circle. Sometimes I felt like a piece of Port Salut. Not that I smelled like a . . ." He smiled wryly and went on: "Silent curiosity! That's what people usually feel when they catch sight of someone like me."

The serviette he had tucked inside his shirt collar was slipping. He tucked it back in and shook his head as he looked at me.

"And disgust. Sometimes disgust."

I probably ought to have protested.

"But not fear," he added quickly. "Not hostility, and never fear. Other than the obvious fear of having children like us. And do you know why?"

Nobody felt the urge to guess.

"There aren't enough of us to make anyone nervous," he said slowly, stressing every single word. "Persons of restricted growth simply do not constitute a threat. Insofar as we still exist. I mean, there are methods of eliminating us before the political majority in this country regards us as being capable of sustaining life . . ."

One of us should definitely have said something.

"So I expect we will soon be a phenomenon for the history books. Not a threat. Our friends over there, on the other hand . . ."

He nodded towards the woman in the headscarf and her travelling companion. They were the only ones who had managed to keep a table for four all to themselves. They ate their food as it was placed in front of them, without a word to each other or to the waitress.

"A really lovely couple," said Magnus Streng with a smile. "They look normal in every way. A little extra skin pigment, different headgear and a different name for God are the only things that distinguish them from us. When it comes down to it. But it's enough. And why?"

Nobody answered this time either.

"Because there are a lot of them. Because there are more and more of them around us all the time. Fear, ladies and gentlemen, is often a question of quantity. Just as none of us is afraid of one buzzing bee, but we all panic when the swarm arrives."

"Well, a swarm is obviously more dangerous than just one bee," mumbled Geir.

"Not necessarily!"

Magnus Streng leaned forward.

"Ask a beekeeper! Go to the expert! *Ask a beekeeper!*"

I had some difficulty in seeing the similarity between a bee and a Muslim, and topped up my glass of water.

"What is worse," Magnus Streng continued eagerly, "is that once we have been frightened by the swarm, we regard every bee that comes along with suspicion. And once we are afraid of bees, it's only a small step until we are afraid of every buzzing, flying creature among our fauna. That, my friends, is what is known as collectivism. Dangerous stuff. Kari Thue over there, now I should think she's a woman who's been stung a few times. Kari Thue is a frightened woman."

He looked at her with something approaching sympathy.

"I have to talk to you!"

I almost jumped. The businessman whose name I couldn't remember was leaning over Johan. The man was still clutching his laptop; I was beginning to wonder if he took it to bed with him. His medium-length hair was blond and thick with expensive streaks, something that would probably have looked quite good if he hadn't been too old for such vanity, and overweight into the bargain. The combination of smooth skin, a noticeable double chin and a youthful haircut made him appear soft, almost feminine. And if his intention was that other people shouldn't hear what he was saying, then he failed badly. He was whispering so loudly that he could be heard from several tables away.

"Talk away," said Johan without looking up from his meal.

"Not here. I really do have to talk to you."

"In that case you'll have to wait. I'm eating."

"It's important. Come with me."

He was no longer whispering. Instead there was an ambiguously threatening note in his voice. He straightened his back and assumed an expression that I imagine could be effective in some board meeting. Here it just looked comical.

"I'd like to make you an offer," he said. "A particularly lucrative offer."

Johan grinned and put down his spoon.

"I see. And what is this offer?"

"Not here. Let's go to —"

"As you can see, I'm sitting here having my dinner."

"You've finished. Come with me."

"No. I'm going to have another cup of coffee. Besides which, I've just decided. I don't want to talk to you. Not now and not later. I'm actually quite happy sitting here. Go away."

"A million," said the man. "You could earn a million kroner."

Johan started to laugh. He wiped his mouth and looked up at the businessman.

"Now that's what I call an offer," he said, getting slowly to his feet. "An offer worth considering. Thank you for dinner. And for the company."

He nodded briefly to each of us before holding his hand out to Magnus Streng. The doctor looked surprised as he extended his own large, chubby hand.

"I'll speak to you later," said Johan, before turning on his heel and following the man with the laptop.

"Steinar Aass," said Magnus Streng, pulling a face when the pair had just about reached the lobby. "Not exactly a man to do business with."

The pieces fell into place as soon as he mentioned the name. Steinar Aass was what the newspapers liked to call a financial acrobat. The man had been sued a dozen times for overstepping every mark you can think of when it came to financial regulations, but the cases never got as far as court. This could of course be due to the fact that he was a persecuted, but entirely law-abiding citizen. Another explanation could be the notorious undermanning and lack of resources in the economic crimes unit. *Dagens Nœringsliv*, on the other hand, had almost, but not quite, managed to nail Steinar Aass in a seven-page article last summer. They had followed a trail of money from a criminal gang in Norway to enormous investments in land in Brazil. Along the beautiful Atlantic coast this money completed a rotation or two with the help of Steinar Aass and three of his friends from Akers Brygge, before it was miraculously removed from the washing machine as legitimate capital.

"Bloody hell," said Geir, stretching his neck. "You're right! It is him!"

The waitress moved around the table pouring coffee. I felt the caffeine hit home. My eyelids were no longer so heavy. The pains in my back that had plagued me for several hours were easing. Magnus Streng looked as if he were thinking about something before he placed a hand on the waitress's arm.

"I don't suppose I could have a little drop of cognac, miss? Last night I had a really good Otard, which would definitely do the trick."

She smiled and nodded.

Now that we had got used to his eccentricity, we were all smiling at Magnus Streng. Even Mikkel's gang had given up on the uncertain sneering grins with which they had previously received the little man. Only Kari Thue had maintained her forbidding expression whoever she was looking at. With the exception of Mikkel, of course. I suddenly discovered that she was no longer making a point of ignoring us. On the contrary, she had actually started glancing over at our table. I couldn't really work out which of us she was most interested in. But she definitely wasn't smiling.

"My colleagues over there," said Magnus, interrupting my train of thought. He nodded over towards the table where all the other doctors were sitting. "They have been unusually pleasant, I have to say."

I didn't think there was enough evidence to support the idea that the other seven doctors were pleasant. Whenever they had left their rooms, they had more or less stuck together, or sat alone buried in a book. Two of them had laptops, and had used their time on the mountain to make preparations for a conference that had started long ago, as far as I knew. Once they had taken care of all the cuts and injuries that first evening, they had more or less removed themselves from our little community at Finse 1222. And I had hardly seen them exchange two words with Magnus Streng.

"They've left the entire arena to me," he said gently. "Something for which I will be eternally grateful. Oh look, here comes our friend. Already!"

"Three million," said Johan with a broad grin, sitting down again.

"That was quick," said Geir. "You got *three million*?"

"No. Obviously I don't want to do business with his sort. I was just curious."

He looked at the glass of cognac that was just being placed in front of Dr Streng. The waitress looked at him enquiringly and he nodded.

"I wanted to know which of my services could possibly be worth so much money. When he told me what he wanted, I managed to get him to treble the price before I started laughing."

"And what was it he wanted?" asked Magnus Streng, his nose buried in the brandy balloon. "Transport, I assume?"

Johan stared at him.

"Yes. If I drove him to the nearest town with a road link to Oslo, I would get three million kroner. He has to be in Brazil before Saturday, he reckons, because his youngest daughter is seriously ill. Apparently. When I refused, all of his kids were suddenly desperately ill. That didn't help much either. I assume we're talking about sick money rather than sick kids here . . ."

Although I was following the conversation, I was also trying to keep an eye on the couple that I was no longer sure were a couple. They had started talking to each

181

other. They were leaning forward, looking agitated and seemingly disagreeing about something.

"Three million," said Berit, savouring the words. "Would it have been legal? I mean, could you have accepted that amount of money?"

Everybody except me looked at Magnus Streng. He was gradually acquiring the status of an omniscient being, a reference work who knew something about most things. Nobody seemed to be paying any attention to the fact that Geir Rugholmen was a lawyer.

"Well," said Magnus, smacking his lips. "We do have freedom of agreement in this country. If the man paid entirely of his own free will, then that would probably be absolutely fine. However, if you had to demand the money, then I think the question is whether that would offend against common decency. Like in a poker game, or some other wager. But you said no?"

"Of course."

"But could you have done it? Would it have been possible for you to get to Haugastøl in this weather?"

Johan shrugged his shoulders.

"I could probably do it if the snowmobile held. And there's no guarantee that it would. I've never gone on a long journey in such extreme cold. It's a completely unnecessary risk. I never take *unnecessary* risks. Besides which . . ."

Everyone around the table was following the conversation between Johan and Magnus with interest. I was trying to listen to what was going on between the two foreigners at the same time. The odd word reached my ears, but I didn't recognize the language. I know

182

enough Turkish to be able to identify it at least. Nor was it Arabic. Nefis has already started teaching Ida this third language so that later in life she will be able to relate to the Koran without troublesome interference, as she occasionally says with an ironic smile.

"Besides which Steinar Aass wouldn't have lasted five minutes," Johan went on. "I would have arrived in Haugastøl with a dead man."

The thought seemed to amuse him. He took the glass of cognac and sipped at the contents. He was still smiling broadly, as if he had just taken somebody in completely.

"Excuse me . . ."

The Kurd, or perhaps I should say the man I had thought was a Kurd up to now, had got to his feet. He approached our table hesitantly, looking from Berit to Geir and back again. Then he smiled stiffly at Magnus Streng and Johan. He avoided looking at me altogether. This made me wonder if I was wrong to assume that he didn't know I had seen him draw his gun.

"I'm sorry to disturb you," he said. "But I wondered if my wife and I might put forward a request?"

He spoke such good Norwegian that at first I didn't understand what he was saying. He had almost no accent; if it hadn't been for his appearance and old-fashioned clothes, I would immediately have taken him for a Norwegian. It was of course slightly embarrassing that I had failed to notice this earlier, after more than twenty-four hours in the same hotel.

"Of course," said Berit. "How can I help?"

"We would really like . . ."

He stroked his beard and looked over at the woman. She was still sitting at the table. From time to time she glanced up, but only briefly, before casting her eyes down once more in a way that now seemed demonstratively servile, given what I had seen earlier.

"We would really like to be moved to the apartment wing," he said quietly.

"I see," said Berit with a frown. "I can . . ."

Everybody except me looked at Kari Thue.

"I can understand that," Berit said in a friendly tone of voice. "But I'm afraid it's impossible. We've allowed all the entrances to become blocked with snow. Besides which I have to say . . ." she hesitated and looked at Johan. He shook his head almost imperceptibly. ". . . that it would be indefensible in any case to let anyone go outside in the present circumstances. Yesterday we did open up a passageway between the two entrances, but it's been blocked by snow again for a long time. So . . ."

She raised her shoulders apologetically.

"It's not possible."

"It's extremely important to us," said the man.

"As I said, I can understand that. But it's just not possible to —"

"But if we make our way across at our own risk? If we could just have a little help to clear the snow around the entrance, then —"

"I would stop you," Johan said calmly. "And if it became necessary, I would lock you in. There is nothing to discuss. Nobody is going outside. Nobody. OK?"

The man swallowed. He ran his hand over the thick beard once again. A few seconds passed before he nodded.

"I understand. I'm sorry to have disturbed you."

"I can see why they don't want to be here," Berit mumbled once the man had gone back to his table. "Hardly any of us can cope with Kari Thue. It must be worst of all for them."

Everyone around the table murmured in agreement.

But I thought I knew better.

I didn't think the armed man was afraid of Kari Thue.

I didn't even think he found it unpleasant to be in the same room as her. On the contrary, Kari Thue's aggression the previous evening had reinforced the role he wanted to play. There were completely different reasons for the fact that he and the woman in the headscarf wanted to move across to the apartment wing. They wanted to be in the same building as the passengers from the mystery carriage.

I didn't quite know why, but of course I was beginning to have my suspicions.

CHAPTER
FOUR

Roar Hanson was becoming more and more of a puzzle.

The meal was over, as Magnus Streng had cheerfully declared after a warm and slightly too long thank-you-for-dinner speech. Geir and Berit had once again tried to persuade me to accept a proper bed. Since we were fewer in number than yesterday, I could have a room of my own. I refused.

As soon as dinner was over I allowed myself to be hauled up the three steps into the lobby. I feel like a child in a pram whenever other people take control of my chair. The very last thing I want is to feel like a child. It was bad enough being one. In other words, the idea of someone carrying me up to another floor was unbearable. In the end Berit gave in and suggested they should swap one of the short sofas in the Millibar for a longer one from Blåstuen. That would give me the opportunity to lie down, at least.

I agreed, but had to wait until the lobby was empty before I lay down. Falling asleep in the chair with other people around was one thing. Lying down in full view was something else altogether. As I sat there trying to suppress one yawn after another, I felt like the hostess of an all too successful party that no one wanted to leave. It was very noticeable that the atmosphere had lifted once again. Presumably this had something to do with the fact that the bar had been open. With all this day had brought, I suspected that even the most abstemious of us might have gazed too deeply into the glass. And I certainly didn't begrudge them that.

"Could I . . ."

My eyes snapped open.

There he was again — Roar Hanson.

"Sit down," I said, not quite as pleasantly as earlier.

"Why did you lie?" he asked brusquely.

"I didn't lie."

"You did. You denied that Cato Hammer had been murdered."

"No, I didn't, in fact. When you . . . aired your suspicions I asked you why you thought he had been murdered. I denied nothing."

He sat down hesitantly. It seemed as if he were trying to reconstruct the conversation we had had before the fourteen-year-old in red started screaming about her macabre discovery in the delivery bay. He must have had a good memory, because he seemed noticeably less reproachful when he sighed, leaned forward with his forearms resting on his knees, and started again:

"I know who murdered Cato," he said so quietly that I only just heard him. "And keeping that knowledge to myself is a great trial."

I was a police officer for more than twenty years. I haven't worked it out, but since I was involved with murder investigations for the majority of those years, I

187

am unlikely to be exaggerating if I say that I have dealt with something like two hundred such cases. In almost every one, someone like Roar Hanson pops up. Someone who claims that he knows. Not infrequently it's the perpetrator himself, trying to make himself immune from suspicion, a tactic so stupid that there ought to be a warning notice about it on anything that could possibly be used as a murder weapon. I have yet to meet an investigator who doesn't immediately turn his or her attention to the person who maintains that he knows. People should also remember the ninth commandment. Thou shalt not bear false witness against thy neighbour.

Roar Hanson didn't look as if he were bearing false witness.

On the contrary, he was showing all the signs of spiritual torment. His skin was damp and sickly grey, and his hair was so greasy that it was plastered to his scalp in lank strands. His eyes were red-rimmed and watery, although I couldn't decide whether he was actually crying. He let his head droop between his shoulders. Anyone else would no doubt have laid a consoling hand on his back. Instead I moved away a fraction.

"I should have done something back then," he said.
He paused.
"What?" I said as indifferently as I could manage.
"I should have . . ."
Suddenly he straightened up. He rubbed the back of his hand across his lips. It didn't help a great deal. He

still had a thick white deposit at both corners of his mouth.

"It was when the two of us were working in the Public Information Service. I mean, Cato was . . ." He took a deep breath and held it as if he needed to brace himself. "I really can't understand why I didn't raise an objection at the time. Why I didn't do anything. And Margrete . . . I can't bear it. Of course I couldn't have known, but it seemed so . . . unthinkable that he would . . . You are a police officer, aren't you? Is it true what they're saying?"

The Public Information Service?

For meat and poultry? Fruit and vegetables?

I had no idea what he was talking about. In my eyes he looked as if he were about to tip over into some kind of paranoid psychosis; he had started looking around as if he thought somebody was about to attack him the whole time. Since the closest people were sitting several metres away from us and were involved in a noisy game of Trivial Pursuit, it was quite comical. Sometimes he struck himself hard on his injured shoulder, as if pain could be driven out by pain. Since it was impossible to make any sense of his disjointed narrative, I decided it was appropriate to lie.

"Yes," I said. "What people are saying is true. I am with the police. You can talk to me."

"Do you believe in vengeance?"

"What?"

Roar Hanson leaned even closer. I could feel small, sour puffs of his breath on my face. I didn't blink, but tried to lock his eyes with mine.

189

"What do you mean?" I asked slowly.

"Do you think it's ethically defensible to avenge a great injustice?"

As I searched for the answer he wanted, I saw Adrian coming towards us. His cap was pulled so far down that I couldn't see his eyes at all. Since I had realized long ago that he and Roar Hanson weren't exactly fond of each other, I raised a warning hand to make him stay away.

It didn't work.

"Why the fuck are you sitting here?"

Adrian thumped the priest on the shoulder. I didn't even have time to protest before the boy hissed:

"Stop bothering Hanne, OK!"

"Adrian," I said sharply. "He's not bothering me! Go away!"

It was too late. Roar Hanson got up slowly, like an old man. He blinked a couple of times and a controlled, composed expression came over his face. The smile he managed to force was so strained that his lips disappeared between his teeth.

"No," I said quickly. "You can't . . ."

He didn't hear me. I didn't take my eyes off him until he set off up the stairs, and disappeared.

"Why did you do that?" I said to Adrian, trying not to sound as livid as I felt. "That's the second time you've disturbed . . . *destroyed* a conversation I was having with that man!"

"But I . . . I thought . . ."

It was only a few hours since Adrian had been a weeping little boy. When he came strolling across the

190

floor to face up to the priest, he had regained something of the truculent, aggressive persona he wore as a disguise. Now he seemed completely helpless once again, utterly incapable of grasping my lack of gratitude.

"Yes, but . . ." he stammered. "But . . . I th . . . I thought . . ."

"Thought? Yes, what *do* you actually think? That I'm completely helpless? And what exactly have you got against that man? Has he done something to you? Have *you* done something to *him*?"

There were too many questions for Adrian.

He went off without saying a word.

When I think back, I can see that lives could probably have been saved if the boy hadn't come along and interrupted Roar Hanson's incoherent story.

But of course I didn't know that at the time.

Fortunately for Adrian, I have to add. I was already so furious with the boy that I didn't even realize where he'd gone.

BEAUFORT SCALE 6

STRONG BREEZE

Wind speed: 25–31mph

Making progress in a headwind is very laborious. Driving snow reduces visibility to less than one kilometre. It is difficult to face the wind for any length of time without some kind of protective covering. Most people should not venture out onto the mountain at this or higher wind speeds.

CHAPTER
ONE

I tried to get to sleep. Perhaps I tried too hard. For several hours I had longed for this moment, when I would be left alone in the lobby. Berit had found me sheets and blankets and a pillow, and I had counted on falling asleep the moment the three Germans, very reluctantly and with snivelling protests, were packed off to bed by the staff at midnight. The bar had closed at ten. Mikkel's gang had started throwing paperback books soaked in beer onto the crackling fire down in Blåstuen. They managed to create quite a lot of grey, acrid smoke before three of the staff came rushing in and stopped them. The beer taps were then turned off immediately.

Sleep just would not come.

I was comfortable. The sofa was nice and firm, and long and wide enough so that I could turn over without too much trouble. The bedclothes smelled faintly of chlorine and apples. My eyes closed, but still the pictures in my mind's eye kept me awake.

Not only had I decided to leave the murder of Cato Hammer alone until the weather improved and the police were able to take over what was essentially a fairly simple case, even if it was quite tragic, I had in fact also managed to persuade Berit, Geir and Magnus Streng that this very temporary suspension was the only sensible course of action. A murderer among us was bad enough; we didn't want to frighten him or her unnecessarily.

And yet I still couldn't help thinking about it.

Irritatingly, I had started to regard Cato Hammer with a kind of benevolence. I couldn't understand why. It's a long time since I stopped feeling sympathy for murder victims just because a crime has been committed against them. I have bent over far too many corpses for that. I have met far too many of the dead who, while they were alive, headed straight for their demise with their eyes wide open, greedy, dulled to all feeling, and without a thought for anyone but themselves.

However, the victim's background can make me feel for them. The circumstances surrounding the crime. You could call it the extent of the dead person's own guilt, however politically incorrect that might sound. For many years I put everything I had into the job. The murder of a gang member with countless violent crimes to his name was the focus of exactly the same persistence on my part as the crime against a defiled and murdered eleven-year-old girl.

But my emotions were reserved for a minority.

Fewer and fewer as time passed, I must confess.

Cato Hammer had been a posturing peacock, the kind of attention seeker I have never been able to stand. Normally I would be able to disregard the man and concentrate on the crime, which of course was something I had decided not to do in this particular case. And yet there was something about him. I couldn't get his face out of my mind as he lay there on the kitchen worktop, soulless and naked, if not literally then at least figuratively. The surprise in the dead eyes was so genuine, the expression of happy astonishment so striking that I still couldn't shake off the idea that he really had seen God waiting at the end of that white, shining tunnel.

Nonsense, of course.

Irrational sentimentality, due to the fact that I no longer had anything to do with dead people. The sight of the murdered Cato Hammer had definitely touched me.

At least the man had never harmed anyone but himself.

Unlike Kari Thue.

I caught myself hoping, with surprising sincerity, that she was the one who had killed Cato Hammer. A warm, shameful pleasure spread through my body at the thought.

There wasn't a shred of evidence to suggest that she was a murderer.

But Nefis gets so upset whenever she hears her.

Otherwise, Nefis hardly ever gets upset. Nefis is Turkish, a lesbian, a professor of mathematics, and thus fairly pragmatic about most things in life. At the same time she carries within herself a wondrous, childish faith, a certainty of a divine presence; she has lived with this certainty for so long that it is unaffected by knowledge and intelligence. It is strange, of course, and during those early years we would sometimes quarrel about it. Only when I gradually came to realize that it was really to do with the fact that Nefis had a childhood that was worth remembering did I understand that I had to let it be.

For Nefis, Islam is the strict love of her father and the sound of the soles of her brothers' shoes on the floor as they laughed and chased her around the palatial house where she grew up. Islam is her mother's reproachful wailing and forgiving hugs. For Nefis, faith is the presence of her three sisters and everything else that is beautiful and dignified; her maternal grandparents out in the country, the smell of books in her father's great library, and the musical voices of the muezzins from the minarets. For Nefis, Allah is the power that made her father miss her so much after two years of curses and rejection that he finally gave in; in spite of everything, a lesbian daughter is a gift from God, and he just couldn't deny her for all eternity, even though she loved a woman and had also started to enjoy good wine. Nefis's father has seventeen grandchildren, but Ida is the youngest and the only one with ice-blue eyes and her maternal grandmother's hair. She cannot be loved too much, worshipped too deeply, and all this is Nefis's faith and religion.

For me, God is someone who never glanced in my direction.

If he had existed, he would never have allowed me to live as I did for the first eighteen years of my life. When I finally found the strength to break with my family, with my neurotic, snobbish, prejudiced, dry-as-dust

198

academic, pseudo-Christian and utterly Norwegian family, I saw no sign of the Lord then either. The only thing I discovered was a resigned, sorrowful certainty that I had done something right.

Breaking with your family is the most dearly bought liberty.

It means breaking with parts of yourself.

Breaking *off* parts of yourself.

Kari Thue encourages that kind of thing. She stomps around on delicate ground in spiked shoes. She opens up opportunities for young girls who do not have the maturity to understand the consequences of these opportunities. For Kari Thue, Islam is a straitjacket to be broken out of, and she does not believe in people like my Nefis.

It makes me furious. But it doesn't make Kari Thue a murderer. At least not just like that.

I shifted my position on the sofa.

At any rate, there was no longer any reason to worry about who might be up in Trygve Norman's apartment in the wing. After the violent events of the day, we were effectively cut off from the passengers from the mysterious extra carnage. Berit had assured me that the two men from the Red Cross who were over there would ensure that nobody went up to the dark, narrow corridor where the armed guards were, outside the cordoned-off apartments.

I wouldn't have needed to bother about it any more, had it not been for the two Kurds.

It was impossible to find a comfortable sleeping position.

Although the man appeared to have accepted the fact that his request to move had been turned down, I wasn't convinced. I would have felt much happier if I had known exactly what role those two were playing in the midst of all the secrecy.

Whether they were hunters or guardians, I mean.

Time I stopped thinking. I wanted to sleep.

I opened my eyes.

It was as if the sound of the storm had altered. The wind was still angry and howling, but I was certain the thuds and blows were coming less often, and with less ferocity. Since it was impossible to insulate the hole in the wall properly, there was a new freshness in the air indoors, a chilly draught that had not completely disappeared despite the fact that the heating had been turned up and fires had been lit.

Berit had said that the storm would start to ease early tomorrow evening. Perhaps even in the afternoon. I thought it seemed as if a change in the weather was already on the way. I tried to absorb the monotonous roar of the storm, like a lullaby telling me that everything would get better, that everything would turn out all right in the end.

I thought about Ida and fell asleep.

Just before I dozed off I noticed Adrian coming back. He lay down on the window ledge and pulled a blanket over him as he had done the previous night, and I hadn't the energy to say anything.

CHAPTER
TWO

"Hanne! You have to wake up!"

I didn't know where I was. It was a long time since I had slept so deeply. The journey from the land of dreams was long and winding, and for several seconds I tried to focus on the man who was crouching beside me, his hand on my shoulder as he whispered again.

"You have to wake up!"

"What's the matter?" I mumbled eventually. "What time is it?"

"Three. Almost three."

"I'm asleep."

"Roar Hanson has disappeared."

I tried to sit up. Fortunately Geir had learned his lesson and didn't try to help, even though I must have seemed very confused.

"Roar Hanson," I repeated mechanically. "What do you mean, he's disappeared?"

Eventually I managed to sit up. Geir slid his bottom onto the sofa where I had been lying, and leaned forward.

"He shares a room with Sebastian Robeck."

"Seb — What are you talking about?"

I sank back against the cushions. Sleep just didn't want to let go of me now it had finally got a firm grip.

"That doesn't matter," hissed Geir. "He's just one of the blokes from the church commission. They were sharing a room. But when Sebastian Robeck got up for a pee half an hour ago, he discovered that Hanson's bed was empty. It hasn't been touched. He never went to bed."

"A different room," I mumbled. "He's probably gone to bed on his own somewhere. Since the carriage fell there are a few empty rooms."

"That's what I thought. But this bloke, this Sebastian, he said something about . . ."

I waved my hands to get him to move back a bit. My tongue tasted dry and stale, and I grabbed my jacket to look for some chewing gum.

"What did he say?" I asked quietly, rubbing my eyes with both hands. "Is Adrian asleep, by the way?"

Geir glanced over at the window and nodded.

"Roar Hanson had said something," he whispered. "Tonight, just before everybody went to bed. He told his roommate he had a little errand to do, but it would only take quarter of an hour. He . . ."

He suddenly looked up.

"Here he comes," he whispered, pointing.

Berit Tverre was moving silently across the room. I threw off the covers and managed to get into my wheelchair before she and her companion reached me.

Fortunately I had gone to bed fully dressed. A sharp smell from my own unwashed body made me roll the chair back as the man held out his hand. He lowered it again, shrugged his shoulders and introduced himself anyway. I mumbled my own name.

"What's all this about?" I said, shaking my head violently; it didn't help much. "Why the drama? It's the middle of the night, and as there are plenty of empty rooms . . ."

"He asked me to wait," Sebastian said so loudly that I had to shush him. When he continued, his voice was considerably more subdued. "He said he was going to sort something out or meet someone, or maybe he said he had an errand to do. I can't remember properly. But the strange thing is, he asked me to wait. It was only going to take quarter of an hour or so. I asked him why, but he just repeated that I had to wait."

"But were you intending to go somewhere? Why would he ask you to wait — surely you were going to bed anyway?"

"Of course."

The man scratched his armpit and a furrow of discontent appeared at the top of his nose.

"He asked me not to go to sleep. To stay awake until he came back."

"Why?"

"I've no idea."

"Did you ask him?"

"Yes. But he just asked me even more insistently to wait."

"And what happened?"

The man squirmed.

"I fell asleep. I was just so worn out."

His voice had a complaining, almost guilty undertone.

"I can't see that you've committed any sort of crime, exactly."

I tried to stifle a yawn. Tears sprang to my eyes. I picked up a bottle of Farris mineral water from the coffee table and had a drink. At the same time I swallowed my chewing gum.

"What shall we do?" asked Geir. "Start searching?"

Silence.

"Let's wait," said Berit eventually. "The last thing we need is to wake everybody up long before they've had enough sleep. Hanson has probably gone to bed in one of the other rooms. He might have come back, seen that Sebastian was asleep, felt like reading for a while, and decided to go to a different room so that he wouldn't disturb him."

"Are the empty rooms open?" I asked. "I mean, don't you have to collect the keys from reception?"

Berit gave a resigned smile. "We gave up on that early yesterday. Everything's open. We've put out piles of clean sheets. People have to make their own beds if they want to change rooms. Easier for us, of course, but it also means we have less control. But what could we do, we . . ."

"It sounds eminently sensible. And I agree with you. Since it seems probable that there is a perfectly natural explanation for Roar Hanson's disappearance . . ."

I stopped. The others were looking at me. All three of them knew I was lying. We were all thinking the same thing: the fact that another member of the church commission had disappeared during the night under slightly mysterious circumstances, almost exactly twenty-four hours after his colleague had been shot dead, was suspicious to say the least. I also assumed that I wasn't the only one who had noticed Roar Hanson's unstable state of mind. As far as both Sebastian Robeck and I knew, the priest could have smashed a window and jumped out into the bitter cold of his own free will.

Or something along those lines.

". . . we'll wait before raising the alarm. If we wake people up now, I'm afraid it could cause an even bigger catastrophe than . . ."

It was impossible to finish the sentence. And nobody tried to help me out.

"Could we meet here at . . ."

It was now ten past three.

". . . six. No, half past six should be fine. Most people will still be asleep then. And we can take it from there. OK?"

Nobody protested. They padded away, each to his or her own space, and I lay down again. Adrian was lying in exactly the same position as when he had settled down three hours earlier. Before I had time to fear insomnia, I was in a deep, dreamless sleep.

It's strange, what people can cope with.

BEAUFORT SCALE 7

NEAR GALE

Wind speed: 32–38mph

In a headwind it is necessary to lean forward over the skis and press the ski poles down with some force, even on level ground. It can be difficult to stay on one's feet in strong gusts of wind. Drifting snow reduces visibility to only a few hundred metres. Problems orientating oneself in the terrain. Skiing on the mountain in a wind this strong will be extremely arduous for most people.

CHAPTER
ONE

The clock insisted that it was morning; 06.20, explained the luminous numbers on my mobile. My body protested with some tenacity. I was just as far gone when the monotonous mechanical noise tried to drag me from my sleep as when Geir had woken me a few hours earlier.

My back was aching. A fire was running downwards from the small of my back, disappearing into a pain I could no longer feel. For a moment I wondered if I had regained my mobility. If so, it would be a miracle of biblical proportions. A heavy-calibre projectile had severed the spinal cord between the tenth and eleventh vertebrae, and it was beyond all hope of healing.

I tried to sit up. Although the sofa had seemed like a good idea, I couldn't lie there all night. At home we had a 120,000 kroner bed from Auping, ordered especially to take into account Nefis's and my weight and height. Even that can sometimes give me problems. Right now I doubted briefly whether I would be able to pull myself up into a sitting position.

I just about managed it.

"We'll start with those rooms we know are empty," said Berit quietly, frowning as she noticed that Adrian was gone.

"The boy went off a while ago," I mumbled. "I've no idea where."

"Geir's already started searching," she said. "And Sebastian Robeck insists on helping. We'll see if luck is on our side. Hopefully he'll turn up in one of the beds."

"How many rooms do you actually have?"

Her smile was resigned, and didn't reach her eyes.

"More than I'd like at this particular moment. First of all we'll take the storerooms, the cubby holes in the cellar, the workshop and the technical rooms. And the attic. With a bit of luck, people will sleep late today. After everything that happened yesterday, I mean. If they're all as tired as I am, they'll sleep until twelve! I just hope we can find Roar Hanson before we have to start waking the guests."

I was thinking precisely the opposite. If we found the priest in a room that wasn't a bedroom, I had a bad feeling about the state he would be in. Since I very much doubted that he'd embarked on some amorous adventure, given the circumstances, for the time being I was clinging to the hope that he had found a bedroom all to himself. In which case it would be more difficult to find him without starting to wake other people.

Berit ran a hand over her ponytail, which was caught up in a blue band. There was something helpless about the movement, a childishness that formed a stark contrast to the strong face with its intense, blue, open gaze.

210

She talked about us as *guests*.

Only a handful of us had ever bothered to thank Berit and the rest of the staff for their help during this dramatic interlude. Many people had commented that the food was good, but most were so preoccupied with themselves as victims of an accident that they took everything for granted. Some people complained about the beds, others about the fact that the dogs were constantly allowed to come down into Blåstuen, when they weren't really supposed to be in there. A married couple in their fifties had struck a chord when they said that the selection of diversions available was poor; there were counters missing from most of the games, and there were far too few packs of cards. When the cheerful, friendly woman in the kiosk pointed out that such things were on sale, the woman pursed her mouth haughtily; she certainly hadn't asked to end up in a train crash on the mountain, and she definitely had no intention of spending her money because of it.

Berit had dark circles under her eyes. A weary, almost sorrowful expression had settled around her mouth during the course of the night.

As far as I could see, it was only in the kiosk and the Millibar that anyone asked for payment. So far not one single credit card had been asked for to cover accommodation or food, not one guarantee had been requested. The staff had worked from morning to night. So far they had all functioned as a combination of spiritual mentor, nurse, child minder, waiter or waitress, wailing wall and cleaner.

Only Magnus Streng had clearly expressed the view that Finse 1222 must be one of the country's most generous and charming hotels, ever since he first waddled in from the platform and set to work bandaging wounds and putting broken bones in splints.

We really were an ungrateful lot.

We really were Norwegians, the majority of us.

And yet Berit Tverre was still referring to us as guests, and she even managed a wan smile before she hurried off towards the stairs. As far as I could see, she was heading downwards.

I listened to the wind. During the night I had been sure that the storm was abating. It was no longer attacking us with the same fury. It was as if it had gradually realized that the buildings at Finse could be lashed, they could be buried in snow and severely damaged, but they could never really be conquered. The buildings around the little railway station between Hallingskarvet and Hardangerjøkulen had been built in an era when things were allowed to take their own time, by people who knew the mountain and the caprices of the weather gods better than they knew their own children. I discovered to my surprise that the lower part of the windows facing out towards Finsevann were covered in solid snow. I didn't really know, but I assumed it must be three or four metres down to the ground in summer. Maybe more. Only through the upper third of the windows could I still see whirling snow, as if it were in some kind of madly spinning centrifuge, grey-white flakes illuminated from inside against the pitch-black morning sky outside.

212

The wind had not begun to die down; we were in the process of being buried in snow.

There were no longer thick walls against which it could batter. Up to now the snow had piled up in enormous drifts a couple of metres away from the walls facing the lake. I presumed this had something to do with both the wind and the heat from the buildings, but there were ramparts of air between us and the terrifying quantities of snow. Now these were being filled in. A covering of driving snow had settled around the building, protecting us from the worst of the onslaught. Only from the side wing, which was the highest part of the hotel as it was on a slope, could I still hear the familiar creaking from the walls.

I didn't know whether I ought to be relieved or afraid.

I had no idea how much snow could actually fall from the sky once it had really started to play up.

CHAPTER
TWO

Nobody came.

True, Berit had only just been here, but otherwise I was completely alone in the lobby. The chef and his two colleagues were already in the kitchen. From time to time I heard the clank of metal and other human noises, blending with the monotonous background roar of the storm.

It was making me feel hungry.

But most of all I was tired.

I'm used to getting up at six o'clock, but this felt like one o'clock in the morning. I couldn't stop yawning, and my eyes were streaming. That's why I noticed the dog that came rushing in as more of a blurred movement, a pale yellow shadow moving at full speed across the floor. Before I had time to wipe my eyes with the back of my hand, the dog was already halfway between the stairs and the Millibar, while I sat there in my wheelchair without a clue about what was going on.

Suddenly every sound disappeared.

A fuse had blown. It was as if my body didn't have sufficient energy to keep all my senses working. It was more important to see, and I saw. The whole thing can't have taken more than three or four seconds, but once again I had the experience of registering every detail. Every single one. It was neither the Portuguese water dog nor the nervous setter that was hurtling towards me. Nor was it the poodle, which I hadn't actually seen at all since the first evening.

As I am always sitting down, I have a different perspective on life from other adults. In a literal sense as well. This can often be valuable; I see things that others miss. But I also miss some elements that others see. In many ways I see the world as a child sees it.

The pit bull terrier is not exactly a large dog. A fully-grown male can weigh up to thirty solid kilos, but since there is no breed standard, the variations are great. At any rate, they are banned in Norway. However, since the similarity with other fighting dogs is so striking that they can easily pass for a different breed, there are still plenty of them around.

The specimen that was hurtling towards me was more monster than dog. Its chest was broader than the length of its legs, and from its enormous mouth lolled the longest tongue I have ever seen on any creature. I don't really know why, but I realized immediately that the dark patch on its yellowish-brown, short fur was blood. When the animal was just five metres from me I could see that its teeth were dripping with pale red saliva, splashing around its mouth every time its front paws hit the floor.

The eyes were colourless: clear, with an almost imperceptible hint of pale, pale blue. It looked as if the dog were blind, yet could see at the same time. Its gaze was fixed on me, but only as if I were sitting at the end of a dark tunnel, and there was nothing else in the room.

Fortunately, there was.

Suddenly I could hear again. A faint, muted thud as something soft and solid landed on the floor. Although everything I have read since about fighting dogs and their behaviour maintains that the dog should not have allowed itself to be distracted, it did. It didn't take its eyes off me, but a slight turn of the head made it lose its rhythm and stumble without actually falling.

I just wished I was able to use my legs. I realized the only way I could defend myself would be to lift my foot and kick out just as the dog was about to take its final leap. If the dog got anywhere near my face I was lost. Every ounce of my strength and concentration was therefore focused on this one impossibility: raising my knee and extending my leg in front of me with full force and at exactly the right moment.

The miracle didn't happen.

I was still crippled, just as I will be until the day I die.

And I couldn't understand where Mikkel had come from. He was a metre away from me with the beast underneath him. His right arm was locked around the dog's neck, with the crook of his arm across its throat. His left hand, clenched into a fist to avoid the jaws, pushed the nose upwards until Mikkel jerked his arm in a sudden, violent movement. The dog's neck vertebrae snapped with a crunching, meaty sound. The paws scrabbled spasmodically at the floor a couple of times before Mikkel got to his feet, kicked the corpse and mumbled:

"Fucking mongrel."

I leaned over to my left and threw up.

He made no attempt to help me. He didn't offer me water, didn't ask if there was anything he could do. He was obviously intending to leave the dog where it was, but he half-turned and said:

"I think the ptarmigan's bust. I had to jump over the desk and I knocked it down."

He tugged at the waistband of his trousers and walked away.

On the floor in front of the reception desk lay a shattered winter bird, a sad heap of white, tufted feathers. It was the companion of the stuffed raven, which was still standing there with its wings outstretched, gazing into space with its dead eyes. The noise that distracted the dog must have been the little ptarmigan falling on the floor. I thought it was strange that I had heard only that soft thud, and nothing of the storm, nothing of Mikkel. I could only imagine what he might have been doing hidden on the other side of the desk, where only the staff were allowed, early in the morning, without giving away his presence.

But I hadn't the strength at that moment.

Mikkel, the lout from Bærum, had saved my life.

And Berit was running across the floor. When she caught sight of the dog lying there dead, she stopped and put her hands up to her head. Only then did I notice that she was crying. It was unlikely to be out of sympathy with the yellow monster with blood around its mouth and froth along the thick, shining lips.

CHAPTER
THREE

They had found Roar Hanson behind the third door they opened. Fortunately Berit was there at the time, because she was the only one who knew that the remote room in the cellar had been made into temporary quarters for the dangerous dog from the train. The owner, a man of about forty who had more or less kept himself to himself since the accident, used to go in and see the dog every two hours. He had taken it upon himself to keep the room clean, and according to Berit he seemed conscientious and decent. At night the dog was alone behind a locked door, from bedtime until the owner got up.

He hadn't got up yet. Fortunately.

Roar Hanson was dead, but it wasn't the pit bull that had killed him. Although it had looked that way at first.

CHAPTER
FOUR

We had learned one thing, at any rate. Roar Hanson's body was not moved to the kitchen, the delivery area, or anywhere else where people might trip over him. For the time being he was rolled up in a tarpaulin packed with snow and ice in a room a few doors away from the room where he was found. The door was locked with a key and an extra padlock. Cato Hammer's body had also been moved there during the quiet hours of the night. The dead dog had been removed from the floor in reception, but I hadn't bothered to ask where it had gone. The room where the dog had been locked in with the body of the priest had been emptied and cleaned. The owner had a key. Since his surprise at finding the dog missing would probably be more than enough, at least he wouldn't have to be faced with an empty room covered in blood and shredded newspaper before he was given the sad news about the animal's demise.

I still felt dizzy and sick.

"I just think we're in the middle of a Roald Dahl short story here," said Magnus, who seemed to be so excited he was verging on the euphoric. "I have examined the body very carefully and my goodness . . ."

He took a deep breath and let the air out very slowly between his front teeth. A low, whistling hum filled the room, which was extremely small.

Berit Tverre had allowed us to use the office behind reception. As I understood it, the chef had finally put his foot down when it came to any further use of his kitchen domain. I can't say I blamed him. The stale smell of unwashed bodies was distinctly unpleasant in this small space where three desks, office equipment, shelves and files were all over the place in a complete mess. Even if only a few of us had managed to bring our luggage and toiletries from the train, it should still have been possible for most of us to keep ourselves clean. It was as if we had all allowed ourselves to fall for the cliché: it was OK to stink in the mountains.

Magnus was waving his arms excitedly. Large rings of sweat under his arms were framed by a circle of dried, grey, bodily salts.

"Fascinating," he shouted, clapping his hands softly. "A real live story!"

I was presumably the only one who knew what he meant, even though I was also the only one who had not seen Roar Hanson's body.

Berit had produced a flip chart. Magnus found a clean sheet of paper and drew a sketch of an adult, so quickly that the marker pen squeaked across the paper. He didn't have quite enough room for the legs, because he had made the torso exaggeratedly large.

"The feet are of no interest in any case," he said, drawing a circle on the figure's stomach, just below the ribs and above the navel. "This is what we're going to focus on. You see . . ."

He put the cap on the pen and used it as a pointer, short and chubby just like him.

"The dog only licked the body. It licked it clean, so to speak. Not that I know much about dogs." He smiled, almost coquettishly. "But I have read a little. *Canis familiaris* is an exciting creature. A tamed dog, but still with much of the wolf about it. To varying degrees, of course, but this example of the pit bull breed is a fighting dog."

"The owner said it was a cross breed," Berit interrupted.

"Mongrel, pit bull . . . only a DNA analysis could determine the difference. However, this one was so big that I choose to believe what I want to believe. Well. In any case."

He banged the marker pen against the paper.

"Fighting dogs are, as the name clearly states, dogs that fight. With a very short fuse, you could say. Powerful body, immensely strong jaws. And yet we have seen really sweet pictures of dogs faithfully and patiently guarding small children, even tiny babies; these children can tug away at the dog's ear, and yet they are just as safe as they would be in their mother's arms!"

He looked from one to the other for confirmation that we had all seen pictures like this. None of us nodded.

"These dogs are first and foremost a danger to other dogs. As we saw when we arrived at the hotel, in fact.

222

The more peaceful animals were absolutely terrified as soon as that yellow creature showed its teeth."

"What are you getting at?"

Geir looked unhappy. The lines around his eyes were more pronounced than before, and his stubble was well on the way to becoming a full beard.

"If the dog didn't kill Roar Hanson, then why are we wasting so much time on it?"

"Just bear with me on this," Magnus Streng said mildly. "I'm trying to draw a timeline here. And that means we have to understand what really happened. You could actually help me on that point."

"Me?"

"Yes. What did you do when you opened the door?"

"To the room where Roar Hanson was lying?"

"Yes."

"I . . ."

Geir looked at Berit, who shrugged her shoulders.

"Berit said the dog seemed dangerous, and that I should be careful. So I opened the door just a little bit. As best I could. I saw Roar Hanson. He was just lying there on the floor, and I realized at once that he was dead. Nobody lies down on —"

"And the dog?"

"The dog? It growled and stuck its nose through the gap in the door. Because it wanted to get out, I presume."

"And you were frightened, of course."

Geir frowned and looked at him blankly.

"He was frightened, wasn't he?"

The doctor turned to Berit. She tried to hide a smile, but said nothing.

"Well, I mean, it was barking like mad," Geir exclaimed. "And showing its teeth!"

"So what did you do next?"

"Well, I was convinced that that bloody animal . . . It was covered in blood, for God's sake! I thought it had gone for Hanson and killed him! I was terrified!"

"I can totally understand that," Magnus nodded reassuringly. "But what did you *do*?"

"He opened the door," Berit said slowly. "When the dog tried to get out through the door, he kicked it. Hard. I heard the crunch."

"Aha," said Magnus, raising his index finger in the air. "You reconfigured the monster's code! With your well-aimed kick you . . ."

He broke off and looked at Berit.

"Do we know what the dog was called."

"Muffe."

I must have been overtired, because I laughed. The others looked at me as if I'd lost the plot.

"Muffe," I repeated, and I couldn't help smiling. "A pit bull?"

"But it was a sweet little doggy," said Magnus eagerly. "Muffe wasn't dangerous at all! Not to people, at any rate. Here we have one of the closest relatives of the wolf; it spends several hours locked in a room with a body, and it doesn't help itself. It licks off the blood, it lies down next to the body and gets covered in more blood, but it doesn't start eating! A friendly pet when it comes to human beings, ladies and gentlemen, that's what our little Muffe was!"

"Maybe he was full," said Geir sourly.

"Maybe. But what happens when you land your doubtless well-aimed kick is that his already short fuse runs out. He is afraid, angry, in pain, terrible pain, but instead of attacking, which is his real instinct, he runs away. Up in the lobby, he spots Hanne. Whether he was completely possessed by that time and wanted to hurl himself at your throat . . ."

He nodded in my direction before turning back to the flip chart.

"We simply don't know. Perhaps Muffe just wanted to be comforted."

"It didn't look that way," I mumbled.

"Get to the point," said Geir, whose mood was deteriorating noticeably.

"This," said Magnus, pressing his marker pen against the red circle on his sketch. "This is a wound caused by a murder weapon I have never come across before, to tell the truth. It certainly wasn't a dog. As you can see, the entry wound is . . ."

Presumably he suddenly realized that all we could see was a slapdash sketch.

". . . or to put it more accurately: having examined the deceased, I can tell you that the entry wound is relatively large. Seven, eight, nine centimetres, in fact. Then the wound narrows as it goes further into the body. It's sort of conical. The liver has been penetrated. An organ that contains a great deal of blood, the liver. It's very critical if it's ruptured."

His face creased into a serious expression before he shook his head and regained his enthusiasm.

"I can't be absolutely certain, of course, pathology is far from my speciality. It is well known that the internal organs have the troublesome capacity to move around. And yet all the indications are that the murder weapon looks like this."

He turned to a clean sheet of paper and drew a pyramid.

A pyramid with a very pronounced point.

"A crowbar?" said Geir enquiringly.

"No, no, no. I can say with comparative certainty that the weapon was this shape because I turned the body over. And I discovered . . ."

Suddenly he tore off the sheet with the outline of a man on it. He held it up in front of him for a moment before handing it to Berit with the blank side uppermost. Through the paper we could still make out the red strokes of the pen and the large, gaping hole he had drawn on the midriff, above and to the right of the navel just below the ribs.

"So now we are looking at his back," Magnus said seriously. "I found a lesion. Here."

The pen was pointing at the exact centre of the circle.

"So the weapon didn't go right through the body. But almost. Just a few millimetres short. The bleed on this side indicates that the object was pointed at the end, but slender."

"Not to mention sharp," I said.

"Exactly. Sharp. And slender."

"But what on earth *is* it?" asked Berit, pointing at the drawing of the alleged weapon.

"I don't know," said Magnus. "I do have a theory, but of course I can't know."

"But you said something about Roald Dahl?"

"Well, it's definitely not a leg of lamb," I said.

"No."

"I know it gets on your nerves," said Geir with an air of resignation. "But I still have to ask: *a leg of lamb?*"

"It's a story," I said quickly. "It's about a woman who kills her husband by hitting him over the head with a frozen leg of lamb. The police come, and while they're looking for the murder weapon, she cooks the leg of lamb and serves it up to them. They simply eat the evidence. She doesn't get found out. She gets away with it."

"But what's that . . ."

"It's an icicle," said Berit slowly, moving her hand towards the drawing.

"Yes! *Yes!*"

Magnus raised a fist in the air.

"Genius! A murder weapon that disappears as it *melts!*"

"You can't know that," I said.

"No, that's what I said. It's just a theory. And like other theories, it has to be proved. But like other theories it can also be regarded as probable, if no other explanation can be found and if other circumstances support it. As far as I'm aware, no one has found anything in the hotel that looks exactly like this."

He punched the drawing.

"Yes, but we haven't looked for anything," Geir protested, in a foul mood and impatient to bring the meeting to an end. "Besides which, I'm bloody starving. And thirsty. And tired."

Berit sighed and nodded.

It seemed as if no one had the strength to see the seriousness of the situation. Certainly most of what had happened since Wednesday afternoon had been excessively dramatic, and it was possible that some of us were becoming immune. The human psyche has a blessed ability to shut out things it is unable to cope with. However, the murder of Roar Hanson signalled a brutal paradigm shift in the situation at Finse 1222, and I didn't have the impression that the others realized what had to happen now.

While Berit and Geir were close to collapsing with exhaustion, Magnus appeared to be enjoying himself. Not over Hanson's death, but over the burlesque details he thought he could see in the murder. I wasn't at all sure about his icicle theory. Not that it mattered much. Murder number two wouldn't be all that difficult to clear up either. Quite the reverse, in fact; there were fewer suspects now than when the link between the hotel and the wing still existed.

When the carriage fell, we were relieved of the problem concerning the passengers on the top floor. I no longer had the energy to concern myself with how things were going in the apartments. Judging by what had happened, those of us in the hotel itself were still with Black Pete.

The murderer.

It was highly improbable that Cato Hammer and Roar Hanson had been murdered by two different killers, although there were troublesome differences in the methods and circumstances that might well indicate that I was wrong. However, the links between the two victims were so numerous that I was convinced, at least for the time being, that we were dealing with one and the same perpetrator.

I had counted on the fact that Cato Hammer was the only one he wanted to kill. A disastrous mistake.

"Any news on the weather?" I asked.

"It's supposed to improve over the next few days," said Berit. "The wind will begin to drop this afternoon. But the heavy snow will continue. At any rate, no help will arrive before this time tomorrow. At the earliest."

"Tedious," I mumbled.

"You can say what you like about all this," Magnus said cheerily. "But you certainly can't say it's tedious!"

"It's tedious that we're going to have to find the killer before the police get here," I said, much louder. "It's tedious that the tactic of leaving him in peace went wrong. Extremely tedious that Roar Hanson's family has lost a husband and father because of a serious error of judgement on my part."

I don't know what I had expected. A feeble protest, maybe. Perhaps a tentative indication that the responsibility was not mine alone.

Nobody spoke.

"You kept saying this was going to be easy," said Geir, slightly more amenably.

"For the police, yes. They have the resources in terms of personnel, they have registers they can use, and in addition they have incredibly advanced technology. They have computers, tactical teams, and not least the right to use force when necessary. The police are quite simply in the best position to do what we pay them for: to investigate crime. Personally I have only got a mobile phone." I rummaged in my pocket. "That's the only thing I can use to find the perpetrator and prevent a possible third murder. That and a complete bloody mess."

Berit coughed discreetly.

"Er, no, you haven't . . ."

I looked from her to the phone.

"There's no reception. The masts must have blown down. Or been smashed by the wind. I don't know. Johan says he can try to get over to the Red Cross depot and fetch a satellite phone, but because it wasn't absolutely necessary, I said no. For the time being."

"Right," I said, closing my eyes. "In that case I've got . . ."

"You've got us," said Magnus Streng, striking his chest. "At least you've got us, Hanne!"

I almost had the urge to stand up and give him a hug.

Thank God I'm not capable of doing such a thing.

BEAUFORT SCALE 8

GALE

Wind speed: 39–46mph

The mountain is boiling. Lichen and branches from the trees are carried along by the wind. It is extremely difficult to ski. Almost impossible to carry skis over the shoulder. Driving snow reduces visibility to less than one hundred metres. Impossible to orientate oneself in the terrain. Very difficult to follow even clearly marked trails. Do not go out skiing!

CHAPTER
ONE

Rarely has it been so good to feel water on my body. Over and over again I dipped the flannel into the big hand basin without wringing it out, then simply held it over my shoulder and let the red hot water flow freely.

Berit Tverre was starting to get to know me. I didn't like it. But I had still said yes.

She had produced a plastic chair with metal legs, three towels, a soft flannel and some soap. All without asking. She had put the whole lot in the ladies' toilet that I had already used a couple of times with considerable difficulty to empty my bags. When she asked me to go with her half an hour after our meeting, when everyone was having breakfast, I hesitated. Then I realized she would be furious if I didn't do as she said. By the stairs she held open the door of the Ladies and explained:

"I've put out some clean clothes for you. They're too big, but they'll have to do. I'll stand here and watch the door until you've finished. Take as much time as you need."

In front of the two cubicles was an area containing a hand basin and a mirror, big enough to allow me to get undressed, move across to the plastic chair and get clean again. Without any help from anyone else.

It was difficult to refrain from groaning with pleasure.

I couldn't remember when I last stank like this. It felt as if I had acquired an extra layer of skin, smelly, thick flakes of sweat and stress. Stripes of grey soap and dirty water ran slowly down my body, down the legs of the chair and across the floor. I couldn't understand how I had got so dirty, so *filthy*. In spite of everything, I hadn't been in contact with anything except my own clothes. Gradually the water began to run clear. The soap began to lather up, but I just couldn't stop. The bandage around my thigh was soaking wet and pink. It didn't matter.

Nothing mattered any more, and I fell asleep where I sat.

Presumably I was only out for a fraction of a second; I woke because the flannel fell on the floor, and I was wide awake.

We were down to 117 residents at Finse 1222.

In other words, 116 suspects, although of course it was out of the question that any of the children had been involved. Nor did I believe that Geir, Berit or Magnus were mixed up in the murder in any way, but my years in the police service had at least taught me that unpleasant surprises await those who draw over-hasty conclusions.

I still had hopes of Kari Thue.

I wasn't going to draw over-hasty conclusions.

If Magnus Streng's theory that the murder weapon was an icicle turned out to be correct, against all expectation, then this would significantly reduce the number of suspects. I wanted as few suspects as possible. A weapon like that . . .

"It can't be an icicle," I mumbled to my reflection.

Perhaps it really was true. Was ice even strong enough? Wouldn't an icicle snap if it met resistance from human flesh and tissue? Plus, and even more importantly: wouldn't an attack with an icicle be quite easy to ward off, even for a mentally and physically broken man like Roar Hanson?

Kari Thue was a feeble, skinny anorexic.

If Magnus was right, I was looking for someone who was strong and quick, and who had no fear of bad-tempered dogs. The perpetrator had chosen to kill Roar Hanson in a room containing a pit bull. Or, if the murder had taken place somewhere else and the body had been moved to the dog's room later, someone who felt sufficiently at ease with fighting dogs to haul a bleeding corpse into a temporary dog room and arrange it neatly before leaving both the body and the dog.

My thoughts touched on Mikkel.

Motive, I thought, scrubbing my thighs until the skin stung.

So far none of us had even mentioned the word. Motive had not been discussed in one single conversation I had had with Geir, Berit and Magnus, collectively or individually. Not once since I saw Cato Hammer's dead body in the kitchen for the first time had any of us asked one another what might be behind the murder. During the meeting in the little office behind reception where Magnus Streng had so enthusiastically put forward his theory about frozen water as the murder weapon, nobody had asked themselves or others that crucial, most basic question of all: *why?*

We simply didn't want to know. We didn't need to know. Until now.

All modern investigation work is conducted on a broad spectrum. Forensic evidence is collected, tactical discussions are held. An excess of information is collected all over the place; the investigators work to complete a jigsaw that could certainly have too many pieces, but never too few. The tiniest piece of information could mean something, every apparently insignificant forensic discovery could be crucial when it comes to solving a case. And yet there is a noticeable fork in the road, that critical counterpoint in every murder case: the moment when the investigator understands or receives confirmation of the actual motive behind the crime.

The motive is the keyhole to the crime, and up to now I hadn't even attempted to find either this keyhole or the key that would fit it.

The water was no longer quite so hot. I picked up one of the towels and rubbed myself dry. I really felt I needed to wash my hair, but that would be too difficult.

As Berit had said, the clothes were too big. But they were clean. I don't think the jeans would have stayed up if I'd been able to walk, but as I was doomed to remain seated, they were fine. The white sweater smelled faintly of fabric softener. The wool rubbed pleasantly against my arms.

I tried to clean up as best I could. It wasn't easy. The space was so small that the wheelchair was trapped between the wall, the door of one of the cubicles, and the chair I had sat in as I let the water run over my body. The floor was covered in water. The place smelled of soap and a lack of fresh air, and only now did I notice that the constant sound of the storm and wind was gone. There were no windows in the toilet, and it was surrounded by other rooms in all directions. I was completely insulated from the noise outside. I sat there for a few seconds with my eyes closed, simply enjoying the silence. Then I stuffed my own clothes into a plastic bag, placed it on my knee and looked around for a while before I knocked on the closed door.

Berit opened it.

"Thank you," I said. "A billion trillion thanks. I think somebody's going to have to clean up in here."

Her smile was the warmest I had seen for a long time. Berit Tverre was a person who liked helping others.

"Have people started waking up?" I asked her.

"A few. Not many. So far we haven't had to say anything. Everything's quiet."

"I'm thinking of testing out Magnus's theory."

"About the icicle?"

"Yes. How would you get hold of such a thing if you wanted to? While all the outside doors are blocked with snow, I mean?"

Berit put her hand to the back of her neck and rolled her head from side to side.

"Our roof is really badly insulated," she said. "Enormous icicles form along the eaves. In the rooms on the top floor, all you have to do is open the window and help yourself. Although the windows will snap off the icicles if you try. They all swing outwards from the bottom. They sort of tip up. And the wind has probably blown down most of the icicles. A lot of the bangs we've heard must have been thick chunks of ice hitting the walls and windows."

"But is it possible to open a window at all in this storm?" I asked. "Wouldn't the pressure from the wind and so on simply push it closed? And even if you managed to get it open, wouldn't —"

"Maybe. I don't know. This weather . . . we've never experienced anything like it before."

I set off towards my usual spot on the other side of the reception desk, in the corner by the Millibar. The bag of dirty clothes was cold and damp against my thighs. Once again Berit preempted me.

"Let me take your clothes. Would you like me to have them washed?"

"No thanks. Just put them somewhere. Where's Geir?"

"He's already started."

"Started what?"

"Looking for the room the icicle came from."

I stopped.

"If it really is the case," she said, "that someone has used an icicle to kill Roar Hanson, it will be obvious that a window has been opened. If it isn't broken, then the room will still be wet from all the snow that would have come swirling in during just a few seconds."

A fleeting smile passed across her face.

"We can think too, Hanne."

I think that was the very first time she used my name.

Before I had time to make an issue of it, Geir came running in.

"Steinar Aass," he said, gasping for breath. "I think it's Steinar Aass!"

He bent down, supporting himself with his hands resting on his knees.

"What is?" I asked.

"He's jumped. He's lying under the window up there . . . in the snow . . . where . . ."

"Calm down," said Berit. "I haven't a clue what you're talking about."

Geir straightened up, took three deep breaths and started again. "Room 205," he said, pointing up at the ceiling, "He's managed to open the window and jump out. I mean, it's not far, and I —"

"205," said Berit, moving away. "If he jumped from there we ought to be able to see him from . . ."

She stopped at the far end of the table. I followed hesitantly. It was as if Berit had only just noticed that the snow was beginning to pile up against the windows. I presumed there were still the remains of a gap between the building and the enormous drifts outside, at least in the corner where the wing was attached to the main building.

Berit clambered up onto the window ledge. Since I couldn't see what she saw, I tried to read her face. It was expressionless, and then she closed her eyes, took a deep breath and said:

"What makes you think it's Steinar Aass?"

Geir climbed up beside her. He had to stand with his knees bent; the window wasn't high enough for him.

"There's a man lying in the snow," he said without looking at me. "It looks as if he was aiming for the big drifts a few metres away from the wall. But of course he missed. Slid down. He's partly covered in snow, but as he's lying where the wind catches most, we can still see him."

"Dead?"

Unnecessary question.

"Definitely."

"How can you know it's Steinar Aass?" Berit asked again. "He's lying face down, and . . . Where did he get those clothes from, anyway? Isn't that . . . That's Johan's snowmobile suit!"

"It was hanging up in the drying room," said Geir. "He took it. Along with Johan's hat and goggles."

"In other words, we're not talking about a suicide here," I said.

They both turned to face me at the same time, I threw my hands wide.

"Nobody dresses like a polar explorer if their intention is to freeze to death. And the jump was far from high enough for him to die from the fall. With the snow and everything. But you still haven't answered Berit's question. How can you be sure it's —"

240

"Look what he's got on his back," Geir interrupted.

"Well," I said. "It's a bit difficult for me to . . ."

"A laptop," said Berit. "That bloody laptop, the one he was always carrying around. When he arrived from the train I noticed it was in a bag like that. With a couple of twists he could turn it into a rucksack."

She pressed her forehead against the window pane and peered out.

"A Brazilian flag on the flap," she mumbled. "You're right. It is Steinar Aass. But what on earth was he doing there? *Why the hell . . .*"

Her voice cracked into a falsetto.

"He was intending to run away," I said tersely.

"Run away? *Run away?* Could he drive a snowmobile? Did he even know where it was? Didn't he realize it would take him hours to dig his way down to . . ."

"Hubris," I said. "A familiar characteristic of people like Steinar Aass. And the stakes must have been high. Incredibly high. He had too much to lose by staying here. Bearing in mind what we know about the man from the newspapers, things were getting too hot for him."

I didn't know how right I was. Just a few weeks later, his business colleagues would be seized and placed under arrest in a major police operation in the Natal province of Brazil. They could look forward to a lengthy trial and an even longer prison sentence, all under conditions that made the prison at Ullersmo look like a five-star hotel. Steinar Aass was actually mentioned in an interview with the leader of the Norwegian branch of the investigation, a week after the raids had been carried out in both Norway and Brazil:

We had serious questions for another Norwegian who could have cast light on some of the biggest transactions into which we are now looking more closely. However, he tragically lost his life in the Finse disaster. His case is currently regarded as being of no interest to the police.

The guardians of the law had chosen, surprisingly enough, to consider those left behind, in this case a Brazilian wife and four fatherless children under ten.

But of course we knew nothing of this on 16 February.

The fact that yet another person had died, before it was even common knowledge that Roar Hanson had been murdered, was all I could think about as Geir and Berit climbed down from the window and stood in front of me, silent, resigned, and with so many questions that they couldn't even manage to ask a single one.

"Leave him there," I said. "Let's hope the snow will cover him before anybody sees him. After all, you have to stand on the window ledge to see him. Nobody does that."

Apart from the South African, I thought.

But I hadn't seen him since the carriage fell. Now I came to think of it, he was the only one who had gone away when I suddenly started speaking and everybody gathered around me. Perhaps he had gone over to the

242

wing in the seconds before the accident. Perhaps he was just scared of Kari Thue, and was staying in his room.

At any rate, I had other things to think about.

It was ten past nine in the morning, and soon the lobby would once again be full of guests and fresh rumours.

CHAPTER
TWO

"I've told you, it wasn't a pit bull! It was a cross breed! A quarter Staffordshire terrier and . . ."

Muffe's owner had got up. Someone, presumably Berit, had shown him where the body was. The man was now standing with the dead dog in his arms, giving Berit hell while occasionally appealing loudly to people walking past.

"Look what they've done! Look! He was locked in. I looked after my dog, I did everything you asked me to do."

Nobody seemed to care. On the contrary, if anyone did stop, it was more to express relief that the beast was dead.

The man started to weep. He buried his face in the short fur and sniffled as he murmured the dog's ridiculous name over and over again. Berit was silent, completely motionless; for a moment it seemed as if she was almost floating. I wheeled my chair towards her without really knowing what to say to the grieving owner.

"This is just crazy," said Veronica. "Who did this?"

She and Adrian were coming out of the kiosk. The boy was dangling a big bottle of cola between his index and middle fingers. He looked scruffier than ever, and even at a distance of several metres I could smell yesterday's drink on him. Since he was definitely not permitted to buy anything in the Millibar, I began to wonder if Veronica had brought an entire cupboard full of booze with her to the mountains.

Her voice was surprisingly deep.

"Who the fuck has treated the dog like this?"

"It's them," sobbed the owner. "It's them!"

He nodded at Berit and me. I raised my eyebrows and pointed at the wheelchair without saying a word.

"Was it you?" said Veronica, looking sideways at Berit.

"No," said Berit, swallowing. "And what's more, I am not answerable to you. Go and get something to eat. Breakfast is served."

"I'll eat when I feel like it," said Veronica, placing one hand on the body of the dog.

The man took a step towards her as if he were harbouring a quiet hope that this girl, dressed all in black and with her ridiculous make-up, might be a witch who could bring life back to the dead body.

"Lovely dog," she said calmly, running her hand over the fur.

"Best dog in the world," said the man.

Adrian said nothing. He hardly even noticed me. Nor was it the dead dog that interested him. His eyes were fixed on Veronica's face, and he had completely forgotten to pull down his cap. His mouth was half open. A thin string of saliva vibrated between his lips with each short, shallow breath.

Adrian was deeply in love. This bothered me, for some reason. I didn't need to bother about the boy any more. His interest in me from the first day had long since died; no one but Veronica existed for Adrian. It wouldn't last long. As soon as help arrived, the boy would be moved to a youth care facility, which would pay more attention to him than either I or his temporary great love.

Or they wouldn't pay any attention to him at all, which unfortunately was more likely.

He wasn't my responsibility, and he never had been.

And yet I couldn't suppress a vague feeling of unease, a nagging sense that this anaemic, antisocial woman wasn't exactly the best influence on Adrian.

And what I disliked most of all was the fact that she was letting him get drunk every night.

"I need to talk to you."

Geir came from behind me, and I jumped when he tapped me on the shoulder.

"It was him!" shouted the dog owner. "He's the one who killed Muffe!"

Veronica spun around. Her eyes narrowed to two lines framed in thick kohl with a cold, almost scornful glint just visible in the middle.

"Are you aware that this is against the law," she said. "There is an animal welfare law in this country and you —"

"And you can shut your mouth," snapped Geir, going right up to her.

She held her ground.

Adrian smiled inanely.

246

"I didn't kill the bloody thing," said Geir. "And if I had, you can be sure I would have had a good reason. What is more, we have bigger problems in this hotel than a dead dog. I suggest you and your boyfriend go and sit down. Any more fuss about that animal and I'll . . ."

Whatever he was intending to do was left hanging in the air. The threat was equally effective. Veronica assessed him with her gaze before indifferently shrugging her shoulders and heading for the dining room. Adrian trailed along behind her.

"Come with me," said Berit to the dog owner, who was still crying. "Let's find a place for Muffe."

She put her arm around his shoulders and led him away.

"Room 207," whispered Geir, bending over me.

"I thought it was 205," I said, slightly confused.

"Steinar Aass jumped from 205. There are clear marks from his shoes on the window ledge, and a piece of the snowmobile suit was caught on a nail. But in room 207 . . ."

He looked around and waved me closer to the reception desk so that we wouldn't be in the way of the people who were beginning to pour in from their rooms.

"Someone has been in there too. The window is open. The whole room is full of snow and ice. Ice, Hanne! Great big, long icicles! Everything that was outside the window has been smashed, either by the storm or when the window was opened. But somebody

247

has obviously managed to stretch to the side and get hold of more that way."

I said nothing.

"Magnus could be right, Hanne! At any rate, someone has been collecting icicles in room 207. You would never find icicles inside a room unless somebody had put them there. Snow, yes. Masses of snow. But ice?"

Still I said nothing.

I had far too many thoughts, far too much to say.

More and more people were coming down from their rooms. It was difficult to gauge the atmosphere. Some seemed to be in a good mood, almost cheerful, while others were walking with their heads down. Two of the girls from the handball team looked as if they had been crying; they weren't quite so grown-up any longer, the adventure in the mountains wasn't so exciting any more and they wanted to go home. The woman who was forever knitting couldn't quite make her mind up where she wanted to be, and was wandering back and forth between the long table and the door of the kiosk. Mikkel suddenly appeared from the stairs. He threw an unfathomable look in my direction before sauntering towards the breakfast room without saying anything.

A new, unfamiliar fear was clutching at my throat. I coughed. Tears sprang to my eyes, and I opened them wide as I tried to concentrate on breathing calmly.

"Is something wrong?" whispered Geir.

"No," I said, meeting his gaze. "But I need a place where I can be alone. The office? I have to have space and time to think. OK?"

"Of course," he said, pushing my chair towards the reception desk.

I didn't protest, and my hands rested idly on my lap.

BEAUFORT SCALE 9

STRONG GALE

Wind speed: 47–54mph

Wind and driving snow make it impossible to make any progress over the mountain on skis. Even with clear weather and a limited amount of driving snow, the strain can be such that a snow cave or cabin is the only salvation.

CHAPTER
ONE

Logic, I thought.

How I was going to be able to think logically and systematically in the chaos of impressions we had all had to deal with, I didn't know. I only knew that I had to start somewhere.

Geir had wheeled me back to the office. The flip chart was still there, and Magnus's red sketch of Roar Hanson's body was still hanging from the pale brown wooden blinds. The big hole in his stomach looked like a gaping mouth. A small Cupid's bow cut into the top of the oval, where the marker pen had caught and come off the paper.

Despite the fact that I had no basis on which to draw one single conclusion, I had decided we were dealing with just one perpetrator. I felt it was out of the question that two murderers entirely independent of one another should strike in the situation in which we found ourselves, with such a limited number of people and over a period of two days. And yet the difference in method was worrying. I was still not completely convinced that Magnus's theory about a frozen spike was correct, but it would probably serve as a starting point for the time being. However, it was difficult to understand why someone would use an icicle when he or she obviously had access to a gun. Earlier I had guessed that Cato Hammer had been killed with a revolver, but of course it could just as easily have been a heavy-calibre pistol.

The Kurds had guns. I hadn't seen his, but the movement of his hand towards the shoulder holster had been unmistakable. She definitely had a revolver. Therefore, I ought to suspect both of them. For some reason I couldn't keep them in focus; their faces slid away every time I tried to add them to the overview of possible perpetrators I had set up in my mind's eye.

I used to call it intuition in the old days.

It could no longer be trusted, of course.

I wheeled my chair over to the flip chart. The pen was lying on the metal lip below the paper, and I slowly took off the cap. *Cato Hammer*, I wrote at the top of the page.

The name told me everything and nothing. Red letters against cheap greyish paper. I tried to see past my own slanting handwriting. A name is an icon. A brief expression of the person who bears it.

I used to be able to do this. Once upon a time I was good.

I wrote *Roar Hanson* under the name of the other priest. Four letters in each forename. Roar and Cato. Six letters in each surname. Hanson and Hammer.

Coincidences. I wasn't looking for coincidences. I was looking for connections.

Both were priests. They had been at college together. They were the same age. They had worked together in the past, and they were working together now. Or rather: their involvement in the church commission wasn't actually a job, I supposed. More of a project, presumably. Cato Hammer was an outgoing person, known all over the country. Fat, jovial and a football fan. Roar Hanson was anonymous and grey, about as exciting as a grand master in chess.

I tore off the sheet of paper. Wrote the names again, this time with Roar Hanson at the top.

I had to start with the person I knew best.

I hadn't exchanged a word with Cato Hammer. All I knew about the man was what I had read or seen on TV. Most public figures turn into paper dolls on the way from reality to representation in the tabloids. Knowing this should of course have stopped me disliking Hammer. But as I've said: I'm not particularly bothered about becoming a better person. Although I have to say that I knew Roar Hanson slightly better. If it hadn't been for Adrian's constant interruptions, I would have known even more. I felt a surge of adrenalin at the thought; I could have shaken him like a rag.

Forget Adrian, I tried to tell myself.

Roar Hanson had definitely found something out. Or rather, he thought he had found something out. The man had been walking around like a living ghost, stooping and almost transparent with despair. Of course I had no way of knowing if he was right in his assumptions about who had shot Cato Hammer. It would have been considerably easier if we had been allowed to complete our conversations; he had been on the point of sharing his suspicions with me on two occasions.

I refused to think about Adrian.

The boy was lost anyway. He wasn't my problem.

Someone knocked on the door.

I didn't want any visitors. Didn't need them.

"Come in," I said.

"Is this where you're sitting?" Magnus asked rhetorically, settling himself down on the office chair behind the cluttered desk without asking if it was OK.

"Yes, I'm sitting here — it's all I can do."

He looked curiously at the flip chart.

"Can I join in?" he asked.

"With what?"

"With this . . . thought game. Because that's what you're doing, isn't it? Thinking?"

I sighed. A little too loudly, A little too demonstratively.

"Hanne Wilhelmsen, my good friend."

His voice had changed character. It had greater depth without sounding contrived, as if there were another man hidden inside that short body. I didn't understand him. He called me his good friend, even though he didn't know me. The constant switching between joker and omniscient sage, doctor and clown, wag and sharp observer was beginning to erode the sympathy I definitely felt for the man.

"Hanne Wilhelmsen," he repeated, clasping his chubby hands at the back of his neck.

The odour of sweat hit my nostrils. It was more difficult to handle now I was clean. He smiled, as if he understood without letting it bother him. At any rate, he didn't lower his arms.

"You can't quite make up your mind," he said, not taking his eyes off me. "On the one hand, you find it difficult to dislike me. My whole . . . appearance stops you from feeling sorry for me. People, by which I mean people in general, are sympathetic towards those of us who suffer the brutal and unpredictable caprices of nature. To dislike me would be to lose the illusion of being a good person, more than anything. Believe me, I have understood this ever since I was a little boy. To be honest, I have exploited it. A great deal."

He beamed. An entire finger could have fitted between his front teeth.

"You and I are basically very similar," he went on. "We are both different from other people, albeit in different ways. What separates us . . ."

Finally he unclasped his hands and leaned forward.

"Do you know what my father used to do when I was growing up?"

I had no idea what old Streng used to do when Magnus was growing up. The need to know didn't feel all that compelling.

"Every evening after I'd had my bath and before bedtime, he used to take me into his office. Every single evening. I would be wearing my pyjamas. Striped flannel pyjamas with sleeves and legs that my mother had shortened. Turned up, I think they say. Always flannel pyjamas. With blue and white stripes. He was a man of the old school, my father. A giant of a man. A real outdoor type. I would curl up on his knee while he

257

leafed through his books. He would show me animals. Ants busily building their anthills. Elephants in Thailand with enormous logs perfectly balanced above their jaws. Hunting lions and grotesque hyenas, cleaning up the savannah and disposing of infectious corpses. Hummingbirds hovering over the most fantastic flowers."

He closed his eyes. His smile changed, as if he were looking back and into himself.

I really didn't understand Magnus Streng.

"We would sit there for quarter of an hour," he said, still smiling and without opening his eyes. "Never more, never less. Then he would close the book and put me to bed. And that is the difference between you and me."

He was right, actually. Nobody showed me books with pictures of animals before bedtime, despite the fact that my father was a professor of zoology. Nor could I recall any flannel pyjamas. However, I had no idea what point Magnus Streng was trying to make. Other than to highlight the fact that he had a kind daddy. I agreed; the difference between us was immense.

"My father didn't say much," he said. "But it wasn't really necessary for him to say anything. The message was clear enough: we are all needed. We are necessary here on earth. Small and large, fat and thin, ugly and beautiful. I was good enough. I *am* good enough."

"You don't know me," I said sharply.

"No," he said, shaking his head. "I've read about you, but I suppose I don't know you. That's true."

"Do you know what the Public Information Office is?"

His smile died away. He seemed confused. Disappointed, perhaps, but only for a moment. Then he leaned back in the chair again.

"Well," he said. "There's a Public Information Office for meat. For fruit and vegetables too, I imagine. And as far as I know there's a Public Information Office for eggs and poultry. And no doubt one for fish. And for . . . Why in the world . . ."

"Could Cato Hammer ever have been involved in something like that? Some project? An — an advertising job? Something like that?"

"Cato Hammer? No, no, no. You mean the Public Information *Service*! The Public Information Service Foundation. That's something completely different."

I tried to think back to the last conversation I had had with Roar Hanson before Adrian turned up. Magnus could be right. Perhaps he had said Public Information *Service*. Not *Office*. Not that the difference meant anything to me.

"Cato Hammer worked there for many years," said Magnus contentedly. "He was a man of many talents, you know. He had a degree in economics as well as being a priest. Such educational combinations are no longer so uncommon. I have a brother who is a qualified engineer as well as a doctor, and you have no idea what an advantage that is in today's —"

"What do they do?" I interrupted him.

"Who?"

"The Public Information Service Foundation!"

"They administer funds. Billions of kroner. Literally, I think. At any rate, it's not a question of *doing* a great deal."

"Who owns . . . Who do they administer this money for?"

"For the church, of course. For the Norwegian church. Some of the problems involved in separating state and church are linked to property. Wealth. The church is rich. The church is a real Croesus. As it has acquired most of its fortune as a state church, allocating all of this causes a serious schism. Possessions. Funds. Property. Houses and church buildings. Does all this belong to the state, to you and me in other words? Or does it belong to the church, so that the faithful can take it with them in exchange for the privileges they have, which are protected by law if we dismantle the entire edifice of state belief?"

It had never occurred to me that the church was rich. On the contrary, I remembered all the fuss surrounding the renovation of the cathedral in Oslo before the wedding of the Crown Prince. If we were to believe the newspapers, the building was on the point of falling down thanks to many years of neglect and a lack of money.

"He was financial director there," said Magnus, his bushy monobrow knitted into a frown. "Or was he an accountant? No, I don't remember. It wasn't until he moved to the church at Ris as priest that he became seriously . . . visible to the masses, so to speak."

He whinnied like a horse.

"Do you know if Roar Hanson ever worked there?"

"No-o . . ."

He drew the word out slightly, scratching behind his ear with his index finger.

"To be honest, I'd never heard of Roar Hanson until today. An anonymous sort of chap, Hanson. Unfortunately he had none of his colleague's charm and warmth."

There was another knock on the door.

"Who is it?" I said crossly; I had told Geir I wanted to be left alone, and he had promised to keep the others away.

"Sorry," said Berit, hesitating before she came into the room and closed the door behind her. "But something's happened. Something that . . ."

She tugged at her ponytail.

"Don't tell me anybody else has been killed," I mumbled.

"No, it's —"

"And don't tell me anybody else has decided to set off on their own."

"No," she said. "In fact, you could say the opposite is true."

"The opposite," pondered Magnus, making a clicking sound with his tongue. "You mean somebody's trying to get in?"

Then he laughed, loudly and uproariously, quite a different sound from the laughter I had heard before. Magnus Streng had a repertoire of laughter that an impressionist would envy him.

"Yes."

I looked from Berit to Magnus and back again.

"What?"

She was fighting back the tears. Swallowing and breathing rapidly with her mouth open. Then she rubbed the back of her hand over her eyes, forced a smile and said:

"Somebody is digging their way down to the main entrance. From outside. They want to get in."

Then she snivelled and added:

"At least, that's the way it seems."

CHAPTER
TWO

Berit, Geir and Johan had persuaded the guests to move down into Blåstuen and Jøkulsalen. Every single hotel room had been checked to make sure that everyone, with the exception of the staff, Geir, the Red Cross personnel and I were located in the lower part of the wing. Magnus Streng had taken his role as chief of security very seriously, and had immediately chosen Mikkel as his deputy. The young gang leader muttered a sullen "OK" as he tried to hide his surprise and something that resembled pride on his sulky countenance for a change. None of the guests was told the truth about why people had to be moved. Geir came up with the explanation that the gap where the carriage had been needed some reinforcement. There were also problems with the structure of the staircase itself since the fall, he lied, and everybody needed to stay away until this had been investigated. Magnus was enjoying his role. I could already hear his exhortations: people must keep calm, there was no need to worry.

This was a big fat lie, and everybody knew it.

Since the accident there had been every reason to worry.

Oddly enough, people had accepted their temporary internment. Even Kari Thue had allowed herself to be sent down to Blåstuen without making a fuss.

Of course it was difficult to know what she was thinking, and she immediately made sure she was as far away from the two Muslims as possible. Over the course of just two days she had managed to acquire her own little court. They followed her into the far corner by the window looking out over the veranda to the south, where she settled down on a yellow sofa with multicoloured stripes, looking for all the world as if she were surrounded by friends. I sat by the stairs leading down to St Paal's Bar, and watched. Everything was going worryingly smoothly.

"It won't be long before they're done," whispered Berit, with one hand on my shoulder. "It sounds as if they're getting close to the door."

I followed her towards the main entrance. Whoever was shovelling snow out there was doing a thorough job. After Johan had decided that it was pointless, dangerous and unnecessary to keep the entrance open, the small windows in the outside door had gradually darkened as a wall of snow built up outside. Now it was getting light again. Since the entrance was protected by a solid porch with benches on each side, it was necessary to dig down on the outside in order to get in under the roof and reach the door.

It was after one o'clock.

The chef had been furious when he was told that lunch would have to be postponed.

I hoped there would be a reason to eat lunch, even after this.

"It's somebody from the wing," Johan mumbled. "They're the closest. It has to be them. And they must have a bloody good reason to come over here. It's minus twenty-four out there, and the last time I checked the wind speed was just below thirty metres a second. And it's still snowing heavily. But they're almost here."

I did my best to convince myself that the situation wasn't threatening. Not for us, at least. Something could have happened in the wing. A revolt, perhaps. Something along the lines of the mutiny Kari Thue had tried to get under way on our side just before the railway carriage came down.

Berit had said there was enough food in the wing where the apartments were, but that it was mostly tins and vacuum packs left behind by the owners of the apartments after each visit. At any rate, it was unlikely that people were starving to death after less than twenty-four hours of not particularly tasty food. At least I thought it unlikely they would set out on the highly dangerous journey between the buildings just to get a better meal.

"My money's on those people from the top floor," said Johan with a yawn. "They're tough, those guys. Strong."

The scraping noise grew louder, almost drowning out the roar of the storm. I could now see movements behind the narrow windows in the door. Something dark against the white light from above. A person busy shovelling snow from the lowest part of the door.

"Hello!"

The shout was clearly audible. It was a man. Several shadows were moving behind him; it was impossible to see how many there were.

"I'm going to try to open the door. Is that OK?"

The voice almost disappeared among the scraping and bumping. Berit walked over to the door. She shouted back:

"Who are you?"

"Let us in! We're . . ."

The answer faded away. Perhaps because of the wind, or perhaps because the speaker wanted it that way.

The man tugged at the door. Berit considered for a moment, then looked at Johan who nodded. He put his shoulder against it and pushed. The wind immediately found its way in, and the snow whirled in the draught. As soon as the gap was wide enough, the first man squeezed through and closed the door behind him. He stood in front of the door as if he wanted to prevent those outside from following him. Or perhaps he wanted to stop us from going out. At any rate his behaviour was striking as he stood there with his legs apart, arms akimbo like a bad-tempered bouncer outside a popular night club.

He was very tall and was dressed in windproof trousers, heavy boots and a mountain anorak. A woollen jumper was just visible under the anorak. Little balls of snow were stuck very close together around the neck. He gasped for breath and took off his hat before unwinding his scarf and pushing his ski goggles up onto his head.

He looked around without saying anything. The frost had nipped at his cheeks in spite of the scarf, hat and goggles. His face was narrow but with strong, almost handsome features beneath the dark greying hair that clung damply to his forehead. He had a rucksack on his back. It must have been heavier than the size suggested, since the straps were cutting surprisingly deeply into his shoulders.

I tried to understand. My brain tried to get this to make sense, searching for a logical connection in a chain of thought that was far too long.

When the man caught sight of me he stiffened before the shadow of a smile passed across his face, and he eventually took a step forward.

"Hanne," he said, letting out a long breath. "I've never been so pleased to see you."

CHAPTER
THREE

When I recognized Severin Heger, I thought about the day I got shot.

Perhaps that wasn't so strange. The last time I spoke to Severin, between Christmas 2002 and the New Year, he was the officer in charge with the police in Bergen. I had known him for a long time. He was a school friend of Billy T's, and used to work in what was known as the police supervision unit, on the top floors at Grønlandsleiret 44. Even though we weren't friends, we had bumped into one another from time to time for almost twenty years. I needed help, and he gave me what I needed to unmask the head of the crime unit in the Oslo police force as a corrupt murderer. During the arrest I was shot. One bullet destroyed me for life. The prosecutor in the ensuing trial made a dramatic point of the cold-blooded attack on a female police officer. Personally, I thought the fact that the corrupt police chief had murdered four innocent people to make sure he didn't lose his position and his reputation was considerably worse.

He was found guilty on all charges.

So it's his fault that I am no longer able to walk.

As I see it, I have only myself to blame.

I was careless, Billy T tried to warn me. He ran after me when I rushed into a cottage in Nordmarka where we knew the suspect to be. There was no stopping me. I was tired. Broken down, in many ways. It was amateurish, rushing in like that. I had already heard the approaching helicopters in the distance; reinforcements were on the way.

The psychologist I was forced to see once I had eventually recovered sufficiently actually to speak to someone maintained that I was driven by a subconscious desire to die. She called it a death wish, I think. Which is absolute crap. I have no desire whatsoever to die. Life hasn't exactly turned out the way I hoped, but in spite of everything death is definitely a less appealing alternative.

I was burnt out, irresponsible, and should have left my job as a police officer before it all went wrong. In fact, I remember that was the last thing I thought before I stormed the cottage: I have to give up this job. I can't do this any more.

I learned my lesson.

Then I got Ida. I'm always with her. I always have time for my daughter. There is a kind of purpose in most things.

The fact that Severin Heger should suddenly turn up during an apocalyptic storm at Finse was considerably more difficult to grasp. Only when I had absorbed what had just happened did the pieces fall into place. My assumptions with regard to who had been hiding in the secret carriage and later in the apartment on the top floor could well be right. They *had* to be right. I glanced over at the door and felt my skin break out in goosebumps at the thought of the kind of person that was on the other side. Then I looked over at the tall man in his winter clothes.

"Hello, Severin."

I just couldn't think of anything else to say.

He didn't even try to give me a hug. His smile vanished as quickly as it had appeared.

"Who's in charge here?" he asked, still out of breath.

"I am," said Berit.

He held out his hand and introduced himself.

"Why —"

"I need an isolated part of the hotel," Severin Heger interrupted her. "Without any through traffic."

Berit's expression was part surprise, part displeasure.

"This hotel is not in a position to offer the highest level of service at the moment," she said. "So we are in fact a long way from being able to accommodate that kind of special request or requirement."

For almost forty-eight hours I had seen Berit Tverre in most moods. Up to now she had never been sarcastic. It didn't particularly suit her brisk style.

Severin opened his mouth to say something, but I got there first.

"Why have you come here? What's happened in the wing? I'm assuming it's you and your friends who . . ."

I glanced over at the door, where shadows were moving outside the small windows. I couldn't understand why the others had stayed outside. Even if they were sheltered from the wind in the deep hollow in front of the hotel, it must be bitterly cold.

270

". . . who were in the extra carriage," I went on. "And who have been staying in the apartment on the top floor. What's happened?"

Severin looked around. I knew exactly what he was thinking. Before he replied, he spent a couple of seconds weighing up how much he had to say in order to achieve what he wanted.

"A small . . . revolution," he said quietly and hesitantly, as if he wanted to buy himself more time.

Nobody said anything, nobody asked anything. Everybody was looking at Severin Heger.

"A child died," he said. "A baby."

"You shot a *child*!"

Geir took a step towards Severin. It looked as if he were intending to avenge the baby's death fight there and then.

"No! No! The baby died last night. Quietly and peacefully. It was sleeping next to its mother, but when she woke up the baby had died. No sign of external violence, no sign of anything at all apart from . . . sudden infant death syndrome?"

He shrugged his shoulders; the gesture was one of resignation rather than indifference.

"Was the baby pink?" I asked.

"Pink?"

"Was she dressed in pink from top to toe?"

"Well. Yes. When they came up to us, a whole gang of them, wanting to . . . I went downstairs to stop them from . . . I went down to talk to them."

He swallowed hard before adding:

271

"Yes. It was a girl. The mother collapsed completely. Acute psychosis, I think. It was like throwing a lighted match into a can of petrol. Panic was threatening to take over completely. Two lads — I think they're from the Red Cross — were doing their best to get the situation under control, but we thought it was best to make a move."

Once again he swallowed hard before repeating:

"It was a girl."

I didn't even know that Sara and her mother were in the wing. To tell the truth I had hardly thought about them, at least not since the hotel lost contact with the apartments.

I remembered the faint smell of sour milk from the baby's clothes. I could see that little face in front of me, yelling and yelling into my jumper straight after the accident, as the temperature dropped and I was afraid we were all going to die.

"She received a hard blow to the head. When the train derailed and crashed."

Nobody seemed to grasp what I was saying. Perhaps I had only thought it.

"But you're armed," said Geir. "Couldn't you keep them away?"

"We are armed," Severin nodded. "But so were they. Axes, hammers, kitchen knives. A drawbar for a sledge! God knows what they'd kitted themselves out with."

"You had guns," Geir insisted.

"Yes. But we are actually very keen not to shoot anyone. The balance of terror, you know. The deterrent effect. Our guns are primarily there to maintain peace.

But these people were totally desperate. They thought we had a doctor, better food, they thought we had . . ."

He ran one finger across his brow and shook his head almost imperceptibly.

"They would have smashed their way through the door, I think. They kept saying we had some member of the royal family with us."

From outside we could hear loud banging on the door.

Severin straightened up. Berit was looking increasingly sceptical. Geir glanced at the policeman with something approaching hostility. Johan was the only one who still seemed impressed that Severin had made his way from the wing to the hotel, and had got here in one piece.

"The situation was quite simply such that I had to bring . . ." He pulled up his sleeve and looked at his watch. Then he started again. "I need a part of the hotel where we can be alone."

He turned to me this time.

As if there were suddenly only two people there, it was me he looked at. When I realized why, for the first time since I was shot I felt a small stab of longing for the job I had done for so long. I was reminded of an affinity between colleagues that even I had felt and once been part of, despite the fact that I had done my best to avoid it for many years.

Severin Heger trusted me. I didn't know if he was still part of the Bergen police in what had been renamed the PST, or if he was a consultant in the growing market for private security. Since I thought I knew what kind of people he was guarding, I assumed that Severin had left Bergen and ordinary police work in favour of the more secret elements of the force. But right now we were both police officers, and he was relying on the fact that I would help him, just as he had helped me on the day I almost died.

"He needs an isolated part of the hotel," I said. "And I think you should help him."

"But who *is* he?"

Berit looked from me to Severin.

"Who are you? Why should I —"

"Berit. Give him what he's asking for."

I was trying to remain calm.

"Trust me. Please."

The shadows outside were obviously tired of waiting. Someone banged on the door again, and Severin had to take a step backwards to stop them from coming in. The look he gave me was easy to interpret.

"The top floor looking out towards Finsevann," I suggested quickly. "From room 207 onwards. Would that be OK?"

"No," said Berit. "That's too much. Too many rooms."

She turned to Severin and tugged at her ponytail again. The gesture was evidently a sign that she was thinking.

"You can have the dog room."

"The dog room?" Severin repeated enquiringly.

"Yes. How many of you are there?"

"Four."

274

"OK. We have a room that's been used to keep a dog in up to now. It was thoroughly cleaned this morning. It still smells of shit and maybe slightly of blood, but it is clean. It's usually the staff dining room. You can have that room."

"How many entrances are there?"

"One. One door. The window is blocked by snow."

"That's no good. We need —"

"Take it or leave it. Both you and those with you out there are welcome into this hotel on the same conditions as everyone else here. I would never have agreed to give you special treatment if Hanne hadn't asked. I can't offer you anything but the dog room."

I looked at Severin and nodded imperceptibly.

"You can lock the door," Berit went on. "It can be locked from the inside. There are several keys, but I will keep those. That means I can come in at any time. I will make sure you are provided with food and water. That's what I can offer you."

"That's probably the best solution," I interjected.

"I assume you don't want anyone to see you," said Berit. "Just as before. Therefore it would be best if you take the opportunity right away. We have gathered all the guests in a different part of the hotel. You can go down into the cellar without being seen."

Severin realized he wasn't going to get any further. He nodded and opened the door. Three men came in. They were wearing layer upon layer of clothing, and their faces were completely covered by goggles, scarves and hats. None of them seemed to want to take anything off. They were all carrying rucksacks, apparently just as heavy as Severin's. If one of them had turned up carrying nothing, that would have given away the difference between him and the others. If one rucksack had been noticeably lighter than the rest, there would be reason to assume that it at least didn't contain weapons. Given the way the four men were dressed and equipped, it was impossible to say who was doing the guarding and who was being guarded.

Severin looked enquiringly at Berit, who moved quickly towards the stairs, waving the new arrivals to follow her.

Halfway across the room he stopped dead and turned around.

"Hanne," he said.

I moved over to him and allowed him to lean over me. When he began to speak his mouth was so close that the words tickled my earlobe.

"Are there two people here who look Arabic?" he asked. "A man and a woman? They can't possibly have been in the wing. She's wearing a black headscarf, he's in a greyish brown jacket and —"

I nodded and he straightened up. His hesitation could be because he was intending to tell me something. It was difficult to tell whether my confirmation of the Arabs' presence was good or bad news.

He decided not to say anything.

But he still gave me a sign. His eyes bored into mine. He held my gaze for several seconds, and it was impossible to look away. Then he blinked three times, and ran down into the cellar after the others.

I thought I understood what he meant.

Just a few hours later I would be forced to trust that I had interpreted him correctly. I had to take an enormous risk based on one look, but of course I knew nothing of this as I sat there listening to the footsteps of five people disappearing down the stairs.

I was thinking only of Sara, the little pink baby who was no longer alive.

CHAPTER
FOUR

Despite the fact that I have never heard an avalanche in reality, I have a definite idea of what it sounds like. If you spend enough time watching the Discovery Channel at night, as is my habit since my back was destroyed, frequently forcing me to get up at the most ungodly hours, you learn quite a lot about disasters. Including avalanches.

When Kari Thue's voice sliced through the room, it reminded me of the first warning that an avalanche is on the way. It is often impossible to see anything but a slender and apparently innocent crack in the snow, but the sound is already there, it comes from deep beneath the snow where the mass is already on the move.

"Where is Roar Hanson? Has anyone seen Steinar Aass? *Where has Roar Hanson gone?*"

Perhaps it had been a mistake to gather all the guests right at the bottom of the building. Up to then nobody had noticed that the ill-fated priest was missing. People had been preoccupied with themselves and their own affairs all morning. His absence was considerably less striking than that of Cato Hammer. As far as I was aware, Steinar Aass had not struck up a single acquaintance during the trip, and I had quietly assumed that nobody would give the man a thought.

By gathering all the guests in one place, we had made sure they were safe from whatever came in through the snow-blocked main entrance. However, this had made it easier for someone to notice that neither Roar Hanson nor Steinar Aass was there.

Kari Thue was the one who had made the discovery. This emaciated, irritating woman was not only wide awake and full of life, she was also smart and constantly on the lookout for ways to erode Berit, Geir and Johan's otherwise undisputed leadership.

"I demand an answer! We all demand to be told! Where are Roar Hanson and Steinar Aass?"

Kari Thue was the almost invisible crack in the snow, just below the top of the mountain, I was still sitting by the door, unable to stop thinking about the baby who came flying through the air and landed on my knee in the crash. Her death had had a greater impact on me than anything else that had happened since Wednesday afternoon. Sara hadn't even reached her first birthday when she died. I reproached myself for not having told the doctors that she might be injured, despite the fact that she seemed to have suffered no ill effects from the hard collision with the wall in front of me on the train. I had no doubt assumed that her mother would ensure that a thorough examination was carried out, but I knew perfectly well that you should never take anything for granted. In my mind's eye I suddenly saw her mother, shouting at me on the train. Her despair at having dropped the child was so great that she barely knew what she was saying. I should have . . .

At the same time, I didn't know what I could have done, and that depressed me even more.

Kari Thue's outburst had triggered the avalanche. The noise level was rising. More and more people were talking and asking questions down in Blåstuen, even though there was really nobody to whom these concerns could be addressed. Berit still hadn't come back up from the cellar, and I didn't know where Geir and Johan had gone. I pushed my chair slowly towards the accelerating spectacle. I would have much preferred to take cover in the office behind reception, and lock the door.

But I thought about Magnus, who had been tasked with keeping everyone calm down there. It sounded as if he had serious problems.

When he caught sight of me by the stairs leading down to St Paal's Bar, he got up with some difficulty from a maroon chair and ran across the room. Despite my depression at Sara's death and the certain knowledge that Kari Thue was going to make things even worse for us all, I had to suppress a smile as he hurried agitatedly towards the stairs. He wasn't built for running, Magnus Streng. Nor for walking upstairs. It was as if his knees didn't work properly. They were too loose to work normally when he was walking in a straight line. Instead he turned his legs in rapid semi-circles from the hips. It looked as if he were parodying a speed walker.

"Here we go again!"

His chest was whistling. He grabbed his throat, coughed and waved his free hand apologetically in the air.

"Asthma," he gasped, "Unfortunately I haven't brought my medication with me. I don't usually suffer at this time of year."

"Sit down," I said, pointing to a chair by the table.

"Yes," he said, catching his breath. "This is actually . . . rather unpleasant."

He tried to moisten his lips before picking up a glass of water someone had left on the table. He emptied it in one draught.

"She sees everything," he groaned. "She remembers everything. I'm bloody certain she'd have won the world championship in Memory."

The noise from downstairs was so obtrusive that I didn't answer.

While the gang surrounding Mikkel had never been anything more than irritating and cocky, the group that gathered around Kari Thue was much more threatening. It now consisted of something like forty people. Kari Thue herself had climbed up on a table, where she had begun to address her followers like the charismatic leader of some sect.

"Things are being kept from us," she shouted, tucking her thumbs into the straps of the little rucksack; I was beginning to wonder if she kept it on in bed. "And I'm asking myself who exactly is making the decisions in this situation, and with what right and authority. We were told that everyone, absolutely everyone, must assemble down here. The insulation packed into the hole in the wall was to be reinforced, they said, and the structure of the staircase checked. But where are Roar Hanson and Steinar Aass? Do they have privileges not extended to the rest of us? Is there some difference between us and them?"

"What shall we do?" I whispered to Magnus.

"I . . . don't . . . really . . . know."

He was gasping for breath after every word. I was seriously concerned; his skin was grey and damp, and one hand was clutching the edge of the table so tightly that the knuckles were white.

Berit came running in.

Some people crumble under protracted pressure. Some cling to others and become like children again, needing consolation and reassuring lies. Some become paralysed. Life has taught me that it is more or less impossible to predict how people will react under great stress.

Choosing soldiers is an art, and Berit Tverre was a woman you would want by your side in a war. She stopped dead on the top step of the staircase leading to St Paal's Bar. During the course of just a few seconds, she had grasped the situation. First of all she crouched down beside Magnus. Without asking him any questions, she took an inhaler out of her pocket and pushed it into his hand.

"Bricanyl," she murmured. "I have asthma too. Deep, calm breaths."

I will never forget Magnus Streng's face as he greedily swallowed air containing the healing micro-particles. He cupped his hands around the rocket-shaped inhaler. His eyes were gratefully fixed on Berit's face. Big, heavy tears slowly trickled from his eyelashes and ran down towards the corners of his mouth. He gave the dosage dispenser one more turn and inhaled deeply.

Once Berit could see that Magnus had the situation under control, she raised both hands and shouted down to the agitated crowd.

"Roar Hanson is dead," she almost bellowed. "And so is Steinar Aass. Sit down. *Sit down!*"

There was complete silence. It seemed as if the weather gods themselves had had a shock; the monotonous roar from outside seemed more distant and subdued. Berit walked quickly down the short staircase and cut across St Paal's Bar. She stopped by the wide opening leading into Blåstuen, where the doors were folded right back so that both rooms formed one big space. Kari Thue was still standing on the table. Most of the others were looking embarrassed, searching for somewhere to sit. The dog owners had settled in one corner, where the three surviving dogs seemed to be getting on well. I couldn't see Muffe's owner anywhere, but a number of people were hidden from me behind the walls between the two rooms. Some were also sitting in Jøkulsalen. The double doors leading into this area were open, so that everyone could hear what was said. Adrian and Veronica must be in there, because I couldn't see them.

"Get down from there," Berit hissed at Kari Thue. "I will not have you treating my furniture like this. Down! *Down!*"

She could have been talking to a disobedient dog.

"What's happened to Roar and Steinar?" said Kari Thue, without showing any sign of obeying.

"As I said, they're both dead. Steinar Aass got the idiotic idea that he could make his way down from the mountain by himself. He froze to death. Roar Hanson . . . He's dead too. There isn't much you can do about that."

"How did he die?"

I had to strain to hear what they were saying. For the first time since the accident I regretted not asking for a ramp from the lobby down to the communal areas.

"*Will you come down from there!*"

Berit was trying to grab hold of Kari Thue's arm. Mikkel, who was sitting at the other end of the room, got to his feet hesitantly. It looked as if he hadn't quite decided what he was going to do. He eased his way slowly between tables and chairs before suddenly speeding up. When he reached Kari Thue, he stopped and put his hands on his hips.

"Do as the lady says. Get down."

"First I want to know what's happened."

"You've already been told what you need to know," said Berit.

"No. You lied to us before. I want to know the truth about Roar Hanson, and I want to know right now."

"You look absolutely ridiculous," said Mikkel. "Stop making such a fuss. Get down. This lady here is in charge, OK!"

Kari Thue looked at him as if he were something she had dug out of the bathroom plughole.

"I seem to remember that you agreed with me."

284

Mikkel had his back to me, but I could make a guess at his facial expression from his posture. His head tilted slowly backwards at an angle, and he made his shoulders look broader by raising them.

"Bitch," he hissed all of a sudden, waving his hand in the air as if to ward off some annoying insect.

He turned around and sauntered indifferently away, mumbling something I couldn't hear. When a couple of his friends stood up to follow him, he snapped at them to stay where they were. I expected him to walk past Magnus and me without a word. To my surprise he sat down on the stairs in front of me, on the bottom step.

"Bitch," he said, without looking at us.

Kari Thue clearly believed that she was leading the battle. In a way she was. With renewed self-confidence she gazed out over the assembled crowd before turning to Berit once more.

"It can hardly be a coincidence if two members of the church commission die within the course of just a few hours. You have already confirmed that Cato Hammer was murdered, although of course you did try to pull the wool over our eyes with regard to his death as well. Which, incidentally, is a fundamental infringement of my rights, and the rights of everyone here. We are snowed in on the mountain under extreme circumstances. Each and every one of us has the right to make decisions in order to save our own lives."

She was speaking on each inhalation and exhalation. This made the brief pause even more dramatic.

"Within the boundaries of the law, of course. I must remind you that we are not on board a ship. You are not the captain. None of the maritime rules of hierarchy apply here."

She stabbed her index finger at Berit's shoulder and took a step back.

"I am not aware of any laws that give you the right to make decisions on behalf of all of us," Kari Thue went on. "Quite the reverse. In the absence of either the police or some other authority, it is up to us to find the best solutions to help us survive. And therefore I demand to be given the information necessary to enable me to take care of myself. I would say that . . ."

"Mikkel," I whispered.

He half turned and ran a casual hand over the handkerchief tied around his head.

"What?" he mumbled.

"Help me down. Down the stairs."

"I would say," said Kari Thue more loudly, "that with the current mortality rate in this place, information about what people are actually dying of is to be considered absolutely vital."

Instead of easing the chair down the three steps, Mikkel simply picked up the chair with me in it, and carried me down before gently placing me on the floor, with no sign of exertion whatsoever. The boy really was as strong as he looked.

"Thanks," I whispered.

He didn't answer.

"What did Roar Hanson die of?" Kari Thue shouted accusingly at Berit.

"You're right," I shouted back as I moved closer to the crowd.

Kari Thue jumped, quite literally. She reminded me of a squirrel, a nervous, quick, alert creature who nevertheless hadn't had the sense to take in enough food. Berit looked at me, slightly confused. I would have liked to have told her what I was thinking.

"You're absolutely right," I repeated instead. "You all have the right to know what people are dying of up here."

I stopped my chair three or four metres from the doorway leading into Blåstuen. I put the brakes on and placed my hands on my lap.

"Steinar Aass froze to death," I said loudly. "As Berit has just told you. As far as Roar Hanson is concerned, all the indications are that he was murdered last night."

The woman with the knitting, who I had eventually realized was one of the lay members of the church commission, burst into tears. She raised the half-finished knitting to her face and sobbed. A man leaned over to console her. The sound of murmuring grew louder, and after just a few seconds everybody was talking over the top of one another. Kari Thue looked as if she didn't really know what to do. It was as if the confirmation that she was right was so unexpected that she had lost her balance, rhetorically at least.

"I was right," she said, talking to the air; no one was listening.

"And what are you going to do about it?" I asked her.

"What did he die . . . How was he murdered?"

Neither of us was talking particularly loudly any more. This was a conversation between the two of us, as

I had hoped. But people were starting to shush one another. They wanted to hear.

"We don't really know," I replied. "But he was stabbed with some kind of object."

"A knife?"

I noticed she was blinking more rapidly now. Whether this was a sign of insecurity or of something quite different and even more desirable, I couldn't say.

"No," I said. "Not with a knife. So what are you going to do? Now you've got the information you thought you had a right to?"

She looked around. Presumably it didn't feel quite so good to be standing on a table having a reasonable conversation with me as when she was hell-bent on deposing Berit. At the same time, it would be a defeat to climb down from her makeshift speaker's podium, as both Berit and Mikkel had tried to get her to do. She chose to start with a compromise, and sat down. It was obviously uncomfortable sitting in that position, like a child with her legs tucked up, because she slowly shuffled towards the edge. Eventually she was standing on the floor. But she didn't say anything.

"I'm waiting," I said with a smile.

"Yes, what are we going to do, Kari? What do we do now?"

It was one of her courtiers, a lady in her fifties with a tan that owed much to a sunbed, who was asking. She had been among the first to attach herself to Kari Thue, that very first evening after the intermezzo with the two Kurds.

Still no answer. Kari Thue swallowed, and the room was so silent that I could hear the wet sound of her larynx moving.

"Look, everybody — look!"

One of Mikkel's gang had got to his feet. He was standing right by the window overlooking the terrace. He waved his hand and went on:

"The weather! Look!"

The terrace had been covered in deep snow for a long time. The door was completely blocked. You could only see out of the top half of the window, although not many people had noticed this as the view had disappeared thanks to the constantly falling snow.

The cloud cover had broken up. It was still snowing heavily, but the light slicing through the whirling flakes was white and intense. It was as if the sun itself wanted to remind us that it was still up there. That it hadn't forgotten us, and that it would soon knock aside this monstrous storm that had already been allowed to torment us for far too long.

Kari Thue was forgotten. Everything but the weather was forgotten. A number of people got up and went over to the window, as if they couldn't really believe what they were seeing. Others clapped their hands and laughed, some tentatively, others light-heartedly. The woman with the knitting dried her tears over Roar Hanson and screamed with joy.

The whole thing lasted a minute or so.

The sky closed up once more. The grey darkness pressed against the windows. The snow reverted to its dirty grey colour, and became a wall of miserable weather once again.

A huge collective sigh rose up to the ceiling.

"The temperature is rising," Geir said cheerfully. I had been so focused on the weather that I hadn't heard him come in. "At the moment it's minus twenty-one, and the wind is already down to twenty-four metres a second. That's only a strong gale! Nothing compared to what it has been."

Like most of the others, I looked from Geir to the windows and back again. It was as if that glimpse of better times was an illusion. There was nothing in the monotonous, limited view to suggest that the weather was likely to improve in the foreseeable future.

"Very good," I said, forcing a smile. "Does that mean they'll be coming for us soon?"

"Well," he gave a broad grin, "everybody will be staying at Finse for one more night. But if it continues to improve, I should think the first of us could probably be heading for town as early as tomorrow."

"Perhaps," Berit added sceptically. "We have no experience of this amount of snow. We don't even know what it looks like out there. The railway lines will have to be cleared, and —"

"Let's be optimistic," said Geir. "I should imagine they'll allocate a helicopter to us after all we've been through. One more night, and then we'll all be off home."

He was obviously ignoring the fact that the police would want to have their say about the chances of our leaving Finse as soon as it became physically possible.

But given the current situation, I didn't think there was any point in reminding him of that.

Despite the fact that the upbeat atmosphere plummeted noticeably when it turned out that the break in the cloud cover above Finsevann was extremely temporary, Geir's optimism seemed to be infectious. Nobody was talking about Roar Hanson's death any longer, nor about the safety of the guests. They were talking about the wind and the weather, and a few had already begun to bet on when the first helicopters would arrive at Finse. People spread themselves out around the seating areas, and many went up to the Millibar for coffee while they waited for the tables to be set for a delayed lunch. Some of the teenagers started singing.

It was hard to understand that this shower had just been told that yet another person had been murdered. On the other hand, a comparatively long time in the police had taught me that people have a phenomenal ability to let themselves be distracted by good news. None of them had any kind of close relationship with either Roar Hanson or Steinar Aass, with the possible exception of the knitter. I wasn't even all that convinced of her honesty when she broke down at the thought of her colleague's death. She was sitting there now with a blissful smile on her face, slurping coffee with lots of cream and glancing constantly at the windows in the hope that God would once again show His grace.

Kari Thue had sat down. She was flicking through a book with an interested expression on her face; I didn't believe for one moment that she was reading it.

The Kurds must have been there the whole time, but I hadn't seen them until now. They came hurrying out of Blåstuen, heading for reception. I followed them with my eyes all the way, but they didn't turn around or give any other indication that they wanted to talk to me or anyone else. The woman kept her head down, while the-man-who-might-have-been-her-husband held her forearm in an authoritative grip.

Magnus Streng was obviously feeling better. I could see him up in the lobby. He was talking quietly to Berit, who suddenly leaned over and gave him a warm hug.

Things were starting to return to something resembling normality. And nobody had asked a question about the really big lie: the need to improve the insulation in the hole left by the railway carriage, and to check the staircase. Not one of the guests at Finse 1222 had any idea that four strange men from the secret carriage were sitting behind a locked door in the cellar. Nobody had even asked why it had been necessary to gather everyone down in Blåstuen.

The whole thing was like magic. You wave one hand dramatically so that no one notices what you are doing with the other hand. In this case it was Kari Thue who had performed a magic trick. Little did she suspect that her performance had made it possible for us to take in the men from the wing and hide them without anyone noticing a thing.

The world really is happy to be deceived.

"You look a bit down," said Geir, patting me on the shoulder. "Come on, I'll help you back up to reception."

292

I didn't know if I wanted him to do that. To be honest, I didn't know what I wanted.

"Cheer up, Hanne! The weather is improving. One more night, and then we can all head for home."

That was exactly what was getting me down.

"I don't know if we can get through one more night," I said quietly, so that the others wouldn't hear. "It's the nights in this place that scare me. So far we haven't had one single night without a murder."

Geir blinked and swallowed. It looked as if he were about to say something. A word of consolation, perhaps. He couldn't come up with anything. Just as well — I was frighteningly right. Instead he followed me as I slowly wheeled my chair across the room towards the stairs leading up to the lobby, and my fixed spot by the Millibar.

"I need coffee," I said. "Lots and lots of coffee. I have no intention of going to sleep again until we've been rescued. The next time I lie down, it will be in my own bed."

BEAUFORT SCALE 10

STORM

Wind speed: 55–63mph

Most people never encounter this wind force and above. Trees fall on electrical cables and telephone wires. Wooden walls creak. Small, light cottages are torn from the ground.

CHAPTER
ONE

"This ought to do," said Berit, putting down a three-litre thermos. "Milk?"

"Normally, yes, but since the intention is to keep me awake, I think I'll take it black. I'm sure it's just my imagination, but I think it works better the darker it is."

The very thought that I wouldn't sleep before tomorrow afternoon at the earliest was making my head feel unbelievably heavy. Geir had suggested I should have a little nap on my own in the small office behind reception. Nobody was going to be murdered at three o'clock in the afternoon when everybody was awake, he insisted with a wry smile. And he was right, of course. Anyway, I said I'd rather not, but I did agree to use the office. One hour in the land of dreams would make me even sleepier. From experience I knew that I could be on the go for another twenty-four hours as soon as I had passed over the borderline between deathly tired and overtired. A strong dose of caffeine would therefore be more useful than a one-hour nap.

"Do you need anything else?"

Berit threw her arms wide as if she could offer me whatever I might wish for. I looked at a dead computer screen and tried to come up with something.

"No. But thank you anyway. You're a marvel, Berit. I'm so impressed by the way you've dealt with all this."

"It's doing you good to be in the mountains," said Geir with a smile, clipping the back of my head before moving towards the door. "You should come here more often!"

It was half past two in the afternoon, and I couldn't really see the humour in what I was planning to do.

CHAPTER
TWO

Sometimes I imagine that I still have feeling in my legs. I have never wanted to bother anybody with complaints about an injury for which I have only myself to blame, so I never speak about that hint of pain that reminds me from time to time of what it's like to stand on two legs.

Not that I usually have all that many people to share my thoughts with. It can be weeks between those occasions when I have to speak to anyone other than Nefis, Ida and old Mary, our housekeeper. This is the life I have chosen, and this is the way my life has turned out.

But now I was sitting alone, and feeling lonely.

It was very strange.

The wound in my thigh was hurting. I mean, really hurting. Of course I realize it was my imagination; I've seen the pictures of the severed nerves in the small of my back. Like porridge, the surgeon had said, peering in fascination at the pictures they had taken when they operated on me.

There is no possibility that the cells below my navel can send any kind of signal to my brain. Communication has broken down for ever, something that I accepted long ago. And yet it was as if I could still feel the searing pain in the wound left by the ski pole. Not like a phantom pain, but like a real injury that hurt.

It was strange to feel so alone.

Cato Hammer must have had many enemies. Perhaps enemies was the wrong word. He wasn't dangerous enough for that. Too rotund and nice. His constant pronouncements were irritating rather than sharp, loud rather than offensive. And yet I was still certain that many people must have felt like me: the man was intolerably self-obsessed in his alleged concern for others.

But that kind of person doesn't usually provoke murder.

The flip chart was still in the corner of the little office. The sheet on which I had written the names of the two victims was untouched. I moved slowly over to the chart and picked up the red marker pen. Beneath the two names I drew a line, dividing the sheet in two. Then I began to add more names.

Einar Holter, the train driver I had never met.

Elias Grav, I wrote.

Steinar Aass.

Sara.

I wished I knew her surname. The way it looked now on the sheet of paper, you might have thought I didn't like the little girl. Not using her surname showed a lack of respect, as if she were worth less than the others. As if she were a dog. Or a cat, with no relatives, no sense of being part of a real family.

300

Rosenkvist, I wrote slowly in my best handwriting. Sara Rosenkvist. It suited her.

Four people were dead, and nobody could be blamed for their deaths apart from this bloody storm. Einar, Elias, Steinar and little Sara Rosenkvist. They had been torn from their lives as unexpectedly as the two who had been murdered. And just as pointlessly. And yet when the police got here, to this cold place, tonight, tomorrow or in two days at the worst, they would concentrate on the two names at the top of the list of the fallen at Finse during the storm of February 2007. They would put all their resources and manpower into the investigation, and within a day or two they would have driven the perpetrator into a corner, and would have made sure he was looking through prison bars for the next fifteen years or so.

What was actually the difference between these people?

Was the fact that Cato Hammer or Roar Hanson had lost their lives worse than the fact that Sara would never grow up? Was Cato Hammer's death a greater loss for his family than the fact that Einar Holter's three children would barely remember their father by the time they were grown up? Why should society put all its resources into punishing the person or persons responsible for two of the deaths, while the others would be forgotten by the public as soon as they were in their graves?

Concentrate, I thought, and had some more coffee.

I stared at Cato Hammer's name and tried to picture him in my mind's eye. However hard I tried to see him as he had been when he was alive, it was only his dead, surprised expression as he lay on the kitchen worktop that had stuck in my memory.

The information meeting.

The thought suddenly struck me, and I realized why. I closed my eyes so that I could think back to that first evening, when only the train driver was dead and everyone seemed relieved and excited following the accident rather than shocked. Before Berit Tverre began to speak, I had seen Cato Hammer disappear behind one of the pillars in the lobby, and had noticed that he seemed different. Earlier in the evening he had been positively bubbling with obtrusive happiness and irritating energy. He had even managed the harsh confrontation with Kari Thue with a self-confident smile on his lips. Therefore, it had struck me as strange that he seemed so serious later on. Depressed, somehow.

Afraid?

When I saw him disappear behind the pillar, I immediately thought it was Kari Thue who had frightened him. I had no reason to reflect further on his change of mood at the time. But now, when I thought back, I became more and more certain that he had seemed just as mild-mannered and smug after Kari Thue's bizarre rant as he had been before he got mixed up in the quarrel between her and the Kurds.

I tore off the sheet of paper and wrote Cato Hammer's name again. Underneath it I drew a timeline, writing in the approximate times of the heated discussion and the information meeting. I used a green pen to mark the first event, black for the second. In green I wrote *happy, eager and patient.* Then I drew an arrow pointing to the right; I couldn't indicate when his good mood had started to deteriorate. With the black pen I wrote *serious, possibly afraid.* After a brief pause I added a question mark after the last word.

As far as I could work out and recall, there was a gap of one and a half hours between the two events. Kari Thue had been in the lobby the whole time. Cato Hammer had been in the hobby room where the prayer meeting had taken place, and the big bridge tournament was under way. I had fallen asleep, but that could hardly have been for more than a few seconds, perhaps a couple of minutes. I was as sure as I could be that Kari Thue and Cato Hammer had not spoken to each other during the period that was marked out on the sheet in front of me.

Kari Thue had not frightened Cato Hammer.

At least not then.

It must have been someone else.

There were far too many people to choose from. And of course Cato Hammer's change of mood didn't necessarily have anything whatsoever to do with the fact that he was murdered a few hours later.

I was stuck, and wearily tossed the pen aside.

There was a gentle tap on the door.

"Am I disturbing you?" said Magnus, and came in without waiting for an answer. "So this is where you are, is it?"

There was no reason to answer either question.

303

"I'm feeling much better," he said mildly, and sat down. "She's a marvellous woman, that Berit Tverre. She finds solutions to most things. What are you doing?"

"Trying to think."

"I see! That can be difficult. Particularly under circumstances like these."

"Yes," I said, although I wasn't sure what circumstances he meant.

He took out his thick horn-rimmed glasses and perched them on his nose.

"What have we here," he said. "A . . . timeline, I imagine."

He leaned forward and peered at it. Then he clicked his tongue, which was obviously one of his many little habits.

"So you noticed it too."

"What?" I asked.

"This . . ."

He smiled and took his glasses off again. The lenses were so sticky I felt like grabbing them and cleaning them.

"This change of mood," he went on, put his glasses down on the desk. "Cato Hammer was cheerful and exhilarated from the time we arrived at the hotel. But he was taciturn and serious when he came back to the information meeting."

"Came back? From the hobby room, you mean?"

"Yes, he was in there most of the time. But not all the time. Me, I was running about all over the place!"

His index finger waved about in the air.

"We had a lovely little chat, you and I! I offered you some wine, but you were determined to stick to your vow of sobriety!"

"I haven't made any vow of —"

"And then I went down to the hobby room. Hammer was there. Full of energy, I have to say. He had a voice, that man. And good humour, thank heavens. Perhaps a little too much good humour and eagerness to get involved. But then he left us. I had just bid six spades, and was sure of taking the game. Later, when I got back to the lobby, Cato Hammer wasn't there either. He arrived just before the information meeting began. But then this building has countless rooms, so he could have been absolutely anywhere."

"Did you ever speak to him?"

"No, I didn't, actually. As I mentioned to you during our little session when we were . . . viewing the body . . . he was my patient. Something I would never have told you if the man hadn't been dead. In such extraordinary circumstances, I must add. I have developed the habit of never speaking to my patients when I meet them outside the surgery, unless they speak to me first. It's simply a matter of discretion. Respect for patient confidentiality."

"And he never did that? He never spoke to you?"

"No. He didn't even say hello. Perhaps he didn't recognize me."

I pretended to yawn. For a long time.

"I'm sure he recognized you," I said eventually, biting my lower lip so hard I could taste the sweetness of blood on my tongue.

Magnus shook his head, lost in thought.

"Hello," I said tentatively.

A deep, wide furrow appeared down the centre of his forehead. He took a deep breath as if he were about to say something, but then sat in silence with his thought, unsure if he should share it.

"One could of course ask oneself," he said at last, "why I noticed that Cato Hammer's mood in particular had altered."

His eyes fascinated me. His unusual facial features drew the attention away from the fact that his eyes were actually beautiful, and such a deep blue shade that they were almost indigo.

"Then I'll ask the question," I said. "Why did you notice that Cato Hammer's mood in particular had altered?"

"Well," he said with a smile. "Let me explain. I noticed because I know something about him."

I nodded and waited.

"I know that Cato Hammer's temperament, this keen commitment he shows in public, has" — he fiddled with his glasses and searched for the right words — "has an excessive level of tolerance and openness towards more or less everything and everybody. I know it isn't entirely genuine. In many ways he was a considerate man. And over-scrupulous, in the sense that he could be tormented by a guilty conscience. As to whether he really was a good person . . ."

His index finger rasped against his cheek, where the stubble had started to form strange, patchy patterns on his skin.

306

"To tell the truth, I'm not entirely convinced that he was."

I wasn't sure whether I should say anything, or just wait for him to go on.

"Of course you have to be very careful with things like that. Very careful."

He gave me a quick look, as if it were me he was warning.

"Judging other people, I mean. Particularly on inadequate grounds, such as those I have. Cato Hammer came to see me three, four times before I realized that all those vague illnesses he kept complaining about were the expression of a very disturbed psyche. Very disturbed indeed. So I referred him to someone else."

His face broke into a smile.

"But I've told you all this before."

"Why do you doubt his goodness?"

"Can I use this cup?"

His hand closed around an unwashed coffee cup; I had no idea who had used it before. I shrugged my shoulders; he placed it under the dispenser and filled it right up to the brim.

"What does being a good person involve?" he asked, rolling his eyes to take the sting out of the banal aspect of his question. "Does it involve doing good? Or, since we human beings are permanently wired to care about ourselves and our offspring, is it more a question of the ability to be aware of our inadequacies and deplore our faults? To take responsibility for the fact that we can't manage to be good, I mean. In other words, is goodness

307

an indication of our willingness to engage in an eternal struggle against the ego, or is it only the victor, the person who has already defeated his egoism, who can call himself good?"

I wasn't really with him. Perhaps I was too tired. Or perhaps I just thought he was talking absolute rubbish.

"I don't really know," I mumbled. "But what was Cato Hammer's problem?"

"He had done something evil," said Magnus, stretching.

The tone of his voice had changed. It grew deeper, and he was speaking directly to me now, not to himself or to an imaginary, more philosophically inclined listener than I had managed to appear.

"What?"

"I don't know," he said briefly. "We never got that far. But he was a tormented person. It only took a few conversations with him for me to realize that he was weighed down with deep feelings of guilt. Which is in itself an indication that he had a conscience, at least. But he never did anything about it."

"How can you be sure of that?"

"Good question."

He leaned back in his chair with both hands around the coffee cup.

"I definitely got the impression," he said, considering his words carefully before proceeding. "I definitely got the impression that he was guilty of something that was punishable by law. Since he had so much exposure in the media, you and I and everybody else would have known about it if he had admitted to such a thing. Even a speeding fine would have ended up on the front pages. Deduction, in other words. Drawing a conclusion on my part. He has never come to terms with himself. And yet he set up this façade of an abundance of love. Something doesn't match. That's why I noticed that sudden seriousness when he came back from the information meeting. It was almost . . ."

He glanced at my notes on the flip chart.

"Fear. He seemed afraid. You can cross out the question mark."

"Greed and betrayal," I heard myself say.

"What?"

"It was something Roar Hanson said. He came to find me twice before he was murdered. It was obvious he wanted to tell me something. Something that would — He said he knew who the murderer was."

"What? *What?*"

The coffee splashed everywhere as he banged the cup down on the table.

"*Did he tell you who killed Cato Hammer?*"

"You're not listening," I said. "He said he knew who it was. He didn't tell me anything. We were interrupted. Both times."

The very thought of Adrian made the heat rise in my cheeks.

"But what do you mean by greed and betrayal?"

His fingers drew big quotation marks in the air.

"That's what he said." I closed my eyes. I always remember better when I close my eyes. "He said that you can make amends for betrayal, but there can be no forgiveness for greed. No, I think it was the other way round. Greed can be forgiven, he said, but never betrayal. Something like that."

"I thought everything could be forgiven," Magnus mumbled.

"That's exactly what I said. The first time he came to find me was before anyone else knew we were talking about murder. Everybody else obviously believed the story about a brain haemorrhage. Roar Hanson, on the other hand, was convinced that the man had been murdered."

"Strange. Very strange indeed."

The coffee was working. I felt brighter than I had for a long time. Absurdly, I was enjoying myself. It was ages since I had talked to someone who made me relax the way that Magnus Streng did. His friendly forwardness and obtrusive friendliness were qualities that would normally have put me off. Instead I was beginning to toy with the idea of inviting him to dinner. Him and his wife, perhaps, if he had one.

When all this was over.

When I finally got home, to everything that was mine.

Of course I wouldn't invite him to my home. I hadn't invited anyone for many, many years. It was Nefis who had friends, not me. She stopped nagging me about it a long time ago. But it would have pleased her enormously.

"I was wondering," I said with a smile. "Do you think you might like . . ."

The pause was too long.

"Might like what?"

"Are you married?"

"Yes," he said delightedly. "I've been married for forty-two years!"

A quick calculation made him at least sixty-two. Probably more. He seemed younger.

"We've had three fantastic children," he said contentedly, taking an oversized wallet out of his inside pocket. "And five grandchildren. So far. My youngest daughter is expecting twins, so soon we'll have seven, my Solfrid and I."

A small plastic accordion tumbled out of the wallet. In every pocket was a photograph: wife, children and grandchildren. Christmas Eve, Norwegian Constitution Day and something that looked like a summer's evening by the sea. He pushed it across to me. I flicked slowly through it. The last picture was a photo of the whole family. Children and their respective partners. Children of all ages, with the proud paternal and maternal grandparents in the middle; a woman with greying hair and fine features had her arm around the bent, abnormal Magnus Streng. Something must have given me away, even though I was doing my best not to show anything other than friendly and polite interest.

"My condition is hereditary," he said calmly. "Achondroplasia. But that doesn't mean my children will necessarily inherit it. There's a fifty per cent chance each time, because my wife doesn't have the condition. Fate has been kind to me, and allowed my children to escape. Not that my life has been particularly difficult. But I'm not so different from other people in that respect; I want the very best for my children."

He had three daughters. They were all pretty women of normal height, with long hair and warm smiles. They were very like their mother, who looked about thirty centimetres taller than her husband.

"I really did hope they would be normal," he said, taking back the bundle of photos.

"Of course," I mumbled. "We all feel the same."

"Not necessarily," he said.

I didn't pursue that comment.

"You started to ask me something," he said.

"No."

"Yes, you did. You said: 'Do you think you might like . . .' Like what?"

"Oh, that. Do you think you might like . . . Do you think Roar Hanson really knew who murdered Cato Hammer?"

"I have no idea. I wasn't the one who talked to the man."

Suddenly he seemed completely uninterested. Indifferent. He stood up and finished off his coffee. Then he put the cup down on the table, once again a little too forcefully, and headed for the door.

"Just one more thing," I said in order to stop him. "Don't you think it's strange that so many of you actually already knew Cato Hammer?"

He looked at me, his face totally expressionless.

"Isn't it a bit odd?" I went on after a brief hesitation. "Geir knew him from the board at Brann. Berit had met him here at Finse before. He was one of your patients. Isn't that a conspicuous series of coincidences?"

"You could see it that way," he said, shrugging his shoulders, "And if you think it makes us all suspects, then you're entitled to your point of view. Personally, I would say that it underlines the obvious: Cato Hammer was an active man. A sociable, bumptious man who knew a lot of people. But right now I could do with a proper drink. Even though it is a little early. I'll see you later."

He didn't even slam the door.

Sometimes I'm an idiot.

All too often, in fact.

CHAPTER
THREE

I could simply lock the door, of course, and let the others carry on with whatever they were doing.

Perhaps I ought to do just that. Despite the fact that the windows in the little office were completely covered in snow, which meant that I couldn't be sure of anything, the weather seemed just as hopeless and unchanging as it had been for two days. But the wind wasn't howling quite as loudly any more. The fact that the temperature was rising had to be a good sign too, of course. At any rate, the storm couldn't continue for ever. I keep myself better informed than most people, and the horror stories about global warming could frighten the life out of those less nervous than me. But I have never heard anyone seriously claim that the mountain regions of Norway are likely to be devastated by continuous hurricanes.

At some point the storm would abate.

Tonight. Or tomorrow. Or perhaps not until Sunday.

Cato Hammer's name in red ink on the greyish white paper now looked almost luminous. I blinked, shook my head and refilled my coffee cup.

Cato Hammer's sin lay in the past.

He must have committed a major transgression.

314

Roar Hanson had been seriously unbalanced, perhaps on the verge of a breakdown. People who are highly strung can say strange things. In addition, his vague, disjointed stories were shot through with religious torment, and to tell the truth I have to confess that I wouldn't have taken much notice, if it hadn't been for the information Magnus Streng had given me about Cato Hammer's medical history.

There was too much that matched, and I was no longer in any doubt.

But it didn't help a great deal.

Do you believe in vengeance? Do you think it's ethically defensible to avenge a great injustice?

I remembered Roar Hanson's words as I closed my eyes. That was exactly what he had said in our final conversation, I could literally hear his tense, high-pitched voice: *Do you believe in vengeance?*

The fact that he asked the question at all had to mean that he himself had his doubts. At any rate, he had a certain amount of understanding of the dilemma. Which once again underlined the seriousness of whatever he believed Cato Hammer to be guilty of.

Greed and betrayal, he had said.

Greed is linked to money. Capital. Mammon.

Greed is a mortal sin for Catholics. But it's hardly something to get worked up about in a society where greed no longer makes people shudder, but is more likely to evoke a nod of approval.

I picked up the red pen and wrote *greed* above the timeline.

Betrayal?

Of course you can betray someone by being greedy.

Roar Hanson must have meant that the victim of Cato Hammer's greed and betrayal was here at Finse.

If he was right, Cato Hammer couldn't have discovered this until several hours after our arrival at the hotel. Strange. I could see him in my mind's eye, going from room to room, chatting and shaking hands as he went. It had struck me at an early stage: Cato Hammer was the person who had the best overview of the assembled party, even if he had once made a mistake with the woman in the headscarf.

The confrontation between Kari Thue and Cato Hammer took place at approximately quarter to eight.

By that time we had already been at Finse 1222 for several hours, or at least many of us had. The last few were not rescued from the train until about five, but at any rate Cato Hammer had had plenty of time to acquaint himself with most people before eight o'clock. But he was as gentle as a spring shower, even after he had been shouted at in front of everybody.

If Roar Hanson was right in his assertion that there was someone amongst us who had good reason to kill Cato Hammer, why did the victim not know this himself? At least not before the information meeting, which began around ten. And even that was far from certain; his change of mood didn't necessarily have anything to do with that. But for the time being, I chose to assume there was a connection.

I tore off the sheet and screwed it up. On a blank page I wrote:

The perpetrator was not recognized straight away.

I sat there for a while, looking at the words.

The perpetrator, I thought. It could just as easily be a man or a woman. Or perhaps not. If it was a woman, she would have to be strong. To kill someone with an icicle must demand both strength and technique, although I am ashamed to admit that I have never thought about how you use frozen water to kill a person.

It wasn't necessarily an icicle.

There was a great deal to suggest that it was an icicle.

But when the murderer clearly had a gun, providing him or her with the easiest method in the world when it comes to killing people, why not use it again? If Roar Hanson was pierced through with an icicle or some other spear-like weapon, why on earth wasn't he shot?

I pushed my hand into the side pocket of my chair and took out the box of painkillers. To be on the safe side I took three, and washed them down with lukewarm coffee.

Cato Hammer was murdered outdoors. Roar Hanson in the cellar. Geir thought it was fairly clear that the murder had taken place in the dog room. There were no traces of blood outside the door. In fact, all the blood was concentrated in the spot where he and Berit found the body.

One outdoors. One indoors.

The wound in my thigh was extremely painful. I couldn't understand it. I realized I was trying to raise my leg.

The two locations where the bodies were found had only one thing in common: they were out of the way. The chances of bumping into anyone outside in the storm at night, and in a locked room containing a pit bull, were negligible. At least if the murderer had noted the dog owner's routine when it came to visiting the animal. I bit the marker pen so hard that the metal buckled.

Both victims went willingly to the slaughter, I wrote, before crossing out the last word and adding another.

Both victims went willingly to the slaughter rendezvous.

It couldn't be any other way. Cato Hammer had been willing to go out of the hotel, in spite of the weather, to meet someone. That must mean that not only the perpetrator, but also Cato Hammer, were keen that the meeting should take place discreetly. Perhaps only Hammer.

It was difficult to see why Roar Hanson would go along with something similar. He had obviously been anxious about the meeting, because he had repeatedly asked his roommate to wait for him. I wasn't sure what Sebastian Robeck might have done if he hadn't fallen asleep.

It struck me that the explanation must lie in something I have no chance of understanding: religion.

Religion.

Nonsense. I really could not understand why the man had gone to meet someone he thought had murdered Cato Hammer, with no protection of any

318

kind, in a room in the cellar where no one could come to his aid.

Did he want to give the murderer a chance? To turn over a new leaf?

The marker pen was running out, and squeaked horribly as I wrote:

Was Roar H. sympathetic towards the perpetrator?

Perhaps I was right after all. Perhaps there was enough of the priest left in Roar Hanson for him to take on the role of spiritual mentor, however stupid and naive it might seem to try and talk a murderer into seeing the error of his ways.

After the railway carriage fell, there were 118 of us in the hotel. Then the four mysterious guests had arrived, but they were under lock and key in the cellar, and did not need to be taken into account. Since both Steinar Aass and Roar Hanson had died, and I still counted myself as innocent, we were now down to 115 possible perpetrators. If I discounted all those under fifteen, I arrived at ninety-seven.

Ninety-seven suspects.

Far too many.

If I were to draw conclusions of a tentative and extremely temporary nature, based on the methods and the scenes of the crimes, then I was looking for someone strong and fit, who had access to a gun, and whose story could arouse the sympathy of a priest. This person must also carry within them a hatred powerful enough to make them murder Cato Hammer, with sufficient will to survive to kill Roar Hanson to avoid being unmasked.

Now I was going too far, of course. Unprofessional.

The Kurds had guns. Mikkel was strong and fit. I had no doubt that Kari Thue's personality made it possible for her to feel hatred. Most of us could probably persuade Roar Hanson to feel sorry for us, at least on a bad day.

I couldn't do this.

The best thing would be to mind my own business, keep my fingers crossed and wait for the police.

However, I did decide to look for Adrian. I had to find out what Roar Hanson had said to him when I was distracted by my annoyance at being given paprika-flavoured crisps, and failed to grasp why Adrian reacted so aggressively to the pallid priest with the white flecks at the corners of his mouth.

At least it would pass the time.

CHAPTER
FOUR

For some reason I was disappointed by the sight that met me when I got back to the lobby.

At one end of the long table right next to the shabby wicker chairs with the tartan cushions that were never used by anybody except the lady who knitted, Kari Thue and Mikkel were absorbed in a quiet conversation. The lobby was so full of people that they didn't notice my arrival. Their heads were almost touching in a display of intimacy that I didn't like. Kari Thue was sitting at the end of the table, Mikkel at the side with his back to me.

Of course I shouldn't let it bother me.

The fact that Mikkel had saved my life and in addition had started to behave in a way that was bordering on the acceptable didn't mean he was someone to be reckoned with. On the contrary, he was high on the list of those I suspected of having murdered both Cato Hammer and Roar Hanson. True, the list was extremely long and I had no evidence against the boy apart from the fact that he was strong and fit, but still: Mikkel was not my friend.

Suddenly he got to his feet so abruptly that the chair fell over. I couldn't hear what he said, but there was no misunderstanding the gesture with his finger.

I smiled. Kari Thue picked up a book with lightning speed and immediately appeared to be so absorbed in its contents that I almost began to doubt what I had seen. But I was still smiling.

Mikkel really was on the way to making important decisions in life.

CHAPTER
FIVE

"Adrian! *Adrian!*"

The boy didn't even bother looking in my direction. He was sitting on the floor between the kitchen door and the dresser with Veronica. I didn't recognize the game they were playing. They had a lot of cards spread out on the floor in a strange pattern, face up. It looked as if Veronica had considerably more cards in her hand than Adrian, which struck me as an appropriate metaphor for their relationship. I no longer believed she was as young as she seemed at first glance, and I found it odd, to put it mildly, that she got any pleasure from hanging out with a kid of fifteen.

It didn't have to be about pleasure, of course. It could be a question of usefulness, or necessity, for that matter; the way Veronica behaved towards her fellow human beings made me look like an open and sociable person. Adrian was the only one of all the passengers from the train who hadn't given the skinny figure dressed in black a wide berth right from the start.

"Adrian," I said again when I reached them. "I need to talk to you."

"Forget it," he snapped.

Adrian and I had certainly had our differences, but the boy must be somewhat oversensitive if he thought our arguments justified such behaviour. I could only imagine that Veronica had persuaded him to go against me.

"Come on," I said calmly. "I really do have to talk to you."

"But I don't have to talk to you."

The young woman was examining her cards. She placed the queen of hearts on the floor before picking up two of the cards that were lying face up.

Two aces.

The boy swore vehemently and threw the jack of clubs on top of the queen, then picked up a king.

"What are you playing?" I asked.

Neither of them answered. I sat there for a few minutes following the game, which seemed increasingly absurd.

"Isn't there somewhere else you need to be?"

He didn't look at me.

"No," I said. "I'm going to sit right here until you're ready to talk to me."

"*There!*" he hissed, banging the ace of spades down on top of the nine of diamonds, which Veronica had just put down. "Ha!"

When he was about to pick up a card, Veronica placed her hand on his.

"Hang on," she said in that deep voice that contrasted so sharply with her thin body. "Look."

She placed four twos on the floor one after the other, gave a little smile and gathered up all the other cards on the floor.

"*Paris*," she said.

"Shit," said Adrian.

I've played a lot of cards in my life, but this was the most ridiculous, incomprehensible game I'd ever seen.

"What do you want?" mumbled Adrian, getting stiffly to his feet.

"I just want to talk to you. In private."

The boy had already smelled less than sweet on the train. By now the smell around his skinny body was so unpleasant that I wrinkled my nose and moved back.

"Look, I haven't got a room of my own, OK! Which means I haven't got a bathroom!"

"That's the most stupid thing I've ever heard. You were the one that chose to sleep in the window. And even if you don't want a room, there's nothing to stop you from using a shower. Any time."

"Haven't got any clean clothes," he muttered. "No point in having a shower."

"Come with me," I said, taking advantage of the fact that he was too embarrassed to refuse.

The smell was so strong that I had no desire to take him into the little office. Instead I went ahead of him towards the wicker chairs that were still unoccupied. Kari Thue was no longer sitting at the wooden table. I nodded towards one of the chairs. Adrian sat down, sullen and reluctant.

"How's it going?" I asked, moving my wheelchair so close to his knees that he couldn't get up without pushing me away.

His mouth took on a sulky expression that presumably meant that I should mind my own business.

"Adrian. I don't really understand what I've done to upset you. You make your own decisions about who you want to be with while we're up here, but it won't be long until they come for us. When that happens, I don't think Veronica will be in as strong a position to help you as I will. I am after all —"

"So you're using blackmail now?"

He looked me briefly in the eye. He was close to tears. His lips were trembling and he suddenly lashed out with his right hand. I don't think he meant to hit anything, but he caught my thigh with a hard blow.

"Sorry," he said, pulling back his hand. "I didn't mean . . . I'm sorry, OK!"

"It's fine. I didn't feel a thing. It's OK."

I wondered what his hair looked like underneath that bloody hat. As if he had read my mind, he pulled the hat off and placed it on his knee before scratching his scalp frantically with both hands, his fingers stiff.

"What do you want?" he mumbled eventually, putting his hat back on.

"What was it about Roar Hanson that made you so angry, Adrian?"

"He was fucking disgusting."

"What was it that was so disgusting about him?"

"Didn't you see him? That greasy hair with a comb-over, and that horrible white stuff at the corners of his mouth. And he stank."

He stopped and lowered his eyes.

"He was coming on to Veronica."

"Yes, so you said. How old is Veronica, actually?"

"Twenty-four. That fucking priest was a pig, running after little girls."

"I don't think twenty-four counts as a little girl, Adrian. If he was into that kind of thing, there's a whole load of fourteen-year-old handball players here."

"They haven't even got tits! Hardly, anyway."

"Unfortunately, that's part of the appeal," I said drily. "If Roar Hanson really did prefer girls who were a little bit too young, then he would have preferred them without tits. But he wasn't like that, Adrian. There's absolutely no evidence to suggest it. And you are far too intelligent to go along with crap like that."

"But he was after Veronica! It's true! I saw it with my own eyes! And she wasn't the only one who thought the old bastard was vile. There were two old women in the hobby room who told him to fuck off as well."

"I'm sure they didn't."

"Well, maybe they didn't say that exactly, but he was all over them and they moved several times. What a fucking . . ."

He couldn't find the right swear word.

"What was it he said to you?" I interjected while he was thinking.

"Said? I don't talk to wankers like him!"

"You did talk to him. Yesterday morning. After you'd been to the kiosk to get me some crisps and cola. He said something to you about washing your hands, I think. I didn't hear properly because I was distracted by the fact that you'd brought me paprika-flavoured crisps, and I don't like them."

Adrian sat motionless, staring into space. It was as if thinking back made him confused. Or perhaps he wasn't entirely sober; I thought I could smell alcohol on his breath. That first morning I had suspected that Veronica had alcohol with her. I must have been wrong. As far as I could see, she didn't drink alcohol at all. She always carried a bottle of mineral water with her, during the evenings too.

"I don't remember," he said, pulling at his hat. "It wasn't anything to do with washing my hands, anyway."

"You do remember," I said.

"He said . . . he said 'watch yourself'."

"Watch yourself? Was that all?"

"Yes."

"Watch yourself as in 'can you move out of the way'?"

"No. Watch yourself as in 'WATCH YOURSELF!' "

His body lurched forward as he snapped out the words, and I moved back in my chair.

"It's odd that I didn't pick it up," I said, taken aback.

The corners of Adrian's mouth turned down in an indifferent expression.

"It's not my fault if you can't hear properly."

He thought the conversation was over. He couldn't get up because of my chair, and tried to push me away.

"Hang on," I said. "I've got more questions."

"But I haven't got any more answers."

"Why do you sleep in the window, Adrian?"

He blushed noticeably. Small patches of pink on his shiny skin rapidly grew bigger.

"What's it got to do with you?"

"Veronica doesn't want you in her room, is that it?"

His whole face was red by now.

At least Veronica had some kind of decency, I thought, if she hadn't even touched the boy. She was setting clear boundaries for the dreams in which he could entangle himself.

"I think," he said, clearing his throat. "I think being near you is OK. At night, anyway."

The reply was such a surprise that all I could think of was to smile at the boy. His face had darkened, and when he tried to get up again, I let him. He had lied to me about what Roar Hanson had really said, but I wasn't going to get any more out of him.

Not at the moment, anyway.

Like other practised liars, he had stuck close to the truth. As a rule it's the sensible thing to do, but Adrian had given me a piece of a jigsaw puzzle without realizing that I only needed a fragment of sky to sense the outline of the entire finished picture.

And I was beginning to understand why he was lying.

It was definitely not a pleasant thought, but if I was right, at least I was on the way to something.

A kind of goal, perhaps.

I didn't really know.

CHAPTER
SIX

It was five past five by now, and there were still two hours to go to the first sitting for dinner. I was starving, and absolutely full of caffeine. I was tired of coffee, myself, and my disjointed thoughts. When Adrian left I had thought I was getting close to something, but now I was no longer so sure. At any rate, a break might be good for me. I had wheeled my chair over to the sofas by the Millibar. The only people keeping me company in the small seating area were the Kurds.

To begin with it was difficult to understand why they didn't spend more time in their room. They never spoke to anyone. Nobody ever bothered with them. They seldom exchanged more than a word or two with each other, and that was in a language I had so far been unable to identify. It was only during dinner the previous evening that I had seen them engaged in something that could be called a real conversation. Now they were sitting bolt upright on the yellow sofa that really belonged in Blåstuen, each with a glass of water in front of them. Even though I had said I had no intention of sleeping tonight, Berit had left the sofa there. Just in case, she said with a smile, and hurried away.

330

One of the kitchen staff came through the swing doors with a large basket full of buns. My mouth started to water, and I had to swallow. He smiled when he saw me, and offered me the basket before putting it down on the counter next to the hot chocolate machine and hurrying back to the kitchen. I took two.

"Delicious," I mumbled, smiling at the dark-skinned man.

The buns were so hot they were still steaming.

The man nodded, but made no move to help himself. The woman kept her eyes downcast almost all the time, glancing surreptitiously around only now and again.

"The storm seems to be on the way out," I said, sinking my teeth into the second bun. "The wind is easing, and the temperature is rising."

The man gave a slight nod. The woman didn't move.

The Germans passed us on their way down into the wing. They had grown tired. One day in the midst of the storm had been sensational, a unique experience to write home about. Now, well into our third day of isolation, nothing was exciting any longer. Their restlessness was not helped by the fact that Berit had restricted the sale of beer. The taps would not be opened until seven o'clock. This was the third time I had seen the three young men get up and move elsewhere in less than twenty minutes, with no apparent goal or purpose.

Bearing in mind all that had happened during these three days, I was more and more surprised by the atmosphere in the hotel. With every harrowing experience that occurred, it took less and less time for people to settle down. Most looked as if they were bored, but there was an air of patience about the tedium. A sense of resignation over the way things were, a quiet conviction that all would be well if we could just get through one more day on the mountain. The brief glimpse of normal weather we had seen out over the lake had of course helped, but I was still fascinated by the way in which the guests appeared to distance themselves from their own horrific experiences, and the fact that two people had been murdered. It seemed as if I was the only one who feared the night that lay ahead of us, the only one who was conscious of the fact that a murderer was still at large, and that we had no way of knowing whether he planned to strike again. The remaining members of the church commission had resumed their bridge tournament, which I found positively distasteful.

On the other hand, we all needed peace and quiet.

I couldn't see Kari Thue, which was just as well. Mikkel and his gang had taken over St Paal's Bar once more, and were idly listening to music, while Mikkel sat with his feet on the table rocking his chair back and forth, a laptop on his knee. Judging by the mechanical sounds and his abrupt movements over the keyboard, he was playing some kind of game.

"Could you all listen, please!"

Bent's voice had grown stronger since the evening before last, when she had told us there was no need to worry. Now she could be heard everywhere; even the lads in St Paal's Bar were startled out of their comatose state and leaned forward to listen.

"The wind has now dropped to a stiff breeze. The temperature has gone up to minus nineteen. There is no possibility of anyone reaching us tonight, but I think we should be prepared to move out tomorrow. Since it is also snowing less heavily than it has been for the past few days, I would like to ask for volunteers to help open up all the exits. The main entrance has already . . ."

I hoped I was the only one to pick up on her hesitation. Only those of us in the know were aware that the entrance had been cleared that morning.

". . . Johan cleared the main entrance this morning when the wind began to drop," she went on after a pause no longer than a breath.

I liked Berit more and more.

"But the opening needs to be made bigger. We also need to clear all the emergency exits. Up to now we have allowed them to become blocked by the snow, which is strictly against the law. I would ask those who are willing to pitch in to go and meet Johan outside the ski room. It's next to the inside porch, if anyone hasn't found it yet. We have clothes and boots you can borrow."

Three men at the table leapt to their feet. One of the handball team raised her hand politely.

"I'd be happy to help!"

"Only adults," said Berit, smiling and shaking her head. "The weather is still pretty challenging. But thank you!"

Mikkel closed the laptop and put it down on the table in front of him. Then he got up slowly and prodded two of his well-built subordinates in the chest. They got to their feet without hesitation and followed him in the direction of the ski room. None of them glanced in my direction as they walked past.

"I think I ought to spare them my input in this particular enterprise," said Magnus with a little smile.

He came and stood beside me but didn't sit down, although there was room on the sofa.

"Instead I would like to talk to you."

He glanced sideways at the Muslim couple, who were still clutching their glasses of water, and had not touched the buns.

"In private," he murmured.

The Kurds didn't seem to have any intention of moving.

The fact that they were still sitting there in the unusual atmosphere that had enveloped them most of the time since the train crash could only indicate one thing: I had interpreted Severin Heger correctly when he looked into my eyes for far too long before hurrying after Berit to lock himself in down in the cellar.

At least, I hoped so.

"We'll go into the office," I said, pushing my chair slowly away from the Millibar.

CHAPTER
SEVEN

"You asked me about the Public Information Service Foundation this morning," said Magnus Streng, munching away at a bun. "And I've given it some thought."

He had helped himself to three buns from the basket as we left the Millibar, and gave one to me. I polished it off in four bites. Even Mary's expertise as a baker fell short of these buns; they were incredibly light, with something that must be raspberry jam and vanilla cream hidden in the middle of the sweet dough as a delicious surprise.

I studied Magnus with interest.

"I've come up with something," he said, swallowing. "Something that happened in the Public Information Service Foundation. I don't remember exactly when it was, but it must have been eight or nine years ago. That's when Cato Hammer was working there."

"How do you know?"

"Well . . ."

Jam and cream oozed down his strong, square chin.

"It was there that people first noticed the man," he said, looking around for something to wipe his chin with.

"I didn't," I said, handing him a wet wipe from the side pocket of my chair.

He shrugged his shoulders and opened up the little wipe.

"OK. Maybe not you. But as far as I know and recall, that case was his . . . breakthrough in the media, I suppose you could say."

"What case?" I said.

"That embezzlement case," he said, slowly wiping his chin.

"Cato Hammer was embezzling money? Embezzling?"

"No, no, no! Just hold your horses!"

He rolled the wet wipe into a ball and placed it on the desk in front of him.

"It was a female employee," he said. "She had psychological problems, and reading between the lines you could see that the whole thing was a real tragedy. A case of kleptomania combined with religious obsession and a weak mind. That's how it was presented, at any rate. Reading between the lines, as I said."

"An unfortunate combination," I said, raising my eyebrows. "But what in God's name has this got to do with Cato Hammer?"

"He was the spokesman when it came to dealing with the media. You have to understand, this was potentially explosive for the church. The people's church, the people's money. And we're not talking about an insignificant amount here. Three million kroner, if I remember correctly. Something like that. Big bucks. Since then we have seen Norway go to rack and ruin, with corruption everywhere and the theft of public resources as an everyday occurrence. But this was at a time when such things were still rare."

"Or at a time when the exposure of such things was rare," I corrected him.

"That's probably true," he said, nodding. "At any rate: Cato Hammer took care of everything. He must have had a position on the board, as I mentioned to you the last time we talked about this. I just can't remember what it was. Anyway, he really put himself out there, as the papers say these days. Not on his own behalf, but on behalf of the institution. He apologized deeply and sincerely for what had happened, and promised a thorough review of the organization to ensure that something like that could never happen again. And in the middle of all this, he showed great consideration and respect for the unfortunate woman. Her identity was protected, her name was never made public, and the whole thing blew over eventually."

"Blew over? Wasn't it a legal matter?"

"I expect it was. But the woman was seriously ill, and perhaps the press was being kind."

We both burst out laughing; Magnus laughed loud and long.

"No," he said, wiping away the tears. "There must have been something about it in the papers. But as I said it's nearly ten years since it all happened, and I don't remember every detail. On the other hand, I remember Cato Hammer very well. He was immediately profiled in a couple of the Oslo newspapers, and was a guest on several TV programmes. In less than a week he had an image: the caring leader. A fine representative for the church's message of love, Cato Hammer. This was at the time when the men of darkness within the church were allowing themselves to be frightened into the light in order to put a stop to homosexual priests. Cato Hammer was exactly what the church needed at a time when many had begun to leave in protest. Gentle and simple and suitably cuddly. He became a pastor just a few months later."

"What a memory you have."

"I've been training it since early childhood! The brain is a muscle, you know. Not literally, of course. But it's worth keeping it in trim."

He smacked his lips contentedly and pushed the little wet-wipe ball around the table.

"Betrayal and greed," I murmured.

"What did you say?"

He looked up, one hand ready to flick the ball. He had placed an empty coffee cup on its side and was trying to get the ball into it. He kept missing, but wouldn't give up.

"Roar Hanson's words," I said. "He was referring to an episode within the Public Information Service Foundation. But it doesn't sound as if . . . Given what you've told me, it sounds as if Cato Hammer . . ."

". . . was guilty of neither betrayal nor greed," he went on as I paused infinitesimally. "More like the reverse, I'd say."

"Unless . . ."

I stopped.

"Unless what?"

"Nothing. Do you remember . . . do you remember what the woman was called?"

"The guilty woman? No."

He gave a brief laugh and finally scored a goal with the ball of paper.

"There are limits," he said. "Even for me. I can't remember a name that was never made public!"

Once again he became absorbed in the little game he had invented.

I had been struck by a thought, but hadn't quite managed to catch it. However, something was different, and it was distracting me. Something had changed radically.

"Listen," I said quietly, shaking my head.

"Certainly," Magnus said pleasantly, his expression surprised. "And what would you like me to listen to?"

"To something that is no longer there," I said.

There was almost complete silence.

The sound of the wind was still managing to penetrate the thick walls, but it had given up the attempt to tear Finse 1222 to pieces. The howling sounded distant and muted, as if it were no longer anything to do with us. We were safe indoors, behind walls that had protected people for a hundred years. This twisted, warped building had seen storms come and go for an eternity without suffering any significant damage. This time the attack of the storm had been fierce. It would take time to repair the damage. But the hotel at the highest station on the Bergen line had withstood the gales as it was built to do, and like the rest of us had relied on the fact that it would survive.

Magnus and I sat in silence for a few minutes, absorbing the fact that the storm was abating. The windows in the small office were still completely covered in snow. We couldn't see the change, but we could hear it, feel it, perceive it with every sense except sight.

"Wonderful," Magnus murmured, almost ecstatically. "It's over. Tomorrow we can go home."

His words jerked me out of an almost physical intoxication. A good dose of endorphins had given me an unfamiliar feeling of happiness, simply because the storm was abating.

The feeling quickly disappeared when Magnus started talking.

"What is it?" he asked kindly, almost lovingly.

"This isn't going to be easy."

"I'm sorry," he said, his voice devoid of expression. "I don't understand."

A deep furrow appeared at the top of his nose.

"There's nothing to be sorry about," I said hastily. "It's just that I can't understand how we're going to be able to leave here tomorrow."

"But the storm," he said, gesturing with his left arm. "It's obviously on the way out, and —"

"There is absolutely no way the police are going to let us leave," I said calmly.

"Not going to let us . . . What do you mean?"

"There's a double murderer among us. It would be dreadful police work if they simply let everybody leave before they've secured all the clues, interviewed everybody . . ."

340

I stopped for breath.

"There'll be an absolute outcry," said Magnus. "A revolution. Mutiny. Nobody in this hotel, with the possible exception of you, me and the hotel staff, will agree to be kept here once it becomes physically possible to leave."

"Exactly," I said.

"And what are we going to do about that?"

I was desperate to go home.

My back was hurting and it was difficult to take a deep breath. It felt as if a vice were tightening around my chest. I was reminded of the reason why I had been on the train that derailed: I was on my way to consult an American specialist about all the problems I was now suffering from.

"I know," I said breathlessly. "But fortunately it will soon be time for dinner."

Magnus Streng got to his feet and came around the table. Then he took my head between his big, chubby hands and placed a feather-light, fleeting kiss on my forehead. He didn't let go, but gazed into my eyes.

"Hanne Wilhelmsen," he said, clearly amused. "Things can never go really badly for a person with your appetite. Come on, let's go and persuade Berit to give us a little aperitif. I didn't get a drink when I needed one, so it will taste all the better now."

When he opened the door and went ahead of me into the lobby, I thought he wasn't waddling any more.

CHAPTER
EIGHT

I'm used to good, homely food.

When I was injured in the shooting, something dramatic must have happened to my metabolism, because my weight plummeted and since then I have remained slim, in spite of an appetite that can sometimes be a real pain, both to me and to others.

Mary is a real expert when it comes to cooking.

However, I have never tasted a better cauliflower soup than the one that was served as a starter at Finse 1222 on Friday 16 February 2007. Small florets of cauliflower, the most boring and tasteless of all vegetables in Norwegian cuisine, lay floating in a soup so rich and strong that I wondered how it was possible to get so much aroma into something that basically tasted of cauliflower with a dash of cream.

"Wonderful soup," said Magnus, asking for more. "The mountain air really does give you an appetite. My compliments to the chef. Once again."

He winked at the waiter, who smiled back.

I put down my spoon. Once more I had allowed myself to be carried down the stairs so that I could have dinner in the dining room. All in all, I had accepted more help from people in the past twenty-four hours than in the last four years put together. Berit, Geir and Johan were also at the table. Just like yesterday.

We were getting into a routine.

"And how are things looking outside?" Magnus asked enthusiastically. "Is it possible to get an idea of the damage?"

Both Geir and Johan had been outside for the last few hours. They looked completely exhausted; Geir was almost falling asleep as he ate.

"It's strange," said Johan, enjoying his soup. "Very strange. Most of the buildings have completely disappeared."

"Has the storm taken them?" Magnus enquired expectantly. "I suppose they're down there somewhere. Under the snow."

Geir gazed blankly down at his bowl.

"At any rate, there won't be any family winter holidays up here. I'd really prefer to let the summer do the job, and melt all the snow away. Which probably means we'll have to wait until August."

He gave a long, drawn-out yawn, without a trace of embarrassment.

"We managed to dig out the snow plough," he went on. "That Mikkel is a real hard man. Tomorrow we can start clearing the platform. It's almost stopped snowing. The wind is still blowing hard, but it's significantly less strong than it was. And it's dropping by the hour."

"The railway company is going to have a hell of a job with the track," Johan muttered. "But fortunately that's not my problem."

"Does this mean," said Magnus, wiping his mouth thoroughly with a large serviette, "that we'll be picked up by helicopter?"

Johan nodded.

"I should think the first group will be picked up early tomorrow morning."

I was still surprised that none of them was thinking about the fact that two murders had been committed.

"How are things over in the wing?" I asked.

"No idea," said Johan with a wry smile, then he leaned forward and said quietly: "In view of what that guy said about the . . . situation over there, I thought it was best to leave them snowed in for a while longer. The last thing we need is that gang storming in here. When I was over at the Red Cross depot picking up the satellite phone, I could tell they hadn't made any attempt to dig themselves out. Nor has anybody else, for that matter."

He grinned and shook his head.

"The biggest building looks like a roof somebody has just thrown down on the snow."

Magnus looked around in bewilderment. Johan must have forgotten that the little doctor was the only one at the table who didn't know about the four people in the cellar. He was in the office when Berit came and told us that somebody was trying to dig their way in, but he had never been told who they were. He hadn't asked. Nor did he do so now.

"Have you had enough, sir?"

The waiter smiled at Magnus, who immediately reverted to his normal, jovial self.

344

"I'm looking forward to the next course," he said, pouring himself another glass of wine.

"You picked up a satellite phone?" I said to Johan, trying to appear uninterested. "Does that mean we can now communicate with the outside world?"

"It should do," he nodded. "But I haven't managed to get it working yet. I don't really understand why. I expect I'll be able to fix it this evening. It's not really a problem, after all. I mean, it's not as if we need to call for help. The rescue services know we're here."

Out of the corner of my eye I saw Veronica come down the stairs into the dining room. As usual, Adrian was trailing behind her. She stopped, looked around and sat down at a free table. Adrian bent down to her. She whispered something. The boy nodded, picked up two of the four chairs at the table and carried them up to the long table in the lobby.

Veronica stared fixedly down at the table. Her black hair hung like a curtain in front of her face, and she didn't look out until Adrian came back and sat down on the empty chair. Now they didn't need to worry about unwelcome companions at their table.

Her make-up was exaggerated. I wondered whether she really was that pale, or whether she used some kind of stage make-up. On the first evening there had been something absurd about the young woman, but now she was starting to lose her grip. The black lines around her eyes were no longer so sharply drawn. Her hair was so greasy that the brown roots along her parting showed up even more clearly. She had taken back the sweater Adrian had borrowed. As she answered the waiter's questions, she kept anxiously fingering the Vålerenga logo on her stomach. She was bouncing her heels nervously up and down on the floor. She still had Adrian's red socks on her feet.

Veronica never carried a bag.

Odd.

I have little pockets here and there on my wheelchair, so a handbag would be superfluous. And I very rarely use make-up. When I was still able to walk, I usually managed with just the pockets in my jacket.

Women who wear make-up don't do that. Kari Thue, for example, never let go of that ridiculous little bag with the straps. She clutched it tightly as if it contained the crown jewels, for which she was entirely responsible. I looked over at the bottom table, where she had gathered her entourage. Five other women were sitting around the table, four of them with handbags that were either hanging over the back of the chair, or at the owner's feet. Kari Thue had placed her bag on her knee, to be on the safe side.

Women take their handbags seriously.

Almost all women. But not Veronica.

On the plate in front of me lay a piece of venison. The sauce was a deep brown colour, almost red. Where the chef had got hold of fresh asparagus during a snowstorm in February was a mystery. I picked up a spear with my fingers and tasted.

"I don't understand this," I murmured, eating it slowly just the way that delicious, tender asparagus should be enjoyed.

Veronica *had* had a bag.

346

I licked my fingers one by one. They tasted of salty butter, with a faint hint of Parmesan.

In the left-hand side pocket lay Adrian's list, his notes on some fifty people and the bags they had brought with them from the train. I had hardly given the list a thought since I saw it for the first time. I placed the sheets of paper on my knee and smoothed them out. The beautiful handwriting flowed over the densely filled pages, perfectly legible. Now that I had a considerably better overview of my fellow passengers than when I asked the boy to compile the list almost two days ago, I was even more struck by how observant he was.

Really skinny woman with even thinner hair and a terrible voice; light brown almost yellow bag, can be worn as a rucksack. Doesn't look heavy. Not very big. Keeps her eye on it all the time!

Fat git with pale hair; laptop case. Brazilian flag on the flap.

"What have you got there?" asked Magnus Streng. "Have you tasted this sauce, Hanne? Cranberry, I think."

I wasn't really listening to him. My eyes moved down the list.

There.

Veronica.

She was one of only six people Adrian had mentioned by name.

Veronica. Cool girl wearing Gothic clothes and an Enga top; black shoulder bag. Not big, but looks a bit heavy. I think she's got a bottle with her. (Hope so, anyway!)

"Your food's getting cold," said Berit, pointing at my plate with her fork. "Eat!"

"If you had something valuable," I said, folding the list up carefully before tucking it back in the pocket, "here in the hotel, I mean, would you have chosen to drag it around with you? In a bag, for example? Or would you have put it somewhere? Hidden it?"

"I've got cupboards I can lock," said Berit with a smile. "And a safe as well. Why?"

"Obviously," I said, trying not to sound impatient. "But if you were one of the guests?"

She popped a large piece of meat in her mouth and didn't answer before she had finished chewing and swallowed it.

"Hidden it, I think. It would depend on the size, of course."

I measured about twenty-five centimetres between my index fingers.

"Well. Carting something like that around involves a certain element of risk. I mean, you could leave your bag behind somewhere, just misplace it. It's probably easier to steal something out of a bag than from a hiding place in your hotel room. On the other hand, it's fairly easy to get into the rooms here. If you're intent on stealing something, that is. We rely on people's honesty, and in principle that always works out well up here on the mountain. Has someone . . . has someone stolen something from you?"

348

"Oh, no. It was just something that occurred to me. A thought. Nothing really. By the way, have you got a list of all the guests? With names and addresses, I mean."

"Yes. I'm assuming things could get a bit tricky when it comes to . . ." she smiled apologetically before going on, "when it comes to who's going to pay. For board and lodging and . . . I'm sure it will be some insurance company. Norwegian State Railway's insurers, or the individual guests'. I don't know. But I have to have the names in any case."

"Could I have a copy of the list?"

"Well, I don't know whether . . ."

"Please. It could be important."

She looked from Magnus to Geir as if they could clarify, in their roles as doctor and solicitor, whether the list might be subject to some kind of rule of confidentiality. Neither of them spoke. I wasn't even sure they'd grasped what we were talking about.

"OK," she said eventually. "After dinner."

"Just one more thing," I said in a whisper. "Do you think you could find out what Kari Thue was actually going to do in Bergen? And whether those people she surrounds herself with are people she met on the train, or if they already knew each other? If they were going to the same place, I mean?"

"Can't you just ask her?"

"She doesn't like me."

"She doesn't like me either."

"But your position means you can camouflage the question. You could say that —"

"OK, OK," she mumbled, her mouth full of food. "I'll see what I can do."

Calm settled over our table.

Veronica and Adrian were also eating in silence. Adrian wiped his soup bowl with a piece of bread, stuffed it in his mouth and emptied his beer glass before he'd finished chewing.

It certainly wasn't the staff who were providing him with alcohol.

Beneath the table, Veronica's red feet were dancing up and down, nervously and continuously.

I stared at her for so long she might have felt it. At any rate, she suddenly looked up. I looked away as quickly as possible, only to realize that Kari Thue was staring intently at me, and with far less discretion than I had shown towards Veronica. Mikkel, whom I hadn't noticed until now, was heading slowly towards our table. Halfway across the floor he hesitated, took one step towards us, then suddenly speeded up and ran up the stairs to the lobby. His two strongest companions sat back down uncertainly at the table just behind Kari Thue, as if they weren't quite brave enough to follow without their leader's permission.

Magnus Streng was insatiable. He ate and ate. I liked him. I liked him very much, but I didn't really know why. I didn't understand the man at all. He was unusually friendly and outgoing, but he also had a unique way of suddenly taking offence that bordered on presumption. Sometimes he almost seemed conceited, or at least over-fond of his superior intellect, his impressive level of knowledge and his memory. One

350

moment he could appear to be wallowing in the misfortune of others, for example when he couldn't hide his hopes that the entire community of Finse had been devastated by the storm. At the same time he showed a concern for other people, an insight and understanding into their lives that I found touching. Magnus Streng was a man who could be deeply serious, which in itself was a rare quality these days.

Now he was asking for even more food. The grease from the sauce was smeared around his large mouth like Vaseline, and I had to turn away.

Geir Rugholmen, on the other hand, was a simple soul.

Face value, that's what the Americans say about people like him.

Perhaps he was the only person among all the adults at Finse 1222 who I could definitely say had not murdered either of the priests. Geir was a genuine man who said what he thought and was in a position to rise above most things. He would be a useless liar, I imagined, quite simply because he wouldn't see any point in lying. It didn't matter to Geir Rugholmen what others thought about who he was and what he said.

He was simple. Totally uncomplicated.

People like that don't commit murder. They turn their backs and move on.

That was what I believed. Absolutely.

It was more difficult to get a handle on Berit Tverre. She had changed over this last couple of days. She had become so different that I barely recognized her from that evening during low season when we came tumbling into her hotel, demanding care, food, lodgings and protection from a storm of which even she was afraid. Absolutely terrified, to be honest. She had changed so radically that it made me uneasy.

While the others at my table ate their way through the main course and dessert, I looked around. My companions were chatting and laughing, relieved because it would all soon be over, and because most things would soon be back to normal. Meanwhile, I let my gaze roam over a collection of people I would never forget.

The woman with the knitting was knitting. The dog owners were watching the clock and keeping an eye on their pets, who were tied up in the lobby, gazing longingly at the aromatic plates from which we were eating. The young handball players were giggling in the way that fourteen-year-olds do, and the Germans were happy because they were allowed to knock back beer and sing drinking songs that made others laugh in embarrassment. The members of the church commission were sitting at a long table of their own; some were drinking wine, others water, and the knitter had a glass in front of her containing a liquid that looked like whisky.

Perhaps it was apple juice.

Perhaps they were just as anxious as I was.

But they were hiding it well, all of them.

I was starting to feel sure I knew who had murdered Cato Hammer and Roar Hanson.

However, one of many problems was that people were not behaving in a manner that matched my theories. They were certainly opening the way for other ideas about connections and causality. Since every theory must be refutable in order to be valid, I ought to dismiss the idea that had been growing stronger in my mind over the past few hours. I ought to start again from the beginning.

I didn't want to do that. Not yet, anyway.

An even bigger problem was that the weather had seriously begun to change. Through the top part of the window in the dining room I could see that it had stopped snowing.

To put it simply, I didn't have much time.

What's more, I had lost my appetite.

I can't remember when I last left good food lying untouched on my plate, but I just couldn't manage a single piece of the delicious venison with cranberry sauce, and asparagus that the chef had got hold of from goodness knows where.

If only the snowstorm had gone on for a little bit longer, I thought; and allowed the waiter to take my plate back to the kitchen, virtually untouched.

BEAUFORT SCALE 11

VIOLENT STORM

Wind speed: 64–72mph

Roads and railway lines blocked. Chaos on the telephone and electricity networks. Severe damage to forests.

CHAPTER
ONE

"He answered no to your first question. This is a written answer to your second question."

Geir handed me a sheet of paper, placed a large glass of strong beer on the desk, sat down on a chair he had moved across from one of the other work stations, and stroked his beard. It now covered his cheeks completely, thick and dark with greyish streaks at the corners of his mouth. He pushed a substantial plug of snuff under his lip. I didn't really understand what he was waiting for. I didn't need him any longer. It was possible that he had read the message from Severin Heger, but by no means certain. If he had, it wouldn't have meant anything to him, so I had no need to worry.

There was just a name; a name and a few simple facts on a piece of white paper.

Margrete Koht, Born 14.10,1957. Died 07.01.2007. Convicted of embezzling 3,125,000 Norwegian kroner in 1998. In-patient at Gaustad Hospital from the date of the verdict until her death.

Margrete, that was it.

During my last conversation with Roar Hanson, he talked about a woman. I had tried to remember the name, just as I had tried to remember everything Roar

Hanson had said and done. The key to the murder of Cato Hammer lay with Roar Hanson. I was convinced of that. I had spoken to him and seen him devastated by mental agony during the last twenty-four hours of his life, and I had hoped that in spite of Adrian's Interruption and the priest's own hesitancy, I might find clues and answers in what remained of him within my memory.

But I hadn't been able to recall the woman's name. It was mentioned in passing, and disappeared in my own confusion about the man's disjointed talk of the Public Information Service, which I thought was an organization that had something to do with meat and vegetables.

It was when the two of us were working in the Public Information Service. I remembered his voice had trembled slightly. *I mean, Cato was . . .* He took a deep breath and held it as if he needed to brace himself. *I really can't understand why I didn't raise an objection at the time. Why I didn't do anything. And Margrete . . . I can't bear it. Of course I couldn't have known, but it seemed so . . . unthinkable that he would . . .*

As soon as I saw the name on the piece of paper, I remembered what Roar Hanson had said. Word for word. I closed my eyes and saw him standing there in front of me. Nervous and shrunken. Watchful glances in all directions. He sat there hitting his painful, injured shoulder as he talked, a middle-aged priest doing penance for a sin that wasn't even his own.

Perhaps he didn't see it that way. He had talked about Cato Hammer's betrayal and greed, but he was just as devastated by his own guilt, his own failure to raise the alarm about something I was beginning to think I had worked out.

"Isn't there something you should be doing?" I asked without looking up from the piece of paper. "Clearing some snow? Digging out some houses? Anything, really."

It was nine thirty on Friday evening.

From the lobby I could hear laughter and quiet music. One of Mikkel's gang had speakers with his iPod, and for the first time since the accident the clearly defined boundaries between the different groups from the train were becoming blurred. Middle-aged ladies were laughing as they bobbed around the floor dancing, celebrating the fact that the storm had abated. The fourteen-year-olds were allowed to sit with the bad boys. Eventually I had felt compelled to whisper in Berit's ear that the boys were busy getting two of the handball players drunk. The church commission had temporarily dissolved itself, and its members were dispersed throughout all the different rooms, relaxed from the effects of red wine and various other beverages. Elias Grav's widow was the last person I saw as I fled to the office, weary of all this happiness. She was still shocked following her husband's death, but at least she had come down from her room and politely asked for something to eat. The cheerful and friendly assistant from the kiosk had put her arm around the widow's shoulders and accompanied her down to the dining room.

Johan still hadn't got the satellite phone working, so I had been left with no choice. I had been forced to ask Severin for help.

When I watched him hurry down to the cellar after the others earlier in the day, I had decided to forget all about the secret carriage. It had nothing to do with us, and that was that. The murders of Cato Hammer and Roar Hanson were a different matter altogether from this business of the men who were determined not to let anyone near them, and who were hardly likely to emerge from their hiding place until Finse was virtually empty. When the rest of us had gone, picked up by Sea King helicopters or trains or all-terrain vehicles, only then would the four men in the cellar leave the hotel and eventually be conveyed to their destination, probably under cover of darkness.

I had decided to file the whole issue in the section allocated to things that were nothing to do with me.

But then I needed them after all.

"My, but you're in a bad mood," said Geir. "I thought you'd cheered up a bit."

He picked up the glass of beer in both hands. His index fingers made patterns in the condensation as he turned the glass around slowly.

"I'm not in a bad mood," I said, still not looking up from the piece of paper giving the name of the woman Cato Hammer had so brutally betrayed, if my assumptions were correct. "I'm sad."

I smiled briefly to take the sting out of what I had just said, and added:

"Did it go all right?"

"Well, I'm not sure I'd put it quite like that." He drank some of his beer. "At first they didn't want to open the door. I had to talk to your mate for bloody ages through it. As far as the gun went, the answer was a flat no. Not that I know what you want with . . ."

I gave him a quick warning look.

He put down the glass and held up his hands, palms facing me.

"No questions. I promise. But it didn't take long for him to understand your query. He was prepared to help with that, at any rate. Eventually he pushed that piece of paper out through a crack *this* narrow" — he measured a centimetre between his thumb and index finger — "before he shut the door again. What was it you actually asked?"

He raised his hands again and stopped speaking.

"They've got the very best equipment," I murmured. "I'm absolutely certain they have the best communication equipment there is. And at the other end there are people who have access to all the information in the world. Data. Registers. Everything. If Severin would just agree to help me, I knew things would work out."

I wasn't sure if I was talking to him, or just summarizing for myself. I had taken out Berit's list of names, and my gaze settled on one of my fellow passengers. One of the guests had a name that didn't help me get where I wanted to be.

But I had made significant progress.

I hoped I had got far enough, and I folded up all the papers and tucked them in the side pocket where Adrian's list already lay. There was a weather report on the desk. Berit had given me an odd look when I asked for it, but had given me a copy without any fuss. One of the staff had mapped the progress of the storm from Wednesday morning until an hour ago. I searched for what I needed. Then I folded that sheet of paper up as well and put it with the others. Unfortunately Berit hadn't managed to find out why Kari Thue was going to Bergen. I suspected that she had forgotten to ask.

"Hanne," said Geir.

"Yes?"

"Do you trust me?"

"Yes."

"I mean, do you *really* trust me?"

I looked up and into those grey eyes. Or brown. Or blue-grey. It was difficult to tell, actually.

I nodded. It was true. I did trust Geir Rugholmen.

"In that case, can't you tell me about those four men in the cellar? After all we've gone through up here, I think I deserve to know."

"You deserve nothing," I said. "Apart from a medal for gallantry. A prize for a victorious campaign against the storm. An award for putting up with yours truly for two days. Which looks like turning into three."

He grinned, and the juice from the tobacco ran down between his front teeth.

"I don't want anything like that. I just want to know what that extra carriage was about."

"I don't know," I said in all honesty.

"Rubbish," he said.

"No, I really don't know. But I do have a distinct feeling."

"Which is?"

"Shall we have a smoke?" I said. "Have you got any cigarettes?"

He looked around, slightly confused.

"Berit will be furious."

"Of course. Forget it. I think they're guarding a terrorist. I think they were transporting a terrorist to Bergen."

"A — a terrorist? But what would . . . *why the hell would they be taking a terrorist to Bergen?*"

"I've no idea," I said. "There are both prisons and military institutions in Bergen as well, you know. At any rate, he was being moved."

"Moved where? And why? What makes you even think there's a terrorist on Norwegian soil? And *on the Bergen train!*"

"Keep it down," I hushed him. "The fact that I'm sharing my theories with you doesn't mean the entire hotel has to know."

"The entire hotel? Everybody here knows about that bloody carriage! And how are they going to explain this, when everybody can just leave and say what they like to whoever they like?"

He took a quick breath.

"You cannot begin to imagine," I said quietly, "what kind of cover stories the authorities can cook up. In the end you almost believe them yourself, in spite of the fact that you know the real truth. I've experienced it myself, Geir."

I left it at that.

In the spring two years ago, I hid the American President in my apartment for several days. This utterly absurd situation ended when she shot dead an FBI agent. That same evening the story was distorted, simplified, and conveyed to the public in a way that frightened the life out of me. But most of all, and extremely reluctantly, I was impressed. There were still only a handful of us who knew the truth about the American President's visit to Norway, and that was the way it was going to stay.

"Believe me," was all I said. "Right now, well-paid and well-equipped specialists are sitting there cooking up a story that all these people . . ."

I jerked my thumb over my shoulder in the direction of the lobby.

". . . will swallow hook, line and sinker."

"But what about me? I mean, I can say what I like when —"

"As I said," I broke in. "I trust you. Besides which, no one is likely to believe your story."

"My story," he repeated. "So far I haven't got a story. Why do you think . . . what makes you think this is to do with a terrorist? Here?"

He was still immensely worked up. A vein was throbbing at the side of his neck, and his face had taken on a different flush from when he had been out in the storm for several hours.

"The scope of it," I said, trying to force tears to my dry, smarting eyes. "The planning needed to carry the whole thing through. The insanity of it."

And the fact that the Foreign Secretary himself is involved, I thought, without saying it out loud. The only reason I could see why they had the minister's telephone number as a contact to inspire confidence in case of a crisis was that they were absolutely one hundred per cent dependent on being believed without any further questions. They needed an authority figure with a voice everyone recognized.

"The insanity."

Geir had fallen back into his old bad habits. He had reverted to repeating what I had just said.

"We talked about it, don't you remember?" I asked. "Outside the cold room? We decided it must be a high-risk prisoner. Who was in a position to be able to make demands. Don't you remember that?"

"I suppose so . . ."

He fished out the snuff with his index finger and threw it in the bin. Then he wiped his hand on his trousers and gulped down the rest of his beer.

"You said it was absolutely ridiculous to move a prisoner by train," he said, suppressing a belch. "You said it had to be every police officer's worst nightmare. And that they must have planned the entire journey taking all eventualities into account. Wind and weather and power failure. Possible escape routes. All the way from Oslo to Bergen."

I nodded.

"But a *terrorist*."

He still couldn't utter the word without looking as if he'd just swallowed a wasp.

"*In Norway?*"

"Souhaila Andrawes," I said drily. "One of the most wanted terrorists from the 1970s. She lived here for several years with her husband and children in a nice little apartment in Oslo before she was discovered and unmasked. And many people also feel that Mullah Krekar isn't exactly an honoured guest in our country. But nobody has managed to dig him out yet. Not that I'm taking a stand on . . ."

I shrugged my shoulders instead of completing the sentence.

"This is something completely different," muttered Geir, looking around for something else to drink. "I'm going for another beer. Do you want anything?"

I did, really. A big glass of good red wine would be wonderful.

"Just a Farris," I said. "With ice, please."

"I won't be long. Don't go. Don't go!"

I had no intention of going anywhere.

Geir was right. The case of Mullah Krekar was something completely different from our current situation. The only threat he posed was that he was still legally resident in Norway, many years after the first attempts to throw him out came to nothing. It was true that Mullah Krekar had given various ministers with responsibility for foreign affairs a headache, but he was hardly a danger to others. At least not in this country.

I could understand Geir's scepticism. I was sceptical myself. But my terrorist theory was the only one that could explain this absurd mystery. The whole thing was so huge, so spectacular and so unnecessarily risky that I couldn't imagine the Norwegian authorities going along with something like this unless . . .

"You're still here," said Geir, putting down the glasses before closing the door. "I've been thinking."

And you interrupted my train of thought, I wanted to say.

I picked up my drink and felt the coldness of the glass. The ice cubes clinked delicately and the wind was now so far away that I could hear the faint hiss of the carbon dioxide.

"You know," said Geir, settling down, "there could be something in what you say. Terrorists have more bargaining power than other prisoners. Much more. They have information about future attacks on civilian targets, about terror cells, about . . . And besides . . ."

He looked thoughtful and seemed to be examining something in the foam on the top of his beer.

"The Americans are stupid," he said calmly.

"I'm not saying that."

"Just imagine the dilemma that would have arisen," he said, addressing the air in front of him and putting down the glass of beer without having a drink, "if a terrorist were seized on Norwegian soil. A Norwegian terrorist blasting his way into a Norwegian embassy, for example. Or the Norwegian forces in Afghanistan having . . . You see what I mean!"

He was animated now, resting his elbows on his knees. His breath smelled of beer and snuff, and he thought for a few seconds before he carried on, making a point of emphasizing certain words.

367

"I'm not talking about some idiot who carries out the odd attack on the synagogue in Oslo. I'm talking about a *real* terrorist. One that *the Americans want*. One they want more than anything! One who has helped to strike a blow against American interests."

Suddenly he leaned back and folded his arms.

"They would never have got him," he said in a surprisingly low voice.

"I . . ."

"They can't have him! Norway would not be able to extradite a terrorist to the USA, however good the Americans' reasons for putting him on trial might be. We couldn't do it, however much we might want to. Neither we nor our closest allies for the past sixty years could do that. A tricky situation for both parties, to say the least. They would never have got him."

"Because they have the death penalty for terrorism," I said slowly.

"Yes. Yes!" He slammed his fist down on the desk. "Which means that we —"

"The USA could promise not to make use of that law," I interjected. "Norway extradites prisoners to countries that have the death penalty as long as we receive guarantees that the death sentence will not be imposed or carried out."

"But they —"

"The USA is a country we trust," I said, raising my voice. "There is no doubt that someone like . . . a central figure within al Qaeda, for example, would have been handed over. Al Qaeda has killed thousands of Americans. *They have the right to demand it, for fuck's sake!*"

Now I was the one raising my voice. I don't know who was most surprised, Geir or me. He smiled sweetly. Picked up his glass. Had a drink.

"I doubt whether the Americans would have made such a promise," he said after an embarrassing pause. "And then everything immediately becomes more complicated. But let's not fall out. This isn't actually my main point."

"So what is your main point?"

With everything that had happened over the past couple of days, I had forgotten that Geir Rugholmen was a solicitor. To me he was a man of the mountains. A local hero in shabby mountain clothes, a resident of Finse.

That was the way I had come to know him.

The way I liked him.

"I thought your speciality was property," I said, more sourly than I had intended.

"That's right," he said, inserting a new plug of snuff. "But my wife is also a solicitor. She deals with completely different issues from me."

There was an invitation in his words. I was supposed to ask what his wife did.

"You said you had more ideas."

"If we toy with the idea that you're right," he said, poking at the snuff with his tongue, "and that there actually is a terrorist down in the cellar . . ."

Once he had actually spoken the words out loud, he started to laugh. His laughter was even more girlish than before. Panting, almost giggly.

"Sorry," he said, raising one hand, "but it's just so ..." He shook his head and swallowed, pulling himself together. "Well," he continued firmly. "If we really are dealing with a terrorist here, then it isn't the Norwegian authorities he should be most afraid of, or hard-hitting interrogations, or a difficult journey over the mountains."

I knew I was tired and I did actually have a damaged auditory nerve, but I was beginning to wonder if I was suffering from auditory hallucinations. Since the storm had abated I had been able to hear a faint rushing sound in my ears. It was as if the sound of wind and whirling snow had attached itself to my eardrum for good. But the deep, monotonous hum that I could hear far, far away had nothing to do with the weather. I swallowed and opened my mouth wide so that my ears popped. Geir didn't appear to notice.

"Our friend the terrorist ought to be afraid of the *Americans*," he said, rubbing the back of his neck. "Not only do they have an ugly history when it comes to liquidations outside their own country, but they —"

"That was during the Cold War. Everything was different during the Cold War, and we ought to be more sympathetic towards —"

"Hanne!"

Geir slammed his fist down on the desk. The glass of beer was still half full. It fell over. He leapt to his feet and backed away to avoid getting wet.

"Shit. Shit! What's the matter with you?"

"With me? I'm not the one who just knocked a glass over!"

"Are you the American ambassador to Norway, or something? Don't you understand what I'm saying? Haven't you realized that the Americans literally kidnap prisoners in other countries and put them in their horrendous camps? If a terrorist really has been caught or sought refuge on Norwegian soil, then it's the Americans he ought to be afraid of! They would go to any lengths."

He pushed the spilt beer across the desk with his hand. It splashed onto the floor. A sweet aroma of malt and alcohol pervaded the room.

"It wouldn't surprise me if the bloody Yanks had a man on the train," he said angrily. "Or several, in fact. If your crazy theory is correct, then I understand why the terrorist insisted on travelling by train. An attack on the railways is much more difficult to cover up than a carefully arranged plane crash. One strike against a plane, and everybody dies. To kill all the passengers on a train, you'd have to . . . Bloody hell!"

The front of his trousers was soaking wet.

"I haven't got any clothes down here," he groaned. "And I don't feel like going out and shovelling snow. Shit."

The noise outside had grown louder. The humming had turned into a throbbing, even roar.

"Quiet," I said. "Can you hear that?"

He stood there with his legs apart looking as if he had wet himself. His expression sharpened, with narrowed eyes and his mouth slightly open.

"A helicopter," he said, fascinated. "They're here already?"

He had forgotten his wet trousers.

I put aside all thoughts of terrorists and American attacks on foreign soil. It struck me briefly that the story of the secret prisoner was a sign of how small the world has become. Even in Finse, the Norwegian mountain village where the train struggles up through valleys so Norwegian that you imagine you can see nineteenth-century paintings flickering by outside the windows; even now, in a snowstorm, in ultra-Norwegian isolation in an old National Romantic wooden building, even here the outside world has made its presence felt. The presence of the terrorist was life's reminder that the world was no longer so alien or so far away; it was here with us, always, and we were a part of it whether we liked it or not.

But I didn't want to think about the terrorist.

Instead I thought about Cato Hammer and Roar Hanson.

CHAPTER
TWO

"They're coming! *They're coming!*"

The lobby was in joyous uproar. People were clapping and laughing as if they were sitting on a charter flight that had just touched down on the runway. A few were raising their glasses in a toast, while others were starting to gather their belongings as if they thought they might be going home in ten minutes. The fourteen-year-olds had already started putting on their outdoor clothes; none of them wanted to miss the spectacle of a heavy helicopter landing on deep snow.

"They can't land," said Johan. "There's no way they can land on this powdery snow. The thing will tip over!"

He was standing at the window by the long table, watching the lights as they approached over Finsevann. The helicopter was low in the sky and moving slowly. The searchlights swept from side to side across the vast expanse of snow. The ice crystals glittered so beautifully in the dazzling, blue-white light that some of the older ladies gasped out loud. As the machine came in above the roof and we lost sight of it, there couldn't have been more than twenty metres between the ridge of the roof and the helicopter. The whole building was shaking, but this time the racket was not a sign of a threatening danger. This noise was a welcome consolation, a greeting from the lives we really lived, far away from both Finse and a storm that we didn't yet know had been given the name Olga.

All those who had seen the helicopter coming ran to the front door. Even Adrian seemed excited. He left Veronica sitting alone by the kitchen door with those stupid cards spread out on the floor. He was chatting enthusiastically to one of the girls from the handball team, as if he'd completely forgotten how cool he actually was.

"They can't land," Johan said again.

A metallic voice sliced through every other sound and most people stopped dead before they even reached the door.

"This is the police. I repeat: this is the police. We are going to winch down three men. Stay away from the station platform. I repeat: everyone must stay away from the platform."

Johan sighed with relief, then ran towards the door.

"Move away!" he shouted. "Inside, everybody! Stay away from the door! Inside, all of you!"

The teenagers protested defiantly. A couple of men started arguing outside the kiosk, and Mikkel had to intervene. The lady with the knitting started crying again, loudly and piercingly. Berit came running from the kitchen.

"Calm down!"

Over the past couple of days Berit had become a new person. She had acquired a strength that surpassed Johan's, despite the mountain man's indisputable

374

physical superiority. From being an ordinary hotel landlady with a pleasant nature, Berit had taken control at Finse 1222.

"OK, we're going to remain completely calm," she bellowed, paradoxically with a smile. "Go and sit down either in Blåstuen or St Paal's Bar — and I mean everybody. Come along!"

People calmed down. They shrugged their shoulders and glanced at one another. Nobody said anything much, but they moved back into the hotel as one man, removing hats and outdoor clothes. A few shuffled along slowly and sullenly, others strutted along arrogantly, heads held high, as if they had been proved right in some way, although I had no idea what this could possibly be.

"This is the police," the metallic voice intoned again. "We are asking everyone to remain indoors during the operation. I repeat: everyone must remain indoors."

Kari Thue was not in the lobby. When I thought about it, I hadn't seen her since dinner. Perhaps that wasn't so strange; I had spent most of the time in the office, and hadn't seen anybody except Geir Rugholmen.

But I didn't like it.

Severin had sent for the police. In the letter Geir had smuggled to him, I had not only asked who had embezzled funds from the Public Information Service Foundation at some point towards the end of the nineties, I had also asked him to inform the authorities that there had been not only one murder at Finse 1222, as they had been told before communication with the outside world broke down, but two.

People moved towards the side wing as the helicopter's rotor blades sent deep vibrations through the battered hotel. The disappointment over the fact that the helicopter had not come for them, that the journey home was postponed, the embarrassment at having got excited and happy for no reason meant that everybody had a long face as they passed by without looking in my direction.

I just stayed where I was in the middle of the floor, waiting.

CHAPTER
THREE

Although one of the police officers gave me an almost imperceptible nod as he walked past on the way down to Blåstuen, none of them seemed to recognize me from the old days. When I saw them, two men in their thirties from the Bergen police authority and an older man from the National CID, I felt a pang. They reminded me of the fact that I had once been part of something different, something bigger than life on Krusesgate with Nefis, Ida and Mary. For a long time I had felt as if that cold, dramatic December night in 2002 was not just the end of an epoch; my break with the police service was just as much the beginning of something new. Something I had wished for. The injury made it possible to create an existence for which I had the strength, a life where I was seldom afraid and never worn out.

When I saw the three officers talking quietly together, using an abbreviated language they were trained to interpret, and with glances only they could decipher, I wondered if I had been fooling myself. These years of silence, these days that were longer than I ever imagined days could be, the nights of loneliness in front of the TV, all these months that followed each other smoothly and without friction, when the only reminders that the year was passing were Christmas celebrations and Ida's wonderful birthdays: was this what I really wanted?

I had thought I had swapped one life for another. After these days at Finse, it struck me that I had actually swapped a vital, ambitious life for an existence in waiting.

During the night I waited for the others to wake up. During the day I waited for Nefis and Ida to come home from nursery. I waited in the company of books, films and newspapers, I allowed time to pass by without really bothering about anything except a little girl who would soon need so very much more than the endless oceans of time I was able to offer her in our closed little universe.

Geir appeared behind me and placed a hand on my shoulder.

"We'll finish our conversation later."

I could feel the warmth of his rough hand through my sweater. I closed my eyes, dizzy with tiredness. Exhaustion. Longing, perhaps, for Ida and Nefis, but also, I realized reluctantly, for another life.

They knew who I was, the police officers.

They didn't know me, but they knew who I was. One of them had merely glanced in my direction, but there was a kind of respect in that look. Admiration, perhaps. The older man turned around. Berit had said he was from the National CID. He looked at me expressionlessly for a brief moment before raising two fingers to his forehead and nodding slightly.

Everyone was to assemble downstairs in the wing.

Including me.

I didn't know for certain who had murdered Cato Hammer and Roar Hanson. But I was quite convinced that I knew who Roar Hanson had suspected. As soon as I began to have my suspicions, it wasn't difficult to find evidence that supported the murdered priest's theory. The man had in fact tried to tell me the name of the person who would later murder him. Grotesquely, there was already a great deal to indicate that he had been right.

But not enough.

I could share my thoughts with the police. That was what I ought to do. They could treat my statement in the way that this kind of statement should be treated, in a targeted process involving facts and speculation, forensic evidence and tactical considerations, rumours, carelessness and precise observation.

That would take time.

A difficult time for everyone in the hotel, and for those who were running it. For Berit and her staff. And for me. I wanted to go home.

Perhaps I should let Roar Hanson solve his own murder.

"Can you organize some coffee for me?" I asked Geir. "The biggest mug you can find."

"It's late. Don't you think you should —"

"Coffee," I repeated with a smile. "I need to sharpen my little grey cells."

"Please yourself," he said without so much as a hint of a laughter line appearing around those chapped lips with brown tobacco juice at the corners.

Perhaps I hadn't been quite as amusing as I thought.

CHAPTER
FOUR

As yet no one from the other buildings in Finse village had emerged from their snowed-in existence. Presumably they were waiting for the all-clear. Besides which, it was late and still bitterly cold. As far as the people in the wing were concerned, the Red Cross personnel had dug their way out and made contact with Johan. After a short conversation with the police, he informed us that everybody should stay calm. They had evidently managed to get the situation under control after the mutiny earlier, and the police wanted to deal with one thing at a time.

One building at a time, if you like.

I closed my eyes and imagined what it must look like out there, with snow so deep that there was no one alive who could remember anything like it. Hurricane Olga had left behind a station community that was neither a station nor a community; most of the houses were invisible, and the railway line had disappeared. And beneath all this, beneath an inconceivable number of hexagonal ice crystals, dry and almost weightless in the biting cold, beneath this immense covering of air and frozen water that stretched from Hallingdal to Flåm, from Hardanger to Hemsedal, beneath all this there were people, tiny as insects, who didn't yet dare to believe that the whole thing was over, and that they could creep out into the world once more.

I really hoped I would leave here in daylight.

I wanted to see it all.

I opened my eyes.

The atmosphere at Finse 1222 was discontented and expectant at the same time. Most people were still affected by disappointment over the fact that the helicopter had not come to begin the evacuation. On the other hand, it was as if the murder of the two priests, from which most people had managed to distance themselves because they couldn't cope with the knowledge that there was a murderer among us, had suddenly become a brutal reality when the investigators arrived. The three police officers brought with them a reassuring, safe air of authority; they came up to the mountain with elements of the society that still existed out there, where there were laws and rules and order. The police were here, the storm had abated and nothing was really all that bad any longer.

People around me were finally able to appreciate what they had lived with, how they had lived. And it was exciting.

I saw them coming.

Kari Thue and her entourage marched in with determination, practically doing the goosestep, with Kari at their head. They sat down at the far side of the room, next to the terrace. Mikkel's gang were no longer so disciplined; they came in one by one, ambling along, the skinniest one with a half-smoked cigarette butt dangling from the corner of his mouth. The older ladies and the handball players, the men with their laptops under their arms, Johan and Berit and the Germans, they all walked past me on their way into the wing to hear what the powers of law and order had to say.

Finally, along came Mikkel himself. As usual, he barely looked at me.

"Mikkel," I said. "Can I ask you something?"

He shrugged his shoulders and took a step towards me, his expression indifferent.

"Like what?"

"Why were you going to Bergen? What were you going to do there?"

"Concert. Maroon 5. Missed it. It was yesterday."

He turned away and carried on walking.

"Mikkel! *Mikkel!* Come back here, please."

Two steps back.

"Did you know Kari Thue before you met her here?"

"Slightly," he said, a fraction too quickly. "But only slightly."

He was determined to go this time, so I gave up.

Adrian and Veronica were still sitting by the kitchen door, next to the green cupboard with gourds painted on it. They were playing their peculiar game and didn't even look up when the knitter from the church commission stood on the jack of clubs.

"May I?" said Geir, placing a hand on my wheelchair.

I nodded, and he pushed the chair carefully down the three steps.

The Muslim couple were almost the last to arrive.

"Stop a minute," I said quietly to Geir, "and let them pass."

People were gathering in Blåstuen. The Kurds went and sat by the window right next to the little half-wall separating the room from St Paal's Bar, on a sofa they had all to themselves for the time being.

"Come along, Adrian," I called over my shoulder. "You too, Veronica."

They really were an odd couple. I was no longer surprised that Veronica had picked out the boy as soon as we arrived. In some ways they suited each other very well: two lost, truculent individuals who refused to be like other people. Who refused to be with other people. Whom other people refused to be with.

But I hadn't forgotten what Adrian said about Veronica the first time he interrupted Roar Hanson in his hesitant attempts to make his confession.

I remembered it very well, because I think he was lying when he said it.

Veronica was still sitting on the floor by the kitchen door. She had picked up the cards, and was shuffling them as elegantly as a poker player.

"You too," I called.

For the first time since I met Veronica, she seemed unsure of herself. On the one hand she wanted to demonstrate her independence. On the other, she was smart enough to realize she would look like a stubborn brat if she didn't go along with everybody else.

The police had arrived. They had issued an order. Everybody was doing as they were told.

383

Including Veronica, once she had thought things through.

Several times during the past couple of days Veronica had reminded me of a cat. She got up reluctantly from the floor with soft movements. She padded across the floor in a slight arc, as if she were on the alert, approaching her prey. Only now did I notice that she had her bag with her once more, a medium-sized shoulder bag I hadn't seen before.

I'd only read about it, on Adrian's list.

"Not there," I said quickly as she headed towards Adrian.

I pointed in the opposite direction.

"There! You too, Adrian. Sit over there by the fire. On the sofa. There's plenty of room."

I pointed to the Muslim couple.

Fortunately both Adrian and Veronica did as I said. I hadn't really expected it to be that easy. The youngest police officer gave me a sceptical look, and it seemed as if he was about to say something. But he closed his mouth.

"My name is Per Langerud," said the oldest of the three detectives, clearing his throat with his hand in front of his mouth. "First of all I would like to take this opportunity to express . . ."

It was probably difficult to find the right word.

". . . my sympathy," he said eventually, "for the incredibly difficult situation in which you have found yourselves over the past few days. I realize that you all want to go home as soon as is humanly possible. And I can assure you that is what will happen."

A delighted murmur rippled through the room. Someone applauded tentatively.

"I did say as soon as possible," said Per Langerud, raising his voice. "Which means when we have carried out the most essential aspects of our investigation. The more cooperative you are, the quicker our work will proceed. But I'm afraid none of you should expect to leave before tomorrow afternoon at the earliest. Perhaps not until —"

"Tomorrow afternoon," shouted Mikkel, getting to his feet. "Fuck that! I'm leaving here as soon as it's light."

"Me too," said the lady with the knitting. "I want to go home. I have to get home. My cat is all alone and I wasn't going to . . ."

"We don't have to put up with this," said Kari Thue, gaining the support of the older businessmen who had been hanging around her for the past couple of days. "What right do you have to stop us from leaving here as soon as it's feasible? You have the right to hold me here only if you have reason to suspect me of committing a criminal offence, which you don't."

"Quiet!" shouted Per Langerud in a voice that broke from baritone to bass. "I can assure you that we have the right to —"

"Fuck it," said Adrian suddenly, getting up from the sofa and taking a threatening step towards Langerud.

The boy looked comical more than anything; he was fifty kilos lighter and at least twenty years younger than the police officer. But still he hissed: "We don't even know if you really are cops. I'm leaving here tomorrow if I have to."

"Are you going to ski?" I asked loudly. "Is that what you're all intending to do? Put on your skis and ski down?"

The younger officers had moved closer to Adrian. I signalled to them to leave him alone. They drew back hesitantly and sat down right on the edge of their seats, ready to leap into action. Several of the fourteen-year-olds were crying and sobbing. The knitting lady had once again buried her face in her handiwork, which by this stage must have been completely ruined by snot and tears.

"You will stay here for as long as the authorities decide you will stay here," I said loudly. "For one thing, you have no way of leaving here under your own steam."

The implacable logic in this simple statement made an impression. The teenagers snivelled and wiped their eyes. Mikkel sat down. It was so quiet that I could hear the click of the needles as the lady from the church commission once again began knitting frenetically, before she suddenly stopped and put down the half-finished sweater.

"You will sit here and listen to what the police have to say."

My voice was trembling, but I didn't know if it was because of nerves or rage. Both, probably. Despite the fact that I felt neither angry nor anxious. Just exhausted.

386

"And nobody is leaving here until the police give us permission to do so," I added when there was total silence.

Per Langerud ran his hand over his chest as if the rough bobbles on the old woollen cardigan would disappear with a little brushing. Adrian was right when he said these men didn't look like police officers. Langerud was wearing knee breeches, slightly too tight, and grey socks that were conversely too loose, and kept on slipping down over his high ski-boots. The younger officers looked as if they were on their way to an *après ski* session at Geilo. Both were wearing blue jackets. I knew they cost around six thousand kroner, and their ski-boots were probably in the same price bracket. You definitely don't buy clothes like that on a police officer's salary. Perhaps they had been told to go off and shop for their own equipment for the expedition, and had taken the opportunity to blow the state's entire purchasing budget.

Langerud took his time. Ran his hand over his chest again. He tried to tug at the tight knee breeches a little with his thumb and index finger. Then he examined his knuckles and shook his head, as if he could hear a strange sound that no one else was able to perceive. Only when everybody had had the opportunity to feel really embarrassed did a forgiving smile spread over his angular face. He opened his mouth.

"Excuse me," I said loudly. "Excuse me, Inspector."

I took a chance on the title. It found its mark. He turned towards me. He looked surprised, annoyed and curious all at the same time.

"I was wondering whether . . . Could I possibly have a word?"

"With me?"

"Yes."

He held out his hand in an inviting gesture.

"Carry on."

"Could you perhaps come over here for a moment?"

He frowned again, his expression encapsulating more feelings than I could read. He probably thought the easiest thing would be to listen to what I had to say. And perhaps the most sensible thing too. At any rate he came over to me, and when I waved my index finger he leaned down and put his ear to my mouth.

He smelled of sweet aftershave and coffee.

When I had said my piece, he slowly straightened up.

It was no longer difficult to interpret his expression. I knew exactly what he was thinking. He was doubtful. What I had asked for was far from normal procedure in a murder enquiry. If either of us had dared to take the time to think about it, we might have realized it probably wasn't even legal. There was at the very least good reason to question the ethics of what I was asking him for. He ought to say no. Both his age and the task he had been given indicated that Per Langerud was an experienced and skilled police officer.

That was why he said yes.

Or rather: he nodded. It was the tiniest, most imperceptible nod, but it conveyed his consent. I had his permission to try, and he turned away so quickly that I suspected he didn't want to infect me with his doubts.

"I have been given permission," I said, rolling my chair closer to everyone else, "to ask a few questions first. Before the police do what they have to do, and we can all go home."

Three police officers, a handful of hotel staff and Red Cross personnel, a gang of girls dressed in red with ponytails, some doctors, Kari Thue and Mikkel, Magnus and the lady with the knitting, the Germans and the rest of the passengers from the derailed train: they were all looking at me, and only at me. I could see contempt and curiosity in their eyes, expectation and impatience, indifference and possibly something reminiscent of fear. But not where I had hoped to see it.

Suddenly I didn't know what to say.

The silence was so strange.

I still had a rushing sound in my ears, but this echo against my eardrums of a storm that had died away was the only thing I could hear in the big room. These people would start kicking off at any moment, they would protest, demand that something must be done, something must be said. I would lose this opportunity in a few seconds.

"Why are you wearing Adrian's red socks?" I asked, looking at Veronica.

Somebody sniggered. Others shushed them.

A fine, slender furrow divided her forehead.

"I borrowed them," she said slowly.

"Sorry? Could you speak up, please?"

"I borrowed them. My feet were cold."

Her expression left me in no doubt of what she thought of me. Her voice, which was already remarkably deep, became even deeper.

"Adrian was cold and I lent him my sweater," she added. "My feet were cold and he lent me his socks."

"But not at the same time," I said. "He borrowed your sweater that very first evening, or at least before he settled down to sleep. You borrowed his socks the following day."

She gazed blankly straight ahead. Her gaze was fixed on me, but it didn't look as if she was seeing anything at all. The thin, crooked line on her forehead was gone, and she was once again a deathly pale creature utterly devoid of expression.

"Whatever," she said, pushing her hair behind her ear.

A contemptuous snort could be clearly heard from the far side of the room. The sound was easy to recognize.

"Kari Thue," I said loudly. "I realize you're impatient. You're not interested in borrowed socks and sweaters. But I can ask you a question straight away. Could you stand up, please? I can't see you very well from over here."

No reaction.

"OK," I said. "But I'm sure you can hear me. How did you know that the storm eased at around three o'clock on the night Cato Hammer died?"

Still she sat there, quiet as a mouse. I couldn't see her, but I suddenly saw a hare in my mind's eye, a little brown terrified hare pressing itself to the ground, thinking it can make itself invisible.

A sense of unease spread around her.

"Answer the question, then."

"She asked you a question."

"I didn't know that the storm had eased at around three o'clock," said Kari Thue, without getting up. "How can you say that I —"

"When the rumour started," I interrupted her. "When people started saying that Cato Hammer had run away, you added weight to the theory of a stolen snowmobile by informing everyone that the storm had eased just then."

"I suppose I must have been awake at about three," said Kari Thue, still invisible to me. "There's nothing odd about it, I just happened to be awake! I noticed things were calmer outside."

"Yes," I agreed. "You were awake. And yes, the storm had in fact eased for a while just then. The weather log confirms that."

Now she got to her feet. She smiled triumphantly at her entourage and they smiled back, with a slight hint of anxiety.

"Exactly. In which case I don't really understand why —"

"However, you did state that you were asleep," I broke in. "In the morning when you came down into the lobby, you complained about how heavily you had slept. You believed it was irresponsible of Berit to let the guests sleep all night. We could all have had concussion, you insisted, and should have been woken up."

"But I —"

"Judging by the evidence, Cato Hammer was murdered at about three o'clock. Were you asleep or were you awake? At three o'clock, I mean. I think you have to choose one or the other, since it isn't possible to combine the two alternatives. When were you lying; then or just now?"

It occurred to me that I liked this. I was enjoying it.

"I was . . . I was awake. But only for a few minutes because I . . . I had to go to the loo. Then I slept heavily."

"OK."

I adopted an indifferent expression before turning my attention to Mikkel.

"So I expect you went to the loo as well. At about three o'clock in the morning on Thursday."

He blushed. He actually blushed.

"We'll leave it there," I said. "For the time being, anyway. But let's ask everybody else: who was awake at three o'clock on Thursday morning?"

An arm was raised. It was one of the staff, a lad of no more than twenty who had spent more or less the whole time since the accident in the smallest of the offices behind reception.

"I was on night duty," he said tentatively. "I was in the office all the time."

One of the doctors gave a sign.

"I was awake for most of the night," he said, without any attempt to disguise the sarcasm in his voice as he went on. "As some people might remember, there was a terrible storm. It kept me awake. But I didn't get out of bed."

Another hand went up. And another. Several more followed. In the end I was able to establish that no fewer than thirty-two people admitted to having been awake for the whole night or parts of it. All of them, except for the lad on night duty, swore that they had remained in their rooms. Most of them had been sharing a room with others, but this didn't really constitute an alibi. Kari Thue was right about one thing, anyway: most people had enjoyed a deep, dreamless sleep after the violent experience and the depredations of Wednesday 14 February.

"And what about you," I said, looking at Adrian. "Were you asleep?"

"Me? Why the fuck are you asking me? I wasn't fucking sleeping. I mean, I was sleeping in the same . . ." He stopped and started again. "I was sleeping in the lobby. Just a few metres from you, for fuck's sake."

"And what about you," I said to Veronica. "As I understand it, you were the only person who begged for a single room right away on Wednesday?"

"I didn't beg," she replied calmly. "Nobody wanted to share a room with me. I got the distinct impression early on that I'm not exactly what you'd call popular."

She looked me straight in the eye.

She didn't mention Adrian. She didn't reveal that the boy would have been more than happy to share far more than a room with her.

That was considerate. Almost kind. Adrian had been holding his breath. Now he let it seep out slowly as he picked at a spot near the top of his nose.

"In that case I am really only interested in you two," I said.

The Kurdish man looked at me in surprise.

"Us?" he said enquiringly, running his thumb over his beard. "We were asleep, of course. I'm afraid we're in the same situation as her. Nobody exactly complained when my wife and I were given a room to ourselves."

The alleged wife gazed at her folded hands without expressing anything at all. A few seconds passed, and she gave no sign of either confirming or contradicting the man's statement.

Another loud snort came from the direction of the window.

"Kari Thue," I said, and had to swallow in order to control my voice. "Is there something you'd like to say? Something you'd like to share with the rest of us?"

Per Langerud cleared his throat. I had almost forgotten him, in spite of the fact that his brooding figure was just a metre away, off to the side behind my chair. I turned my head and noticed him glance almost imperceptibly at his left wrist.

"Two minutes," I whispered with my hand covering my mouth. "Give me two more minutes."

I didn't know if he had agreed to my request before I raised my voice dramatically and said:

"Kari Thue. What have you got in your handbag?"

"That's got nothing to do with you."

"No. But I expect the police will want to know what's in there."

Langerud took a step closer and gently touched my shoulder. I understood the warning, but I couldn't give up yet. Nor did I want to.

"If you have nothing to hide, then I don't see why it's a problem to tell us what's in your bag. I mean, you never let it out of your sight. Is it something valuable? Or is it something more . . . compromising?"

"I don't have to put up with this!"

She was on her feet again, pressing herself against the window with her arms wrapped around that ridiculous bag that looked like a rucksack.

"Nobody . . . nobody can insist on looking in my bag!"

So far she was quite right. Nobody could insist on looking through her things. What's more, I had a pretty clear idea of what was in there.

Presumably she was carrying around some kind of electronic device. A USB drive, perhaps. A memory stick. It wasn't many weeks since I read that she was just finishing a book based on her work on the documentary film *Deliver Us From Evil*. The title of the book was to be *For Ours Is The Kingdom*, and was expected to do well in the bestseller lists in the autumn.

Whenever Nefis is nearing the end of a scientific work, she becomes paranoid about losing any of it. The small diskettes are therefore stashed everywhere, at home and in the car, in her study and in the office down in the cellar, in case of fire, burglary, a computer crash or indeed nuclear war. Nefis and Kari Thue have very little in common. However, I presumed that most writers share the fear that a piece of work to which they have devoted a great deal of time could be lost.

Kari Thue also had something else in her bag. Something she didn't want us to see. It could be something quite innocent, like a packet of cigarettes. Apart from her anti-Muslim crusade, she wielded her sword against all forms of tobacco products, and had played a not insignificant role in shaping opinion when the new smoking ban was introduced. A packet of cigarettes in her handbag would of course be embarrassing. Or she could be hiding something a little more spicy, such as a clever little aid from one of those shops you might prefer to access via the computer in your own bedroom. The bag wasn't large, but it was big enough.

I assumed.

No doubt she had make-up. A packet of chewing gum or throat sweets. A notebook, pens and a little pack of tissues. I presumed that the contents of Kari Thue's bag were more or less typical of her sex, apart from the fact that there was something in it that she wanted to keep to herself at all costs. I intended to let her do so.

All she had done was sleep with Mikkel. She was probably in love with him. He had spent part of the night after the accident with Kari Thue, and had shown a certain amount of interest in the endless, monotonous message she spread. But that was all. The quarrel I had observed between them was presumably a good old-fashioned break-up. Unpleasantly done, of course,

396

dumping someone at a table where lots of other people could hear, but neither of them had done anything criminal.

Kari Thue was still standing up.

The people around her were looking curiously at her bag, which she was clutching to her chest as if it were a beloved child someone was threatening to snatch away from her. Her eyes were big and wet; she was on the point of bursting into tears.

Kari Thue would be allowed to keep her secrets.

Before I met her, when I knew only the hard, impersonal debater from the television, radio and press, I despised her. Now I despised only what she stood for. I felt nothing but sympathy for Kari Thue herself. She was so afraid all the time, without really being aware of it. I have also lived a life where I was constantly afraid without realizing that was what I was. Fear made me withdraw and retreat inside myself. In Kari Thue, the fear created anger, an implacable, stubborn rage that was directed at far too many people.

Ever since Cato Hammer was murdered, I had hoped she would be behind his death. The need to hurt this person, to see her fall, be humiliated and destroyed, the desire to unmask Kari Thue had been so pressing that I had almost thought I could pull it off.

I feel sorry for people like Kari Thue.

But she hadn't murdered anyone.

"Sit down," I said calmly.

She looked at me suspiciously. The tears spilled over. Someone sitting nearby started sniggering. She was still clutching the bag. Her chin trembled and she was biting her lower lip, not daring to sit down.

"You can sit down," I said. "Nobody is going to look in your bag."

People looked from me to her, back and forth, as if we were playing tennis.

"Adrian," I said, and all eyes turned to the new player.

The boy didn't respond.

"Yesterday morning," I said. "Yesterday morning I was sitting talking to Roar Hanson. You remember that."

Adrian leaned back on the sofa with an expression indicating that he had no interest whatsoever in anything that was being said.

"You interrupted us," I went on. "And Roar Hanson said something to you. You responded by telling him to mind his own business, in rather less polite terms. You remember that. Don't you? Adrian? *Adrian?*"

I put all my strength into my voice. The lady with the knitting let out a terrified squeal, but Adrian still didn't react. He pulled out a long strand of chewing gum then stuffed it back in his mouth, showing no interest whatsoever. I carried on:

"I thought Roar Hanson said: 'Wash your hands every day'. Which was of course a peculiar thing to say. But then Roar Hanson was a strange man. After Cato Hammer's death, at any rate. I couldn't really understand why he should be concerned about your hygiene, even if you definitely did need a shower."

398

Like many others, I thought; the air was heavy with body odour and bitter coffee in spite of the high ceiling.

"Then I asked you earlier today what he had actually said, I still suspected strongly that I had misheard. It was difficult to understand why you would react so violently to a quiet admonition to wash your hands."

"I can't deal with this any more," said Adrian, suddenly getting to his feet. "I'm off. I'm not sitting here and —"

"You're going nowhere!"

Per Langerud took a step towards the young lad. Adrian sat down hesitantly. For a moment it looked as if he were weighing up the odds of getting away if he ran for it. They were dire. As indifferently as possible, he leaned back against the cushions.

"Today you said he had told you to 'watch yourself'," I said. "That was probably when I realized what he had actually said." I let my gaze roam across the room. "Because, you see, I am slightly hard of hearing. It isn't really a major problem, but I don't like not being able to see the person I'm talking to. If I get distracted for a moment, as I was during the conversation to which I am now referring, I don't always pick up the whole sentence. With experience and association skills, it's usually fine. But not always."

An impatient whispering began to spread around the room. The smaller children were getting restless. Their parents were doing their best to keep them quiet, but I thought most people seemed genuinely interested in what I had to say.

"This is almost like a word game," I said, looking at Adrian. "You told me the first word he said to you was 'watch'. 'Watch yourself'. Not 'wash'. You insisted that was all he said, but I know there was more since the sentence 'wash your hands daily' doesn't make any sense."

Someone giggled, the knitter laughed out loud.

"So I started working on associations. It was easy. What Roar Hanson said when you came over to us was —"

"You can't know what he said," shouted Adrian. "You're practically deaf, for fuck's sake. You said so yourself! You can't."

Veronica had sat there motionless and silent the whole time, like the wax doll she resembled. Now she placed her slender hand on his thigh, and he stopped speaking at once.

"'Watch yourself with her, she's dangerous'."

I said it loudly and very slowly.

"That's what Roar Hanson said to you when you replied 'fuck you', and it was Veronica he was looking at when he said it."

Nobody said anything. Nobody moved. It was as if everyone wanted to go through my reasoning for themselves, they wanted to double check and work out whether it really was possible to mishear like that. They sat there lost in their own thoughts, their mouths moving soundlessly, tasting the words, the rhythm of the sentence, the uneven rhymes, and eventually they concluded that there was a logic in it.

There was still total silence. Even the children understood that something significant was happening; they clung anxiously and silently to their parents.

"Your socks were wet," I said, looking at Veronica. "That's why you had to borrow Adrian's the following morning. It was Cato Hammer who insisted on going outside. He was so afraid when you made contact that he wanted to get as far away as possible from anyone who might hear you. You sought him out before the information meeting. Told him that your mother had recently died, and said that you wanted to have a serious talk with him. When you met during the night as agreed, and to be honest I don't know where, he wanted to go outside for safety's sake."

I paused, and got the feeling that everyone was holding their breath.

After Cato Hammer's death I couldn't understand how someone had managed to lure him outside. It was only when I realized he must have been the one who wanted it that way that the pieces began to fit together.

"You didn't go far," I went on. "You were probably standing beneath the roof. He was just outside. You weren't wearing any shoes. Most people had been in their stocking feet all evening, once the floor had dried and nobody was bringing snow in from outside. Looking for your boots in the middle of the night would have been much too great a risk. You went out in your stocking feet. When you came back in, your socks were covered in snow, which melted and left them soaking wet."

Everyone looked at Veronica's red socks.

"That's *bullshit!*" Adrian yelled. "They weren't wet. That's not why Veronica wanted to borrow my socks. Her feet were cold, for fuck's sake! That's all — *her feet were cold!*"

She placed her hand on his thigh once again.

"This isn't true," she said calmly.

"Yes," I said. "More or less."

Her face was no longer so pale. I thought I could see a faint hint of pink across her cheekbones and her mouth, which was turning upwards in a slight, almost imperceptible smile.

"But of course a pair of socks is not enough," I said. "Your name is Veronica Larsen, isn't it?"

She just looked at me. That Mona Lisa smile was still there.

"Your name is actually Veronica *K.* Larsen," I said, emphasising the K, "or at least that's how you're registered on Berit Tverre's list of the passengers from the train. And I would guess that K stands for Koht. Your mother's surname."

She shook her head slightly.

I rolled my chair a little closer, while making an effort to look as weary as possible. Presumably I overdid it, because some of the handball players started giggling. There were now three metres between me and Veronica Koht Larsen. I stopped and put the brakes on.

"Finding out your name is the easiest thing in the world," I said calmly, looking her in the eye. "It would just be foolish to —"

"It's true," she interrupted. "Koht is my middle name."

402

"Your mother is Margrete Koht," I said.

Now I was speaking only to her. I lowered my voice. Out of the corner of my eye I could see many of the others leaning towards us, some with a hand behind their ear. I didn't help them; in fact I spoke even more quietly.

"She was employed by the Public Information Service Foundation. An embezzlement took place within that organization. During 1998. A comprehensive deception that damaged the institution, and not only in terms of the financial loss. Your mother was picked out as the guilty party, and was later convicted. I have a strong feeling that she didn't do it. She was either badly taken in, or perhaps . . . persuaded. To accept the blame for something she hadn't done at all."

I think she blinked. I can't be sure, my eyes were dry and smarting, and I was blinking myself the whole time. But I think her eyelids moved a fraction.

"You brought a gun with you on this trip," I said. "Something that is obviously going to make the police wonder if the murder of Cato Hammer was planned. I'll leave that for now."

Adrian flung his arms wide and roared: "Stop it! Stop it, Hanne! Veronica hasn't —"

"No, *you* stop it," Veronica said sharply. "Just shut up, Adrian!"

He glared at her with his mouth open before collapsing. It was as if the air slowly ran out through his gaping mouth until there was nothing left of the skinny boy's body but a limp, soft shell.

"You're wrong," said Veronica, keeping her eyes fixed on mine.

"You shot Cato Hammer," I said. "And you had a gun in your bag, which you kept hidden up in your room until now. Adrian noticed that something was in the bag when you arrived at the hotel. Not all that big, but heavy. He hoped it was . . ."

Adrian whimpered. I stopped, then went on:

"Adrian thought it was something completely different."

She didn't even reach for the bag. It was lying there beside her, on the end of the sofa between her thigh and the armrest.

Not a glance at the compromising bag.

Not even the slightest quiver in her hand. She simply sat there, motionless as always, smiling enigmatically.

I hadn't expected this.

I was sweating.

"You're the only one who's had a room to yourself," I said. "The only one, apart from the staff. Of course you could have hidden the gun in the room and locked the door, but you thought it was safer to leave it in the bag and hide the whole thing. To be honest, I think you felt the revolver was difficult to deal with once you had killed Cato Hammer. You found it hard to look at it."

She definitely blinked this time. The small tip of a wet, pale pink tongue ran over her lower lip.

"But I don't think that's what stopped you from using it again," I said. "It was something quite different that made you murder Roar Hanson with an icicle, and

I will come back to the reason why you didn't choose to use the gun a second time."

"Icicle? *Icicle!* Icicle . . ."

The word ran through the room like a cockroach. At first it was whispered, then spoken out loud, and finally it was shouted; in disbelief and delight, with doubt and a huge exclamation mark: *Icicle!*

"I didn't understand that business with the icicle," I said quietly when Langerud had exercised his authority to calm people down. "An unusual weapon. Difficult to handle. It places particular demands on the attacker, not least in terms of skill and precision. But something Adrian had said came back to me."

The boy was weeping. He had pulled off his hat and was pressing it to his face to muffle the humiliating sobs. I wanted to console him. I wanted to put my arms around him and rock him and say that he'd just been bloody unlucky yet again. I wanted to whisper calming words in his ear and reassure him that at some point in the future he would meet an adult he could trust. One day.

I couldn't help Adrian. Perhaps no one could help Adrian.

"Hanne Wilhelmsen."

Per Langerud placed a hand on my shoulder, and I came to with a start.

"Sorry," I mumbled.

"Perhaps we ought to —"

"No," I said. "No!"

"I think this is —"

"Adrian told me you're a black belt in Tae Kwondo," I interjected, fixing my gaze on Veronica once more. "I thought he was lying. Or that you were lying to him. But it's true, isn't it? You are."

"I am a black belt."

Hence the self-control, I thought, and took a deep breath.

"If anyone could commit murder with an icicle," I said, "it would have to be a martial arts practitioner. You are also a genuine dog lover."

Her tongue ran over her lower lip once again.

"The only time you really bothered about anyone other than Adrian was when the dog died. Muffe. You were furious. You talked about laws and regulations, and you wanted to find out who was responsible. You patted the body and sympathized with the owner. It was a touching show of concern, given how dismissive you have been towards everybody else. Nothing would stop you from going into a room with a pit bull locked inside. On the contrary, you are one of the very few people in this hotel who would dare to do so. Possibly the only one, apart from the owner. That's what I think, anyway."

I smiled briefly, and noticed that I was having difficulty in breathing.

People were no longer sitting quietly. This had nothing to do with a lack of interest in my ridiculous public interrogation, a clear infringement of all Veronica's rights and, moreover, without any perceptible stringency. When some people started whispering, and others didn't even bother trying to talk quietly, when conversations were conducted across the room and grew louder and louder, it was because people were already convinced. Veronica Koht Larsen, the girl with the pack of cards who usually sat by the kitchen door, that scary creature dressed in black who always had that peculiar, grubby lad trailing behind her, was a murderer. The whole thing was so sensational it was hard to keep quiet. This was such a major experience that it had to be shared with others in order to become real.

I didn't know what to do.

The pressure on my lungs was increasing, and once again I felt that searing pain from the wound in my thigh, the pain I shouldn't be able to feel. I closed my eyes and gritted my teeth just as Veronica got to her feet.

The hum of conversation in the room stopped abruptly.

Nobody moved.

Veronica was also standing still. She had looped her bag over her shoulder before any of us had realized what was going on.

"In that case," she said calmly, her voice clear and melodic, "can anyone tell me why the hell I would use an icicle as a weapon when you all seem to think I have a revolver in this bag?"

When the helicopter arrived, most of the guests had thought their stay at Finse 1222 was at an end. Many had fetched their outdoor clothes from various corners and from their rooms, and a few had brought down their small amount of luggage. Veronica was one of them. She had thought she was going home, and had brought her bag downstairs. Now she had slipped her hand inside it in an almost imperceptible movement.

"Good question," I said loudly, and took a forbidden risk. "A very good question, in my opinion. Perhaps you would like to answer it yourself?"

"That's enough," said Per Langerud, moving towards Veronica with his hand raised in a calming gesture. "Let's just take it easy and —"

"Stop."

She didn't even raise her voice.

I was right. It was a revolver, not a pistol. And it was pointing at me. Veronica moved slowly sideways.

Somebody screamed and I closed my eyes.

When I opened them again, Veronica was lying on the ground face down.

The Kurd, or the man with the beard whom I had believed to be a Kurd, was sitting with his knee in the back of the skinny figure, locking her arms with one hand. The woman with the headscarf was also on one knee, holding a revolver in a two-handed grip as she pressed it to Veronica's temple.

Per Langerud roared, and behind me I could hear someone running across the floor. I didn't hear what they yelled, but I yelled back:

"Don't touch them! They're our people! *Don't touch them!*"

The three police officers stopped dead.

"Let her get up," I said, moving my chair over towards Veronica.

408

The woman slipped her gun into its holster and grabbed Veronica's revolver. With a practised, sure hand she opened the gun and spun the chamber around.

"Empty," she said, sounding embarrassed. "No ammunition."

"Exactly," I said. "Empty."

I had gambled with high stakes. Far too high, but I had won. I was so sure that the revolver was empty I had risked other people's lives on the basis that I was right. Perhaps it was best if I stayed away from the police service after all.

But there was no good reason to use an icicle as a murder weapon if you had a revolver. Unless it was broken, or out of ammunition.

Veronica had had one single bullet with her on the train to Bergen.

I didn't need to ask why. I was remembering another occasion, another time, in a completely different life. A man had inexplicably had two bullets in a magazine with room for nine. The explanation was that he had stolen the gun.

There were just two bullets in the magazine.

Both of them hit me.

Veronica had stolen a revolver containing what should have been exactly the right amount of ammunition. I didn't know whether she had planned to kill Cato Hammer on the train, or in Bergen. It no longer mattered. She had done it here at Finse, and when Roar Hanson threatened to expose her, she didn't have a second bullet. But she did have an idea. Veronica was a clever woman, and the refinement of a weapon that actually melted would have been admirable under different circumstances.

In theory, I mean.

Veronica was sitting motionless on the sofa. Her arms were locked behind her back in handcuffs. The three police officers were busy ushering everybody else out of Blåstuen. They had to get people away from Veronica, away from everything that had happened, and the three representatives of law and order were probably wondering how they were going to explain to their superiors what had happened.

Adrian was still sitting in Blåstuen like a forgotten rag doll that a little girl no longer cared about. He had stopped crying. The tears had left wide furrows down his grubby face. His nose was red and swollen, his eyes narrow.

"Go," I said to him. "Off you go, Adrian. I'll come and talk to you later. OK?"

He got to his feet and allowed himself to be led apathetically up to the lobby by Berit.

Veronica didn't even look in his direction.

She looked at me instead.

"My mother didn't do anything wrong."

"Don't say a word," I said. "I'll get you a good solicitor. Don't say any more until then."

"She was far too religious."

For the first time she was showing signs of pure anger.

"When Cato Hammer had been helping himself to funds for several years, and realized things were starting to get a bit uncomfortable, he managed . . . He

410

persuaded her to take all the blame. He knew that she would protect the church, *above everything*. The church was everything to my mother."

The words came pouring out of her. Some sentences sounded dead and flat until she suddenly raised her voice on the odd word. It was as if something had cracked inside the frail girl; she had to speak.

"The church and me, that was all my mother had in the world. She would have done anything for both of us. But when my need for a mother was set against the church's need for protection, I lost. Cato must have gone on and on about how much damage it would do to the church if one of its financial directors was convicted of embezzlement, told her that the whole church would —"

"Veronica," I interrupted her, "I'm serious; don't say any more right now."

"Wilhelmsen is right," said Langerud. "As soon as we're done here, we'll take you to Bergen, and you will of course have access to a solicitor there."

"Mum was just a simple secretary," she carried on, as if she hadn't heard either of us. "A deeply religious secretary with access to a lot of money, and the authority to make payments. Money she never touched! A simple secretary with weak nerves, a great deal of anguish, and a blind faith in God. Both He and Cato Hammer betrayed her worse than . . . worse than . . ."

The tears came. But her voice remained steady.

"I couldn't get my head around the idea that she'd done it," she said. "Stealing money. What would she have used it for? It was a straight confession. Nobody made a big deal out of the fact that all the police managed to trace was 800,000 in a recently opened account. Cato must have given her the money in sheer desperation when it was clear that the whole thing was going to come to light. She said she'd frittered away the rest. I didn't believe that. We never had much money. Then she got . . . She got sick, and she was put in hospital. I was only fifteen years old. *Fifteen!*"

She gasped for breath with a short panting sound.

"For almost ten years she was locked up in a hospital. And she never told anyone she'd taken the blame for Cato Hammer. My childhood home was sold to cover the debt to the foundation. When she finally died in January this year, I found a letter among her papers, a letter she wrote in 1998. My name was on it. When I had read it I decided to —"

"Shut up, Veronica!" I said. "Langerud — do something!"

The big man squatted down in front of her.

"My mother has atoned for both of us," she said expressionlessly. "And I have already paid too much. I couldn't let Roar Hanson destroy . . . He said he was going to . . . He . . ."

"Veronica," said Langerud. "That's enough, OK?"

She looked past him. He gently took hold of her chin and forced her to make eye contact.

"*Be quiet!*"

Suddenly he gave her a feather-light clip around the ear. It happened so fast I would have missed it if I'd blinked.

"Do you understand? *Do you understand?*"

412

"Yes," said Veronica Koht Larsen. "I understand everything. I wish I'd understood it long ago. If only I'd understood everything when I was fifteen, then . . ."

She didn't finish the sentence. She had already talked herself deep into two premeditated murders, despite the fact that I would never pass the information on to anyone. Per Langerud couldn't think that way, and too much had already been said. True, Veronica would not say another word, not for several months, but none of us knew that as she stiffly got up from the sofa.

She no longer reminded me of a cat. The woman who obediently followed Per Langerud through the big rooms in the side wing at Finse 1222 was not moving with stealth and suppleness. Her steps were short and stiff, with sudden moves to the side in order to maintain her balance. Her head was bowed. Even the black, loose clothes around her bony figure seemed greyer now, and made her look like a pencil mark that someone had tried hard to erase.

It suddenly occurred to me that that person was me.

BEAUFORT SCALE 12

HURRICANE

Wind speed: 73–83mph

If buildings are hit a natural disaster will ensue, with the possible loss of many human lives.

CHAPTER
ONE

"The boy will be coming with me," I said.

Berit was making lists of those who were to be evacuated together, and in which order. A decision had been made to start moving people out of the hotel tonight. Nobody would be able to sleep anyway, and the wind had dropped. There was no longer any reason to keep people here. Quite the reverse, in fact. The sooner the hotel was emptied, the sooner work on the repairs could begin. Johan had had help to clear the snow from the station platform. The tractors were dug out in record time. Many of the guests had joined in with shovels and unassailable enthusiasm. As far as I could gather from people coming in with red faces and frozen hands, the platform looked like a giant pool, a deep ice hockey rink with an edging of powdery snow. The electric lines along the track were still buried, and were no longer live.

The helicopters could land.

The first one was expected at any moment.

"The boy will be coming with me," I repeated. "And I'd like to be the last to leave."

"In that case it won't be until tomorrow some time," said Berit.

"That's fine," I said, rolling my chair through the lobby, which was more or less empty.

Some people were outside, some had gone to their rooms — if not to sleep, then perhaps to collect their thoughts after everything that had happened. The bar had been closed since the police arrived, and most people realized this was going to take time. Nobody minded. The evacuation would soon be under way, and that was the only thing that mattered now.

Adrian was sitting alone by the kitchen door. Nobody was taking any notice of him. He had been sitting there ever since Berit led him up from the wing. He wasn't doing anything or saying anything. He was just sitting there with his forehead resting on his knees and his arms around his legs, almost imperceptibly rocking from side to side.

The Kurd who was not a Kurd suddenly came over to me.

"Thomas Chrysler," he said with a smile, holding out his hand. "That was an impressive performance you gave downstairs."

"Thomas Chrysler," I repeated softly, thinking that someone should have come up with something better when they were giving the man a false identity. "From the police security service, I presume?"

He glanced around quickly. No one could hear us. But he still didn't answer. His teeth were even below the bristly moustache.

"I just want to ask you," he said instead, "how you could be sure Clara and I would step in and tackle Veronica Larsen? I mean, you put them there, right

418

next to us. You asked them to sit there, Veronica and the boy."

"I saw you when the railway carriage fell; I saw you draw your guns."

His eyes narrowed. He studied me for a few seconds before breaking into a broad grin. His teeth really were strikingly white and even.

"But surely you couldn't have known that we —"

"Just a minute," I said, raising a hand defensively. "I had my reasons for believing that you were the good guys, OK? A little bird had . . . well, not exactly chirruped in my ear, but at least given me a look that suggested you were to be trusted. Let's leave it at that. It was nice to meet you, but I have to go and help the boy over there. Just one thing first."

Now I was the one glancing quickly over my shoulder.

"I presume you were supposed to keep an eye on the train passengers," I said, suppressing a yawn. "You were working undercover in case someone was after your terrorist's life, weren't you?"

His eyes grew even narrower. His eyelashes were so long they curled up over his heavy eyelids.

"Terrorist?"

The grin cracked into a hearty laugh.

"We didn't have a real terrorist with us," he said without raising his voice. "This was an exercise! Did you think . . . No, no. This was an exercise. A very realistic exercise under extremely demanding conditions."

He was lying.

What he was saying just had to be a lie.

It couldn't be true that this whole nightmare, everything that had happened to do with the mysterious carriage, all the rumours and the unpleasantness, the rebellion in the wing — it couldn't be true that the whole thing was based on a bluff. I couldn't have wasted so much energy on nothing, on an exercise, on a little training jaunt for the security service boys, when I should have been concentrating on one thing from the very first night: who killed Cato Hammer?

"An exercise in what?"

I swallowed and tried to keep my voice neutral.

"In transporting high-risk prisoners by train. You said it yourself."

Once again that experienced look, confidently sweeping the room.

"We live in a new age with new challenges. In fact, you mentioned one of them."

He winked with his right eye. The eyelashes curving over his eyelid made the gesture more comical than confidential.

"Please go now," I said. "Please leave me in peace."

"Goodness," he said, taking a step back. "I didn't mean to —"

"Go Just go."

"OK."

The smile was back. He straightened his jacket, fished a packet of chewing gum out of his pocket and offered it to me.

"No thank you. I want to be left in peace."

"In that case, thank you for your company," he said, starting to move away. "I wish you a pleasant journey home."

Just three metres away he turned around.

"Just one more thing," he said, chewing like mad. "During dinner yesterday I could see that you were wondering what language we were speaking, Clara and I."

I didn't reply. Didn't even look at him. Slowly I rolled my chair towards Adrian.

"Esperanto," he said with a laugh. "Neither of us speaks Arabic well enough, really. Hardly anybody speaks Esperanto, and it sounds nice and foreign. Don't you think?"

His laughter was genuine. He wasn't making fun of me, he was just as glad as I was that the whole thing was over and we were all going home. But right there and then I could have strangled him. I never wanted to see him again.

An exercise. I felt as if I had been conned. Badly conned.

And what was worse, I felt like an idiot.

"Adrian," I said quietly.

But the boy didn't even look up.

CHAPTER
TWO

It was now Saturday 17 February, and the time was approaching one o'clock in the afternoon. Finse 1222 was virtually empty of guests. The big helicopters had been running a shuttle service since three o'clock in the morning. They had come buzzing in from the south-west like dragonflies, heavy as lead, swallowing up groups of passengers before slowly climbing into the sky and disappearing. Magnus Streng was among the first to leave, and he had hugged me so hard when he was saying goodbye that I thought I might sustain permanent damage. I had taken his card, and promised faithfully that I would call him.

"One day," I said. "I'll call you one day."

I never called Magnus Streng.

The dead were taken away in a separate helicopter: the train driver, Einar Holter; the old man, Elias Grav; the priests, Cato Hammer and Roar Hanson; and the terrified Steinar Aass, who was stupid enough to think he could beat Hurricane Olga. Only little Sara in her pink baby clothes had been given permission to travel with her mother, wrapped in a woollen blanket that her mother clutched to her breast as she was led to the helicopter, silently weeping.

And I had actually allowed myself to be carried.

That had hardly ever happened since I grew strong enough to get out of bed on my own after I had been shot. In four years I had allowed someone to pick me up on only a handful of occasions. Geir didn't even ask my permission. He simply picked me up, so easily that it almost felt pleasant, and carried me up the cleverly constructed steps in the snow from the main door, up and out into the fresh air and the intense, white sunshine. On the eastern side of the hotel right next to the snowed-in station building he had dug out a wide sofa covered in reindeer skins, with a view out over Finsevann.

Frozen waves of snow covered the entire lake. On the opposite shore the mountains rose up, and Geir pointed as he named peaks and valleys, even though I wasn't really listening.

Neither was Berit, apparently.

She already knew the landscape and leaned back against the skins. Closed her eyes behind her sunglasses. Her mouth was half-open. She almost looked as if she were asleep; a carefree mountain tourist in the ice-cold sunshine. I, on the other hand, gazed around in fascination. Berit had given me a pair of sunglasses from the kiosk, and refused to take any money. They made me look like an emaciated fly, so it was probably just as well.

The fact that white could be so white surpassed my understanding. The light stabbed my retina like a knife when I took off the glasses to experience the intensity in all its colourlessness.

423

Which wasn't colourless at all, however.

I screwed up my eyes to look at the magnificent view.

The light from the snowdrifts was refracted in the tears that had stuck on my eyelashes like little prisms of water. In this cannonade of light it seemed to me that every single snowflake in the open landscape was rainbow-coloured. Everything around me was shining with small sparks of colour that disappeared before I could get hold of them properly.

Geir was talking and waving his arms around, but I didn't hear a thing.

I was deaf to everything but the view. It was as if I could actually hear the sunshine crashing to the ground and exploding in this overwhelming show of colours that just took my breath away.

I had to put my sunglasses back on.

The reflections disappeared, and once again I was looking out over a beautiful, white, Norwegian mountain landscape.

From where I was sitting I could see over the top of the snow on the right-hand side of the little fortress Geir had built. We were sheltered from the slight breeze that still nipped at the cheeks, and I could see most of the temporary landing pad between the railway track, the hotel and the station. The penultimate helicopter would soon be leaving Finse.

Veronica was walking up the snow steps from the hotel. The handcuffs had been removed. The two younger police officers were each holding one of her arms. From the way she was wobbling across the

424

platform towards the huge machine, she looked as if she needed all the support she could get.

I shaded my eyes with my hand and peered at the hotel.

Per Langerud was coming out of the wing with the South African man in front of him. I hadn't given the man a thought since assuming he must have gone over to the wing before the carriage came down.

The South African was over-exposed in the sharp light, making his face black and unreadable.

"Why . . ." I murmured, then stopped myself.

The man was in handcuffs. Per Langerud gave him an irritated shove to move him on when he stopped at the sight of the helicopter.

"Berit," I said, clearing my throat.

"Yes."

So she wasn't asleep.

"Why has the South African been arrested?"

She sat up and raised herself slightly so that she could see.

"Oh, him. He's not South African."

"Yes, he . . ."

It struck me as soon as I started to speak: nobody had ever said the man with the sharp, sing-song British accent was South African. I had just guessed.

"He's American," said Berit, sinking back against the reindeer skins. She sighed with pleasure, despite the cold that made her wrap the woollen blanket more tightly around her.

American.

He had managed to fool me with a convincing accent.

I tried to remember exactly what Thomas Chrysler had said during our brief encounter when the whole thing was over, and all I wanted to do was take care of Adrian. The words still hurt. *It was only an exercise.* I also remembered Geir Rugholmen's outburst in the office just before the first helicopter arrived: *If a terrorist really has been caught or sought refuge on Norwegian soil, then it's the Americans he ought to be afraid of! They would go to any lengths . . .*

"May I borrow your binoculars?" I said to Geir.

The man I had assumed to be South African was still just as impeccably dressed. I could even see the narrow stripes on his suit through the powerful lenses. The tie was just as neatly knotted, the shoes in which he was ploughing through the snow were just as elegant and shiny as they had always been.

Only his face had changed.

"Why has he been arrested?" I asked, without taking the binoculars away from my eyes.

"Because he was carrying a gun," said Berit. "That's all, I think."

That's all they're telling you, anyway, I thought.

I lowered the binoculars and glanced over at Geir. He wasn't looking at what was happening down below. Instead he was gazing out over the lake, his expression dreamy, murmuring something about kiteboarding.

There's your Yank, Geir, I thought. You were right.

But I didn't say anything.

The South African who wasn't a South African was proof positive that Thomas Chrysler, who certainly wasn't called Thomas Chrysler, had been lying about an exercise that most definitely wasn't an exercise.

I didn't really know what I was feeling. My pulse was beating faster and little spurts of adrenalin were making me breathe more quickly. Perhaps I was furious. Perhaps mostly relieved. I hadn't been wrong, when it came down to it.

As if that mattered.

I raised the binoculars to my eyes again.

The American climbed on board the helicopter. He almost stumbled, but Langerud saved him with a firm grip on his arm before he fell. Once he was inside, Langerud followed him. The rotor blades began to spin slowly with a dull, clattering sound. Berit sat up and shaded her eyes from the sun with both hands.

"The next to last helicopter," she said. "When the last one comes it's your turn, Hanne."

"You must come back another time," said Geir with a smile. "I will personally guarantee to haul you up to the top of Finse on a sledge."

I actually smiled.

The Sea King lifted slowly, as if it didn't quite dare to break contact with the ground. The snow was whirling so violently that we had to put our hands up to our faces and lean forward. Only when the helicopter had reached a height of a couple of hundred metres was I able to look up at the sky again. Suddenly the helicopter picked up speed and headed west, with two prisoners and three police officers on board.

"I mean it," said Geir eagerly. "Come back. I'll make sure I dig out my apartment by then, at least. We can take you out with the snow scooter, Johan's got a fantastic dog team, we can —"

"Was the next helicopter supposed to come right away?" I interrupted him, gazing south-west through the binoculars.

The last Sea King had already put more than a kilometre between itself and us. However, even further away and a little further south I could see something dark approaching through the air.

"No," said Berit hesitantly. "It's due in about an hour. Why?"

I pointed. By now the object was visible with the naked eye. It was flying lower than the Sea King, and following a slightly different route from the rescue helicopter.

"I can hear it," said Geir, squinting at the sky. "It's a helicopter. And it's flying low. Very low."

It was heading straight for us. Halfway across Finsevann, at a height of no more than a hundred metres above the snowdrifts, it veered to the west and headed towards Finsenut in an arc before approaching the landing area in front of the hotel.

"It's completely black!" Geir roared through the racket. "No markings! No identification!"

The snow whirled up once again in a frenzy that reminded us of what the hurricane had been like over the past few days.

"Give me the binoculars," I yelled to Berit, who passed them to me before leaning forward and hiding her face between her knees, with her hands covering her ears.

When the helicopter landed I managed to shuffle forward to the very end of the little snow fortress. I crept right up to the wall and poked my head a little way over the edge. The snow hurt my eyes, but it was better once I had the binoculars in place.

I could see mostly snow. However, I had brief, lightning glimpses of a clear view. I saw the four men from the cellar crouching as they moved towards the helicopter, which clearly had no intention of switching off its engine. It was difficult to distinguish between the figures down below, but I thought the first of them must be Severin Heger. He was almost two metres tall, and his back looked broader than the others'. None of them was dressed in thick winter clothes any longer, even though it was almost minus fifteen outside; they were expecting a warm helicopter.

The snow and the wind were hurting not only my eyes; it felt as if my face was being peppered by thousands of tiny arrows made of glass. I had taken off my mittens to get a better grip on the binoculars, and my knuckles were so cold I was afraid my fingers would break.

Severin had reached the helicopter. He stopped and straightened up slightly before grabbing hold of the next man's upper arm and helping him up the short flight of steps that someone inside had lowered as soon as they landed. I suddenly realized that it was only the man who was just boarding the helicopter who was no longer wearing a rucksack. He hesitated briefly before taking the final step, and looked around him in all directions.

His face filled my field of vision for just long enough to convince me that I couldn't believe what I was seeing. Perhaps it was a second before the driving snow and whirling wind blocked my view of the four men and the black, unidentifiable helicopter.

Perhaps it was half a second, perhaps a little more.

I couldn't have seen what I thought I saw. It couldn't be him.

The man's beard was long and dark, with stripes of grey in an upturned V running downwards from his mouth. The eyes that were staring into my binoculars without being aware of it were dark, with long lashes and a gentle, sorrowful expression. His whole being created a violent, almost paralysing impression, yet the mouth was the most striking element. It was large with unusually full, beautifully shaped lips. Since he was squinting against the light and the driving snow, he was exposing his teeth, which were white and even, forming a sharp contrast with the signs of age in his curly beard.

He was a very handsome man, and I couldn't get my head around what I had just seen. It was even more difficult to understand why the Americans had contented themselves with sending just one man.

Perhaps they hadn't. Perhaps there were more than the man I had assumed was from South Africa. It was just that nobody had discovered them. I closed my eyes tightly to get rid of the tears, then opened them again.

The rotor blades were screaming.

The helicopter began to lift. I defied the cold, and forced myself to look into the chaotic, whirling snow. Everything was white, and for a while I felt as if I had gone blind. I took a deep breath and rubbed my face with my ice-cold hands once the helicopter was high enough for the driving snow to settle, and it became possible to see again.

I was not blind, but it was impossible to believe what I knew I had just seen.

"What was that?" said Geir as the black helicopter disappeared in the same direction from which it had come, flying fast and low, and complete silence once more descended on the mountains.

"I don't know," I said, hoping more than anything that I was telling the truth. I really didn't have any idea what it was.

Also available in ISIS Large Print:

Rupture

Simon Lelic

North London; in the depths of a sweltering summer, teacher Samuel Szajkowski walks into a school assembly and opens fire. Three pupils and a teacher are shot dead before Samuel turns the gun on himself.

As the only woman in her office at CID, Detective Inspector Lucia May is finding it difficult to be taken seriously by her colleagues. When she is assigned the school-murders case, she is expected to tie things up quickly and without a fuss. The incident is a tragedy that couldn't have been predicted and Szajkowski a psychopath beyond help. But as Lucia begins to piece together the testimonies of the teachers and children at the school, a much more complex picture of the months leading up to the incident begins to emerge . . .

ISBN 978-0-7531-8822-4 (hb)
ISBN 978-0-7531-8823-1 (pb)

Dark Country

Bronwyn Parry

For 18 years most people in the small town of Dungirri have considered Morgan "Gil" Gillespie a murderer, so he expects no welcome on his return. What he doesn't expect is the discovery of a woman's body in the boot of his car.

Wearied by too many deaths and doubting her own skills, local police sergeant Kris Matthews isn't sure whether Gil is a decent man, wronged by life, or a brutal criminal. But she does know that he is not guilty of this murder — because she is his alibi . . .

Between organised crime, police corruption, and the hatred of a town, Gil has nowhere to hide. He needs to work out who's behind the murder before his enemies realise that the one thing more punishing than putting him back in prison would be to harm the few people he cares about.

ISBN 978-0-7531-8728-9 (hb)
ISBN 978-0-7531-8729-6 (pb)